PENGUIN BOOKS

TO DIE FOR

Janet Neel is the *nom de plume* of Janet Cohen. She lives in north London with her husband. After reading law at Cambridge, she qualified as a solicitor. She spent some time in the USA designing war games, and then returned to London, where she worked first in industrial relations in the construction industry and then, for thirteen years, as an administrator in the Department of Trade and Industry. As well as being a director of Charterhouse Bank, the Yorkshire Building Society and BPP Holdings plc, she is also a Governor of the BBC and an advisor to the Ministry of Defence. She has also founded and financed two successful London restaurants.

Janet Neel is the author of *Death's Bright Angel*, which won the 1988 John Creasey Award for the best first crime novel; *Death on Site; Death of a Partner*, which was shortlisted for the 1991 Crime Writers' Association Gold Dagger Award; *Death Among the Dons*, which was shortlisted for the 1993 Crime Writers' Association Gold Dagger Award; *A Timely Death;* and *To Die For*. As Janet Cohen she has written two highly acclaimed novels, *The Highest Bidder* and *Children of a Harsh Winter*.

TO DIE FOR

JANET NEEL

PENGUIN BOOKS

PENGUIN BOOKS

Published by the Penguin Group
Penguin Books Ltd, 27 Wrights Lane, London W8 5TZ, England
Penguin Putnam Inc., 375 Hudson Street, New York, New York 10014, USA
Penguin Books Australia Ltd, Ringwood, Victoria, Australia
Penguin Books Canada Ltd, 10 Alcorn Avenue, Toronto, Ontario, Canada M4V 3B2
Penguin Books (NZ) Ltd, Private Bag 102902, NSMC, Auckland, New Zealand

Penguin Books Ltd, Registered Offices: Harmondsworth, Middlesex, England

First published in Great Britain by Constable & Company Ltd 1998
Published in Penguin Books 1999
4

For Gertrud Watson

1

'Thank you. Thank you indeed. Yes, we have you with a table for six tonight. Yes, in a booth. Look forward to seeing you.'

Judith Delves, in the neat inconspicuous black suit befitting the manager of a major West End restaurant, presented raincoats and umbrellas to the expensively dressed pair of young men just leaving the restaurant. It was a brilliant September afternoon, intermittently streaked with rain, and the Café de la Paix had been full that lunchtime. The tourists, who sustain all big London restaurants, were going home to Paris and New York, but the regulars, the Londoners working in the big office blocks in St Martin's Lane and the Strand, were coming back from their holiday houses and big hotels in foreign countries.

The Café was a long ground-floor space running the full width of a large office building and the design challenge had been to avoid the look of an oversize village hall. A skilful mixture of heavily gilded large mirrors and huge 1930s posters against a pale gold background broke up the space without having involved enormous cost. The real money had gone into a long, curving bar, equipped with every storage device a barman could want, and a modern, beautifully equipped kitchen. The Caff, as its regulars called it, could seat 250 and, at lunchtime and after curtain-down in the surrounding theatres, mostly did. Judith Delves turned and with the restaurateur's eagle eye saw instantly that two tables at the back had not been cleared and signalled a busboy, in the long white overall over black trousers that signalled his status.

'Judith.'

Selina Marsh-Hayden, her partner in the restaurant, bright blonde, model slim, turning all heads in her cherry-coloured suit with its exiguous pleated skirt over long legs, pushed through the heavy glass door.

'Hello,' Judith said, trying not to sound accusing. Selina should have been present two hours ago to deal with the lunch reception, but this was not the moment to say so.

'I tried to ring.' Selina made a pretty gesture of helplessness, indicating histories of unavailable telephones and broken-down lines.

'But then I thought, anyway, we had to talk face to face. Can someone look after the place just while we have coffee?'

'I'm not sure there's any point, Selina. I'm not going to change my mind.' Angry as she was, Judith still observed that every last one of the men sitting over their coffee at the bar was watching Selina's legs more or less overtly.

'Yes, but darling, that's the *thing*, you see. *I've* changed *my* mind.'

Judith stared at her and put both hands on the reception desk to steady herself. 'You've what?'

'Judith, *do* come over and sit down and I'll get coffee.'

They both waited until they had before them a cup of the Café's exquisite cappuccino, the milky foam only just not overflowing the top of the heavy earthenware cup, and grated chocolate a sharp brown on the top. 'You were right,' Selina said, when the waiter had gone. 'We *can* do better and I've decided not to sell my shares in the Caff. So we'll be able to stop a sale, won't we, just like the lawyers said, because we've got thirty per cent between us.' She beamed at her friend, fresh and beautiful, her looks enhanced if anything by the faint milky line of cappuccino on her upper lip.

'Thirty per cent does block a sale, yes, just as we've always been advised,' Judith agreed. 'But what's made you change your mind? I've asked you often enough to stand by me and told you we could do better.'

'Oh. Various things.' Selina pressed her hand. 'Mostly I remembered – bit late, I know – that you're my very best friend, and have been since we were babies.'

Judith contemplated her, not unaffectionately. 'You were quite clear you wanted out. What happened, Selina?'

'I told you. Various things.' She took her hand away and dug in her handbag for a cigarette and glanced around. 'We *are* in the bit for the pariahs who smoke, aren't we? Good.' She smiled, lazily, at the young waiter who had sprung to her side with a light. She drew on her cigarette, giving her friend a considering look through the smoke. 'Well, Richard for one. He still wants to sell, of course, because we're absolutely bust. This morning, the laundry actually wouldn't *give* me this week's lot until I paid cash for three weeks back. I only had £20, so I had to look in all Richard's jackets for the other £30. But the trouble *is*, Judith, any money we get has to go to the bank, and it's a joint account – I mean, they'll take mine too. So there isn't much point in selling.'

8

'Did you not realise you – or Richard – were bust?'

Selina and the Hon. Richard Marsh-Hayden had been married for several years, and Judith had been chief bridesmaid and a regular guest in their house, but had always understood that she had no idea how that marriage worked.

'Oh, you can't tell with Richard. He always *says* he's broke but mostly he isn't. Only *this* time he is – I looked at some of his letters. He owes money everywhere, not just to the bank.' Selina drew on her cigarette, irritably. 'You are *lucky*, you know, with Michael. All those chaps at Marshall Deneuve are making a fortune in bonuses, Richard says, and I bet Michael's got it all safely tucked away.'

Judith found herself blushing furiously. 'Selina, we're not ... I mean, we only just ... I mean, I don't really know how Michael feels about ...'

'You've fucked him, though.'

Judith, scarlet, nodded, as always appalled and cheered by Selina's directness.

'Was it OK?'

'Oh yes. Yes.'

'Mm. Have you seen him since? I mean, apart from here.'

'Yes.'

'And done it again?'

'Yes. And we're going away this weekend.' She saw, incredulously, that Selina's lip was drooping, disconsolately. 'Selina?'

'Oh hell. Just don't get married, it ruins everything.' Selina stubbed a cigarette out crossly.

'We're nowhere near that,' Judith assured her, battening down the fantasies which she was determined not to allow to surface. She hesitated and crumbled a piece of sugar into her coffee. 'I wondered, you know, whether it was because ... well, if he was doing it because he wanted to persuade me to sell my shares. He wants to sell his and get on to the next thing. But he didn't have to do that – I mean, when I was the only person holding out, I only had fifteen per cent, so I would have had to sell.'

'Yes, but you were making his life more difficult.'

Judith stared at Selina, stricken.

'*Don't* look like that, darling, it's just that you've known each other – well, at least since Richard and I got married. I know you've always rather fancied him, but he's never ... well, has he? Sorry, sorry, Judith, it's just that men are such bastards, and you've always been sensible and kept clear of the worst. Look, anyway, it doesn't *matter*, you and I aren't going to sell, no matter what any of these bloody men say, are we? All we have to do is tell them.'

Judith took a long swallow of her coffee to steady herself. It was perfectly true that Michael Owens, director of Marshall Deneuve, four years her senior and a very personable six foot two inches hunk of man, had never reciprocated her tentatively offered admiration until the last month. But as Michael pointed out, he had never seen her very much and certainly not registered her as a person until the discussions about selling the restaurant had started. It had been Richard Marsh-Hayden, temporarily flush, who had originally agreed to put up money to enable Selina and Judith to start a restaurant together. They had found, rapidly, that on the basis of the most hopeful budgeting exercise, their own funds were inadequate, and Richard had therefore persuaded Michael Owens, an old school-friend and rising banker, to put in the rest. Michael had only started to take an interest when it became worthy of a banker's attention, and not long after had begun to pay real attention to Judith.

She sneaked a look at her oldest friend who was looking downcast and pettish, and decided in a rush of confidence that all this was, unbelievably, jealousy. Richard Marsh-Hayden, despite his undoubted glamour, was a selfish and boorish husband and had now added insolvency to his other faults, quite unlike the well-mannered, well-off Michael Owens.

'Brian Rubin is going to be very cross though, Selina. It's been in the papers – that the Gemini Group are about to make an acquisition.'

'Well, that's just too bad, isn't it? I'll just go and ring Peter – my solicitor, darling, *you* know – and get him to ring up Mr Rubin, so he can get sworn at.'

'The cow. The bloody cow.'

'Excuse me.'

'I'm sorry, Richard, I know it's your wife I'm talking about. But fuck it.' Brian Rubin was shaking with temper, the olive skin flushed unbecomingly up to the dark, thick, curly hair.

'*I'm* just as pissed off with her as you are.' The Hon. Richard Marsh-Hayden, an elegant blond thirty-eight-year-old graduate of Eton, Balliol and the Welsh Guards, habitually spoke as if reared on one of the rougher North London council estates, all the consonants slurred or missing altogether.

'She agreed to sell.' Brian Rubin threw himself into a chair. 'I've been trying to do this deal for six months and I can't tell you what it's costing in fees. Ah, Judith.'

He rose awkwardly to his feet as Judith Delves, a little flushed, the heavy jaw in the square face set, came in. Richard Marsh-Hayden rose too.

'I'm sorry,' she said, breathless, 'but we were finishing the service. Chef is just behind me.'

Tony Gallagher, a heavy-set blond Irishman, his dirty white tunic unbuttoned at the neck, walked in looking hot. He glanced round the group and said, unapologetically, that the laundry was late, so he had to go on in this jacket, then threw himself into a chair and lit up a cigarette. He made to put his feet up on another chair, but a look from Judith stopped him.

'So where *is* Selina?' Brian Rubin asked, rudely.

'She'll be back soon.'

Judith sat behind her own large desk which took up a good quarter of the available floor space in the cramped office. A PC sat to her right, and that part of the desk was covered with piles of bills held together with rubber bands. Three heavy board-covered day books lay to her left near a small office switchboard. There were two more desks in the room, both smaller, one as tidy as Judith's, the other wildly disorderly, with flowers, papers and two Harvey Nichols bags jumbled together on the top.

Richard went over to look at his wife's cluttered desk, and burrowed through papers and bags until he found her diary. 'Nothing at all for today except Hair. And she'd *had* that done. Where *is* she?'

'She doesn't put everything in that diary, Richard.' Judith spoke without looking up.

'I bet she doesn't.' It was explosive and angry and Tony Gallagher applied himself to be soothing.

'She'll be back. She knows this is important. Where did she go, Judith?'

'To pick up her shoes from that place up the road.'

'When?'

'Well, about ten minutes ago, but she did say she had other things to get.'

Richard Marsh-Hayden made an impatient noise and Judith shook her head slightly at Tony. It was after all Richard's wife whose conduct they were seeking to excuse.

'Michael is on his way,' she said, feeling herself going pink.

11

'Oh good. We'll have *one* major shareholder who is making sense.'

Tony Gallagher stubbed out a cigarette savagely and reached for another, catching Richard's attention.

'Sorry, Tony, but your five per cent is about as much use as a fart in a thunderstorm.' He swung round to look out of the window. 'What's the silly bitch doing?'

Judith began to sort the pile of bills on her desk, treating the question as rhetorical.

'Look, for God's sake, Judith, go and find her, we need to sort it out right now.' Brian Rubin was rattled and didn't mind showing it.

Richard Marsh-Hayden swung round from his furious contemplation of the street below. 'Or you'll do what?'

'Or I'll go and buy some other place where the owners can make up their minds to sell.'

'Get off. You need this deal, you'll run out of cash if you don't get a rights issue off.'

'You don't know what you're talking about.' The response was immediate but defensive, and everyone in the room heard that.

'Yeh, I do. Talked to a man in a brokers this morning.' Richard Marsh-Hayden jabbed a pencil in the air by way of emphasis. 'Look, bugger it anyway, most of us want to sell, there's no disagreement about *that*. Just don't be too ready to tell us how you could go and buy something else tomorrow. You couldn't, you're fucked if you can't buy us, so let's start from there, OK?'

Brian Rubin opened his mouth to protest but Richard Marsh-Hayden had swung back to look out of the window again, both hands flat against the glass, frustration in every line of his body. Tony Gallagher's mouth had dropped open and Judith felt as if hers had too.

'You mean that after all *this* Mr Rubin here can't afford to pay us for the restaurants?'

Richard turned to her, slowly, in an elaborate display of weary patience. 'Thought we'd gone through all of this months ago. Brian is going to raise the money by issuing new shares in his company to the punters on the stock market, yeh? Only you can't *do* that unless you've got something to buy. He's got a lot of restaurants but no cash. Now, we've got two restaurants. OK, and not a lot of cash either, but put the two together and you get a group in which he can sell shares, so he can get cash to keep going and buy some more. But he has to do a deal, or he runs out of cash. Soon.'

'Not that soon.' Brian Rubin had recovered himself, but Richard Marsh-Hayden was implacable.

'You're in trouble, Brian. Don't feel bad, we've all been there, but don't give us any crap either.'

'What sort of trouble, excuse me?' Tony Gallagher, thoroughly alarmed, was looking from face to face, and Richard turned on him in vicious impatience just as a buzzer went.

Judith jabbed her finger on the door release and looked gratefully at the tall man, with a thick mop of dark blond hair, who was pushing the door shut behind him.

'Michael. You up with the latest situation? Right now we're just waiting for my bloody wife. She's gone shopping, would you believe.'

Michael Owens nodded to Richard, kissed Judith who had risen to greet him, and shook hands with Tony and Brian Rubin, carefully lowering the temperature of the meeting. He looked doubtfully at a small cane chair, decided against it and perched on the edge of Judith's desk. 'Could we have coffee?'

'Of course.' Judith reached for a phone to order it.

'Tell him to be quick an' all. No one's got all afternoon to sort this out.'

'Richard, you're talking as if Selina will agree to sell if you just shout at her.' Judith had been up since six, as restaurateurs have to be. 'She only agreed in the first place because you were pushing her. She really wants the same as I do, to be left alone to run the two Caffs we've got and to open a couple more. Then we could raise money ourselves on the stock market.'

Brian Rubin, uncomfortably seated behind Selina's crowded desk, had turned scarlet. 'That's dishonest. And unbusinesslike. She *agreed*, you all did, and I've spent a pile of money, not to say three months' hard work, to get this deal.'

'*I* never agreed,' Judith said, angrily.

'No, but you've been professional about it. Up to now that is, when you've helped to bugger up the whole thing, excuse my French. You could be sued, you know. Interference with a contract.'

'I didn't do any of that. I tried to persuade Selina not to sell her shares right at the beginning, but we never even talked about it again until yesterday.' She looked to Michael for support, and he took her hand.

'You've been absolutely consistent, darling, from day one. But

13

Brian's right, we're too far down the line to go back now. It's just not fair to him, or sensible. So, Richard, do *you* know why she's suddenly thrown a wobbly?'

The question hung in the air and everyone in the room considered Richard Marsh-Hayden, whose relationship with a wife fully as wilful and strong-minded as he had never been smooth. He opened his mouth to be rude but closed it again in the face of Michael's gently enquiring expression. 'No. No, we didn't have a fight, nothing like that. Hardly saw her yesterday. No idea what's itching her, but I agree, she'd better forget about it.'

Michael Owens nodded, plainly having expected nothing more revealing. 'Judith, could we shift this stuff? I haven't got a seat and there's nowhere for Selina to sit either. Can we get someone to take it away?'

'Sorry, Michael, but please not. It's the new tunics and I must check them for fit before they get marked.'

Michael Owens picked up a white chef's tunic that lay half out of its cellophane wrappings on top of the pile. 'It is marked, surely. It says Café de la Paix on the pocket.'

'I didn't mean that. We're going to mark jackets with the names of the chefs and kitchen people.'

'Why?' Richard Marsh-Hayden asked, belligerently.

'Because we keep losing tunics – or at least that's what's been happening while I've been over starting Caff 2.' Judith Delves was sounding ragged. 'So everyone is going to get four, as before, but with their names on, and their pay gets docked if they lose them. Or sell them, or give them to friends, or whatever they've been doing.' She looked round at a sullen and unpromising audience. 'Actually, since we're all waiting, could we check the sizes and then I can get them into the back office ready for marking when Mary is in tomorrow. So Tony – Chef – would you try the large? And I'll try the medium.'

Tony Gallagher didn't move, plainly in a bad temper, and Brian Rubin reached for a package.

'I'll give it a go – I can tell whether it's right. We use tunics like these. *And* we mark them, you're right there, Judith.' He pulled off his elegant Armani jacket and hauled on a chef's tunic, cursing at the buttons. 'Bit big if anything,' he said, hunching himself into it.

'Nah.' Tony Gallagher reached for another packet and helped himself and replaced his tunic with one of the new ones. 'About

14

right. You need the room in the shoulders, see, if you're working rather than modelling.'

'The medium size is OK.' Judith sensibly ignored the last part of the sentence.

'Hadn't you better try it on a bloke?' Richard Marsh-Hayden asked.

'They're unisex, and I wear medium, that's why. But do please try one, Richard.' She watched as Richard unpacked another jacket and put it on. 'Comfortable?'

He struck a model pose, shoulders twisted round. 'Yup. Not bad at all. Come on, Mike, you got one too.'

Michael Owens took off his jacket and found a large size and put it on, over immaculately cut trousers, and lunged forward, neatly and fast behind an imaginary foil.

'Fits well,' Judith said, professionally smiling at him, admiring the quick athletic movement.

Tony Gallagher, upstaged, jabbed a finger towards the door, and they all heard the click of high heels accompanied by a rustling of paper. Judith pressed the lock release button and Selina Marsh-Hayden was in the room in a cloud of Diorissimo and a rustle of bags.

'I *really*, really am sorry. There was this huge, huge queue, and I had to have my shoes back, they've been there *months* and there's this little notice that says they'll *shred* them or something if you don't take them away.' She smiled round the group, unapologetically. 'Goodness, what are you all dressed as? Is this a game? Can I play?'

'Be my guest. I've lost a day so far on this nonsense, I may as well waste a bit more time.' Brian Rubin had had enough.

Selina picked up a packet labelled 'small'.

'*Do* try it on, Selina,' Judith said. 'Then I can put them by for marking. There's no point marking the gloves or the towels – everyone uses them, so they can go down now, please, Tony. In the hoist,' Judith added as the service lift rattled up, loaded with coffee and biscuits, and Tony Gallagher, with poor grace, exerted himself to unload it and substitute packets of rubber gloves and piles of tea towels for the journey to the kitchen.

She looked in appeal at Michael Owens, who nodded reassuringly and took off the white tunic he was wearing and organised the other two men to carry through tunics to the small inner office.

'It fits fine. Bit loose but then I'm quite small.'

15

Selina was wearing her tunic over the short cherry-coloured skirt, and looked, Judith thought wistfully, like the model she had once been, the top buttons becomingly undone in a way which would have got her fired at once from the Café de la Paix kitchen.

'Get it off, Selina,' her husband said, testily. 'We need to get shot of this nonsense.'

Selina took off the jacket, taking her time, handed it regally to Tony Gallagher and took the chair he had been sitting on, leaving him with the rickety bentwood chair on which he sprawled, legs splayed, in an open bid for dominance. The three other men in the room, after a single annoyed look from Richard, ignored him and fixed their attention on Selina. She hooked a strand of blonde hair, delicately highlighted, behind one ear and gazed back at them. 'Well, I'm sorry I didn't do this earlier but then there are lots of things I didn't know before.'

'Like what, for fuck's sake?' her husband snarled.

She tucked the blonde hair in again, and addressed herself to Michael. 'I was talking to this *friend*, who's a very successful businessman. Anyway, he *said* that we – Judith and me – would be mad to sell, everyone loved the Cafés and we ought to go on and build up a chain. Why let someone else do it?' She looked under her eyelashes at Brian Rubin who was sitting, hunched and tight-lipped, behind the bookkeeper's desk. 'He asked what profit we were making and when I told him he said it wasn't *enough* for somewhere like the Cafés and something must be wrong with the costing, or we weren't being careful enough. But we could sort that out, he said.' She blinked sweetly at them all, inviting them to share her conviction, and her husband drew a breath in through his teeth. '*And*, as I've always said, haven't I, Judith, it's *so* much more fun running our own business than working for someone else—although it's been very kind of Brian to offer – that I thought I'd rather stay as we are.'

'We can't do that, you silly witch,' her husband exploded, and she stared back at him.

'Who says?'

'I bloody say.'

Tony abandoned his sprawl and crashed forward on his chair. 'I told you, Selina, I want to work for a bigger group. You won't have me if you want to go on on your own.'

Selina, cool again, pushed bags aside and rested her chin on her hand. 'You have to give up your five per cent if you go, remember?'

16

It was quite clear from Tony's expression that he remembered all too well. 'That's not fair.'

'Yes, it is. And it's in the shareholders' agreement.'

Michael Owens had sat absolutely still while battle raged, waiting his chance. 'Selina, I invited Brian to join us because he has a major interest in all this, but if this is a discussion better held among us as shareholders, I am sure he would rather leave us to it. We *do* need to understand better what has prompted you to change your mind. You've far too much sense to have abandoned a route we all agreed just because of a chat with someone.'

This appeal to reason silenced the group, as it was intended to. It was Richard Marsh-Hayden who took charge. 'Tell you what, Brian, it would be better if you left us to . . . to discuss among ourselves, yeh?' Judith made to protest but Michael touched her hand and she stopped. Tony did not speak, but his expression suggested he was seeing the last lifeboat starting its motor, as Brian Rubin left, angrily expressing a hope of a successful outcome and a quick one.

As the door banged behind him, Richard swung on Selina but she faced him down. 'What this man *actually* said, darlings, was that on our turnover we ought to be making a lot more margin and we would find we had a leak somewhere.' She looked round the group who were all staring at her. 'Don't you see? We may be selling the Caffs *far* too cheap. I mean, I'm not saying I'll never sell, but Judith and I have worked our butts off and I'm not selling for less money than we ought.'

'Selina. We can't afford to go that way. We need the fucking money.' Richard Marsh-Hayden was only just keeping his hands off her.

'You mean *you* need the money.'

'Hang on.' Michael was sitting still, in contrast to everyone else in the room. 'The business needs the money. We are close to breaching our banking covenants. Which means, Tony, that we are close to giving the bank every excuse for calling in our overdraft. So either we have to put up more money – and that may not be convenient for all of us – or we're bust. Can't pay our bills.'

'You could put up some cash,' Tony said, sullenly.

'I could. But equally we're being offered a good price and there's always an alternative investment.'

'And one which'll pay off a bloody sight better in the long run.' Richard Marsh-Hayden was too anxious to leave the point alone.

'This one *will* pay off if we just wait a bit and find what's happening to our profits,' Selina insisted.

'Maybe so,' Michael said, calmly. 'But we are where we are, and I have to say I don't think we can get round this corner without a cash injection. Which I would be unwilling to provide.'

'And me,' Richard said, grimly.

'I couldn't,' Tony confirmed, watching Selina.

'Well, I could put up some,' she said.

'Don't be so bloody silly,' her husband said, violently. 'You're overdrawn on both accounts, so unless you're selling your favours you can't either.'

Judith cleared her throat. 'I would be prepared to put up £20,000 just to see if we couldn't do better.'

Michael's left hand jumped convulsively and he turned to look at her. 'I don't think you've taken this line before.'

'I know, and I'm sorry. But it's my money from Dad. I don't want to sell now, you all know I don't. I agree with Selina, we're selling too soon and for not enough cash.'

'Selina?'

'I'm not going to give up. We can get by with Judith's cash.'

'I see.' Michael shook his head at Richard and Tony, then sat, in thought, refusing to hurry. 'In conscience then, I think we must tell Brian Rubin that the deal is off. Thirty per cent of the shareholding – Selina and Judith – don't want to sell, so we can't deliver enough votes to get any kind of special resolution through.' He looked round to make sure he had everyone's attention. 'I have to say that I think we may face legal action from Rubin. He's spent a lot of money.'

'Well, too bad,' Selina said, rudely, releasing tension. 'I'm sorry you're pissed off, boys, but you'll be glad in the end, I promise.'

2

Francesca Wilson, Bursar of Gladstone College, wife to Detective Chief Superintendent John McLeish and mother of William McLeish, aged twenty-one months, was sitting on her bed, gazing at a small test tube. She put it down, looked unseeingly at her son who was rubbing her expensive night cream into his right knee-cap, and read, for the tenth time, the printed instructions.

'That,' she said, stunned, removing the jar from her son's hands and substituting a bunch of keys and a toy car, 'is undoubtedly a purple ring. I'll write to the *Lancet*.'

'Why?' William had only a few words and this was the one he used most, on a random basis along with 'No'.

'Because we only thought of it four weeks ago,' Francesca said, dazed, as if to a fellow grown-up. 'And I'm only eight days late,' she added, wonderingly. 'We'd better tell Daddy.'

'Daddy.'

'Oh dear.' Francesca recalled all the instructions about how to introduce your child to the fact that he would have to share his parents with a sibling. Watching William dismember an ancient and cracked pair of sun-glasses he had found in the drawer by the bed, she remembered that she had been pleased to welcome her next brother Charlie but progressively disillusioned by the arrival, at just under two-year intervals, of Peregrine and the twins, Jeremy and Tristram. William would be two and a half when his brother arrived. Or his sister, she thought with a surge of hope. Or his twin brothers, a second disheartening thought suggested.

'Ma.' William had looked up and seen her face and was clambering feverishly on to her lap.

'No, it's all right, Will, don't worry. Look here's Susannah and I know you are going off to see Tim and Lizzie. I'll just ring Daddy – no, sweet, you go and find a biscuit, I'll come down.'

William's Daddy, blast him, was in a meeting as usual and this was not the kind of message that could be left with a secretary. She thought of ringing her mother, but decided she couldn't. This was the sort of news a husband had to receive first. But it was impossible to sit at home contemplating a future so utterly changed. It would have been easier if it had been one of her days at Gladstone College; the financial and administrative affairs of an all-women university college left little time to worry about the future. She remembered then, with pleasure and relief, that she did have an errand to do and a sibling to see, even if she could not tell him her news. Tristram, one of the twins, was at twenty-eight beginning slowly to make progress as a tenor in classical opera. He had toured Eastern Europe in a small experimental company, singing lead or second lead parts; indeed she had been to Budapest to see him as Cavaradossi in *Tosca*, wearing grubby jeans and a doubtful blond wig. He had caught an agent's eye and was now at the Coliseum with *Tosca*, but not of course as Cavaradossi. He would be appearing as one of the villainous Scarpia's henchmen, once in Act One and once in Act Two with about four bars in each act if she had that right. Fortunate, however, to get the job at all in so distinguished a company, and she could easily ring him up and see if he was free for lunch.

Three hours later, after a satisfying encounter with Gladstone College's principal banker and a trip to the National Portrait Gallery, she headed across two sets of roads, making for lunch at a spot highly recommended by friends. 'Very nice with kids, don't mind them at all, and the steak frites is to *die* for,' one of her fellow parents had assured her. She stopped outside and gazed at it doubtfully; it looked rather smart with lots of gleaming brass and polished tables. But inside she could see two women, each with someone of about Will's age climbing all over them. She pushed through the swing doors and stopped, startled. A very tall young man, with dark red hair, dressed in several layers among which at least one waistcoat and two shirts were discernible, was bent over the reception counter, considering a document.

'Matt?'

The young man straightened up and stared back at her. 'Wonderwoman!' He swept her into his arms and kissed her warmly. 'What are you *doing* here, Fran?'

'Lunch with a brother who doesn't seem to be here yet. What are you?'

'Seeing a client.'

'Who is?'

'Chef.'

He was economical with words, she remembered, entirely uncertain whether she was glad to see him or not. 'I didn't realise you were a grown-up solicitor.' Attack had always been the safest policy with Matt Sutherland.

'Qualified two months ago.'

'And you have your very own clients already.'

'Yup. At least one. We know his family.'

Since the clients of Peter Graebner's firm were drawn predominantly from the criminal classes of West London, this was not necessarily a recommendation.

'What's he done? Knifed the washer-up?'

'Not yet.'

He was not going to tell her, she understood, and he was quite unselfconsciously pleased to see her. They had had a brief affair six months before and she was in retrospect thoroughly shocked by herself, nor least because this clever, infinitely competent tough was, at twenty-six, two years younger than the youngest of her own difficult siblings. Matt had left his native New Zealand at twenty-one to live entirely on his own in a foreign land, unlike her pampered brothers, and it showed.

'You want a drink while you wait? I get staff rates here.'

'I'll buy,' she said firmly, needing to get control of this party, and followed as he strode across the restaurant.

'Chef is under threat of dismissal?' she needled, as he sat down.

'No. It's a commercial dispute. I need to eat. You may as well look at the menu too, I take it the brother is feeding you.' He scanned down it rapidly.

She perched awkwardly on the seat, very conscious of him.

'Have the lamb, it's good.'

She looked up, startled to see a blond, solidly built man of about her own age, in immaculate white overalls and hat. Huge hands, she noticed, scrubbed clean with short, bitten nails.

'Worth knowing,' Matt observed. 'Tony, this is an old friend, Francesca McLeish.'

'Pleased to meet you.' Tony Gallagher nodded to her, as royalty faced with a respectable commoner, but his attention was not with her. 'A last word, Matt?'

'Surely.' Matt slid out of his chair and moved away. She watched them, interested; every line of Tony Gallagher's body was tense, the big hands jabbing the air to make a point, in sharp contrast to Matt's easy fluent body language. A head poked out of an unmarked door and Tony Gallagher went reluctantly, head still turned to instruct Matt.

'An Irishman,' she said, enquiringly, as Matt returned.

'Father is. Was, rather. Died in a fight. Tony's a good bloke. Does 150 covers at lunchtime every day. Between twelve thirty and two-fifteen.'

'With help, I assume.'

'Oh sure. But he's the gaffer. Kitchen's about a hundred degrees, the size of a couple of garden sheds.' He signalled a waiter and, without consulting her, ordered a glass of the Chardonnay she drank for preference as an aperitif. She considered, for a moment, asking for something else, but decided it was more dignified to accept it.

'Does Chef own the place?'

'He has a small shareholding.'

'Who owns the rest?'

'The two girls who started it and their men. The girls – Judith Delves and Selina Marsh-Hayden – work it, the men are the money. That's Judith, floor-managing today.'

'Interesting to meet her.'

'You won't. She's avoiding me. Sorry, got to see a man. I'll be back.'

He went off towards the kitchen and she watched his back, acknowledging that she had been shaken up by the encounter. It's sex, she thought, crossly; if you've slept with someone, even if you both gave each other up, your relationship with them is never quite simple again. And men, as the eldest sister to four brothers had every reason to know, were still close enough to their animal origins never quite to let go a woman they had once had. Even if they too, in their rational mind, felt the whole thing had been a mistake, they still did territory-marking things like order, without asking, what you had always drunk when with them. She sipped the Chardonnay, grudgingly, and was both disconcerted and pleased to discover that it tasted terrible. Not corked, she decided, sipping it again, nothing wrong with the wine that a bit less oak in the process would not have fixed, but this was familiar territory. She truly was pregnant, she realised, and for the next nine months all alcohol was going to taste like decayed fruit juice and go straight to her head.

'Frannie, I'm sorry to be late.'

'Tris. Not at all.' She reached up to kiss her youngest brother, Tristram, last-born of the twins who had so disconcerted their mother and father twenty-eight years ago. Well, it must have been a very mixed moment for her mother, she thought in a flash of fellow feeling, *twins* when there were already three children, and the father was known to be a poor life risk. Indeed he had died when the twins were six, and even she, the eldest of the siblings, only twelve. She looked at her brother carefully; he had struggled with a heroin addiction for a couple of years and, though all hoped this was comfortably behind him, they still studied him closely when they saw him, looking for the tell-tale signs. But he looked well and cheerful, and she relaxed; months of touring had evidently not strained him and he had this prestige minor role at the ENO and a couple of concerts to occupy him. He would always be a musician and opera suited him better than the pop music world in which their formidable sibling Perry was a solidly established international figure.

'How's it going? You want to drink my wine? No, it's perfectly nice and it's paid for, I just don't feel like it.'

'Waste not, want not,' Tristram said, cheerfully, and took it from her, glancing automatically round to see if he had been recognised. He had, it was gratifyingly clear, by just enough of the aficionados, and satisfied he turned his attention to her. 'We need to eat a bit quickly, sister mine. I've got an understudy rehearsal.' He looked at her under his eyelashes and she understood she was being slow.

'Darling, who are you understudying?'

'Guess.'

'*Not* Cavaradossi?'

'Well done. Not, you understand, that if old Alan develops a nasty – perish the thought – I'll actually get to sing, not if they've got time to ship someone else in, but it's a start.'

'If old Alan drops dead in mid-performance they'll have to use you.'

'Yes, won't they? Enough to tempt anyone to crime.'

'No, Tris, please not. Do try and remember where I am married.'

He burst out laughing in mid-sip and was still blowing his nose when Matt Sutherland, looking like a giant question mark, arrived at their table. 'Matthew, this is my brother Tristram.'

'Well, of course it is. Sorry, I expect everyone says that.'

'Yes, they do,' Francesca agreed. 'Even if only two of us are gathered. Bit less with Charlie but then, of course, he's sort of blond where the rest of us are dark.' She realised she was chattering, but something about the bright-eyed interest with which Tristram was watching Matt was unnerving her.

'I know your mother, of course. I'm the Refuge's solicitor,' Matt said, hastily. Oh God, she thought, he really is young, a full two years younger even than Tris, our baby.

'Yes indeed, I know just who you are,' Tristram said, briskly, his interested look unswerving.

'You're working down the road from here, Fran says.'

'That's right. In a very small part,' he added, elegantly.

'Scarpia's henchman. Never can remember his name. Polenta? Carpaccio?'

'Matthew,' Francesca said, crossly, as Tristram considered him, thoughtfully. 'The character is, of course, called Spoletta.'

'Close then.'

'Not very. Does your client no longer need you?'

'Not right now. Ah.'

They followed his gaze; every fibre of him pointing like a retriever. And no wonder, when you saw what he was looking at: the back view of a pair of superb slim long legs and a very short pleated crimson skirt and neat jacket topped by vivid blonde short hair. She was standing talking to Judith Delves, the blonde hair swinging elegantly as she moved her head. She turned suddenly, in response to something Judith had said, and gazed across the restaurant. The front view was even better, Francesca conceded, small straight nose, blue eyes, perfect skin. But short-sighted, she understood, ungracefully pleased to have found a flaw – the girl was squinting to see. Francesca followed the direction of her anxious stare and saw that a heavily built dark man, half risen from his chair, was urgently signalling. The girl in the crimson suit lifted the flap on the reception counter with the ease of familiarity and disappeared, past Judith Delves.

'*That* was Selina Marsh-Hayden, co-founder of this place,' Matt observed.

'Who absolutely didn't want to meet the gent at that table.'

'She didn't, did she? He's called Brian Rubin.'

'A fellow restaurateur,' Francesca said, smugly.

'How did you know that, Wonderwoman?'

'Don't call me that. He was in the paper this morning. Owns the Gemini chain.'

'Mm.'

'And perhaps, who knows, wishes to buy this one here? And the other one they own across the river. To add to his little chain.' Francesca was beginning to enjoy herself, watching Matthew fidget.

'I'd forgotten you were so smart. I'll stop interrupting your lunch and go and eat. Nice to meet you,' he added punctiliously, nodding to Tristram.

He went away to join a table at the far end of the long room and she determinedly turned her attention to Tristram. There appeared to be a new and different girlfriend. English this time. She and her mother would wholeheartedly have welcomed any steady young woman of any nationality, but these qualities did not appear to be on offer; this one, too, in the fine tradition of all Tristram's women, was beautiful, or near offer, and struggling to make her way in opera, and necessarily self-obsessed.

'Nice place, this,' he was observing, sunnily, the subject of his sex life concluded. 'I thought I'd get Perry to take us all here. You know he's coming in the back end of next week? He's going to see the show and a quick understudy rehearsal, then take me and anyone else who's interested – which is absolutely everybody of course – out to dinner afterwards. I thought here – it's close.'

'And very nice.' Francesca had collected herself sufficiently to take in the glittering brass, the rapid, unobtrusive but not unfriendly service and the military precision with which the whole enterprise was run. The food, too, had been excellent, precisely cooked and flavoured. 'It may not be so good if it's going to be a part of a bigger chain.'

'Well, it isn't before next Thursday, presumably.'

'This is true. Don't wait, Tris, if you have to run. I thought I'd just sit here and have coffee and I can wait for the bill.'

'Do you mind? Sorry, but I need to pee and I've only got ten minutes before we start again.'

She waved him off, with an elder sister's easy command, and looked round to order a coffee and a bill. Both arrived, surprisingly, in the hands of the woman Matt had pointed out as one of the joint owners, and Francesca pulled herself together to say how much she had enjoyed the meal.

'Thank you indeed. Look, excuse me, but aren't you Francesca Wilson?'

'Yes, I am.' She considered the other woman. 'I'm sorry, my mind's a blank, I can't remember where we met.'

'At Gladstone's Founders' Day.'

'Oh, no wonder. There were thousands there, weren't there? Do you have time to sit down? Matthew Sutherland – who is an old acquaintance – says you and a partner started this place. It's very nice.'

25

'Thank you again. Yes, that's right. I'm afraid I need to go and join the others for a meeting. I just wanted to say hello. And Tristram Wilson is your brother? He's just booked about sixty people in for next week.'

'That'll be all right,' Francesca said, amused, understanding why the owner of this nice place had done her the honour of bringing the bill personally. 'Another brother – an unspeakably rich rock artist called Perry – is the host and will be paying. Or his studio is.'

'Good heavens.' Judith Delves stared at her and she grinned back. Not pretty, she thought, face too square and podgy, but a nice smile and a clear direct personality. And about her own age, thirty-four or so. Judith handed her the change, orthodoxly presented on a plate, and she packed it away, aware that her hostess was trying to say something.

'You started here some years ago?' she suggested, helpfully.

'About four. Look, I don't have any time now and I'm sure you don't either, but might I ring you? At Gladstone? I just ... well ... I'd like to consult someone sensible and female, who has worked all her life.'

'Of course,' Francesca said, somewhat taken aback, and handed her her card as Bursar and Fellow of Gladstone. She could see Matthew Sutherland hovering and decided that discretion was the better part of valour; whatever the temptation to stop and gossip with him, there was still unfinished business there and she would be better to stay out of his way.

Judith Delves paused outside the office to compose herself. She and Selina had agreed to meet the rest of the shareholders and the potential purchaser one more time in the hope, as Michael had put it, smoothly, of finding a way forward. What he meant, she feared, was a way of getting her and Selina – or one of them – to agree, after all, to sell their shares. She heard footsteps behind her and turned; it was Michael, in full fig as a corporate finance star, in a beautifully cut dark suit, blue shirt and blue Hermès tie, the dark blond hair cut very short to conceal the fact that it was beginning to thin. Nothing, however, concealed the strong elegant bones of the face and the athletic ease of the way he moved, or the clear wide blue eyes. A very attractive man, she thought, her heart thumping, and she was unbelievably lucky to have attracted him.

'Darling,' he said, kissing her 'Are we all wasting our time?'

'I still want to hang on,' she said, dry-mouthed and anxious.

'Well, I know that, my love, I might wish it otherwise, but it isn't news. What about Selina? If you are going to hang on you can't afford to have her wobbling.'

He *isn't* furious, she thought with a lift of the heart. He's frustrated but he's still going to be reasonable, and not give me up. 'She was clear she wanted to hold on when I saw her this morning.'

'Oh dear. Well, I would have liked to get both of us out of this, but if it is not to be . . . Well, I need to be back in an hour, so let's just go in and see what's what. Dinner tonight?'

'Oh yes.' She remembered, abruptly, that she was substituting for a sick night manager, but decided that whatever and whoever she had to pay to get that shift covered tonight, she would do it.

'Good.' He put his hand on her cheek and kissed her hard on the mouth, leaving her trembling. 'Come on,' he said, slightly breathless himself. 'Let's get this lot out of the way.'

They walked in, his hand in the small of her back, so she felt warm and supported, to a scene that could well have formed a tableau depicting 'Failure' or 'Dissent'. Brian Rubin was on his feet, pink blotches sitting high on his cheekbones. Richard Marsh-Hayden was leaning against the window, forehead and both hands flattened against it, and Tony Gallagher was standing menacingly over a chair in which Selina Marsh-Hayden, perfectly made up, elegant legs stretched, was sitting, admiring her new pair of lizard skin shoes.

'Afternoon, everyone. Is there coffee?'

The figures in the tableau moved; Tony Gallagher went heavily to the phone, Richard flung away from the window, and Brian Rubin greeted him noisily, claiming that he was glad to have another major shareholder present who knew what he wanted from one minute to the next.

'I *do* know what I want,' Selina said, sweetly, turning one ankle the better to admire the clasp on the shoe. 'I told you, and there's no point going on shouting. You've all had a go, and what I want is to carry on and work with Judith until we can float the company. Or until somebody offers us a very much better deal than they have so far.' She smiled at them all, sweetly and implacably, and Judith was suddenly reminded of the seven-year-old Selina, refusing, equally serenely, to take any part at all in the Christmas play unless she was the Virgin Mary. She sneaked a look at Michael, who was plainly cross, but with Selina, not with her. Brian Rubin, curiously, was less angry; the bright colour had died down and he was considering

Selina with wary interest. And Tony Gallagher was in a panic, sweating round his hair-line. She was just considering this phenomenon when Michael spoke.

'Fine. Well, not fine but that's your privilege, Selina. I think it's probably not the right day to discuss it, but as a major shareholder and a director I have to say that I need to assure myself that our trading position is tenable. We all need to be clear about that, we're all directors. Brian, as you can see, there isn't a deal, perhaps you and I can be in touch next week.'

'No point me staying here now,' Brian Rubin agreed. He shook hands with a startled Judith. 'I think you're both making a mistake, Judith, Selina, but I've not got anything else to persuade you with.' He picked up his jacket and banged his way out, and they listened while his steps died away down the stairs.

'I'll see you later,' Michael said, kissing Judith, and nodding to Selina.

'I'm going to get in touch with my solicitor,' Tony Gallagher said, and left, thunderously, leaving Selina, Richard and Judith looking at each other.

'Will you excuse us, Judith?' Richard said, heavily.

'Don't bother,' Selina said, calmly. 'It's not going to do the slightest good. Why don't you go and play with your awful friends while Judith and I do some work.'

He went over to her, fists clenched, and Judith braced herself to intervene, but Selina stayed sitting, unperturbed, and just waited till he turned and went. The service lift rattled and Selina bestirred herself to extract the coffee and hand a cup to Judith, who found she had to sit down. Selina's hands, she observed with admiration, were completely steady.

'Right then, Judith,' she said, brightly, 'we'd better make a plan, hadn't we?'

3

Detective Chief Superintendent John McLeish crept through the semi-darkness and blinked in the strong light, which revealed his brother-in-law's recumbent body, red stains all over the wide-sleeved white shirt. He edged himself forward as Tristram stirred and turned slightly on to his side.

'Perry. What's happening? Is Tristram OK?'

'Up to a point. He has just been tortured, but has loyally not revealed the whereabouts of his fleeing friend.'

'Ah.' McLeish flinched at a basilisk look from his wife and slid into his red plush seat. He considered the stage where Tristram, now propped on one elbow, was expressing his defiance to a large sullen man in a vast sweater bulging over trousers anchored below a substantial tummy. There had been no time at all to read the summary of the plot provided by his wife that morning, and he could not now ask for any more guidance. Not while Tristram was singing anyway, so he relaxed to listen. He was more used to Perry's high, beautifully placed tenor, but Tristram was a formidable rival. Like Perry, he seemed to be able to turn up the volume to an astonishing level, and like Perry he appeared not to strain at all on any note. But surely it was a more fluent and supple voice; surely Perry could not easily reach those top notes? He looked thoughtfully at Perry's profile and decided he was right; there was a stiffness about the jaw that said that Perry was not wholeheartedly pleased with his brother's beautiful, polished performance.

A large lady in a long shapeless skirt topped with an enormous cardigan flung herself at Tristram and an impassioned duet followed, during which they definitely quarrelled; the music told you that even without Tristram's rejecting gesture. Then Tristram tottered to his feet, apparently much restored by some news brought in by a messenger, and was taken from the stage hurling defiance.

McLeish could bear it no longer. 'Perry, what *is* going on?'

'Napoleon has been victorious at Modena, so Tris feels much, much better.'

'Perry.' A joint hiss from mother and sister silenced Perry who made a graceful gesture of apology.

A heavy young man in a boxy blue suit and pony-tail standing at the back of the box, twitched the curtain helpfully. 'Can't follow it neither, Chief Super,' he confided, and McLeish recognised Perry's bodyguard. Even at an understudy rehearsal on an off-night a bodyguard, or attendant, was needed to keep Perry's fans at bay. 'Tell you what though, the big girl's the heroine. Tosca.'

'Thanks, Biff.'

There was enough of her to make two heroines, she was nearly old enough to be Tristram's mother and she could have swept him off his feet any day. But once you got over the first visual shock you ceased to notice the size 22 hips; the soprano voice was magnificent and she was a great actress.

The heavy pressed his attention on her, having incautiously dismissed his underlings, and McLeish sat bolt upright as she seized a knife and stabbed him, leaving him dead. No, no, he thought, critical sense reasserting itself. She'd been holding the knife wrongly, you needed to get right under the ribs to kill and the way she'd been going the point would have bounced off.

The director called a halt and Tristram emerged blinking, still bloodstained, to receive instructions. The large lady was looking tired, as well she might. The heavy, miraculously restored and smiling, revealed himself disconcertingly as a friendly, good-tempered middle-aged bloke.

'Not bad,' Perry said in his ear. 'The big bloke. Tends to go flat in the top of his register, though.'

McLeish, who had heard nothing amiss, accepted this information as gracefully as he could. His wife and her family were all musicians, and had no idea how much detailed knowledge informed their everyday life and conversation. Ordinary, sensible questions about matters musical tended to be met with a slight pause, followed by the preoccupied frown of people asked to explain some routine part of living, like how to walk, or eat, or chew gum. It was intensely excluding; McLeish had found only one fellow sufferer, a colleague married into a large Welsh-speaking family. They went into Welsh all the time, having no idea they were doing it, the man had complained, and when challenged would assure him that nothing more interesting was being discussed than a better way to repair the car. It didn't help, you just *knew*, he had said darkly, that the wife was reciting your shortcomings as a lover, father and provider, and her brothers were offering sympathy and suggesting early divorce. McLeish considered his own brother-in-law cautiously. 'Is that the end?'

'No.' Perry uncurled himself from his chair as the lights went up to reveal a scattering of stage hands and representatives of Management dotted about in the stalls. 'End of Act Two. It's all they're going to do tonight, and now they're allowed off for dinner. Come on, let's collect the rest of them.'

'No one has even recognised Perry,' Francesca said, with interest. 'Oh, spoke too soon.'

McLeish looked across to where two young women had outflanked the bodyguard and were demanding Perry's autograph. He was at his charming best, explaining courteously that he had come only to hear his brother sing, attending to their twittering cries of amazement and discovery with a patient smile.

'Just as well,' Francesca observed. 'He'd have been absolutely miserable if no one had approached him.' She gave her husband an anxious sidelong look and he braced himself for whatever demand was to come. 'Darling, are you really tired? I mean, can you manage the dinner?'

'So long as it's food and it gets served pretty quickly. Where *are* we eating?'

'At Café de la Paix. I told you. The place I went to with Tris? It's very large and stays open very late. They're just going to cordon off the back and feed all forty of us.'

'There are forty people in this show?'

'Including stage crew, chorus and hangers-on like us, easily.'

'Then we wouldn't be missed?' he suggested, hopefully.

'Well, only by Tristram, who is the reason we are here.' His wife was finding herself in the usual tug of war between husband and brothers. 'I mean, *you* could go home – they know you work very long days. I really couldn't, it would be mean.'

'Even though you're pregnant?'

'I haven't told the brothers, or Mum. I mean *I* know I am, but it's awfully early – practically the morning after – and they might think I was being optimistic.'

'Well, I don't want you going by yourself. I'm OK, provided it doesn't go on too long.'

Francesca reached up to kiss him, and he hugged her warmly, relieved to have been forgiven for being late.

'Oh good.' Perry had shaken off, charmingly, his admirers. 'Warms

31

my old heart to see it. Make her tell you the rest of the plot, John. It ends in tears.'

'Tristram ends up dead. So does Tosca.' Francesca had evidently decided to keep it simple.

'Well, she'd killed a copper, hadn't she?' McLeish pointed out. 'Can't imagine why they hadn't searched her.'

'John. You weren't paying attention. She snatched the knife from the supper table over which he had planned to seduce her.'

'What can he have been thinking of?' McLeish, suddenly feeling much better, his headache eased, enquired. 'The Police Complaints Authority would have had him on toast.'

Francesca, always serious-minded, started to explain that the system for entertaining complaints against the police was not strongly developed in nineteenth-century Italy, then realised that her husband and brother were laughing at her.

'I shouldn't think there is any point in hurrying,' Perry said. 'None of us will get fed anything until the cast get there.'

'We might get a drink,' McLeish pointed out.

'There is that.'

The bodyguard indicated that he preferred to keep Perry out of crowds, even a small docile crowd such as attended understudy rehearsals. McLeish sympathised with him; Biff was an ex-policeman and, like him, professionally averse to unnecessary risk. And it was certainly pleasant to saunter out of a near-empty auditorium into a clear summer night and walk quietly up the street and round the corner. 'Is this place going to manage to feed us all?' he asked his wife under cover of Perry's informed monologue on the problems of recording opera. 'When you were here last you said you thought there was a certain amount of tension among the shareholders.'

'The kitchen will be all right. Or perhaps not, come to think on it. Chef is a shareholder and wasn't getting what he wanted.'

'That was why Matthew Sutherland was there?'

'Yes,' she agreed, self-consciously, and he considered her thoughtfully. Like all good policemen, he was a creature of very highly attuned instincts, and he had feared there had been an emotional entanglement there. This was one of the penalties of being married to a lively, talented, insatiably curious creature like his wife, but he didn't want any of it going any further. 'Ah. Now that is interesting.' Francesca had found a distraction. 'One of the proprietors – not the beautiful one – the worker bee, Judith Delves, is receiving.'

They were behind Perry, who was deploying just enough personality to get himself recognised, but while two passing waiters were struck dumb, Judith Delves was pleasingly unfazed. She summoned a minion to take Perry and the bodyguard to where the party was, confining herself to the observation that it was particularly nice to see him and she hoped he would have a good meal. Perry turned to collect his sister, and Judith Delves smiled at her. 'Nice to see you, Mrs McLeish. This is your brother?'

'One of them,' Francesca said, just as Tristram arrived through the door in a rush. You would know them anywhere for siblings, McLeish conceded, even though they were less alike than when he had first met the whole talented awkward crew six years ago. The same thought reflected itself in Judith Delves' expression and like others faced with Wilsons *en bloc* she could not help staring. But she recovered fast and turned courteously to him.

'I'm Mrs McLeish's husband,' he said, pleasantly. 'There are two more brothers and they all look like each other.'

'Four brothers-in-law. Goodness!' The ring on her finger flashed as she found his name, the pencil just hesitating for a moment as she took in his title. 'That's fine,' she said, sensibly ducking 'Detective Chief Superintendent' in the vocative case. 'Monica will take you through.'

Whatever stresses there may have been among the shareholders were not reflected in either the food or the service, McLeish thought, contentedly, an hour later. They had been fed very promptly – indeed the first course, on which the cast, chorus and stage crew had fallen like starving wolves, was placed before them well before the last stragglers had sat down and drink had flowed, plentifully, from the first moment they arrived. McLeish, replete and comfortable, surveyed the party benignly, half listening to Perry, diagonally opposite him, conversing earnestly with the Russian Tosca. He realised that Judith Delves was hovering and indicated as much to Francesca. His own attention was promptly claimed by Biff who, it turned out, was trying to extract a brother-in-law from possible involvement with one of the South London gangs. This was a problem of immediate interest and he took the man to a quiet spot at the end of a table, armed with a bottle the more readily to get the story.

'Very nice food,' Francesca said, warmly, as Judith slid into the chair beside her. 'Are you worn out?'

'I am tired but not by this. I was so glad to see you tonight. I had just decided to ring you up at Gladstone and ask if I could come and

33

talk to you. As an Old Girl, as it were.' She stopped, not out of diffidence but to decide how best to proceed.

'And what would you have said?' Francesca prompted.

'I would have started by explaining our situation here – except that I imagine Matthew Sutherland told you about it?'

'No. Matt's very correct. I *did* notice Brian Rubin having lunch, but only because I read the City pages.' She hesitated. 'Does Mr Rubin want to buy you?'

'Not only that, but we'd actually agreed to sell – well, all the others had. I only have fifteen per cent of the shares, but that wasn't enough to block a sale if push had come to shove.'

'And it had?'

'Yes, but now it's all changed. My friend Selina, with whom I started this place, has decided she doesn't want to sell, so that makes thirty per cent against a sale.'

'Which would block it – the other shareholders can't get a special resolution through.'

Judith nodded and made a long arm and reached for the wine. 'I don't drink normally when I'm working,' she said, defensively.

'But you're done for the evening. We're almost the last and we're eating pudding.'

Judith smiled. 'Not quite. I get to cash up and see the kitchen cleared.'

'Not Chef?' Francesca, with her habitual interest in the detail of any commercial enterprise, asked.

'Chef has gone. Early.'

'In a huff?'

'He is always in a huff at the moment.'

Francesca considered what she was being told. 'So you may not be able to keep him?'

'That's one of the problems.'

Francesca opened her mouth and closed it again, remembering the lesson painfully learned, that you got better results by listening than by talking. The noise level at Tristram's part of the table had risen and people were starting to bang the tables. Francesca looked apologetically at her companion, but the noise rose to a crescendo as Tristram, making graceful gestures of refusal, was dragged to his feet and over to the piano.

'What I'm worried about is Selina.' Judith was oblivious of these manoeuvres and Francesca settled herself to concentrate.

'Your partner? The very dashing blonde. Who changed her mind?'

34

'She's gone away, you see, and no one knows where she is. She said she wanted to think and she took a week's holiday. And she didn't tell Richard – her husband – where she was going either. He asked *me* today did I know where she was. Well, he must have been pretty desperate to do that.'

'And she hadn't told you?'

Judith Delves glanced irritably at the preparations round the piano on which the small dark man was playing a series of chords.

'Not bad,' Francesca said, professionally, and Judith looked at her, puzzled.

'Not bad for pitch. Most pianos in public places are way off. Not that it would worry Tristram much; he's had worse and usually with me playing. Sorry, please go on about Selina.'

'She told me she would be spending a couple of days with her mother, but carefully didn't say where she would be for the rest. But she said she'd ring up every day and she hasn't. I thought, you see, that she was probably doing her thinking with some man.' She caught Francesca's look. 'I've known Selina for ever, since nursery school. That's how she *works*.'

'But now you're worried.'

'Well, her mother rang up yesterday, looking for Selina. And Richard doesn't know where she is. And the prospective buyer, Brian Rubin, doesn't either because he asked Richard.'

'Judith, what worst precisely do you fear?'

'I don't *know*,' Judith Delves said, crossly, 'I'm sorry, I can hear I'm sounding wet. But I'm being driven mad by everyone asking where Selina is, and Brian Rubin ringing up three times a day, and my solicitor wanting to know what to do.'

'My policeman husband would suggest you report her missing.'

'He looks nice.' Judith glanced across the restaurant to where John McLeish was hunched, looking like something carved from granite, patient, silent, waiting while Biff struggled with his story.

'He's easy to talk to. Only not just now – he's doing something, that's what he looks like when he's working.' Francesca hesitated. 'But Selina could still be with this other man somewhere?'

'That's much the most likely answer. But she hasn't phoned.'

Francesca thought, frowning at her coffee. 'Or she isn't calling because she daren't tell you she's changing her mind about selling again?'

She saw that she had hit a nerve. 'Yes,' Judith said tight-lipped after a pause. 'I hadn't thought of that.'

Francesca was hesitating over words of comfort when the huddled group round the piano scattered, leaving the pianist with an older woman leaning over to turn the pages, and Tristram, arranged gracefully to one side of the instrument.

He opened his mouth to sing and the restaurant fell slowly silent. It was a golden tenor like Perry's only higher, and smoother. Well, that was the training. And he had a far better range these days than his brother, and with success was acquiring Perry's staggering ability to communicate with an audience. He was doing the 'Il Mio Tesoro' from *Don Giovanni*, and doing it superbly; it was right in the fat of his voice, and he sang it absolutely simply, letting the music speak for itself. John McLeish, finalising a complex negotiation about arrangements to interview Biff's brother-in-law, felt tears at the back of his eyes as Tristram sang of love and deep content. He looked across at Francesca, who was watching her brother, with her own look of love and content, and read her mind. It had been worth the time and resource expended on this wayward star to extract him from the drug culture. The song ended and in true tribute the audience was silent for a minute before applauding. McLeish took the chance to finish with his interviewee and work his way back to his wife. He was deeply disconcerted to find her glaring across the room with a gargoyle face, eyes crossed, cheeks blown out, teeth gritted. Startled, he looked to see Perry moving awkwardly for once, backing away from the piano.

'Fran! If the wind changed . . .'

'Sorry. I needed to stop Perry singing and stealing Tris's thunder.'

'Would he have?' Judith Delves asked.

'Yes. You must not have siblings, Judith.'

'No, I don't, actually. Just Selina.' The voice changed colour and Francesca patted her hand.

'You could consult John,' she suggested, as if her husband were not there and he tried to look obliging and receptive.

'No,' Judith Delves said, firmly, 'I'm sure you're right, Francesca. She just doesn't want to talk to me.'

John McLeish let a decent pause elapse to make sure that nothing more was required of him, and decided to take his wife home. She was looking pregnant, pulled down, the eyes enormous beneath the arched eyebrows, so exactly like her brothers. He chivvied her to her feet, allowing a decent five minutes to say goodnight. Standing back from the noisy farewells he noticed that Mrs Wilson was looking very carefully at her only daughter and he made a mental note that his mother-in-law ought to be told as soon as possible that there was indeed another grandchild on the way.

'*Bonjour*. I am afraid we do not open until eleven thirty.'

'Westminster Health Inspectors.' The big man showed his card, and the young French waiter nodded uncomprehendingly.

'You wait here, please?'

'Just take us to the kitchen, sunshine.'

'Excuse me, please.' He gave ground before the incoming trio, looking wildly around. 'Ah, Chef, Chef, *on vous demande*.'

Tony Gallagher, in white overalls, hatless and unshaven, was making for the coffee machine. He stopped, reluctantly, as the visitors advanced in a phalanx, the big man in the lead.

'Morning, Chef.'

'Ah, Mr Aylwin. Good to see you.' He looked longingly at the machine. 'Can I give you coffee?'

'Later. Kitchen still through here?'

'Yeh. We haven't moved it.' He watched, surly, as his visitors surged through the small door, pointing like retrievers. His kitchen was only four years old and had incorporated the health inspectors' every whim at the time. And he, personally, went through the chillers every day with the sous chefs to remove anything suspect his staff had tucked away, or forgotten about. He forced a cup of black coffee out of the espresso machine before catching up with the inspection team. He hesitated, but he picked up the kitchen phone and summoned Judith Delves, who appeared inside a minute, not looking much better than he felt.

'Were you very late last night?' he asked her, grudgingly, as they both watched inspectors peering hopefully into immaculate ovens, lifting the lids of scoured saucepans and kneeling to peer into corners of the floor. All experienced restaurateurs know that speech is a waste of time with health inspectors; you can tell them until you are blue in the face that the washer-up does the floor, every night, with enough disinfectant to sanitise a hospital, and they will still get down on their hands and knees to look along the edges of the tiles. It is, as all reluctantly admit, the only way for an inspection system to be effective.

'We were rather.' Judith was cheered by any civility from her disgruntled chef. 'People started singing. We had a lot of Mozart and Puccini.'

'Glad I'd gone.'

She remembered belatedly that Tony was tone deaf. And he had gone early, she recalled.

'What about the rubbish?' she asked, anxiously. 'Have you looked this morning?'

Staff bullied to keeping up operating theatre standards of cleanliness would still leave inadequately tied bags of rubbish in the wire cage outside the back door, in the simple belief – to which all experience ran contrary – that the employees of the local authority would take them all away without leaving any behind, or dropping any live matter to rot just outside the kitchen. A sub-routine had therefore been installed at Café de la Paix involving Chef, or the presiding sous chef, checking the rubbish area every morning.

'I was late – bloody traffic. Didn't look. Jacques should have.'

'Can you go round the outside?'

'Better you do. *They'll* notice if I've buggered off.'

This made sense. Judith faded cautiously backwards out of the inspectors' sight lines, and moved swiftly out of the restaurant door. She hesitated, doubled back to commandeer a waiter and a couple of plastic bags and walked swiftly, just not running, out the front, round the corner and down the narrow steps to the side entrance. As they arrived the back door burst open and a hatless sous chef rushed out.

'Pardon, Madame. J'étais en retard.'

She nodded, out of breath herself, and the three of them, working as one, picked up odd dirty pieces of paper, half a cabbage and, wincing, the remains of two chickens. They had just straightened up from their task when they all heard several sets of feet scuffling in the cement corridor inside. They arranged themselves hastily in attitudes of people who had just stepped into this dank basement alleyway for a breath of fresh air and a conference about the day's menus. The large chief inspector was first out of the door and his habitual expression of doubt and suspicion deepened as he took in the tableau.

'Miss Delves. Nice to see management getting their hands dirty.'

Judith, who had done an inadequate job of cleaning decaying chicken off her hands with the edge of a plastic bag, smiled as pleasantly as she was able and said that indeed her duties were many and various and the council rubbish collectors were, as she would know, not entirely reliable. The three inspectors peered at every corner and the big man wrinkled his nose.

'Mm. You could do with washing this yard with disinfectant.'

'We did. Yesterday.' Tony Gallagher was standing at the back door.

'I'd do it again, laddie, if I was you.' The big man was writing a note, and Judith scowled warningly. One did not argue with the men of the Westminster Health Inspection team. Tony frowned back and she understood that something had rattled him.

'Right. What about this freezer?' The big man had spoken to his note-pad as he finished recording their shortcomings.

'Which freezer?' Judith asked, instantly alarmed. Freezers and their contents are a potential death trap but even the best-organised restaurants have to keep emergency supplies and ice-cream frozen, not chilled.

'Not the store freezer,' Tony said, promptly. 'They've been through that. The old chest freezer.'

'The one we're throwing away.'

'That one.'

'But it's empty,' Judith said, puzzled, following them into the dank passage, mercilessly lit by harsh overhead strip lighting.

The chief inspector sighed. 'It's switched on, and locked, Miss Delves. And your lad here says he doesn't have the key.'

The five of them crowded under the uncompromising lights and gazed at the chest freezer, eight foot long and four foot deep, the red light glaring from the panel on the right-hand side. Judith looked anxiously at Tony; if there was anything to hide he would surely know better than to try and stall the inspectors with a device as feeble as losing the key.

'Did you have to use it for the party last night?' she asked, hopefully.

'No. No one's used that freezer since we cleared it. Couple of weeks ago. We left it propped open with a couple of towels. You saw it.'

She had indeed, she recalled, but not that recently. 'I thought Broughtons had taken it,' she said, hearing herself sounding idiotic. 'Sorry. The keys are hanging on the kitchen board, surely, Tony? So you – or whoever – could give them to Broughtons when they come.'

'The keys aren't there now.'

She looked at him; he was very angry but that was all she could see.

'We'll need it open,' the big man stated, unequivocally.

'Yes, of course you will.' Judith pulled herself together. 'I'll look

39

for the spares. I'm sorry, will you come up and have some coffee while I do that?'

The big man gave her a sharklike smile and motioned an underling to the fore. He produced a clanking chain from his pocket and fiddled about for a minute. The lid sprang open and the three inspectors bent hopefully over to peer in. The chief made an exasperated noise and stood back while his underlings pulled out a pile of black plastic. Judith moved forward, but could not find a space between the waiters, and Tony turned to snarl at the two sous chefs and the preparation hand who had crept to the kitchen door to watch.

'There's something in here.'

'Miss Delves?'

Judith moved forward and found herself looking at one of the big heavy-duty plastic rubbish bags, tied at the top.

'Oh dear.'

'Looks as if someone dumped the rubbish in there.' Mr Aylwin observed and reached out a hand to prod. Not this morning, though, that's solid.' He motioned to an underling who untied the bag.

'Chief.'

'What?'

'Oh, Christ. Oh, Jesus Christ.'

The big man shouldered his way past Judith, putting her to one side, and looked into the depths of the freezer, and stopped, motionless. 'Miss Delves.' He reached out a big hand and pulled her forward. 'Do you see what I see?'

'Selina! Oh, Selina!'

Tony Gallagher came up at his elbow. 'Let's get her out,' he said, huskily.

The big man gazed into the freezer, and shook his head. He put out a restraining hand. 'Where's your phone?'

Wordlessly they took him into the kitchen and gave him the phone and watched while he dialled 999, giving his underlings, both white and looking sick, a look of magisterial disapproval. He finished the phone call and said into the air, without looking at either Judith or Tony, 'You'll need to close.'

Judith and Tony gaped at him, then looked at each other.

'It's a health risk,' Tony said, idiotically, and started to cry and giggle at the same time, while Judith numbly sent messengers to the front desk and told the kitchen staff, clustered together anxiously, to get some coffee down Tony and go home.

'No,' the chief inspector said, uncompromisingly. 'You'll all have to stay till the police get here.'

Everyone looked at him as if he had addressed them in a foreign language, but slowly they understood, and kitchen staff started to organise coffee and to press food on their weeping chef. Judith, crying herself and shaking from shock, looked round for the chief inspector. He had vanished from the kitchen, leaving his pallid assistants eating coffee and cake. Blowing her nose, she followed him to the passage to find him looking down on the livid, bloodstained face under the bright blonde hair.

She made an incoherent noise which attracted his attention. 'I'm going to close the lid,' he said, not looking at her.

'Are you . . . are you quite sure she's dead?'

'Oh yes.' He closed the lid gently, not banging it, and stood silently, and she realised he was the only person there who had thought to say a prayer for the soul of her departed friend.

4

It was a hot day in the City, the sun glinting on the cross on the top of St Paul's, but Richard Marsh-Hayden and Michael Owens, sitting in the hushed, thickly carpeted office on the top floor of the Marshall Deneuve building, were wearing jackets in the air-conditioning. The uniformed manservant who brought in a tray with coffee and biscuits paused to make a fractional adjustment to a blind to cut out the sun, turning the room into a self-contained space capsule.

Michael Owens, as the host, poured the coffee. He felt heavy and tired, but Richard, who had never carried excess weight, seemed to have lost half a stone since he had last seen him. He also seemed not to have bathed, or shaved, and the blond hair hung ragged and greasy into his eyes.

'I still can't believe it.' Richard had tasted his coffee and pushed it away and was speaking through a mouthful of expensive biscuit. '*And* I spent the morning trying to do all the things you're meant to. I got a death certificate, of course, in the end. Our lawyer – Wiggins – managed to bang into their heads that we had a business to run here.'

'Or at least one to sell.'

'Yes. The shares are left to me, with everything else. But the bugger is I can't do anything with them till Wiggins gets probate. Could take months apparently.' He reconsidered his coffee and reached for the sugar bowl.

'I'm so terribly sorry. About Selina.'

'Yes. That. Thanks for your note, got it this morning. I miss her, I bloody miss her. It didn't mean anything, you know, when we had these fights. And the worst thing is that the last thing we did was fight. I was so pissed off with her changing her mind about the sale. And now she's gone and she never even said goodbye.' He gazed into his coffee, his face creasing up as he snuffled painfully. 'Christ. Sorry.'

'What's to be sorry for? She's your wife.'

'*Was* my wife.' Richard fished a dirty handkerchief out of his pocket and studied it, looking unsuccessfully for a clean patch. Michael, reflecting that Richard's personal habits had always left something to be desired, produced a laundered one of his own. 'Thanks.' He blew his nose and wiped his eyes, making a thorough job of it. He stuffed it into his pocket and gazed drearily at the discreet blinds. 'I know she was a bitch. But I loved her.'

They sat in silence, the epitaph echoing in the room, until Richard sighed and sniffed. 'And she's left me right in it. The shares are mine, but so's the overdraft and the Harvey Nicks bill and the Access and the Visa, you name it. Only I haven't got anything to pay with and I can't sell her fucking shares, Wiggins says.' He took another cup of coffee. 'I know it's bad to think like that, with her only dead on Friday.' He paused and stared at the tray. 'Well, longer than that, but I only knew then. Oh, fuck it.'

'Rich, why don't you let me get my driver to take you home?'

'Because it's fucking worse there. The bank can't ring me up here and I don't have to open bills.' He hesitated. 'Mike, I know you've always said that you here don't lend on property but at the price my stuff is right now, you couldn't lose.'

Now *that* was probably true, Michael mentally agreed, but bankers are only fairly interested in the security for a loan, lending primarily on their assessment of the borrower. And in that context no worse bet than Richard Marsh-Hayden could be imagined. It wasn't that he was grossly extravagant, or at least not in the usual ways. He neither gambled on horses nor went in for ocean racing, but he was chronically unwilling to deprive himself of any of the things he was used to – skiing holidays at the best hotels in the most fashionable resorts and during the most expensive periods of the year, or meals in London's most expensive places. He had only a moderate London house in a good part of Fulham, but it had been reorganised and refurbished regardless of cost a year ago, when he was already having difficulty finding the interest on the huge mortgages that encumbered his small portfolio of secondary commercial property. Michael had thought censoriously more than once – well, about once every month – that, rather than put himself under such financial strain, he personally would have forgone the skiing holiday, and abandoned the hand-made kitchen and exquisitely redone plaster ceilings in the high living-room. Not that he had to make that choice, but after all he had grafted in a way that Richard never had. As a young graduate in a merchant bank he had worked fourteen hours a day for years doing all the overnight drafting and negotiations with clients, typists and printers to get the work done that fall to junior staff in a merchant bank. With no thanks, and shit poured in buckets from on high if, in a moment of exhaustion after three hours' sleep, you let a nasty through.

The prospect of taking Richard's affairs to the credit committee particularly at this moment stiffened his resistance and he got his mouth open to formulate a gracious but definitive sentence of refusal on the bank's behalf. But he saw that Richard had not been hopeful; he was sitting, shoulders slumped, watching a flicker of sunshine that had somehow penetrated the bank's defences, his expression utterly bleak.

'I could lend you a bit personally,' he heard himself say. 'Against your shares in the Caff,' he added, anchoring himself feebly in the slippery slope. He and Richard owned thirty-two and a half per cent each of the shares, making a powerful sixty-five per cent block between them. Richard's chin lifted as he looked out of the window, and Michael watched the man he had known for thirty years, since their first day at prep school, struggle with a set of conflicting emotions.

'They're hocked already.'

'You're not allowed to,' Michael said, shocked. 'None of us are. It's in the Articles.'

'Aren't bankers wonderful? It's in the Ten Commandments, you can't do it, see.' He slid his eyes sideways. 'I owed my builders. And Wade – you know, the plumbers. And they don't piss around, they'd put in a writ and I was about at the end of the road with the counter-claim for unfinished work, cheque's in the post, sorry, girl-can't-have-posted-it-I'll-give-her-a-rocket routine. You know.'

It occurred to Michael, as it had before in dealings with Richard, that possibly the dividing difference between one man and the next lay not in class or colour, nor upbringing, nor dealings with women, but in their attitude to money. He would personally find being chased for a debt intolerable. Richard, even if he didn't exactly enjoy it, regarded it as routine, like being in the Army where you were always having to shave or eat meals when you weren't particularly hungry.

'Who did you hock them to?' he asked, wondering which of Richard's friends or acquaintances had decided to take this particular risk. He guessed at the answer just before Richard, gazing studiously out of the window, gave it.

'Brian. Brian Rubin.'

'With an option to buy?'

'Yeh.' Richard had seen his expression. 'But only if you all agreed, of course. He knew you could refuse to register a transfer to him.'

44

He picked up a biscuit and crammed it into his mouth. 'After all, it is in the Articles.'

It was indeed; the Articles of Association had been carefully drawn up to avoid a situation in which the original members of the company, all of whom were friends or, like Tony Gallagher, were vital to its future, might sell shares to people less involved. It had occurred to Michael at the time that either, or both, of the improvident Marsh-Haydens might seek to charge their shares in return for a loan, but he had assumed that no one would lend on the basis of a charge which he could not enforce. But of course this calculation did not apply in the case of someone who wanted to buy the business. A potential purchaser, even if he were not able to get his name on the shareholders' register, could use a charge on the shares to force the legal owner to vote them in favour of a sale.

'How much? I mean how much did he lend you?'

'Nothing like the full value.'

A thirty-two and a half per cent shareholding had cost them £162,500 four years earlier. Richard, who would not normally have been able to find that sort of cash, had had a lucky sale of one of the less secondary properties, a small supermarket in Acton, right at the top of the market.

'But how much exactly?'

'Two hundred thou. Well, it was a life-saver at the time.'

'Which was?'

'Oh, about six months ago.'

Or, to put it another way, at about the time Brian Rubin had first tentatively started discussions about buying the Caff. It said much about both borrower and lender that Richard was so soon broke again, and that Brian Rubin had felt able, in view of his reported cash flow difficulties, to find such a sum. He must have been very keen on the deal then and must, like Richard himself, have been in deep trouble when the deal foundered on Selina's change of heart. Not only would he not be able to buy the two restaurants and get in new money, but he would have the greatest difficulty getting his company's £200,000 back from Richard. Not a lot to be done with an option over shares in a private company where thirty per cent of the shareholders were determined to keep it in private hands, and not even to put you on the register. A further set of questions occurred to him.

'What are the terms? Are you paying interest? When do you have to repay?'

'Ah, well, it was only to tide me over, or that's what I thought.' He looked out of the window. 'I'm paying interest at ten per cent.'

'That's reasonable. What about repayment?'

'That, yes. Twelve months after the loan, or he takes the shares.' He looked sideways at Michael who was trying to keep his face still. 'Well, he wants the business and he didn't want to be left with the whole thing up in the air for ever. He gets them if I die, as well.'

'So in six months' time, your shares are forfeit to him? Jesus, Richard.'

'Yeh, I know, but the whole sale should have been over.' He looked sideways, hopefully. 'You could lend me some against Selina's shares. They're mine, in two months, or whatever.'

'Have you tried Brian Rubin?'

'He'd jump at it. But he hasn't any cash. Or not this month, which is when I need it.'

Michael nodded; this went to confirm market gossip about the current financial state of their potential purchaser.

'Let me think about it. I'll come back to you by the end of the week.'

Francesca gazed, exasperated, at the weeping second-year student in front of her. The young woman had come to her, as Bursar, seeking a grant or a loan to enable her to continue her studies at Gladstone. The Hardship Fund, established by an outgoing senior tutor, amounted to just over £5000 in total, counting accrued interest, and had to be used very sparingly indeed if it was to meet the potential needs of the four hundred young women in residence. This one had come, pale and tear-stained, bearing letters from her bank, dressed in old torn jeans and a chewed-looking sweater. Which had made Francesca suspicious; she had an eye for clothes and had admired this particular undergraduate's style. It had not taken more than ten minutes to establish that such of the young woman's student grant as the college did not take in advance for residence, most of a student loan and all of a grudgingly extended overdraft had gone on her back. Repentance had been expressed, reform tearfully promised along with a holiday job that would set her right with the world again, and Francesca didn't quite believe any of it.

'I think this needs a little more thought, Christina. From both of us. But this college does not allow its students to starve or be sued for debt, so you are not to worry about that. Come and see me tomorrow.'

She escorted Christina, now doing no worse than sniffing, to her outer office and raised an eyebrow at the secretary she shared with two other people.

'Three messages, but all from the same person. Judith Delves.'

'Oh, goodness, yes. She is one of our Old Girls and her partner was found in a deep freeze.'

'Well, she really, really wants to talk to you, but I said I couldn't interrupt the college meeting. And then you had Christina.'

'Indeed, I did. I'll do Miss Delves next, thank you.'

What Judith Delves wanted was to talk to her with an urgency which meant that she was prepared to drive out, now, to Gladstone College in the thick of the morning traffic. Sensible alternative propositions like waiting until the evening when the discussion could take place at her house in West London, and/or talking to a good lawyer, were plainly a waste of time, so Francesca agreed, commiserated on Selina's death and organised a sandwich lunch. Feeding the afflicted often helped and never hindered. She found herself wondering whether Judith Delves was in a state to be driving a car and was much relieved when she presented herself undamaged but pale, swollen-eyed, looking very plain without make-up and with her hair flattened and messy.

'I am so sorry,' Francesca said, leaning to kiss her. They were not really on those terms but the other woman looked in need of all the comfort she could find. She sat her down on the visitors' sofa which was wedged into a corner of her small office, and uncovered the plate of sandwiches, on which Judith fell with the appetite of someone who has missed a few meals.

'I'm sorry. I've eaten much more than my share.'

'No matter.' Francesca, who found hunger one of the principal symptoms of pregnancy, lied gallantly. 'I expect you've barely had time to eat. What a dreadful thing to happen.'

'Yes. Poor Selina. Who could do that? Strangle her, I mean.'

The newspapers had not been explicit about the manner of the death, and Francesca was relieved not to have had to ask. A further question did however present itself.

'How long – I mean, do you know when she died?'

'No.' She stared ahead of her, unseeing, at a very dark nineteenth-century lithograph of the college. 'I last saw her in the evening about

47

ten days ago. The day you were in for lunch. I don't suppose you saw her.'

'A very beautiful blonde in a very smart cherry-coloured suit?'

'You did see her. Oh, I suppose Mr Sutherland pointed her out.'

Matt Sutherland must have fallen even further out of favour, Francesca thought, and hesitated on how to proceed, but Judith forestalled her.

'I came to see you because I don't know what to do. And I've asked people about you – they all say you've got very good ideas. And, well, you're at the college and I'd met you.'

'And done a party for my brother, and anyway Old Girls have some call on a Bursar's time. I'll be glad to help if I can.'

Judith Delves looked back at her thoughtfully. The sandwiches seemed to have restored her; she looked less puffy and her hair had somehow stopped flying about. 'You read Law?'

'Yes, but did not go on to qualify. I got a good place in the Department I wanted in the Civil Service. I've *done* a lot of company and insolvency law in the DTI though.'

'That's what I'd heard.' She paused but only to think how best to tell *her* story. 'I don't want to sell the company, you see, and Selina's shares are left to Richard. So he's after me to agree to a sale now on the basis that I'll have to agree when he owns the shares, however long that takes.'

'Even after all this, you don't want to sell.'

'Even *more* after all this. Selina was murdered, and I've known her since we were three. And someone killed her, not long after she decided to stay with me and not sell the restaurant.'

'So, you're damned if you'll sell.'

'That's right.'

'Mm.' Francesca considered her guest uneasily; the emotional response was entirely understandable, but the facts appeared to be against her. 'Take me through it. You have fifteen per cent, Selina has – had – fifteen per cent.'

'Richard and Michael have thirty-two and a half per cent each. They had thirty-five per cent each, but we had to find five per cent for Tony. Chef.'

'And Selina's shares are left to Richard? Yes? Who is trying to persuade you to sell before probate? What do the Articles of Association say?'

Judith Delves leant over and fished a weighty tome out of her briefcase and handed it over. 'Where the sticker is.'

The Articles provided that in the event of death the shares were to be treated as non-voting unless and until probate or Letters of Administration were issued. Francesca frowned and moved back a couple of pages. 'Ah. You don't have to register a transfer if you don't want to. Collectively, I mean.'

'No, we don't but I can't believe the others would refuse to register a transfer to someone who is already one of our shareholders. As Richard is.'

Francesca laid the tome aside, the better to think, and found herself back in a lecture hall, on a spring morning, listening to a distinguished barrister saying that the point about a largely statute-based area of activity, like company law, was that it didn't have the barnacle accretion of precedent and case law that attached to Contract or Tort. If there was ambiguity or doubt, opportunity was usually taken by the government of the day to legislate, hence the plethora of Companies Acts. So, take it that there was no way that that fifteen percent could be voted in advance of probate. But seventy per cent of the remainder wanted to sell; could they do that without the blocked fifteen per cent? She reached for a calculator and established that even with Selina's shares not voting Judith still only had seventeen and a half per cent of the remainder, not enough to block a sale. She gazed at her calculations, unseeingly, hearing the trained clear voice in her head. On the other hand, it had said, where no specific provision is made, the principles of Equity must still obtain. And where was Equity now that he was needed? Well, surely *not* on the side of anyone trying to rush through a sale both against the last known wishes of the testator and the wishes of a substantial minority.

'I think you could get an injunction to stop any sale ahead of probate,' she said, reaching the end of her thoughts. She realised that she had gone too fast and took Judith carefully through her reasoning. 'So you could go to court to stop a sale.'

'Michael would hate it.'

'Michael Owens? With thirty-two and a half per cent?'

'A very orthodox banker and hates hassle and lawyers. If I even hint that I might go to court he would insist Richard waited for probate.'

'Judith, sorry, but won't you have to sell anyway once probate is here?'

'Not necessarily. I've been a bit slow but I have now understood that Brian Rubin has to buy a small restaurant chain and has to do it

49

fast, or he could go broke. So I thought that if I could find a way of delaying he might go away and find something else to buy. And now you've thought of a way of holding the whole thing up – you are brilliant.'

Francesca gazed at her. 'I may not be right,' she said feebly, then thought about it. 'No, actually, I'm sure, at least that you have enough grounds to go for an injunction, and then you've got your delay.' She stood up, the better to think, and felt instantly dizzy. 'Damn.'

'Francesca! Are you all right?'

'Perfectly,' she said, breathlessly, gripping the desk, feeling the darkness recede. 'I'm pregnant, not ill. I just got up too fast. All I need is something more to eat.'

'I *am* a pig.' Judith Delves briskly settled Francesca in a chair. 'I've eaten all the food. Let me go and organise some for you.'

'I can get another load from the canteen and if you can find coffee and sugar right now I'll be fine.' She watched while Judith Delves commandeered someone else's secretary to go to the canteen, and made coffee herself, automatically cleaning up the mess round the little sink.

'Judith, what were you going to do if the sale had gone through? Were you going to work for Brian Rubin?'

'I don't like working for other people. I was going to start again with a smaller restaurant. If I could get the money together. It would have been – well, may still be – a terrible sweat.'

'Was this realistic?' Judith blinked at her. 'Sorry, I mean did you have any money lined up?'

'Well,' Judith was looking rather pink, 'I'd talked to Michael Owens about perhaps using some of the money he was going to make to invest – everybody would make a very nice profit from the sale, you know, more than double their money in four years, that's not bad, is it?'

'Bloody sight better than the lot who invest the college funds do, I can tell you. Did he seem willing?'

'Not really.' Judith was blushing in earnest, and Francesca waited, with interest, until the other woman found a way to continue. 'What happened was that he . . . that we . . . started going out together.'

'Never having contemplated this before?'

'No. We didn't know each other well and every time I saw him he had a different girl with him. Very attractive girls.' She looked across

50

at Francesca, still rather pink, and a little anxious, but obviously pleased with herself.

'So, as sensible men do, he got tired of airheads and looked around for someone who knew how to run their own life,' Francesca said, encouragingly, liking her. 'So where are we now, as it were?' She understood the question was too abrupt. 'How old is Michael, by the way?'

'Thirty-eight. Four years older than me.'

'And perhaps finding that it's time he settled down?'

Judith smiled at her gratefully. 'Well, that's it. And it does seem to be me he wants to settle down with, even though he could have all these dazzling blondes.'

'They *do*, you know, sensible men. You should see some of the creatures that litter the past of my good husband. So what are your plans now?'

'He's got this house. In Hampshire. He bought it last year when he got some giant bonus. He says it was just the house he'd always wanted, going cheap, so he bought it and let it.'

'So his plan would be to marry and install you there?'

Judith went scarlet. 'It's rather . . . well, I mean we haven't known each other very long.'

'It still sounds like the right working assumption,' Francesca said, briskly, and blinked as the other woman started to laugh.

'I absolutely knew you would be the right person to talk to. I had a tutor like you; she treated anything difficult as an administrative problem. It's very comforting.'

Francesca, taken aback, considered her. 'Romeo and Juliet as seen by a senior civil servant?'

'Yes. Precisely. So sorry, yes, I think that is his plan. To find someone to sort out the house and have children. And Michael wants to do a lot of entertaining. That's part of the point of the house.'

'So he is going along happily in the expectation that you will devote yourself to the country life and his affairs?'

Judith gave her a hunted, hostile look.

'I'm only asking.'

'I suppose I thought I would get the house right and have a child, and then look round and buy another business. Or start one. After all, *you* work.'

'Not full-time. Even with just the one child. Mind you, I worked until the night before, but I got ill after William was born – he was

51

one of those that never slept. I was extremely lucky to get this job. I'd have been counting paperclips in some backwater of the DTI otherwise.' She stopped; this was no time to upset her visitor further, and she wished she had not embarked on this line of conversation.

'But you're having another one.' Judith appeared interested, rather than distressed.

'Well, yes, but I ... we ... didn't want Will to be an only child. And I think I can manage two and a job with not much more difficulty than one and a job. But you do need a husband pulling in the same direction. John does, most of the time. He knows of course that we would be a bit pressed without my salary.'

'Michael, I have to say, earns enough for several people.'

'The trouble *is*,' Francesca said, warming to her subject, 'that most men, if they were honest, would rather be free to work much too hard while the wife handled all the domestic side. I can see that my John would be happier if he didn't always feel under pressure to help at home on top of a very heavy job.'

'Does he say so?'

'No, he wouldn't. But I see something else too. I'm not a career asset to him at all, quite the reverse. The colleagues hate him sloping off after only a twelve-hour day, because it's his turn with Will. Or refusing to take a posting outside London, because of my job – he doesn't know I know all this, by the way, but I do, some of them take the trouble to let me know. And if that is true for the Metropolitan Police, I bet it's even truer for merchant bankers.'

The other woman was looking stricken and she tried to think of a way of softening what she had said. She gave up; a truth that she herself had recognised, out of the corner of her eye, was now officially sanctified by research done in America. She had read the summary conclusions in *The Times* only that morning; employers had, as one man (and one woman, too), confirmed that the best opportunities went to the employee whose domestic situation allowed them to snatch them, with no whingeing about the needs of dependents.

'So you don't think that's going to work?'

'Well,' Francesca said, slowly, recognising yet another unpalatable truth about her own situation, 'you would have a better chance than me, if you could keep your own business, so you didn't need your boss's approval and were able to delegate everything you could afford to, and to go home when there's a crisis ...' She hesitated. 'Look, tell me more about your man, Michael. He was one of your original backers, wasn't he?'

'Yes, but I didn't know him then. He was brought in by Richard, Selina's husband. They'd known each other since Summerfield.'

'So Michael went to Eton as well?'

'No. No, he was meant to but his father ... well, something went wrong, and he lost his job and left them. So Michael went to Sevenoaks, on a scholarship, then Cambridge. Then into banking.'

'To make a lot of money.'

'Yes,' Judith said, slowly. 'Yes. To make enough money so he could have a big house and garden and send the children to Eton.' She looked at her hostess. 'And a châtelaine for the house, I know that, of course, but I've just seen it differently.'

Francesca reached for some more coffee to give her time. 'So Richard Marsh-Hayden brought him in to Café de la Paix and they put up the bulk of the money, presumably?'

'Selina and I put up £20,000 each, but we got extra shares for it.'

'Sweat equity. So Michael must have liked the look of you, even then.'

Judith laughed. 'He didn't spend that much time thinking about any of it. He had a huge tax bill that year. He was only thirty-four but he'd done some enormous bond, and he was just looking for somewhere to invest the loot. I tease him about it now – he thought Selina was wonderful and could make anything work. I'm not sure he even saw me.'

'He's a banker. He checked, he liked the look of you as a business person even if it took him four years to see you as a female person.'

Judith nodded, her face soft with remembering. 'I always thought *he* was very attractive, but I ... well, he wasn't taking much notice and he wasn't at the Caff very much. He's very busy, he was working awful hours – I mean worse than we do at the Caff – and at weekends he used to go off with the Territorials.'

'Really? Had he been in the Army?'

'No, but he always wanted to be. Like Richard. Well, like his own father. Only he said he could not afford it, he needed to make his fortune. So he became a banker and Territorial.'

'When did he find time to court you?'

Judith blew her nose, looking much better. 'We decided to do a second restaurant out of the profits, and we needed cash. So Richard made him come to a couple of meetings and I had to tell him all about it. This is just over six months ago. Then we got this offer for the shares, and we all had to spend a lot of time on it, and after that, well ...' She was blushing, and Francesca grinned at her.

'Events moved quickly.'

'Yes. Really *very* quickly.' Judith looked down. 'I mean, I was afraid I'd made an awful mistake – I'd always fancied him and I thought . . .'

'That you'd gone too fast? I keep saying this, but he's a banker, your Michael, and they don't usually have ill-considered affairs with their associates.' She smiled kindly on her visitor, feeling many decades older, but realised Judith was amused.

'He wasn't in banking mode when we . . . well, the first time. He was just back from a TA weekend.'

'Ah.' Francesca, momentarily wrongfooted, started to laugh. 'I see. Conquering hero stuff. What fun.' She considered this history soberly, remembering her grandmother's edict that if you had nothing pleasant to say you should remain silent. She reached for a sandwich – the affairs of Gladstone College would not permit her falling over in the office – and munched, keeping an eye on her guest.

Judith was staring into space. 'I suppose there isn't a lot of point in delaying a sale for eight weeks,' she said, bleakly.

'Oh, I don't know.' Francesca swallowed the last corner of the sandwich. 'The horse may talk. Do you know the story? It's about Louis XIV who is said to have condemned some felon to death but the man pleaded that if the most Majestic would spare his life he would teach his horse to talk.'

'Louis XIV's horse?'

'The felon didn't have one. So the King agreed and gave him a year to achieve this. The man's friends were naturally concerned but he pointed out that in a year the King might be dead, or *he* might be dead, or the horse might be dead. Or the horse might talk.' She met Judith's considering look. 'I'm not being critical; that story is the justification for procrastination when action offers no possible advantage.'

'That is how I heard it.' Judith nodded, looking amused and not at all plain. 'You've been very kind, Francesca, and I feel a lot better. May I talk to you again?'

'Of course.'

They kissed with real affection this time and Francesca stood to wave as Judith got into a big Volvo Estate, the more expensive model of the one she drove herself.

*

'I'll come to the Caff.'

'No. I don't want to talk here. I'll come round your place now, when I've changed. Say three fifteen.'

'OK, Tony, that's fine.'

Matt Sutherland put the phone down and stared at it, thoughtfully. He pressed a buzzer.

'Peter. You in?'

'Demonstrably.'

'I mean, are you free? For a consultation with your Associate.'

'Come on up.'

Matthew prided himself in being able to do all three flights of stairs to Peter Graebner's eyrie at the top of the building in under a minute, but it had the disadvantage of leaving him unable to speak when he got there. He slumped into a chair, sucked in a breath of almost pure nicotine and started to cough.

'Penalty of all this keep-fit nonsense, my boy. Just sit there till you can breathe. I could open a window.'

'That'd spoil it,' Matthew managed to say; and his senior partner looked at him over his glasses.

'It is, I take it, the Marsh-Hayden murder which has brought you to me.'

'It is.' Matthew had a final cough and considered the top of the desk which was piled with even more papers than the day before. Peter Graebner himself, small with curly grey hair sliding back from a high forehead, looking like a distinguished rat, was huddled behind the big desk, surrounded by overfilled ashtrays and a Dickensian collection of writing implements. He pushed up his bottle-thick spectacles and peered at his colleague.

'Tony Gallagher works in one of the two restaurants, I understand.'

'Supervising chef for both, but mostly does his shifts in the West End.'

'And do we think he was involved in the murder of Mrs Marsh-Hayden? The Hon. Mrs, I should say.'

'We bloody hope he isn't coming in to tell me he did it.'

'*Don't* let him do that, Matthew. We'd have to pass him on somewhere else, much less well qualified than ourselves. Do you have any reason to suppose he did it?'

'Well, she was found in his deep freeze. Inside a black plastic bag.'

'Really? Along with the ice-cream and the emergency steaks?'

'You didn't read the papers? All the management fell over themselves to point out that it was an *old* freezer, not in use.'

Peter Graebner considered the point, chewing one arm of his glasses. 'Except it was. In use, I mean.'

'They meant not officially. Not for anything else.'

'I expect that makes me feel a bit better. How long had she been there? Ah no, I see, they probably don't know.'

Matthew nodded approvingly. 'You're catching up, knew you would. She'd not been seen for a week or so, or not by anyone they've found.'

Peter meditated, leaning back in his chair, cigarette drooping from his lips. 'There's a husband of course. Our client, despite his casual attitude to frozen storage, won't be the first person the police are looking at.'

'No.'

'You are sounding doubtful? Ah, I remember now, you told me. They are trying to sell the restaurant. Or so your client hoped.'

'Yeh. And the deceased was the one who was holding up the sale.'

'Oh dear.' Peter's chair tilted forward, and Matthew understood that his attention was now fully engaged. 'How did she die?'

'Strangled.'

'Mm. And he's a Gallagher. Martin Gallagher is, let me see, half-way through a sentence for aggravated assault. And Kevin, the younger one, is away for assault and battery, I remember. What a pity. Hoped that was a brand saved from the burning.'

The six-partner law firm had been founded by Peter Graebner, who had trained originally for the rabbinate, but had decided, abruptly, that his proper duty lay with ensuring that the poor and the deprived had access to the same panoply of legal rights as any of their more fortunate contemporaries. Among his other assets he had a compendious memory which rendered him independent of the firm's up-to-date and efficient computerised systems.

Matthew sat upright. 'You're assuming Tony did it?'

'Well, someone did. But the husband's the best bet, Matthew, remember. Statistically.'

'That's true, isn't it?' Matt said, gratefully, as the phone buzzed and a voice announced that Mr Gallagher was here now, for Matthew.

'Try and get her to call you Mr Sutherland in front of the clients, will you?'

Matt clattered downstairs to receive his client, who was sitting staring out of the window. He had changed out of his chef's whites

56

into a navy bomber jacket, and he was unshaven, his jawline tense. Matthew was disconcerted suddenly to see him as one of the dangerously aggressive men who were part of their regular clientele rather than a key manager at two major restaurants.

'Afternoon, Tony.' He led him into the small interview room and sniffed, turning out an ashtray and a copy of the *Express* which, he saw, unfortunately featured his client on the front page.

'Trouble is, they got a stock photo. For articles, like.'

Tony had secured a good deal of favourable publicity for himself and the group, but, as always, there was a downside. Most papers did indeed have good, recent pictures of him and of the highly photogenic Selina and had not hesitated to use them. Matthew studied his client anxiously.

'You saw the police?'

'Couldn't miss them. I threw a wobbly when the health inspector found the body, but they took a statement today. Just about how long since I'd looked inside the freezer, like. They want to see me again, so I thought I'd talk to you first.'

'I could come with you, if you'd rather,' Matt offered.

'I might. See, there's something a bit difficult.'

Matt caught his breath. 'Tony, you know that we're all officers of the court, I mean . . .'

'If I topped her, not to tell you? Well, I didn't, don't worry, mate. But we *did* have words, Madame and me, the evening she went off the air. I don't want to find myself fitted up. It would suit some to blame the staff, I can tell you.'

Matthew breathed out slowly and organised his pad and pen. 'What sort of words? And when?'

'The Thursday you was in, before she disappeared. She come down to the kitchen and she was asking all sorts of questions – how many of this, what had that cost. So after a bit I ask her what she's getting at, and she goes huffy and says she's just checking on plate costs. So I tell her if she's got anything she doesn't understand we'll go through it in the office only not right now when I'm checking staff for the service, yeh? She gets right uptight and says something that gets on my wick so I tell her to piss off out of my kitchen. And she says I better remember it isn't me who owns the kitchen, so I call her a silly tart who ought not to be in the restaurant business. Or any business.'

'Mm. To which she replied?'

57

'That this restaurant wasn't going to be sold until it had been made as profitable as it should be, and I'd better remember that and who was in charge.'

'Was that all?'

'I said she wasn't in charge, whoever else was, being too busy getting her face in the papers and going shopping. But that was it.'

'Anyone else hear any of this?'

'There was a sous chef and a commis in. They may not have heard the words but they could have hummed the tune. And they'll have said something, 'course they will.'

'That's the right bet, yes.' Matthew finished his notes and looked at them. 'You really wanted to sell, Tony, didn't you? Why? You reckoned to get a better job?'

'That. And I need the money.'

Matthew hesitated. 'I'd better know. Why do you need it?' His client's eyelids flickered, betrayingly, and Matthew waited for the lie.

'I want to buy a house. Put down a big deposit, see.'

'Just for yourself?'

'What? Yes. Might have a mate to share.'

Tony Gallagher lived in his mother's council flat which had more rather than less space now that both brothers were being otherwise accommodated by the state. The silence lengthened, but Matt was not at all uncomfortable with a hiatus.

'I owe it.'

'To whom?'

'Some people.'

Matthew waited, patiently.

'It's a bet, isn't it?' Tony finally volunteered.

'And they want paying.' This was familiar territory but Tony stood to get £30,000 for his share; he must have been betting substantially.

'Yeh. Thought I'd got it back Saturday but the cow fell over in the last race at Doncaster. I had a Yankee with three winners.'

'How much do you owe?'

'A bit.'

This was not a promising scenario. Selina Marsh-Hayden had been standing between his client and enough money to save said client from a beating at best. And they had quarrelled. And her body had been found in a deep freeze in his client's back office, as it were.

'You'd better have a lawyer with you when you talk to the fuzz,' he said, soberly. 'You want Peter?'

His client gave him a long careful look.

'You my lawyer or not, sunshine?'

'I'm your lawyer. I'm good but I've been qualified all of three months, while Peter's been at it for thirty years.'

'Yeh, he's good. But I'll stick with you.'

5

Judith Delves had spent the first hour of the morning sorting out staff rotas. For a wonder there had been enough staff both on the floor and in the kitchen to ensure that she would not be needed over the lunch service, so she had decided to get into the office. She knew that six months at the new site had left a gap here but was startled by its extent. Mary was an excellent bookkeeper, in the sense that all the data got into the system, bills were paid, receipted and filed, VAT returns were made, correctly and regularly. But none of it had seemed to join up in her mind, no alarm bells had rung as the operating margins slipped and the overdraft crept up. Arguably the best bookkeepers were like that, accurate recording machines. But what had Selina been *doing*? Well, numbers had never been her strong suit and she had presumably just not looked hard enough. Too busy chatting up the customers, Judith thought, instantly regretting the lack of charity towards her recently and horribly murdered friend. And come to that, she reminded herself acerbically, what had *she* been doing? She had been busy for long hours off site, but she could at least have got here and looked at the numbers, or checked the bank balance. She had done neither.

'Judith? I'm sorry to interrupt you. I know you said not to, but Richard's on the phone.'

Judith lifted her head from the pile of print-outs she was examining and made a neat mark in the corner.

'Richard. How are you?' And *what* a stupid question, she thought, appalled, to ask of a man whose wife had recently been found strangled and deep-frozen. Mercifully he ignored it, driven by his immediate needs.

'Could you . . . that is, would you come round? I've had the police here, looking through Selina's things, and I . . . Well, there's all this stuff and I can't . . . I can't work out what to do with any of it. Her mother's coming round later, but . . .'

She waited to hear what the 'but' was, but his voice trailed away. 'Of course I'll come, Richard. About twenty minutes in this traffic.'

It took longer, but by the time she arrived Richard seemed to have himself in hand. He took her into the immaculately decorated living-room. He had made himself a cup of tea, the television was on, and the dismembered crusts of a pizza lay on a plate beside it on an expensive glass coffee table. She had always found him alarming; his family was now poor but still very grand, in a faded way, and Richard had been brought up in a cold echoing palace in Shropshire in the full confidence that the eldest son of such a family could do anything he liked. Whatever the vicissitudes of his adult life, he still paid no attention at all to the niceties of conventional behaviour, or worried for one minute about what other people might think. He and Selina were alike in this, being prepared to conduct any aspect of their lives in public, regardless of the number or composition of the audience. Typically, he did not thank her for coming, or ask if she wanted tea, which she would have liked, but plunged straight into his principal preoccupation.

'She's got an awful lot of stuff. Clothes, I mean. Whole spare room's full. I need to sort them out.'

The spare room was a decent twelve foot by fourteen foot and one long wall was entirely made up of expensively designed cupboards. Richard was pushing sliding doors as she took in the dressing-table, glass top covered in a wild profusion of make-up, perfume, cotton wool, scissors and paper handkerchiefs. In the cupboards, clothes were hung in scurried rows and shoes tumbled all over the floor as the doors opened.

She started at the left-hand corner, trying to get a feel for what was there. Everything seemed to carry a designer label and of course they were all in a size ten or less. Indeed, you needed to be as slim as Selina and to have legs at least approaching her length to wear clothes like this, she thought, gazing enviously at a very short, very pretty A-line skirt which had probably stopped six inches above Selina's smooth, brown knees. She glanced at Richard and saw that he was staring intently at the racks of clothes.

'Bloody expensive.'

'She always looked wonderful.' This at least was a tribute she could pay ungrudgingly. 'You helped her shop, didn't you?'

'Sometimes.' He was still staring at the cupboards as if they might escape, and she decided she must get him downstairs again.

'How much you reckon this lot cost, Judith?'

'What?' Well, if no one of the family wanted them, selling them was not a stupid idea; she would ring up one of the up-market Nearly New shops that she occasionally saw at the back of Selina's glossy magazines.

'A suit runs about £800, doesn't it?'

'St Laurent, yes, about that, Nicole Farhi a bit less, Jil Sander a bit more. I don't know what you would get through a Nearly New shop, but say a third of that.'

'She didn't go to those places,' Richard said, and she understood they were at cross-purposes. 'So.' He pulled himself to his feet and went down the racks of clothes, counting. 'Twenty-five, say. That's twenty thousand fucking quid. An' that's not all. Shoes. What do they cost?'

'She buys – bought – Magli. About £150 a pair.' She was watching him anxiously, but he squatted down without ceremony and conducted a rough count in the bottom of the cupboards, occasionally hauling out a pair, impatiently. 'About fifty. That's another, what, £7000-odd. Fuck. And we couldn't even pay the milk bill.'

Judith cleared her throat nervously. 'Richard, I think you should leave this to me and Selina's mother. If she doesn't want . . . well, all of it, then I'll arrange for what's left to go to a Nearly New.'

He cast a final baleful, puzzled look at the cupboards as he stood aside to let her pass – his upbringing had at least included a sound training in formal manners, she reflected.

'Would you like a cup of tea? I could make it.' Judith, in serious need of sustenance, decided she would have to ask, and thankfully found tea and biscuits.

Something was worrying Richard still, she thought, watching him prowl around the small kitchen.

'The police found some letters,' he said, abruptly, looking out of the window. 'To Selina. Before we were married.'

The ground was very uneasy here, she could feel the tension in his body from several feet away.

'Some from blokes, of course.'

'Well, of course,' she said, promptly, and then wondered. If she had been a person who kept letters, what would she have had to show as correspondence with the opposite sex? Two notes from a boy half a head smaller than her, with spots, at the nearby boys' school. And several letters and notes from Ben, with whom she had had an entirely unsatisfactory affair eight years ago now. And to call it an affair was doing it a favour; his letters had been the best part of the whole thing.

'Richard. Do you want to keep them, or . . .?' Or what, she thought, panicking.

'Police took them. There was only a few. Wonder why she kept them?'

At least the conversation had become rational again. 'Don't you keep letters?' she asked.

'Not on purpose. I find the odd thing down the back of a drawer, whatever.'

'I used to, then I threw them away. Or all I could find. Perhaps Selina just didn't find these.'

'Yeh.'

This, she saw, had hit the right note and he was looking more cheerful. She glanced at her watch. 'What time did you say Selina's mother was coming?'

'Oh Christ. Now, or pretty soon. Can I go out and leave you to it? We spent most of yesterday together and it didn't do either of us much good. Yeh? Thanks, Judith . . .'

Michael Owens sat in his big office behind a substantial mahogany desk, space all round him, feeling trapped and slightly sick. His secretary put her head round the door.

'I've just talked to Margaret – that's Mr Judd's secretary. She says he's in a meeting, then he's getting a plane, but he *will* get back to you today. He's been ever so busy, she says.'

'Today?'

'That's what she said.' They looked at each other; Susie preferred to do her job and keep her head down, but she was not a stupid or unsympathetic young woman. 'I know that's what she said yesterday, and the day before, but maybe he is very busy. Her boss.'

'Maybe. Thanks, Susie.'

'More coffee?'

'That'd be nice.'

He waited, looking out over the City, the great high towers thrusting up from the Wren churches and the nineteenth-century banking palaces that still persisted. He had fallen in love, conclusively, the first time he had seen the place, as a graduate trainee accountant, and for over fifteen years it had returned his love, and he had been happy. Until this bloody awful last year when he seemed to have lost his touch. The bank had failed, publicly and conclusively, four months ago, to get a flotation under way. It had been his client, his responsibility, his baby, with substantial success fees for the bank and himself, and all his team riding on it. And the client turned out to be an incompetent manager and perhaps worse than that. The flotation had had to be pulled at the last minute, with all the underwriting in place and fees incurred all over the City to the underwriters, the lawyers and the sodding useless reporting accountants who had not been doubtful or cautious enough. Well, it was a banker's job to see the wider picture. He hadn't been on top of it enough and had left the details to a not very experienced young assistant director, who had not known enough about where to look. He'd been bloody well too busy himself, running half the department and harassed by everything. He stilled, resolutely, the familiar interior monologue; there was no point in it, what's done was done, he'd had bad luck, happened to everyone at some time, and he'd made enough money for the bank that he could weather it. Just. But the débâcle had put him out of the running for head of corporate finance, and an impressive tough, just younger than him, had been brought in from Warburgs to run the department. And Simon had made it arrogantly clear that everyone, but particularly those who had been involved in the mistakes of that year, had to earn their ticket, no matter how senior they were, or what their past contributions.

Now was the time to bring in a really good high-paying innovative deal, or it would have been. But the one – the big one, the one that was going triumphantly to redeem all past errors – was going sour. It was a good idea, a deal whereby a problem division in one big retailer, not previously a client of the bank, would merge with a similar one in different ownership, and he had devised a very clever financing structure to facilitate the merger. And the retailer to whom he had taken the idea had been more than enthusiastic; for the last four weeks his people had been working flat out, and the phone had gone a dozen times a day, either to him or to the bank team he had put in place. But the buzz was gone, and he hadn't managed to speak to the managing director, or the finance director, since last week. And the finance director's staff weren't returning phone calls from his juniors either. You could tell yourself that they were just regrouping, and would be back on all the phones tomorrow, but his years in the City told him otherwise. They'd decided not to do it, or, worse, much worse, decided to do it with someone else, leaving him with nothing to say and four weeks' intensive work by a three-man team unpaid for.

He got up and reached for his address book, the bank's client list and the *Financial Times*. What you did at these points was to go through everything, any contacts you had – and he had plenty – to find a couple of ideas that might work. And you started with the clients, because you knew them best and they wouldn't usually drop you in it, take your idea and run. He found however that he couldn't start, and he couldn't face assembling his team, telling them the bad news, and starting them working on ideas. The best of them wouldn't even do that for him, they would be poached by other busy directors, that was how you progressed and made money in corporate finance, by getting yourself to where the action was. He was supposed to be one of the chaps who found the action, and today he couldn't do any of it.

'Susie? I'm going to the gym. Just for an hour.' His back ached with tension, and he knew he needed exercise to ease it up, so he would go, little though he felt like it. And then have lunch with Judith, he needed a break. Then he remembered she was off site, with Richard, and set off wearily for the gym, commandeering his bastard boss's driver to take him.

Brian Rubin and his financial controller were sitting side by side at a table. A PC blinked at them from one end, then, ignored, swallowed the contents of the screen, substituting a series of starbursts.

'It's a bit better this week.' Diana, in her forties, thin as a whippet, putting a son through boarding-school, had been with him for years and knew exactly what variables mattered. 'Take's up, by, what, £5000. And we paid the VAT last week.'

'So, who do we pay, outside the necessaries?'

'No one. It's only £5000, Brian, we hang on to it in case next week isn't so good.'

'That's right, isn't it?' Brian Rubin said sadly; he was a natural optimist and also liked people he dealt with to be happy. 'Well, maybe we'll do even better next week.'

Diana eyed him. 'It's tight, Brian. What's happening with this deal? We can't go on long like this.'

'No, no, I know.' He hesitated, but Diana had every right to ask, and there wasn't anything else she didn't know. 'The bugger is that Selina's husband has to wait till the lawyers have got everything together and got probate before he can sell the shares to me. Could take weeks.' He considered her. 'You think we can hold out for six or eight weeks, Diana?'

'If the take stays up, yes. The bank sees the management accounts every week, they know the music by now. I don't think they'll increase the overdraft but they'll hang on if it isn't getting any worse and they can see a way out. Just. If no one sues. But we have not to spend a penny anywhere we don't have to. We can forget the redecoration schedule.'

'Bloody right,' Brian agreed, heartily. He gazed fixedly at the piles of bills, thinking hard, then he sighed, and Diana, who knew him very well, waited, apprehensive. He reached over to his jacket and slowly extracted a bill from his wallet. He gave her a sidelong, little-boy look. 'There's one here.'

'Your Visa?' She took it from him and scrutinised it. 'We won't get this past the auditors. We don't buy uniforms at Harvey Nicks, at £800 a throw. Janice has been going it a bit, hasn't she?'

'No. Yes. I'll pay it back, but I'm skint – personally as well. And I need to use it.'

'You'd do better to cut it up. Or, at least, cut up Janice's card. Doesn't she understand what's happening here?' She gazed at her boss, indignant on his behalf. He was a good ten years her junior and she felt responsible for him and totally identified with all his interests.

'Look, Di, leave it, will you? She's been having a bad time and this deal was going to solve a lot of things.'

'Brian, you may not be able to wait for this deal to happen if she goes on spending money like this.'

He got up and stared out of the window. 'Thing is, Di, it wasn't Janice. Those things.' He waited, then turned to see her open-mouthed and struck silent. 'It's not what you think. See, Selina – Mrs Marsh-Hayden – was always being a bit dodgy about the sale, kept complaining that any money she got would be taken by her husband to pay his debts. Well, I thought she was probably right – not a lot in it for her. So we went shopping, so she'd have a few goodies of her own, to sweeten the deal.' His voice trailed away as she stared at him. 'Well, I can't tell Janice any of that, can I? Not now. Not when she's pissed off with me anyhow, wants to know whether Joshua's going to be able to go to Stonefield, yatter, yatter, yatter.'

'Are you mad, Brian?' Diana said, getting her breath back. 'Was Selina blackmailing you?'

'Nah, not really. Just giving me a hard time, and getting a bit for herself off the deal.' He took a deep breath. 'Anyway, Di, I can't tell Janice she can't use the card. She knows what the credit limit is and she's going to pay the school deposit off it, whatever I say. So we have to pay some off, yes? I'm sorry, it looks stupid now.' He gazed at her hopefully. 'I'll buy you lunch. Downstairs, where it's free.'

'John.'

'Sir.'

John McLeish had been summoned to see his Commander, and came carrying the notes on a case he had managed to complete that morning and reduce to a tidy package such as even the CPS could not, he hoped, make a haggis of. He stopped at the door; there was a heavy senior man, whom he did not know, sitting at the table.

'This is Superintendent Hall from Special Branch. Detective Chief Superintendent McLeish. You can tell him everything.'

John McLeish nodded politely to the Special Branch man and listened while he unfolded his story. 'Sorry,' he said after three minutes. 'Let me get this straight. Your royal charge was having a walk-out with Mrs Marsh-Hayden, whose body turned up in a freezer in West End Central's patch. When? No, not the body, the walk-out. Six months ago? Was it still going on?'

'We don't think so. And we ought to know. But we don't want the whole of the Met tramping over the back history so we're asking for "C" division's co-operation. Sorry it took us a while to make the connection.'

'I know the restaurant. I ate there last week with my wife and two of my brothers-in-law.'

'No personal connection though?' the Commander asked, sharply.

'One of the partners knows my wife slightly,' he volunteered, hopefully.

'If we kept you away from anyone Francesca knows slightly you'd be on your ownio in a tower,' his boss said, heartily, and McLeish understood wearily that he had just added another burden to his case load. He acknowledged the obligation and escorted the Special Branch man to the lift, returning to face the Commander.

'Sorry, John. How *is* Francesca?'

'Pregnant.' He had known the man for fifteen years, there was no need to keep key facts from him.

'Well done, John, we knew you had it in you.'

He managed to raise a polite smile for the traditional Metropolitan Police benison before heading for his own office to call for everything anyone had on the Marsh-Haydens and the Café de la Paix.

6

'So that's all I know so far, Bruce. And this is all we have. Photograph of deceased when in life, and a post-mortem picture. She was strangled, and deposited in a deep freeze in the basement of her own restaurant shortly after death according to Forensic.'

'They had to defrost the body before they could cut.'

Detective Inspector Bruce Davidson, a stocky, black-haired Scot, who had known John McLeish for many years, gazed at the small pile of exhibits. 'It's no' a suicide, then?'

'I'd guess not, but we'll need to look at that carefully.' McLeish, lips compressed with tension, was sitting on the edge of his desk going through messages, handing some back to his secretary with instructions, and packing the others into a briefcase.

Davidson laid the photographs side by side and considered the contrast between the assured blonde smiling teasingly into the camera, eyes wide, and the congested distorted lifeless mask, the eyes closed in death. 'Poor lass. A pretty one.'

'That's right. Said to have been the mistress of one of Special Branch's charges – no, not *him*, thank the Lord, one of the cousins. Not current, they don't think, but just the same . . .'

'Keep that off the file, will we?'

McLeish paused in his labours and looked across at him. 'Yes. It's bad practice, but *if* there's going to be anything in the papers it'd better not have come from here.'

'So why *have* we got the case then, John? For the lads' ears, I mean.'

'Can we leave it vague? Blame it on the AC.'

'Nae bother.'

'And could we solve it by tonight, do you think, Bruce? I'm supposed to be in Glasgow tomorrow.'

'I'd mebbe better get started then.' Bruce Davidson gathered up the slender file and made to go, but John McLeish motioned to him to close the office door.

'Your godson is going to have a little sister.'

'Away! Well done, John.' He caught his superior a eye and

managed not to go on. 'I'm glad it's to be a girl,' he said, heartily. 'Francesca decided, did she?'

'*She* thinks it's twin boys. I'm just trying to take a positive view.'

'That'll slow her up a bittie.'

'I'd not put money on it. See you in a few minutes.'

The room was enormous and air-conditioned, high in one of the new blocks at Bishopsgate, overlooking Liverpool Street Station. Twenty people could have met comfortably in it, but even with four thinly spaced at the top of the large oval table Brian Rubin was sweating.

'So I hope all that is clear,' he said, in peroration, leaning forward winningly. 'We would hope to be able to complete the sale next week, after a formal vote. And Richard here would give an undertaking to transfer the remaining fifteen per cent when he gets probate.'

The broker was not listening to him, but was reading the marked passage in Café de la Paix Ltd's Articles of Association. 'I'm not altogether comfortable, Brian. And it's not an easy proposition to explain to investors. Who, as you must know by now, can only cope with the Janet and John stuff.'

'But this isn't *complicated*,' Richard Marsh-Hayden said, irritably, and Brian Rubin, although in agreement with the sentiment, regretted that he was seated just too far away to kick him.

The lanky broker at the top of the table said uncensoriously that anything was too complicated for the simple souls of the investing institutions. If you couldn't chop it up and serve it out in bite-size bits they just went and did something easier. And you had soured your market.

'So what *am* I supposed to do?' Brian Rubin asked, rhetorically.

'Keep on trading in your admirable restaurants. Keep the money coming in until . . . well . . . until all the Café de la Paix shareholders are free to sell.'

The problem was that the cash coming in fell short of that required to keep suppliers in a state of barely simmering discontent, and to give the bank the interest on their loans. As these people ought to know, Brian Rubin reflected, angrily.

'I'm sorry to rush you, but I am due in a meeting. Can we get you a car? No?'

Brian and Richard found themselves outside on the pavement five minutes later in a state of mutual frustration.

'What the fuck am *I* supposed to do,' Richard asked, bitterly, of the surrounding air. 'Wait for the bank to call in *my* loans?' He pulled irritably at his collar, sweating in the warm sun.

'They'll carry you, won't they?'

'Well, they can't do much else. They're better off waiting for probate.'

'Did Selina . . . is there any cash as well as the shares?'

'You must be joking. She had some from her trustees, wouldn't tell me how much, but she spent it. I'm going to post them all her credit card bills. See if they'll do those at least.' He hesitated. 'I asked Michael Owens if he would lend a bit on her shares. He's thinking about it.'

The advantages of having that sober banker tied financially into a sale were considerable, and Brian Rubin was cheered. 'He's known you a long time, hasn't he?'

'Since we were nine. Never lent me any money. Not sure he's going to start now.'

'I would if I could, you know, Rich, against those shares. But the fucking bank took it all this month. I don't know how they expect me to stay in business.'

They parted, gloomily, and Brian slid into his car just as his mobile started to ring. 'Hello.' The voice was as irritatingly cool and detached as the rest of the broker's personality. 'Is Richard Marsh-Hayden still with you?'

'No.'

'Mm. Brian, we think you should consider looking elsewhere for a deal.'

'I bloody *have* looked elsewhere. Café de la Paix is the only thing around.'

'I know it's disappointing. But it occurred to us there may be another problemette here. Don't know how well you know Marsh-Hayden? It's his wife that was murdered, and most murders are domestic. And if, God forbid, that's what happened then he can't inherit those shares anyway. Chap who did the killing mustn't benefit. Makes sense really. Brian?'

Brian Rubin was sitting in the car, heart hammering and an odd ringing in his ears. 'Yeh, I'm here.' He rallied. 'But then the shares just wouldn't get voted, and the Café shareholders who want to sell would still have a majority.'

He heard the man at the other end take a long, careful breath.

'Don't say it,' he pleaded. 'You'd never get the institutions to commit.'

'Would make a difficult introduction to the placing document, yes. I've asked Joscelin to do a trawl, on the chance we know something or someone you don't. Very bad luck.'

'Shit.'

'I agree. But you never know. In six months' time all this will be past, one way or another, and if you stay in touch you could get the Caffs a good deal cheaper than now.'

'So, we've no idea when she died?'

'That's the point about deep freezing, John. It stops all the processes from which I might have been able to offer you an approximate time of death. There was no decomposition, until we got the corpus thawed out. The murderer had had to fold her up to get her into the black bag as well.'

John McLeish considered, despondently, what he was being told. 'So she'd have been put in the freezer immediately – I mean, right after she died.'

'Yes, I think so. When I say there was no decomposition, well, that's almost right, but it probably took twenty-four hours to freeze the corpus to the point where nothing could happen. So there are some signs.'

'What about rigor?'

'Oh, all *that* happened. Or the rigor did. She was put into the freezer on the side doubled up – knees up to the chin – so he must have done all that before rigor set in. Then it set in and didn't wear off until we defrosted the body. So she probably went in within a couple of hours of death. But as to which day she was put in, well, you're back to police work, John. And you, Inspector.'

Bruce Davidson received this as a signal to join in. 'Thanks, Doc. Now, you reckon she was strangled from behind. With a rope?'

'No. See, here.' He jabbed a finger at one of the photographs spread all over his desk. 'Cloth – it didn't cut as a rope would have. Even a tea towel – something like that.'

'What's the blood?' John McLeish was bent over the photographs.

'Her own. A nosebleed. All that' – he indicated the blotchy picture – 'is hers.'

'Might have got on the murderer's clothes, though.'

71

'Difficult to move a body with a nosebleed without getting it on yourself. He might have waited, though. It would stop, you know, a few minutes after death.'

Yes, McLeish thought, suddenly in the scene, seeing a heavy figure relaxing as the struggling creature in his hands went limp and heavy, but he wouldn't have *liked* waiting, would he? He'd have wanted to shift the body immediately from wherever it was he'd killed her and get it hidden. So the best bet is he got some of her blood on himself. He saw Doc Smith look at his watch.

'Anything else useful? Sorry to badger you ahead of the report, Doc. Did she struggle?'

'Yes, poor girl. Torn fingernails, bits of white cotton under them: but probably not very effectively. Not easy to struggle, you know, if you've got someone behind you who knows what they're doing. You can't scratch their eyes out, or kick them in the goolies . . .'

'So he knew what he was doing?'

'Or she. Deceased was a small woman. About eight stone and chicken-boned. Strong girl could have done it.'

'Take long, would it?' Davidson asked, seeing McLeish disconcerted.

'Four to five minutes. And the victim probably didn't make a lot of noise.'

'Could she have scratched the murderer's hands?'

'She could, but there's no traces under the fingernails. Her first instinct would have been to try and loosen the noose, do you see? Get some air. So she seems to have pulled at the cloth that was strangling her and she may have pulled at his wrists as well. There are two sorts of fibres under the nails, it's all in the report.'

'She didn't get at the murderer's hands at all?' McLeish asked, coming out of his trance.

Doc Smith, on the edge of his chair to leave, changed his mind. 'Sit down, Inspector Davidson. There. Now I'm coming round the back of you with my handkerchief – dear me, not that one, but I've a better one here. Now I'm putting it round your neck – it's too thin, but it'll do for demonstration purposes – and I'm twisting it. What can you do?'

'I can dive forward, pushing the chair into your stomach and breaking your grip.'

'You're young, you're a policeman, you've had a moment to think about it and you're not really choking. Try again.'

Davidson put his hands to his throat to loosen the noose and Dr

Smith tightened it sharply. Davidson reached behind over his head to make a grab but could only find air.

'I'm leaning back. And I'm still tightening the band.'

Davidson reached behind his own neck and tried to impede the strong hands, clawing at the wrists and finally succeeding.

'Very good, Inspector.' Doc Smith was out of breath and wheezing distressfully. 'But you only just managed to get to my hands, and you're bigger and younger than I am, not an eight-stone female. And you weren't really running out of air or frightened.'

'Sit down, Doc, for God's sake.' McLeish guided him anxiously to a chair. 'My Commander will never forgive me if I've done in our best doctor.'

'Flattery will get you a very long way.' Doc Smith sat down, still wheezing, but turning a better colour. 'I've made my point, I hope. You're not looking for a gorilla here, male or female.'

'And I'm grateful.' McLeish eyed him uneasily. 'I'd like to go and talk to Forensic, but . . .'

'I expect to live, John. Ask that young woman to give me some coffee. Stimulates the heart.'

They went over to Forensic after waiting to see a coffee into the hands of the police surgeon. Some of the paperwork had caught up with them by then; Bow Street had sent over everything they had and they stopped for a preliminary run through, comparing the statements. They agreed that the statement from Antoine Dhéry would need immediate investigation. Antoine was a sous chef – I must get a grip of the hierarchy, McLeish observed – a French native with not very good English but nonetheless clear that the deceased had come in to see Chef about 5.30 p.m. on the Thursday and they had had an argument, from which the deceased had retired pink in the face and angry. Chef had also been agitated, according to Antoine, observing that management was a pain in the backside and an obstacle to progress in all institutions. Davidson fished out three other statements to confirm that Chef was not a Frenchman like his sous chefs – whatever they were – but Irish born, Tony Gallagher. His own statement confirmed that he had indeed had an argument with the deceased but had forgotten about it as soon as she had left the kitchen.

McLeish thought about Tony Gallagher and the unidentified cotton under the dead woman's nails all the way to Forensic, up to the moment when he was staring at the enormously enlarged fibres through the microscope.

'What's that bit of green?'

'A thread. Same stuff. Bit of the design on the tea towel. These bits *here* are different, they don't come from a tea towel. Different cloth, stronger, closer weave.'

'A uniform perhaps?'

He had hardly been surprised after this to discover from Judith Delves' statement that the kitchen staff at Café de la Paix all wore white jackets, as provided by management, and that all tea towels were white with a green logo. 'Start with Gallagher,' he said, and Davidson left to run him to earth. 'Get him here, not the restaurant.'

He waited, reading as fast as he could while Davidson made phone calls.

'He's bringing his solicitor,' Davidson reported.

'Who is it?'

'Graebner. In the person of Mr Matthew Sutherland, our old friend.'

'Yes, of course,' McLeish said, remembering that Francesca had told him Matthew was advising the chef at Café de la Paix. Well, even the cocky Matthew could not have expected a murder investigation. He sighed; he found Matthew tiring, but on the other hand and in fairness, that young man had saved a life the last time they had met by deciding precisely where danger lay while he himself had been still hesitating.

He shook hands with Matthew and asked him how he was, only because it gave him and Davidson the chance to observe his client, Tony Gallagher, in his late twenties, fair, stocky, carefully dressed in a good jacket and tie which could not disguise the wide shoulders. And he had enormous hands and a good, strong grip. The dead girl would have been almost as tall but nowhere near his weight and no match for those big hands, the palms so wide and thick as to make the long fingers look stubby.

He started gently, taking Gallagher through his previous statement, then moved on to ask about the kitchen jackets and tea towels, observing that Gallagher was showing no surprise at this line of questioning, nor was his solicitor. Well, Sutherland was a clever lad and would have known there would likely be something under the fingernails. And Gallagher had all the details clear. There were at least five dozen tea towels, to his knowledge, stored in the linen shelves, next to the kitchen staff's tunic jackets, the waiters' aprons, and all the spare paper goods – napkins, lavatory paper, and so on.

Anyone could pick up a tea towel as they passed, yes, and it would go quite unremarked.

Armed with the information, transmitted by a phone call from Forensic, that some of the fibres beneath Selina's fingernails did match the jackets worn by kitchen staff, they moved on to what he hoped would be more useful ground. There were, he was depressed but not surprised to learn, no fewer than eighty white jackets on the go, each kitchen person had four issued individually, but the laundry was done centrally; everyone stripped off their jackets at the end of a shift and dropped them into a giant wicker crate supplied by the laundry, which was collected every morning. All laundry including the tea towels went in the crate, yes. A kitchen shift consisted of ten to twelve people, so every morning twenty to twenty-four were taken away and, yes, twenty to twenty-four returned. Except on Sundays, and no, Detective Chief Superintendent, all kitchen staff changed every day, but by Tuesday morning there would hardly be a clean jacket on the shelf. The laundry fortunately arrived at 9 a.m. just ahead of Tuesday's incoming day shift.

'So every jacket gets washed every four days?' Davidson asked.

'Yeh. Yeh, must be right.'

It was a full two weeks now since Selina Marsh-Hayden had been missing. If her murderer had dropped his jacket into the laundry, along with the tea cloth, both would have been washed three or four times in heavy duty bleach and detergent. Not a lot left for Forensic to do anything with.

'Are all the jackets the same?'

'Different sizes, but yes, small, medium and large. Some of the girls wear small, I wear large, so do about half the blokes. The rest wear medium.'

'But they're all the same design and material?'

'Design, yes. We had a new batch the other day, like I told you. They go into holes after a bit with what the laundry uses and I told Judith we needed some new ones. You can't work with your elbows out and the cuffs frayed. And the Health don't like it. The material was different. Bit lighter.'

'So it's the laundry who provide the jackets?' Davidson asked.

'And all the linen. It's a contract, isn't it, they provide it, launder it and replace them in the end. Costs a fortune, but saves a lot of hassle.'

McLeish thought about the process as described, and remembered the gleaming kitchen and immaculate storage rooms he had been briefly shown that morning when he had paid a site visit. 'Where do you put the dirties then? Where is the laundry box, or crate?'

There was a slight pause and Matthew Sutherland uncrossed his long legs and crossed them the other way.

'In the passage. Down the back.'

'Where the old freezer was?'

The freezer in which the body had been found had been moved from the dank corridor to the Forensic laboratories. Neither at the time on site, nor with extensive forensic effort in the laboratories, had any fingerprints been revealed. Or indeed anything much at all, except that the top and sides had been wiped clean before a faint recent accumulation of dust. Whoever had done *that* could hardly have failed to notice the panel light indicating that the freezer was on, so the working assumption had to be that it was the murderer who had cleaned the surface with his victim chilling inside.

'Yes.'

'So anyone dropping dirty laundry in the basket could have seen the freezer. Would no one have noticed it was on?' It was a point that had bothered him when he read Gallagher's statement.

'They would of.'

'Sorry?'

'Except that some bugger had put a pile of black dustbin bags on the top of the cabinet. I saw them but didn't bother to shift them. We've been waiting, oh, three weeks, for Broughtons to fetch it away. I'd just stopped seeing it, know what I mean. It was the Health shifted them, and then they saw the light was on.'

McLeish had an unpleasant but vivid picture in his mind of the big man opposite him stripping off a torn jacket with blood on it and chucking it and a tea towel into the laundry crate, secure in the knowledge that by the next day it would have been laundered – in bleach and very hot water – along with the rest, destroying any evidence. But would he have dared? What if the body had been found that very night, by some accident? What if the bloodstains had been so widespread as to be remarkable even to the disillusioned eye of someone sorting soiled kitchen laundry? Another question occurred to him.

'When did the new batch of jackets come in?'

'Two weeks ago – tell you what, I can get it exact, or Judith can. It was the day we had a meeting in the office, me, Judith, Selina, Richard, Michael, all the shareholders.'

There was a distinct note of pride as he explained the meeting, McLeish observed. Perhaps the extension of a shareholding democracy was the answer to crime prevention. Tony Gallagher's background could hardly have been less promising, or more violent, but here he was, with his stake in a successful business, working as hard and conscientiously as any son of an orthodox property-owning middle-class family. 'They were delivered then, were they? On that day?'

'Must have been. They was all still in packets then, so was the new tea towels and gloves. And we moved the tea towels and gloves, sent them down in the hoist, but Judith said not to send the uniforms until we'd tried them for size and marked them. We tried them on then, see, while we was waiting for Selina.'

McLeish blinked and extracted a description of the incident. Gallagher's sardonic account of Selina's arrival reminded him of his next question.

'I understand you and Mrs Marsh-Hayden had an argument. What was it about?'

The man's eyes glazed. 'Can't really remember. I told the other cop . . . policeman.'

'And I'd like you to tell me, so I understand it.'

'Yeh. Right.' He licked his lips and glanced at Matt Sutherland, who was sitting absolutely still. 'Tell you the truth, I didn't really know what she was on about. She was asking why the plate costs on the steak dishes were high. I ended up telling her she didn't know what she was talking about. Well, she didn't. *She* never got her hands dirty doing the hard graft, working out costs, me and Judith – Miss Delves – done all that.'

'So what happened?'

'She went off.'

'Anyone else hear all this?'

'At the beginning there was Antoine. And a wash-up. You could ask them, if they heard.'

This last came out with a sudden access of confidence and Bruce Davidson realised they had been round this loop, and Gallagher knew no one had heard – or was admitting to have heard – any detail of the conversation.

'What are these plate costs Mrs Marsh-Hayden was asking about, then?'

Tony Gallagher considered him, warily. 'There's a rule – well, it's not a rule really, but close – that the costs of the raw material – yeh?

77

the food, know what I mean – must not be more than one-third of the menu cost. Without VAT, that has to go on top, see? So if your menu price less VAT is a tenner, everything that goes on that plate has to cost less than £3.30. And that means everything, parsley, presentation, the lot.'

Bruce Davidson did a swift calculation. 'That's a two hundred per cent mark-up, isn't it?'

Tony Gallagher had got involved in the detail and relaxed a bit, uncrossing his arms. Matt Sutherland was sitting absolutely still, but there was nothing relaxed about him.

'Yeh. What we say is: one-third for food, one-third for labour, one-third for rent, rates, management, and profit.'

'So if I'm paying a tenner for a steak?' Davidson, genuinely interested, asked.

'You're not eating at the Caff!' Tony Gallagher was pleased with his joke, and Bruce Davidson beamed at him.

'Away. What's a steak cost there, then?'

'£15. But that's with pepper sauce and frites.'

'I'd do better in Glasgow. And if I wanted a wee drink?'

'Three quid if you stick to the house wine.'

'And that costs you what?'

'£5 a bottle and we get six glasses.' Gallagher was enjoying himself, expanding the technicalities of his trade.

'So the plate costs are even lower if it's booze?'

'Nah, not always. On the better stuff, say that's £12 on the menu, that probably costs us £6. Some things you can't get that much of a mark-up. No one'll buy them. So there's some things on the menu where the plate costs are over a third, some where they're less. But you keep to a third over the whole menu.'

'Tell me where the costs are less than a third and I'll remember not to order them when I go out,' Davidson said.

'I'll tell you but you'll still order them. All the punters do. Coffee. Tea. Soup. Pâté.' Tony Gallagher was consulting an invisible menu. 'Side salad – except in winter. Anything with eggs, soufflé, omelette, Eggs Benedict. They're buggers to do, but the punters will pay good money for them.'

Davidson considered him with genuine interest. 'So what do I order if I want to be sure the money's in the food?'

'Steak. Chops. Grilled fish. Our steaks, now, they cost £4.80 each today. Put on the frites and the sauce, which has wine *and* cream, and the salad, you're up to near enough £6. Well, you can't get £18 for that dish. We charge £15, so the plate cost is forty per cent. And sometimes it's worse – if you have to keep a steak too long, or it gets cooked wrong, you just have to put it in the pâté, or the bolognaise, and you never get the costs back.'

Bruce Davidson gazed at him, shaking his head in admiration. 'So *that's* the sort of thing Mrs Marsh-Hayden was trying to think about?'

'That's right,' Gallagher agreed.

'What did she think you could do different?'

'Oh, she didn't say. Just hinted.'

'At what?' McLeish asked and saw Gallagher stiffen. Matt Sutherland looked up warningly.

'Well. She was hinting someone was on the fiddle. Asking about the supplier, was he honest? Did we check deliveries? Christ, who doesn't?' Matthew Sutherland coughed, and Gallagher's confident delivery faltered. 'Stuff like that,' he finished, lamely. 'Stupid stuff.'

'Did she often come to the kitchen?' Davidson managed to sound honestly puzzled.

'Nah. Only to swish round saying how *lovely* everything looked.'

'So you resented her bothering, then?' McLeish asked calmly.

'Yeh, I did.' He cast a sidelong, defiant look at his lawyer. 'Pissed me off. But I forgot about it – can't worry about rubbish like that when you've got two hundred covers to get out.' He hesitated and addressed himself to Davidson. 'I'd like to get back to set up if you've got all you want.'

'Remind me, what time was it that Mrs Marsh-Hayden left you that day?' John McLeish asked.

'Five thirty. I'd just come on.'

'Did you see her again at all, anywhere, after she walked out on the conversation?'

'No. I went to get into whites.'

'You went to the laundry room?'

'Yeh. Then to the men's changing. And she wasn't in there, no. Then into the kitchen, where she wasn't either.'

There was a lie in there, McLeish thought, the man had hesitated over the laundry room and speeded up confidently as he described his return to the kitchen. He considered Matthew Sutherland, who was studying his notebook as if an exam question depended on it.

'How long did it take you to change?'

And there it was, the hesitation, the slight colour over the cheekbones. ''Bout . . . well, I dunno, fifteen minutes. I shaved as well. I hadn't been working that day, so I'd got up late and not bothered.'

79

'So it would have been five forty-five, or so, when you arrived back in the kitchen?'

'Maybe nearer six. I'm a slow shaver.'

And in that gap Tony Gallagher had done something he didn't want to tell the police about.

'Selina was around all evening, you know, after we had our little tiff. She was on duty. Didn't come near me – or the kitchen, too busy flirting with the customers.'

'What time did you – do you all go home?'

'Me, I went at twelve – kitchen closes then. I didn't see her. I don't know when she went.'

They took him through the statement again but without improving their understanding. The gap remained but, as Gallagher pointed out, Selina Marsh-Hayden had been seen alive and well for several hours after the quarrel, so they let him go.

Hours later, McLeish extracted himself from a liaison meeting with Scottish colleagues which he had managed to transfer to London. A message had been particularly brought to him from Francesca, reminding him that she was due at a Community Association meeting at 6 p.m and their nanny was out from five thirty by special concession. He stared at it, momentarily boggled by the idea of trying to explain to the assembled hard Glaswegians the reason for his need to close the meeting by 5 p.m, then remembered that the only decent plane back to Glasgow left at 6 p.m. He breathed again and took the group rapidly through the rest of the agenda, wondering if there was any way of persuading Francesca not to involve herself in these activities.

Francesca walked into the large dusty church hall and stopped, looking doubtfully to see if she recognised any of the dozen people there assembled round a trestle table with a tea urn.

'Ah, Mrs McLeish.' The local representative of the Church of England, clad in baggy trousers, sweater and clerical collar, seized her hand in a firm muscular grasp. 'Nice to see you. We welcome your expertise. We've also been fortunate enough to find a local solicitor to help us.' He turned, beaming with professional enthusiasm, to greet a tall young man who emerged from the passage at the side of the hall.

'Ah. We've met.' Matt Sutherland gathered her into his arms.

'Why are you here, Matt?' she asked, extricating herself.

'Because of the nursery. We need it for the Refuge kids.'

'Of course.'

The community centre putatively housed in four vandalised ground-floor flats in one of the grimmest council blocks in that part of West London was only a hundred yards from the Refuge for which Graebners were the official solicitors. Not a very difficult connection to make, but one she had not even thought of.

'You could send your William if we can get the funding.'

'Indeed.' She took a deep breath. 'And the next one.'

'What next one?'

'The one I'm going to have in about eight months.' She had, she saw, severely disconcerted him and there were interested observers around them. 'We thought we'd better get on with it,' she said, generally, to the group. 'My son is nearly two and I'm not getting any younger.'

The vicar tied himself up in a complex sentence in which he seemed to be suggesting that she hardly looked old enough to be a mother at all. Francesca gracefully acknowledged this muddled tribute, avoiding Matthew's eye. The vicar turned away to greet another newcomer and she sneaked a look at Matthew, who was struggling to conceal laughter. She grinned back, suddenly comfortable with him.

'How's things, Matt?'

'Your husband and his merry men are harassing my client.' Matt had no small talk, she should have remembered, she thought crossly.

'A woman got strangled and John sees finding murderers as more important than not hurting people's feelings.'

'Yeh, but my man didn't do it.'

'Then I am sure he has nothing to fear.' Dear God, what was it about Matthew, she was sounding like the Chairman of the Magistrates Association.

'You sound like your ma,' he said, gloomily, confirming her fears. 'The Caff's falling apart. Tony's lost two sous chefs and a commis in the last week. They don't like being hassled and they can get jobs anywhere, tomorrow.'

'Customers still rolling in?'

'Yeh, but they aren't getting a meal in front of them fast enough. So that won't last.'

'John's very quick,' she said, defensively. 'And when he's got his man it'll get back to normal.' She looked up at him, six inches taller than her, looking annoyingly young and righteous. 'Unless it was your client and then they'll have to get another head chef. He's good though. I agree.'

'Tony could go somewhere else tomorrow. As your friend Judith Delves does not seem to know.'

'Not my friend,' she said, on the back foot, but rallied. 'And I bet your Tony couldn't get another job that easily. Any prospective employer would wonder, fair or unfair, what was going to crop up in their deep freeze.'

Nor had Matt much sense of humour where a client was concerned, she remembered, as he gave her the kind of look with which John Knox might have favoured Mary Stuart.

'We'd better not talk about it.'

'That's right, Matt, let's just get a community centre going here. I have eight months, roughly.'

He smiled, reluctantly. 'Shouldn't be a problem, Wonderwoman.'

Tony Gallagher looked round the small group in the kitchen and exploded. 'How the fuck are we going to do 250 covers tonight?'

His staff looked back at him, lost for a response. Indeed, with no sous chef, two commis, and only one chef de rang and one wash-up, there was no rational answer, unless all 250 people booked in on Friday were going to be content with a very plain steak and one of the puddings the chefs had made up on the day shift. Tony looked round him and picked up a knife, and his staff shrank behind the limited cover available.

He looked beyond them to the passage. 'Jean-Pierre, François. *Attendez.*' The two figures that had been trying to slink past unobserved stopped reluctantly and turned to face him as he advanced carrying the knife. 'You'll have to stay. Both of you. Sorry, but you'll get double rate.'

Both men protested, in a mixture of French and English, that this would be their third consecutive shift, that double rate meant nothing given the iniquitous English custom of deducting tax at source, and that they were moreover both on the very busy day shift tomorrow, when another 250 people hoped to eat lunch. Would Chef prefer that these went unfed? Chef leapt at this unwisely conceded opening, pointing out that tomorrow was another day, and one on which he would personally use all his influence to ensure that replacements

82

worked the shift. But now, at 6 p.m. this day, he needed another two commis and two more sous chefs, so they would have to stay; clean jackets awaited them together with whatever they would like for staff supper.

The two conscripts reluctantly returned to change, and the rest of the kitchen staff resumed preparations for the evening rush, watching out of the corner of their eyes Chef, face mottled with temper, assembling his utensils and stocks for the onslaught.

7

In New Scotland Yard, John McLeish, who had been in since six thirty, was beginning to feel that he had a grip on the case. He understood who was who, and several of his preliminary ideas had been blown out of the water by a reading of the various statements assembled for him. Bruce Davidson was sitting at the other side of the big table which occupied about half the space in a very decent-sized office.

'These letters,' McLeish said, indicating a ring-binder with each page sheathed in plastic. 'I see Marsh-Hayden took the line that all three men were old flames, dating back to before they married.'

'In his place I'd have hoped they'd been written before Selina had even set eyes on me.'

'Somewhere here it says they'd known each other since they were children. Anyway, what did Mr Marsh-Hayden think?'

'He was taken aback, it says here.' Davidson had found the relevant part of the statement and was reading it carefully. 'He knew all three of them, apparently.' He hesitated. 'The letters are rather the same. No, I mean they're different, but . . .'

'But the subject matter is much the same,' McLeish suggested. 'What they hoped to do, or had done and hoped to do again with Selina Marsh-Hayden, as opportunity offered.' Bruce Davidson was the resident expert on matters sexual and his opinion would be useful. 'Did you read them all? Anything, well, out of the ordinary, which might have turned rough?'

Davidson reached over and turned up a page on one of the letters. 'This bloke's a little near the line.'

McLeish read four paragraphs, thoughtfully. 'Mm.'

'He didn't last long, though. The third letter from him is a long moan about how could she give him up. See here.'

' "How could you destroy this precious thing that was growing between us," ' McLeish read. 'What *can* he have meant?'

'The poor bugger had to take it somewhere else, any road,' Davidson said.

'We ought to check him out.'

'He's married and living in South Africa. They're all well over five years old, the letters, I mean.'

'So we're assuming she gave up having men – or at least men who wrote to her – once she was married?' McLeish asked.

Davidson grunted.

'You don't think so?'

'Old habits, John. No. It would surprise me if she'd given them up.'

'We need to see the husband,' McLeish said. 'And quickly. No alibi, broke, and she was standing between him and a pot of cash, *and* she may have been playing him up as well.'

Davidson said smugly that he had arranged that this should be the next interview. And just over an hour later they were contemplating Richard Marsh-Hayden in his own living-room. The room was orderly, if not particularly clean, surfaces cleared, cushions plumped up, coffee promptly offered. The man himself looked drawn and tired and ill, but he had himself in hand as well as his surroundings. As he had let them in, he had picked the post off the doorstep and disposed instantly of the leaflets, flyers and free newspapers into a bin kept near the door, placing the rest on a beautifully shaped, curved table seriously in need of a polish beneath a mirror surmounted by a faded gold eagle. A soldier's tidiness, McLeish thought, and was unsurprised to find, as they talked over coffee, that Richard Marsh-Hayden had served three years in the Welsh Guards.

'I have the statement you made to my colleagues at Bow Street.' McLeish decided it was time to lead into the business of the day.

'Yes. Forgotten what I said, but it was true.'

'Can we go through it again so I get the detail right. You last saw your wife at about 11.30 p.m. on Thursday, just over two weeks ago?'

'Yes. We'd all had a meeting, rather a cross one, in the office. Then I went to see a mate. Then I came back about six thirty for a drink. Selina was on duty and I'd said I'd eat with some of the lads at White's. We finished, oh about ten, and there wasn't much doing, so I came over to the Caff about eleven thirty, and Selina and I had coffee. And a row.' His face crumpled suddenly and both policemen waited stolidly while he recovered himself. 'I mean, not a real screamer, but I was pissed off. So I went off to a club I know and had a few and played a bit. Then I thought I'd better get my head straight and I went to the baths in Porchester Street and had a kip

85

there in the steam. Got home about ten in the morning and she wasn't there.'

'Were you surprised?'

Richard Marsh-Hayden looked at him quickly, the sharp jaw looking even narrower. 'What do you mean?'

'Were you expecting her to be there?' McLeish asked, evenly, noting the sore spot.

'Yes, I was. So I was even more pissed off. Then I made myself a coffee and remembered she had muttered something about going off early. She was going to see friends, then her mother in Bideford for a few days. So I just thought she'd gone and I thought, bitch not to leave me a note and that I wouldn't ring her up, I'd wait till she rang me.'

'What about her car?' This was a point which had puzzled both of them but the detective inspector who had initially taken a statement had not appeared to find it remarkable that all through this time Selina's car had been on the forecourt outside the house.

'She said she wasn't going to bother with it. Her mother's got a spare one there – grotty old Citroën.' Richard Marsh-Hayden was not looking at either of the them. 'Sorry, I need a pee.' He watched, tense, as Davidson glanced at his watch and, leaning forward to record the time the interview was suspended, switched off the tape. 'That's so you can't patch extra bits in, yes?'

'That's the principle,' McLeish confirmed.

'Won't take long. You want the phone? Paper?'

They indicated they were content to sit; Davidson gave his superior a quick sidelong approving glance which McLeish acknowledged. The story was extremely thin and left Richard Marsh-Hayden without an alibi for the night on which his wife had disappeared from all her known haunts.

Marsh-Hayden appeared looking better, the ragged blond hair combed off his face.

'So. Yeh. Look, we – Selina and I – we yelled at each other a lot, it isn't . . . it doesn't . . . well, I only ever hit her once when she'd really got up my nose.' He studied their professionally stony faces. 'We fought, we didn't bottle it up.'

'What did you fight about?' McLeish asked.

'Money mostly. Not having it. Selina had no idea – I mean, she bought this fucking dress to go to one of her mate's parties. I mean, she's got cupboards full. Seven hundred-odd quid, and we couldn't pay the fucking milkman. That's the time I hit her. And that's why I was so pissed off with her before ... when ... week before last, because we can't keep going here' – a gesture took in the living-room with its careful joinery and expensive lighting – 'and she was banging on about putting more money into the Caff. When we had an offer of four hundred thou for our shares. She could have had all the frocks she wanted.' He stopped, hands clasped between his knees, looking beyond them out of the window on to the small, perfectly arranged, paved garden.

'Very good-looking girl, of course, from the photographs,' McLeish said into the silence.

'Yes. Could've worn a flour sack and still looked good, but they don't think like that.' Richard Marsh-Hayden was still staring out of the window, but he had relaxed, slightly.

'Your wife had changed her mind about selling her shares. Quite recently?'

'The day before ... before ...'

'Before you last saw her. Why, do you think?'

'No idea.'

'I understand that she had felt it might be possible to make a greater profit and get a better price.'

'She'd been talking to some wanker, but she'd have come round again.' He glanced at their unmoving faces. 'She was holding up the sale because ... well, because two things. She was pissed off with me, and she felt ... she said that if we sold, the money would just go down the cracks. *And* she didn't trust Brian Rubin – the chap who's buying. He'd promised her a job, but he wasn't offering a director-ship, or not to her, and she thought she'd lose out.' He stubbed out his cigarette and lit another immediately.

'Was she right?'

Richard looked at him, startled.

'Yes,' he said, slowly. 'Yes, she probably was. He wasn't that interested in pulling in the faces.'

'Faces?'

'People whose faces you know. The fashionable punters. Pulling them was what Selina was really good at – and looking after them when they were here – and he didn't care much about all that. He looked at this place – and the other new one – as a big cash cow, middle-class people wanting good value, who didn't give a shit about the fashionable crowd. Rubin just wanted bums on seats, push 'em through, get the tables turned. Selina would have been bored. And done it badly.'

That sounded, McLeish thought, like a very shrewd but not unloving view of the dead woman.

'But you still thought it was a mistake on her part not to sell?'

'Yes. She's not – she wasn't interested in working that hard. She'd have come round, when she thought about it slowly. She is . . . was . . . a clever lady, she could have had a shop which she wanted and not so much hard graft.'

'What would have happened to Miss Delves?'

'I thought – though Judith never said – that Brian Rubin had offered her a deal. Work for him for six months, then go on his board.'

'Is it possible, do you think, that your wife was only negotiating to see if Mr Rubin would offer her an arrangement she wanted, rather than lose the deal?'

'Could be,' he said, slowly, thinking about it. 'I was too bloody angry with her, that's the trouble.' He coughed on his cigarette, and tears appeared at the corners of his eyes. He fished out a very dirty handkerchief and blew his nose, copiously.

McLeish waited till the man had got himself in hand and braced to discuss the restaurants, then changed the subject.

'I need to ask you about the letters that were found among your wife's papers.'

'I told your people all I know.'

'You hadn't seen them before?'

'No, but I knew the people who wrote them.' He lit a cigarette and drew on it deeply. 'I'd known Selina since we were children. She did what she wanted until we married. If anyone'd asked me I could've told you she'd had a walk-out with them, and a few more besides.' He gave them a sidelong look. 'I wouldn't like to see a list of everyone I've had, sometimes not really meaning to except just at the critical moment.' He stubbed the cigarette, half smoked. 'Or the ones where I wanted to and didn't get there, for that matter, if you know what I mean.'

McLeish decided he probably had no real idea what Richard Marsh-Hayden's sexual life had been like. Davidson, who was looking just perceptibly smug, probably did. But the point at issue here was whether Selina Marsh-Hayden had continued to have affairs and, if so, whether her husband had known, and if he had known, had minded enough to kill her.

'You said that you had occasional rows with your wife. Were they in connection with other men?'

'No. Well, we had one, but that was my fault. Ex-friend of mine who was after her, and I didn't see she was trying to get rid of him without upsetting *me*. No. We got on in bed, you see. Important to both of us.'

It was clear that he had loved his wife and was miserable without her; well, that had applied to many people who had nonetheless murdered their wives. But this one was not going to crack, not today, he had himself well in hand. They needed to know a bit more about the late Selina Marsh-Hayden before they could usefully probe further. And there was plenty of legwork that needed doing first. McLeish ended the interview and asked for the usual undertakings about not leaving London without notifying the police.

'Can't afford to, Detective Chief Superintendent. I'll either be here, or on my knees to a bank manager.'

'These, not *these*, John, come from one of these jackets. The white one.'

It was an hour later and McLeish and Davidson were up to their elbows in forensic scientists.

'From one of the new jackets that were waiting to be marked the day before Selina disappeared. There were eighty of them,' Bruce added, helpfully.

McLeish sat down, the better to consider the point. 'So, if the threads come from one of these jackets, Bruce, we need all eighty rounded up and examined.'

'Sergeant Willis and a DC are doing that now. It's no' at all popular at the Caff.'

'Delicate plants, are they?'

'There's a whole kitchen shift with nothing to wear on top. And seven waiters.'

'There won't be many threads missing.' It was Doc, sounding weary. 'It'll look like a snag and if it's been laundered you may not even be able to see it. And even if you find the jacket we're not going to be able to do much with any stains. *If* we even see any stains. My guess is the laundry use heavy duty bleach – the fibres are pure cotton. Laundered four times and overlaid with other stains. No, not a chance.'

'Thanks, Doc. You just made our day.'

'And he wore rubber gloves, John. Look at the prints off the plastic bag.'

McLeish peered obediently through the microscope. 'Where did the gloves come from?'

'Kitchen at the Caff,' Bruce Davidson said, gloomily. 'They've got thirty-one pairs down there and they order them in packs of twenty-four when they think they're getting low.'

'Who wears them? Not people cooking, surely,' McLeish asked.

'Mostly wash-ups. But they're kept next to the spare overalls, and anyone can pick up a pair. Leastways anyone who had any reason to be passing.'

McLeish acknowledged the caveat, and realised his audience was showing signs of restlessness. 'Doc, we need not keep you while Bruce and I engage in fruitless speculation. Thanks for your help.'

They walked out of the depressing basement and got into the waiting car. It was a warm morning again and McLeish yawned. 'Sorry. Early start.'

'Thank God it's Friday?'

'It is, isn't it. But I'm going to come in tomorrow – I'm just not far enough up the learning curve on this one.'

'I'll be in too.'

'Thanks, Bruce. I'll try and get you time off in lieu. Look, tell you what's itching me. The jackets were still in the office, right? So anyone who had access to the office could have picked one up.'

'Yes.'

'And, indeed, possibly, perhaps, killed her up there and stuffed her into a bag. Oh, hang on. The office is on the first floor, isn't it? Is there by any chance a lift?'

Davidson flipped through the report. 'I doubt it's big enough. It's a wee block and tackle job, apparently used for moving food from the basement storage to the kitchen on the ground floor.'

'Doesn't sound right. We need to go and look at the place.'

Judith Delves, who had been in the restaurant office since six o'clock that morning, decided she was becoming less and less efficient and needed a second breakfast. It was clear that the business was paying dearly for the six months she had spent building Caff 2 across the river. It was ten thirty, the restaurant was not yet open, but the day staff were in, and waiters in long white overalls with the green Café de la Paix logo were setting up tables, placing vases and fresh flowers and polishing up cutlery as it came out of the plastic baskets from the washing-up machine. The bar, where light snacks were served, was not yet in action; the grill, dismembered, lay soaking in the sink, and a barman was rearranging and polishing glasses, working at speed, obviously running late. Reluctantly she walked over to the kitchen, hearing raised voices as she approached the serving counter. Tony Gallagher was not there, to her relief, and she asked Antoine for poached egg on toast. He nodded, pushed bread under the grill and reached for eggs and butter, while she considered the kitchen staff.

'How many short, Antoine?'

'I have only one commis, and no one on vegetables.'

'I'll join you. At least to get the prep work done.'

Antoine made a complicated gesture with a spatula that combined gratitude for the offered help with disapproval for the necessity of accepting it. It was all too clear, she thought, wolfing her eggs on toast, that no properly regulated kitchen in a major restaurant had Madame chopping vegetables, but needs must with 180 booked for lunch and 250 for dinner. Including, gratifyingly, the overnight tape of messages told her, a party of twenty from the English National Opera cast. She finished her breakfast and stripped off her jacket, substituting one of the white uniform jackets. There was no point in her volunteering to help during the service; she had not worked under pressure in a restaurant kitchen for eight years, and would be too slow and get in the way, but she could make a useful contribution to the prep work. Indeed, an hour and a half later, with the aid of a processor, she had worked her way through fifty salad-based starters and got them into a chiller, and prepared enough of the five varieties of vegetable which were served with all hot entrées to cover the likely requirement of the lunch shift. Antoine and two chefs were working furiously six feet away from her, getting fish, meat and sauces prepared. She straightened her back, which was aching from the unaccustomed physical work, and decided it was time she got into proper clothes to cover her shift as floor manager. The pâtisserie chef, mercifully, had got in that morning, a competent girl of twenty-two, and rows of stiff, beautifully presented puddings were being fed into another of the big chillers. The food lift lurched up, at her elbow, with big tin containers of ice-cream brought up from the freezer to sit in a chiller, so that the ice-cream could be scooped easily and tidily rather than hacked out to emerge in a less than elegant shape on the plate.

'Madame. *Il y a deux hommes qui vous demandent.*'

Policemen, she thought, from their back view, as she glanced through the serving hatch. And one of them, as they turned to look at the back of the restaurant, revealed himself as Francesca McLeish's husband, looking quite different in the light of day. She had not remembered how big he was, taller than Michael's six foot two. And bigger-framed, with lots of dark hair and what was just recognisable as a broken nose, carefully reset. She watched him; he was standing absolutely still beside his smaller colleague and both had every ounce of their attention bent on the back wall of the restaurant.

'Good morning,' she said, lifting the serving hatch, and just avoiding knocking Antoine's flying elbows as he manipulated four big pans at once; John McLeish turned to her, and she saw that his eyes were hazel, not brown, as she had expected.

'Miss Delves?'

'Yes. We've met.'

'Indeed. My colleague, Inspector Davidson.' He allowed a courteous pause for them to shake hands but his attention, she saw, was still on the back wall. 'We have just noticed that the restaurant is larger than the rest of the building.'

'Yes,' Judith said, taken aback. 'There's an extension on the back of the block which goes up to the first floor, then stops. So, yes, the restaurant goes into the extension – in fact, the kitchen is there at ground-floor level, then we use the bit below for storage and the bit above is our office.'

'Does the basement go right under the building? I mean, how does the access to the basement work?'

'Only through our bit. The rest of the basement is services and pipes and so on, and the landlord has the right to come through to inspect.'

'But he has to come through your back door.'

'Which is in the basement. There is no access to the back directly from this floor.'

'How do you get down to the basement?'

'Stairs. And we have a pulley lift for goods going to the kitchen.'

'May we look?'

She hesitated, and he caught it. 'Or is it inconvenient?'

'Well, it's the service, you see. We're short-handed today and I will have to floor-manage for a couple of hours. But come in quickly, I'll show you.'

She took them round the back door of the kitchen, a plain door marked 'Private', and showed them the pulley lift, whose use was being helpfully demonstrated as it came up loaded with a tray packed with steaks. McLeish, looking enormous in the confined space, stood back to let a sous chef snatch one tray at feverish speed, taking no notice of them. The pulley lift occupied a space about four by four feet wide and about four feet high, enough to take two trays side by side.

'Does it go anywhere else? The wee lift?'

It was the younger man, the Glaswegian, and she blinked at him. 'Ah yes. Up to the office. We use it to send up coffee and the odd meal.'

'And there are stairs to the office at the back too?'

'Yes, that's right. We – the office people – all come in by the basement entrance. It's self-contained from the rest of the first floor. I mean, we don't have access to the rest of the building, nor they to us.'

'Very hard work doing two flights of stairs in the mornings.'

She had seen this coming, but nonetheless felt sick. 'No. We take the lift. No, of course not this one. There's an old two-person lift right at the back, which goes up the outer wall.' She had their full attention and it was an uneasy experience.

'Can we see it?'

'It doesn't stop on this floor, you see, which is why I didn't think about it straightaway.' She was babbling defensively and stuttering, she realised, and steadied herself by taking a deep breath. 'Or rather it would stop, but we built over the door because we need a clear space there.' They were both watching her, absolutely immobile. 'So you could walk down or up to see it.'

There was a pause which seemed to go on for some time and in which she was very conscious of her stained, sweaty jacket; beetroot had featured heavily on the day's menu.

'May we start in the basement?'

She led them down the echoing concrete stairs and felt them stop, briefly, behind her as they passed the laundry hamper and the roped-off passage where the old deep freeze had rested.

'There.' She pointed to the glass door which housed the small lift that dated back to the sixties when this part of the building had been put up. 'It's a bit erratic and very slow, but we've never bothered to do anything about it.' She peered through the glass; the lift was there, so she pressed the button and they waited while the doors creaked slowly open and she stepped aside to give them a clear view. Neither of them spoke, but both were looking at the patch of dirty carpet on the floor and the stain at its edge about three by three inches, which under their attention might as well have been lit in Technicolor.

'They didna look here. There's nothing in the report, nae mention even.'

Judith hastened into speech. 'I'm sorry, but I wasn't here when they came. And I didn't . . . d . . . d . . . didn't look at my feet – I mean the carpet.'

'Right. Miss Delves, I'm afraid we'll have to come back, mob-handed. You'll need to stop anyone using this lift.' A bell, pressed in irritation two floors up, sounded as he spoke and Judith looked up, distraught. 'If you would explain to your colleagues, Miss Delves?'

There was no hint of impatience in his voice, but the whole feel of the personality had changed. He had withdrawn inside himself, focused on the stained carpet, and she and his chagrined Scots colleague were there only to be told to do things. Chilled, she ran up the two flights, arriving out of breath in the office to tell Mary, the bookkeeper, that she would have to walk down to lunch and to take the opportunity of a quick change into a respectable shirt and jacket. She arrived down, clasping the morning's stained coat, and dropped it automatically into the laundry basket, turning round into John McLeish's concentrated, all-observing gaze. She looked back, feeling suddenly cold, but the moment was broken by Inspector Davidson cursing at his mobile telephone. She offered him the staff pay-phone and some coins which he accepted, ungraciously, still in a flaming temper. He could just be heard venting displeasure in snarling Glaswegian, but she and John McLeish seemed to be stuck where they were.

'When the new uniforms arrived, they were delivered to the office, I believe?' He was watching her face and it occurred to her how few people did that openly, and how intimate it was.

'Yes. We needed to check and mark them.'

'And then they were sent down to this floor? How?'

'Well . . .' She tried to think. 'Anyone going down just took a load. Tony – that's Tony Gallagher – did come up and collect his two. He's very hard on jackets – well, he works very long hours and he sweats a lot – I mean, everyone does, but he's Chef . . .'

'And a big chap, I've met him. But the last night anyone saw Mrs Marsh-Hayden – the Thursday . . . what was the situation then? The uniforms were still in the office?'

'Yes. They were only delivered that day and it certainly took twenty-four hours to mark them and get them all down here. And Mary found we were short – oh, you know all that?'

Inspector Davidson came back, face like thunder. 'We'll have a team back here by three o'clock.'

'After the service,' Judith said, in relief, and wished she hadn't, as they both turned the cold enquiring gaze on her. 'Sorry, but we are having great difficulty in getting the customers fed.'

'I can see that,' McLeish said, nodding. 'And I'll get out of your hair. I've some more questions for you, but they can wait while you run your business. I'm going to leave Inspector Davidson here. Good luck with lunch.'

He was out of the back door before she could say anything sensible and she rushed thankfully upstairs. Francesca McLeish had been right, she reflected: her husband, however alarming, was a man who respected women's work and capacities. She paused at the bar to ensure that Inspector Davidson was offered a sandwich to keep him going through his lonely vigil and plunged into the task of greeting and seating the long line forming at the reception desk.

'I'm so sorry, I'm afraid Mr Rubin must just have stepped out. Can he call you back?'

John McLeish, in the traffic at the top of St Martin's Lane and close to Brian Rubin's office, was irritated; this particular interview needed doing and would fill in time nicely until the Forensics troupe could get back and investigate the lift. He remembered a salient fact from a statement. 'Will you say to him that Detective Chief Superintendent McLeish is in the area and will call by in about ten minutes in the hope of seeing him.'

There was a pause at the other end and the voice said, brightly, that Mr Rubin had *just* come back in and would he like a word?

'Be delighted, Chief Superintendent. I could come round to you. No? No, I don't mind doing it here, we'll find a room.'

John McLeish replaced the phone and grinned at the detective sergeant who had been sent up hastily to substitute for Davidson 'We're not after money, so we get to see him.'

'I saw that Mr Rubin was said to be under serious financial pressure.'

This one was young and keen and highly thought of but new to

McLeish, so he started to explain how he preferred to conduct an interview while the car crawled up St Martin's Lane and round to Charing Cross Road.

They were admitted to the headquarters of the Rubin empire – the third floor of an unreconstructed building in the back streets by Neal Street – only after a careful inspection through a locked door. As they entered a blonde woman in her forties was answering three phones at once, with the invariant response that Mr Rubin was not here, at the moment, so sorry, could she take a message. No, the finance director was at a meeting, so sorry, but his secretary would take a message if that would be helpful. She put two calls on hold and pressed a buzzer to summon Brian Rubin, who emerged from an inner room and beckoned them in.

'Sorry about all this.'

John McLeish introduced himself and his sergeant and sat, as invited, at one side of a decent-sized table, on which were piled official-looking drafts. He considered his host; lively, overweight, dark, and harassed.

'Coffee? Sorry, just push that lot along. Fourth draft of the sale and purchase agreement, would you believe? I told your people all about it.'

'You did indeed and I don't need to go over all that ground again. I can see you're busy.'

'Not that busy. Not now. What's the world record for getting probate of a will, do you know?'

McLeish, taken aback, said he thought a couple of months would be good going, and Brian Rubin groaned.

'Be bloody lucky if I'm here by then. Will you try Manners again, Diana? At the bank, yes?'

The blonde woman put down a tray of coffee and gave him a weary look. 'He's in a meeting.'

'So he isn't going to ring. Fuck. Don't post those two letters then. OK?' He caught McLeish's interested eye. 'Post's terrible these days.'

The man, McLeish observed, was in no way crushed by his financial difficulties. 'I need to ask some more questions about your proposed purchase of Café de la Paix and your relationship with the various parties.'

'Ask away. Saves me worrying who's on the phone.'

'Why did you particularly want these two restaurants?'

'Well, I thought they were for sale. And I can make more money than the sellers.'

Interesting that he spoke as if the deal were still on, McLeish observed.

'They've got trouble in there somewhere. They ought to be making near enough twice what they have been in the last six months. They've got plenty of turnover, plenty of punters coming through the door.'

'Why do you think they're doing poorly? Not charging enough?'

'No, no, no.' Brian Rubin's whole body moved to reject the suggestion. 'They're well up to what the traffic'll bear. No, there's a scam going on at Café de la Paix. Or more than one. Plate costs – that's food costs, OK? They're way too high. So the scam's probably in the kitchen.'

'How would it be working?'

'Could be anything. Most probably back-handers from suppliers. Or stuff going out the back door for cash. Or else meals not charged. That's worse, because it means the floor staff's in it too. They don't put an order through the till and take the bill in cash and split the profit with the kitchen, who record the food they used as spoilt or unsuitable.'

'Can any of these be done without Chef knowing?'

Brian Rubin thought, saw the point and hesitated, tongue caught between his teeth. 'No. No, not really.'

'So you assumed that the head chef was involved. But I understand from the statement I've seen that it was intended that Mr Gallagher would join your group.'

'And if he'd ever tried anything like that in one of my kitchens, he'd be out. I assumed he knew that.'

'But you didn't discover precisely what was going on?'

'Nah. Can't get close enough till you own the place. And I needed his five per cent shareholding, so I didn't want to hurt his feelings. Before he'd signed off, that is.'

'And the owners didn't know, you think?'

Brian Rubin helped himself to coffee and a couple of biscuits.

'Well, look at them,' he said, through crumbs. 'The blokes – Marsh-Hayden and Owens – they weren't involved, they weren't there. And Selina, God rest her, didn't really *do* numbers.' He swallowed the last half-biscuit noisily and swilled it down with the last of the coffee. 'Now, Judith Delves, she knows her stuff, but she'd been over the river getting the second one going, hadn't she? Bit of a mistake there – it's a good outlet, but it's very big and it's too far away from the mother ship and they don't have enough managers to go round.'

'So you were getting them cheap?'

Brian Rubin looked at him, wounded, the brown eyes wide. 'That's not right. No, put it another way. I knew I could make more than they were, but that's the only reason for buying a place, that you can make more cash out of it than the next man. But they knew I needed *them* so I was paying extra for that. Came out about even, I reckon.'

McLeish fell silent and thought about Brian Rubin. A tough nut, that was clear, but in this context that was in his favour. Unlikely to have been panicked into a murder to save his deal.

'You are still hoping to be able to complete the purchase, then?'

'Yeh. Richard Marsh-Hayden still wants to sell, so does Michael Owens, I've spoken to them both. If I can just talk a little man at the NatWest into carrying us for – what – two months, until Richard Marsh-Hayden can deliver his wife's shares, yes, we'll complete.'

'At the agreed price?'

'Yeh. No point spitting in the soup, and souring the deal. I wouldn't be surprised to find they're losing – ooh – five thousand a week, but what the fuck. Forty thousand's not a lot to worry about if I can get a rights issue away.'

'If Mrs Marsh-Hayden were still alive, what would you be doing?'

Brian Rubin considered him, alert. 'Same as I am now, only quicker. She'd have changed her mind back again. Or Richard would've changed it for her. She wasn't much of a business person really, it was an ego trip for her.'

'She had been advised she could make more money, I understand.'

'Yeh. She said.' Brian Rubin looked weary.

'Mm.' McLeish took him, pro forma, through his movements on the day and evening that Selina had last been seen. He had left the shareholders' meeting in a really bad temper, he conceded, and gone back to his office. Where he had received a phone call from Michael Owens (sensible bloke that, for a banker) indicating that he had better regard the deal as off.

'I shouted the odds, told him I'd send them a bill for a hundred thou which is somewhere near what my out-of-pockets and fees come to, but he wasn't shifting. Yeh, and I did go down to the Caff later, around nine o'clock, to try and talk some sense into Selina, but she was swanking around charming the punters, so I went home. Can't prove it, just like I told the first lot of you, because Janice and the kids were staying with her mother.'

'But you continued to hope Mrs Marsh-Hayden would change her mind?'

'Yeh, I did. And when everyone kept telling me she was away and not in touch, I thought I was getting the runaround. But Richard said let her alone, she'd get over it quicker, and promised to let me know the second he heard from her. I believed him – I knew he was desperate for the deal too. I mean, he's even worse off than me, I'm trading, no thanks to the banks, whereas he's in property. Can't sell and can't even let, all his stuff is secondary property in the City where landlords are giving away a year's rent even with the good stuff. I stayed close to him, and we were at the Caff the night before she was found.' He paused, and stared at McLeish. 'That's where I've seen you before. You were there.'

'By coincidence. My brother-in-law was entertaining us.'

It was plain that Brian Rubin believed not a word of this. 'Someone had reported her missing then?'

'Well, not officially, and not to me. I really was there as a guest. But I'm sure various people had started to worry. She'd been missing for a week by then, after all.'

Brian Rubin was watching him, and sat back in his chair. 'You're pretty senior, aren't you? And Scotland Yard. Is it because of Richard's father?'

The fact that Richard's father sat in the House of Lords (every day for the attendance allowance) had not featured anywhere, but Mc-Leish was grateful for the idea, and observed vaguely that this was a complicated case, returning to his notes to prevent Rubin asking for further and better particulars. He looked up to find the man bright-eyed with interest.

'So your wife's that tall, dark girl, who looks exactly like her brothers, yes? The party looked like fun. Tell them I want them to go on coming when I own the place, I'll make them a deal.'

Whatever Mr Rubin's shortcomings, shortage of nerve did not feature among them. McLeish, avoiding discussion, asked a couple more routine questions, but realised he needed to put all this together quietly. 'Thank you, Mr Rubin. I may need to talk to you again at any time. You won't leave London without letting us know?'

Four thirty in the afternoon is the dead time in any restaurant. At Café de la Paix the lunchtime kitchen shift was setting up and doing prep work, but the wash-ups had been sent home to get a break before reporting again at 7 p.m. for the staff meal. A skeleton waiting crew was covering the floor, and in the office Judith Delves and a bookkeeper were working on two computers.

'Judith, that's the bills. No point writing the cheques, is there? The overdraft is very close to the limit.'

'No, that's all right.' Judith did not look up. 'We got a £20,000 extension. But I paid the butcher, so that's £12,000 gone. Do cheques for £8,000.'

The bookkeeper looked at her bent head, then looked in the tray in front of her. 'I thought the bank only offered it on the basis the sale was . . .' She faltered as Judith looked up.

'That's right. And I accepted. Last week.'

'But . . . oh, I see, you thought that after all Selina would change her mind.'

'No. We needed the money, to keep going. I'll go and see Mr Andrews, but if he asks all you say is that with poor Mrs Marsh-Hayden gone you imagine the sale will be going through quickly.'

Mary Cameron thought about it, anxiously. 'So you are selling.'

'Not necessarily. But in any case we have to keep the place going. If we collapse we'll get a very poor price.'

Mary's face cleared. 'That's true. And I'm sure Mr Andrews will understand *that*.'

Judith, who did not share her confidence and had no intention of telling her bank manager the full story, nodded, avoiding looking at her colleague. The phone rang and she picked it up. 'Yes, darling. No. Don't worry at all. I've got everything to do here. I'm sorry, it's been so busy today, I will first thing tomorrow.' She put the phone down and sighed.

'Was that Michael?' Mary asked.

'Yes. I haven't done any of the things we agreed I'd do, and he's done all the things he said he'd do.' She felt and sounded defeated and the older woman nodded.

'Usually it's the other way round with men. Enjoy it while it lasts.' She packed up her various bags and talked her way out of the office.

Judith, concentration broken, went down to the kitchen, trying to decide whether she needed food or coffee, or a drink, now that she and Michael were not to meet for dinner. She was looking out into the September afternoon, watching the wind lift the rubbish in the gutters, when John McLeish found her. She was looking very tired, he thought, and not quite of this world, off in some preoccupation of her own.

'Is this convenient? I've come to collect Inspector Davidson.'

100

'Thanks for the sandwiches, Miss Delves. Very welcome. We've done with the lift.'

'The lift?'

'We've taken the carpet of course.'

'Oh. Oh, of course. Was it . . . is the . . . did you find anything?'

'We'll know more tomorrow morning. For the moment I just have a few questions, if I may?'

'Of course.' She cleared a space on the table and offered coffee, which they refused.

'The back door. Who has a key?'

'I do. Tony does, Selina does . . . did. Mary – our bookkeeper – does.'

'Anyone else?'

'Not of their own but, of course, we keep one in the till. So the night manager on any evening can lock up.'

McLeish frowned, seeing another piece of routine he had not sorted out. 'Who unlocks in the morning?'

'Usually Mary. She comes in at eight thirty.'

'And who locks up at night?'

'Well, it varies, I'm afraid. The kitchen is cleared by the wash-up who does the floor and puts the bags out. Then he goes and asks the night manager who should come down and lock up.' She was looking anxious and watching his face.

'And sometimes that doesn't happen?'

'I'm afraid sometimes – and I've done it myself – we give the key to the wash-up and he does it, and brings it back.' McLeish made a note and looked up to see her suddenly pale. 'You mean someone got in that way?'

'Possibly. Is there just the one key in the till? Yes? Who uses the till?'

'Nearly everybody,' she said, slowly. 'Or nearly all the floor staff.' She thought again, biting her lip. 'Oh dear. And the kitchen too. I've seen staff open the till to get change for the phone.'

'Would you notice – would anyone – if the key was missing?'

She was ahead of him. 'Not unless you actually needed to use it, no.'

They sat all three in silence for a minute.

'You must think us terribly careless. No, it is careless, it's awful. You know, you just get into bad habits.'

'When the running of the business takes precedence over everything. Yes.'

'Or even doing the accounts.' She hadn't meant to say *that*, he saw.

'Had you got behind?'

'Yes. Months. Oh, not cheques and bills, but on the management accounts.'

'Is that what you've been doing all day?'

'Yes.' She was looking down, tense and anxious, and he decided to take a risk.

'I understand that Mrs Marsh-Hayden thought there might be a fraud somewhere in the business.'

'There was. There is. Though she can't have known any details given the state the accounts were in.'

She was extremely angry, he realised.

'What sort of fraud?'

'Oh.' She got up from the table, knocking over her chair, a big girl, taller and heavier than Francesca, but not unlike her physically, needing to discharge energy. 'The usual. In the kitchen.'

'Chef?'

She stopped, staring out of the window. 'Has to be,' she said, eyes narrowed, watching something on the street, and he got up noiselessly to see what it was.

'Gallagher,' Bruce Davidson said in his ear, and they all watched, fascinated. The man was moving carefully, like a soldier in hostile territory, keeping to the middle of the pavement, close to the little groups of tourists who were ambling along the broad pavements, glancing over his shoulder. From above, the pattern was absolutely distinctive; it was a man on the run making for a safe home. He ducked into the main restaurant door with a final glance over his shoulder, and the policemen looked at each other.

'Someone's after him,' Davidson said, bristling with interest. 'Shit. Excuse me, Miss Delves.' He scrabbled in his pocket for the phone. 'Davidson. Aye. We are. Can he wait? No? We'll be there.'

'Forensic?' McLeish asked, still watching the street.

'Aye. You know what they're like, want to be home with their tea before it gets dark.'

'There,' McLeish said, quietly, and Davidson came and stood beside him, both men just far enough from the glass not to be visible to someone glancing up at the window.

'Aye. Now there's a face I've not seen for a bit. Will we go down?'

'You go. I must see Doc.'

Davidson nodded and left at a run while McLeish turned round.

'Miss Delves? I'm afraid we've been called away. May we come back tomorrow?'

'I'll be here.' She looked both young and smitten, like Francesca, when things were going wrong, and he stopped on his way.

'Don't do anything tonight. About whatever it is.'

She blinked at him, roused from her preoccupation. 'No. I need to go home for a bit, anyway. And I need to think. Do come tomorrow.'

'We'll be as unwelcome any time? I hear what you say.' He left her tired but just smiling and he plunged down the stairs to find what Doc Smith had done for them.

8

'Frannie?'

'Tristram m'man. Where are you?' Francesca, sitting at her own kitchen table struggling, crossly, with the in-tray, welcomed the diversion.

'At the flat. Brother Jeremy just arrived.'

'How?'

Jeremy, Tristram's twin, was working in Hong Kong for Price Waterhouse, and his siblings had begun to resign themselves to never seeing him in England again.

'Well, darling, on an aeroplane. So I've got him a ticket for tonight – he kindly seemed to feel it was worth it even to see me perform for thirty seconds at a time, and I'm buying him dinner afterwards with some mates at the Café de la Paix. Both of us want you. And John of course.'

'Oh, Tris, I'm not sure we can come. John's in charge of the murder there. Darling, do wake up. Body in freezer? Oh, you don't mind that. Oh well. No, look, I'll talk to John, but we can't both come, anyway. Susannah's out. But I'll definitely get to the show, so get a ticket for me.'

Michael Owens drove up the long drive and parked the BMW in front of the main door of the flat-fronted Georgian house. He was smiling to himself and had been since he turned off the main road.

'So here it is.' He leant across and kissed Judith. She returned his kiss, attention distracted by the sound of an engine.

'Oh, it's a man mowing the lawn.'

'Yes.' Michael agreed. 'It'd better be. Costs the earth. I need to find a regular gardener – you know, someone who comes for a couple of days a week. I want to do some replanning before the winter.'

Judith got out of the car, the better to confront the house. It was a formidable Georgian building, originally a rectory, with additions at the side, so that there were now – in estate agents parlance – six bedroom suites, a nursery suite and a garage with service flat above, which was the only part of the house currently occupied. She took a deep breath; she had not been quite expecting the sheer size and solidity of the building. Set in a small park, it had its own very definite atmosphere; it would not have surprised her at all to find the housekeeper, butler and full supporting cast arranged on the semicircular steps. In practice the reception committee was limited to a middle-aged woman who greeted her with open curiosity, and showed every sign of being prepared to take her round the house herself, until dissuaded by Michael.

She looked round the hall, in the echoing silence that greeted the departure of Mrs Stevens. The house was clean, shabby and lifeless. On a little table by the door lay a pile of envelopes which looked like the incoming post at Café de la Paix. Like much of the Café's correspondence indeed, this lot would consist of bills sent in by the army of people deployed in keeping the house clean, the furniture polished and curtains hung at the windows. Michael was tearing open envelopes, increasingly tight-lipped. He caught her eye.

'You know what they say, that the first hour in any weekend house is spent in paying bills. And unblocking the sink.'

'Can we have coffee before you show me the rest? I'll unblock the sink if we have to.'

The sink, like the rest of the vast kitchen, was a bit shabby but clean and not blocked. She ran water into the kettle, looking round her with a restaurateur's eye. Planning a kitchen held no terrors for her; the rules of what had to go where in relation to what were inexorable. She had been well taught and had designed the kitchens at both the Caffs, making a few alterations only to suit Tony Gallagher who had an unalterable objection to electric ovens of any sort. There was plenty of space and no problems that the expenditure of about £20,000 would not solve.

'Wonderful space for having people to dinner, I thought.'

That was the problem, she realised. She had been a good cook once. But for her, now, meals came out of a big restaurant kitchen, plated ready for her approval, or indeed cooked specially for her if there was nothing on the menu she wanted. The tiny kitchen in her own flat contained everything she was likely to want in terms of cooking equipment and space, now and for ever. But Michael disliked it and his own cramped kitchen with equal fervour, openly hankering for a large farmhouse kitchen with built-in mother as Selina had once maliciously observed. His own mother had remarried after his father left, dragging him round three countries and a series of houses. Mrs Trent, as she now was, lived in a small flat within sight of Harrods, with a tiny kitchen from which nothing more demanding than tea, toast and the occasional boiled egg ever emerged.

She made them both coffee, fighting down panic. 'Can we go and look at the rest?'

'Oh absolutely. It's all a bit like this, though, I warn you. The people who owned it had been here for yonks and hadn't spent any money on it. It's always touch and go whether the electricity works. I just haven't had time, and not really the inclination either. This is a house to live in.' He put his arm round her as he opened the heavy oak door to reveal a huge, shabby, cold drawing-room with long windows on to an overgrown terrace and a magnificent view beyond it.

'Wonderful room,' he said, contentedly, arm resting on her shoulders. 'I love it. Needs everything doing. There's a dining-room of course – through there.'

There was, and it would easily have housed twenty people. The study – the other side of the dining-room – would have made a fair-sized classroom, and was lined with books, every one of which was in need of a bookbinder's attention. She sat on the enormous heavy, lumpy chair which wobbled unstably as she moved. There was a full-time job here for a small army of carpenters, masons and decorators, all of whom would need direction. Combining this role – if indeed she was being asked to – with running the two Caffs looked impossible. It was an awkward journey from the West End, although, she realised, not very difficult for the City; the trains were direct into Waterloo from this part of Hampshire and the journey to Bank undemanding thereafter. She looked out of the window, over the substantial partner's desk, the leather stained and wrinkled, in need of careful replacement by some craftsman who, experience suggested, would need not merely paying but coaxing to fix it. Beyond the desk, framing the wonderful view, hung curtains, faded to a dirty pale red and shredding where they hung. She saw, not the view, but the immaculate mirrored surfaces and glistening brass of the Caff and the half-dozen waiters, who spent the first hour of the day dusting, to keep it like that.

'Darling?'

'Sorry, what did you say?'

'I didn't. I thought I'd wait till I got your attention. You do like it, don't you?' He was sounding desperately anxious, and her throat muscles seemed to have become paralysed.

He got up, abruptly, and came round her side of the desk, and she looked up at him. 'Come here.'

She pushed her chair back and walked into his arms, feeling, gratefully, the heavy muscle in his shoulders and upper arms and the flat stomach as his hands moved down in the small of her back, pulling her to him. She remembered suddenly the first time, the time he had bent to kiss her goodnight, gently, on the lips. She had responded and he had put both arms round her and kissed her in earnest. She had helped him undo the buttons of her dress so he could get at her breasts and had herself, more confident than she had ever been with anyone else, undone his trousers for him. They had ended in bed joyfully, where she had had a better time than she had believed was possible. And from that day she was hooked, she thought, her breath coming short as he felt for the nipple on her right breast.

'Let's go upstairs.'

'Oh yes.'

The first time, she thought, as they both tore off their clothes, he had taken off her clothes and she had been almost sick with excitement and pleasure as he pulled down her knickers, kissing her stomach. But this, now, was pretty good too and he made her come, watching her face, before he came in. She was unbelievably lucky, she reminded herself afterwards, arranging herself so she could lie comfortably beside him, touching at every part.

'You know I want to marry you.'

'Oh, darling Michael.' She started to cry and he kissed her.

'Was that a yes?'

'Oh darling.' She was feeling sick, she realised, incredulous. Here she was in bed with the man of her dreams, who wanted to marry her, and she was terrified.

'What is it? Come on, let's sit up, I'll get you a cup of tea. There's a kettle somewhere and milk, Mrs Stevens puts it out when I come down, because it's a day's march to the kitchen. We'd need a little one up on this floor, I think, just for drinks and tea.'

She sat up, drinking tea, and felt her courage return. 'Were we – I mean, was the plan that we would be here at weekends?'

'Well, we could certainly do that for a bit.'

'Until what?'

'Well, until the Caffs are sold.' He reached over and stroked her bottom. 'I know you don't want to sell, but darling, that's what it's going to come to. You – we, that is – overspent on the second Caff, well, we should have seen that, and it's taken longer to wash its face than you thought. And the mothership isn't making quite the same money it used to, is it? So we would need, at the least, to refinance. Only Richard, who owns not far short of fifty per cent with Selina's share, can't afford to do any of that. Nor can Tony. So, honestly, we don't have that much choice.'

Judith felt her breathing contract. 'Other people manage. We could borrow more.'

'Yes, but where would that leave Richard? He's bust, he needs the cash.'

'Well, he could find another shareholder, who would buy his shares. Like you for instance.'

He took his hand off her bottom and she moved towards him, but he rolled over. 'I'm going to get up. I need a pee.'

She lay, angry with herself for disrupting the moment, but when he came back, wrapped in a towel, he was looking tired, not angry, and sat on the bed facing her.

'Judith. Let's go through it again. Not a lot of people want shares in a private company. You know Richard and I did it because it was tax-efficient and it wouldn't be the same for someone buying now. Look, if both Caffs were doing really well we could put the company on the stock market. Just. Then Richard could sell enough of his shares to keep back the wolves for a bit, but . . .'

She sat up, propping pillows behind her and pulled the sheet over her breasts. 'But the Caffs aren't doing that well at the moment. So, why can Brian Rubin do it – by buying us out?'

'Because he's putting them together with the nine he's got. It's a bigger group. And he thinks he's cleverer than us; he thinks he can make more money on the sites.'

'And people believe him.'

'Perfectly respectable brokers behind him, they're happy with it.'

Judith looked at him, silenced and mutinous, feeling about eight years old.

'In any case, darling, if we want children – and I do, and I assume you do – we'd better get on with it. I mean, you're thirty-four. Of course I could afford to buy Richard out, but . . . well, I can't see how you – how we – are going to do all this if you're stuck in that bloody place six days a week.'

I did not know he disliked it that much, she thought. 'Michael, when you put up the money – for the Caff – what did you think was going to happen?'

'Oh, well. I put it up as a punt, because, well, I'd known Richard for ever, and I liked the site and it was a Business Expansion Scheme, so that was sixty per cent of my cash back straightaway, from the taxman. And Selina was very keen. I thought she'd bring in the punters. And I thought – and I was right, wasn't I? – that you'd put in the work. I didn't know you very well then, but I could see that much.'

'So what's different now?'

'Well, you're not just Selina's friend who does all the work. We're going to get married, I hope. And I want you to have time for me and our life, and you won't if you go on. And we've got a good offer so you'll get a fair return for all your work.'

For sense and logic it could not be faulted, she thought, hopelessly. But the Caffs were hers, her creation. Without her the whole enterprise would not be there, hundreds of people every night would not be sitting down being well fed and made welcome.

'I'd . . . well, not exactly been happy, but I'd accepted that the Caffs would belong to someone else,' she said hesitantly. 'But now, I can't seem to manage to. I mean, if Selina had changed her mind back again, then I'd have been disappointed, but I'd have agreed. I think. But she was murdered, Michael, and that changes everything. I feel I'd be letting her down.'

His mouth was set in a thin straight line as it did when he was upset. 'For Christ's sake. She let *you* down, I mean, you did all the real work.'

Judith acknowledged wearily a direct hit. Selina had tended to appear and do sterling work in greeting and chatting for about half the hours of any shift when she was on duty, rather than arriving fifteen minutes before the shift started and leaving half an hour after it stopped, as Judith did.

'And her murder needn't have had anything to do with the Caffs at all.' Michael could see he had an advantage.

They looked at each other properly, Judith felt, for the first time since she had seen Selina's dead bloodstained face in its black plastic frame. She rubbed her eyes to dispel the vision, and Michael took her hand.

'I've been telling myself it was a prowler,' she said, wearily. 'Someone who walked in off the street and hid and waited. We had one in the early days, you remember? He got in when a kitchen hand left the back door open to get some air and we found him in the morning. Couldn't get out and had settled down to cook and eat most of Chef's carefully reduced stock which was waiting for the next day and four steaks out of the chillers. So I thought it had happened again, only this time . . . this time . . .'

Michael gathered her into his arms as she wept. 'I'd just like you right out of it,' he said, holding her. 'It's a bloody awful thing to say, but Selina – getting killed like that . . . it's very revealing. It's reminded me that it's a rough business, the people who work there are rough. Straight off the streets, some of them.'

'Only the wash-ups,' she protested, tears drying. 'And they come from the hostel, and as you know one of them turned out to be a terrific sous chef, who was just down on his luck.'

'You aren't listening to me, are you? Please, Judith, have some sense.' He drew in a long breath. 'At least have some consideration for Richard.'

She thought, drearily, of Richard Marsh-Hayden. He had not seen Selina, wreathed in plastic in the freezer, but he had gone to the morgue, and presumably had seen her before . . . well, before she could be laid flat in a position of decent repose.

'He won't want to have anything to do with the Caffs,' she acknowledged.

'That's true but it's not what I mean. The police always assume the husband did it. Because ninety per cent of the time it is someone in the family. If it's murder.' He was looking longingly out of the window into the sunlit garden. 'I don't want to talk about all this. Could we, possibly, manage to have a nice day, and go round the garden?'

Matthew Sutherland fought his way to the surface; the duvet had somehow got wound round him and he could momentarily not find his way out. He untied the Gordian knot by rolling out of the low bed, duvet and all, groping for the alarm, then realising it was a telephone he could hear.

'Didn't wake you, did I? Tony Gallagher.'

'Christ. Yes, you did. What time is it?'

'Nearly eleven thirty. Sorry, but the service starts soon and I needed to get you.'

'You're at the Caff?' Matt was slowly finding his way.

'That's where the service is, yes. I'm on double shift because we're fucking short again. You got someone with you?'

'No such luck.' Matthew had managed to unwind the duvet and get himself on to the edge of the bed, sitting up, both eyes open. 'What's up?'

'Fucking busies.'

'They're with you?' Matt was instantly awake.

'Nah. But they're bugging me.'

'Harassing you?' He listened to an exasperated indrawn breath. 'Want me to come over?'

'Thanks, mate. See, it's not exactly harassment but I can't afford the grief, they're digging about where it's better not, know what I mean?'

Matt, thoroughly baffled, understood the question to be rhetorical. Nobody, including possibly Gallagher himself, could have known what he meant but it would wait. And after an evening drinking with some of his peer group in the criminal law fraternity he needed the time he had to get breakfast down and get himself showered and shaved and the washing done and a couple of shirts ironed. Somewhere between toast and his fourth cup of coffee, in the cluttered, grubby kitchen/dining-room, he understood abruptly that his student days were over. He was a working solicitor, decently if not generously paid, and he had clients who needed him at weekends as well as all hours during the week. He put the cup down, collected laboriously all his dirty clothes, towels and sheets, and shoved a load into the ancient, slow, temperamental washing-machine he had acquired with the flat. He looked at it doubtfully as it laboured into action, disentangled all his shirts from the remaining pile and went out in search of a laundry, an electrical showroom and someone to come in and clean the flat.

At a quarter to two he walked in through the doors of Café de la Paix in a mood to take on any giants he might meet. He had brought off a double with the proprietor of the dry-cleaners. He had entrusted him with eight shirts and a suit, and agreed to employ one of the daughters-in-law of the house as a cleaner for four hours on Thursdays. She would, of course, pick up and return any cleaning and laundry while she was at it. Flushed with success he had bought a Miele washing-machine, in honour of Francesca McLeish, a paragon of domestic efficiency, who always bought heavily over-engineered expensive German machines. He felt grown-up and in control and beamed at the girl on reception as he asked to see the chef. After ten minutes he was irritated, and after twenty, seriously annoyed, not least by the explanations offered for Gallagher's absence.

'I know it's lunchtime. But he's expecting me.'

'I am sorry, but 'e is not in the kitchen even.' The girl was flustered and there was no point harassing her, so he went to look in the kitchen himself; no sign of his client but a sous chef, gazing trancelike into space over his pans, said that Tony had popped up to the office after the bulk of the service. The man had been half asleep, he realised, as he went round the back and tramped up the two flights of stairs – the lift seemed to be roped off. Tony's complaints about being short-staffed must be true.

The door to the office was closed but he could hear voices so he walked in. His client was in profile to him, bent over straining and scarlet-faced under the rough blond hair. He was wearing a T-shirt and a pair of navy socks, his jeans, pants and trainers were draped on a chair, and he was talking disjointedly to assist him in his task of pleasuring a thin, pale blonde, bent beneath him over a desk, Chef's tunic protecting her hips from the sharp edges. Matthew withdrew, closing the door, hoping not to have put his client off his stroke. He went through the kitchen door, nodding to the sous chef now occupied with a late order, and sat at a table to drink coffee and read the paper, torn between irritation and admiration. It was now 2.30 p.m. and his time was being wasted, but you had to admire a man who could do that after cooking 150 lunches.

'Sorry, mate, things to do.' Tony Gallagher dropped into a seat beside him, wearing clean jeans and a sweatshirt. He had showered, Matt noted, hair sleeked down and damp, and he looked understandably tired out and pleased with himself as he loaded sugar into the coffee which had appeared in front of him.

'I did come up to the office.' Matt was not disposed to let clients get away with holding him up.

'That was you then? Thank Christ for that. Not that I'd have taken any shit from anyone here, whatever had been going down, know what I mean? There's only me, Antoine and two commis on tonight to feed the five thousand. Anyway, sorry, but I got an unexpected offer.' He narrowed his eyes at the pale blonde, now upright and more or less clothed in a very short skirt as she walked, self-consciously, past them. 'Not enough of that around.'

'Indeed,' Matt agreed. 'Better for you than going on the beer.'

'Been doing a bit of that too.'

'You called me.' Matt decided to call the meeting to order.

112

'Police bothering you?'

'They're stirring things up. Talking to people.'

Matt waited, unmoving, while his client struggled with himself.

'See, like I told you, I owe a bit, here and there. They've been talking to those people and that just makes hassle for me. And I got enough of that.'

'Tony, can you give it to me straight? *I've* got things to do as well, like get fixed up for tonight, now you've given me the idea.'

'Yeh, sorry.' Gallagher, galvanised by this straightforward appeal to masculine solidarity, managed to find the words. 'I have the odd bet, yeh? Well, it's not been a good season, and I owe the bookies. Well, one bookie really. He's carried me, fair play to him, and he's let me go on, see if I can get it back, but ... well, I haven't and there's other people behind him, know what I mean, and anyway, I'm on a deadline. And having the fuzz asking is just bad news – I mean, they ... the people I mean ... think I've asked for protection, like. And I wouldn't do that, I told them. But they rung here, just before I called you. The Yard got one of the people out of bed at seven o'clock – I mean, it's a liberty.'

'The Yard?'

'That's what the man said. And they'd know the difference.'

Matthew sat, considering this disordered narrative. A few facts, he decided, would clear his mind. 'How much do you owe?'

'Five thousand quid?'

Matthew looked at him, wordlessly.

'Nearer ten.' Gallagher looked away, across the restaurant, colour patchy over his cheekbones, and lifted a hand to indicate that some more coffee would be welcome.

'Who else knows?'

'No one. Haven't told a soul.'

'Mm.' Matthew sat, slumped, considering the implications. He waited until the waiter bringing coffee had come and gone. 'If it's the Yard asking, it suggests it's connected to this investigation.' He hesitated. 'You always been a betting man, Tony?'

'Yeh. I usually win, though.'

Well, Scotland Yard had been remarkably quick. John McLeish was a clever bloke of course, had to be, or Francesca would never have married him. He shook his head to clear it of the sudden vision of Francesca in the same position as the pale blonde. He'd been both sorry and relieved when the affair with her had stopped; he hadn't had enough of it, neither of them had, but it was high risk for both

113

of them and had no pay-off other than the obvious. In particular you wouldn't, man or girl, want to cross John McLeish. He hauled himself back to his client's immediate problem.

'So the Yard probably knows by now how much you owe. And for how long.'

'If we'd of sold this place when we meant I'd have paid it off.'

'You'd promised that? The people you owe?'

'Yeh. And now they know there's been a problem, and the fuzz are in. I'm in deep shit.'

Deeper indeed than he had realised, Matthew thought, soberly. He had visited in hospital a previous client who had owed too much money for too long, and he would himself have gone a long way to avoid that fate. But worse than that, Tony Gallagher's obvious need for cash, now, meant that he had a sound motive for disposing of Selina Marsh-Hayden, who was standing between him and the way out of his difficulties. And Gallagher came from a family which always resorted to violence to settle its conflicts with the outside world, as two siblings serving longish sentences amply attested. Gallagher gestured to a waiter, signalling a need for one of the sticky cakes on display at the bar, affording an excellent view of the powerful shoulders and muscular upper arms, developed from heaving heavy saucepans and loads of food around all day. Selina Marsh-Hayden, taken from behind, would have been no match for him at all. The image of the pale blonde came unbidden, and with it the alarming possibility of a further complication.

'Tony. Was there ever anything sexual between you and Mrs Marsh-Hayden?'

'Nah.' Gallagher was looking uneasy and there was colour over his cheekbones. Matthew waited, silently, while his client fidgeted. 'I tried it on,' he said, finally, 'and she turned me down.' He looked at Matthew, who thought he had been registering only patient interest. 'Nah, nah, mate.' He patted him reassuringly. '*Nicely* she done it. Said she still fancied me – but it wasn't on, not working in the same shop, surely my Dad would have told me that. Well, I had to laugh, because of course he did. When I was fourteen. She was a goer though, Selina. Would almost have been worth going to work somewhere else.'

'So she didn't confine herself to her old man?'

'Nah. Him neither, mind. There was a blonde tart, used to come here, late, with him. Like Selina, only not as . . .'

'Pretty?'

'Confident, I guess. She knew she had us all where she wanted us.' He brooded, silently. 'She was a pain in the ass sometimes – in fact a lot of the time – but she was a pleasure to the eye. They say that in Cork, you know.'

Matt, who had been thinking on different lines, considered his client. 'I can't do anything about the police, Tony. They've got an investigation to run. They just have picked up somewhere that you were in debt to the bookies. They've got contacts.'

'What am I going to do, Matt?'

The man was not only a client but a contemporary in a fix, and Matt bent his mind to the problem. 'If they come after you, the police'll know who it was.' Gallagher's look told him this would not be much use. 'We could ask for protection.' *That* wasn't going to meet the case either, he could see. 'Make a deal,' he suggested.

'I did. And couldn't deliver, so they're not going to trust me, are they?'

'Well' – he lowered his voice – 'this place will still get sold, won't it?'

'Yeh. But when?' They looked at each other and Gallagher sat up. 'You could tell them. You was acting for me on the sale.'

'Yes, I could.' He thought. 'Well, I'd have to talk to Peter, but I don't see why not. I'd be representing you and explaining your position, that's what solicitors do. They want the money, don't they, rather than risking trouble by beating you up?'

'I guess so. Yeh. Particularly after a visit from the fuzz.'

'Ah. So that was useful, as it turns out.'

'I'd never have thought it, but you got a point. Thanks, mate, do it quickly, can you?'

'Gallagher owes £9740 now, interest running at ten per cent a month,' Bruce Davidson reported smugly, replacing the phone. 'I sent Sergeant Willis, he knows those people.'

'Well, well, well.' McLeish, who had been working all day, consulted a chart, and looked wistfully out of the window. 'No alibi, or not much of one, from eleven o'clock on the last day Selina was seen until about four in the morning next day. When he rolled home to Mum who would have heard him come in.'

'Come a trial, she'll have heard him come in whenever he needed her to.'

'I expect that's right – he's the only one of the brothers bringing

115

home a pay packet, isn't he? My bet is, Bruce, that she was strangled sometime after the kitchen closed. In the office, and her body put in the lift and run down to the basement and unloaded into the freezer. By someone she knew, I think.'

'What, she arranged to meet them?'

'I think so. Much more likely than a vagrant – as some of the other shareholders have suggested. It would have had to be someone who knew the place. To find the lift and the freezer.'

'You think this was all carefully planned?' Davidson was sounding doubtful, and McLeish shook his head.

'Not necessarily. I mean, you couldn't have banked on the freezer still being there. Remember, it was supposed to have been taken away. No, the best bet is someone who knew the place well and who took advantage of all its features – including an old freezer which wasn't meant to be there. And who Selina knew, and wasn't worried by.'

'That's right. You'd not sit down and turn your back on a stranger, or someone you were scared of.'

'This also assumes she was killed because she was holding up a sale. The timing favours that, but we ought to hold in our minds the possibility that she was murdered for quite other reasons.' He considered his associate, who was looking restless. 'We're going to have to catch this one using our brains and very old-fashioned policework, Bruce. I had a call from Doc just before you arrived. Forensic did all the towels and jackets; as they thought, they couldn't find a thing. Nothing left to test and couldn't find any missing threads.'

'We'd found all eighty of the jackets too.'

'Yes. So the murderer's jacket is in that lot, but the laundry's destroyed all the evidence. So no help at all there, it's back to motive and alibis.'

Bruce Davidson thought about it, gloomily. 'So we start with the husband, who doesn't have an alibi, and then have a look at the rest of the shareholders.'

'None of them has an alibi. Judith Delves and Michael Owens went home individually and at different times to their own flats, and can provide no evidence at all of what time they got in. Richard Marsh-Hayden can prove where he was for some of the time, but not all – I've got a team checking. Tony Gallagher ... well, he's no better. And the outside chance, the one who wanted to buy the shares, Brian Rubin, is in the same case.'

'Unusual, that,' Davidson said, thoughtful.

'Yes. And lucky for whoever did it.'

'Mebbe they all ganged up, and agreed that nobody was to have an alibi?'

'Thanks, Bruce. It's time we stopped, when you're thinking like that. I have to go, anyway, I'm babysitting.'

'If you wanted to get letters from a lover, where would you have them sent?'

They were settled, cosily, drinking tea, Francesca with her feet up on the sofa and he in the big comfortable chair they had chosen together as her wedding present to him. Francesca, who had undone the top button on her trousers in the interests of accommodating someone that, as he observed, could not be much more than an inch long, considered the point.

'To Gladstone. Marked "Personal", then no one would open them.'

'Not to home? I don't usually open things addressed to you.'

She gave him a look of amused affection. 'No, but if it was marked "Personal" you'd *ask*, wouldn't you? Who was it from? Anything interesting? Any husband would. So no. Anything which comes here you may open in the confidence that it is a gas bill or an offer of a free *Reader's Digest*.'

'I maybe ought to have a word with the office at Gladstone.'

'I haven't had any letters like that for years,' she said, wistfully.

He considered her; they had met when she was a driven twenty-eight-old divorcée, working for the DTI. She had married her first love and had no option but to divorce her husband when she was twenty-six years old, he having left her for another woman. She had had three years on her own, living and loving as she pleased, before he had met her.

'What sort of chap does write letters?'

She burst out laughing. 'I was waiting for you to ask that. I don't think you've ever written as much as a line to me – though you may, I suppose, have written to others? No? Well, when I used to get letters – when I was young – they were sometimes from chaps who liked writing about sex. But mostly they wrote because they were married and couldn't chat on the phone, and wanted to make a date or simply keep in touch. I mean, one can't ring up married men at home, so sometimes your only hope was a letter.' She had gone rather pink, and he hauled himself out of his chair to move her feet

117

over so he could sit beside her. 'Put like that,' she said, with a burst of her always disconcerting honesty, 'it doesn't sound much fun. Nor was it – I am very glad to be married to you, no matter how burdened we are.' They both started uneasily at a faint cry from their principal burden, who they had hoped was still finishing his afternoon rest, but it did not persist and they relaxed.

'So a man who wrote letters to a woman's office address would have been married?'

'Oh, not necessarily. They could be single and just like to write, or don't mind writing if that was what was required. The ones who are writing only to fix a date, or who are saying things like "Last night was very precious to me", *sans préciser plus*, are likely married.'

McLeish checked an entirely inappropriate giggle at her coolly detached view of a complex activity, and reflected humbly that in a limited field his wife was probably fully as expert as Bruce Davidson. 'Where would you – would she – would anyone have kept letters like that at the office. What if someone tidied up and found them?'

'No office I've ever been in gets tidied to that extent. Surely, you have a drawer where you keep the masculine equivalent of make-up, sanitary towels, medicaments, decayed combs, etc.'

'Old love letters. Yes, OK. I don't keep the love letters, but I could easily. Jenny'd never bother with the bottom drawer of my desk.'

'And much safer there than at home. Where did *she* – Selina – keep them, by the way?'

'We found everything else you list in her desk, but no letters. So either there aren't any more, or we haven't found them.'

'In a filing cabinet? Disguised as something else?'

'Now there's a thought.' He moved her feet, got up and found a notebook while she watched him with love.

'I do like a methodical man.'

'Only way in my trade.'

'Only way in most people's, just very few accept this boring truth. You wouldn't like to make another cup of tea?'

So he did that, in the big comfortable kitchen which you found in every house occupied by the family into which he had married.

'You do have to go and watch Tristram tonight, I suppose?'

'Oh darling. It means I can see Jeremy too. You don't mind really.'

'No, I don't mind.'

*

118

Some hours later, Francesca, arm in arm with Tristram, who was as high as a kite on nothing more chemically advanced than a good performance, stopped outside Café de la Paix, struck by doubt and anxiety.

'You go ahead, Tris, I'll wait for Jeremy.'

Tristram, with acolytes, swept ahead, giving her the chance to ascertain, furtively, that none of the principals in the Café de la Paix cast were visible. With luck, her presence would go unnoticed and any complications with her husband would be avoided. He had not asked where they were eating after the performance and she had not told him, but it would all too obviously be better practice for the wife of the principal investigating officer not to visit the locus of the crime at this point.

She waited for Jeremy, who had done his best to cast aside all restraint and was wearing a beautiful figured leather jacket, looted from Tristram's wardrobe. It was amazing how much occupation affected genetics, she reflected; Tristram and Jeremy were fraternal twins and very like each other, yet everything about Jeremy said conservative solicitor, or banker, despite the jacket. Conversely, no matter how sober his suit, no one would ever take the expressive Tristram for other than an artist. She slid in, behind Jeremy, to a place at the long table at the back, banking on the assumption that the waiting staff would have needed to have seen a customer more than twice to be confident of recognising them. She had now met most of the *Tosca* cast, so conversation at the table flowed easily, as did the food and wine. But she was aware that their table was receiving favourable treatment; it was impossible not to observe that two of the tables nearest to them were becoming distinctly restive, and that waiters were giving them a wide berth. She watched out of the corner of an eye, thinking smugly that they had been wise, at Gladstone College, to change over to self-service, but finally laden trays and smiling, gracefully apologetic waiters arrived there, followed by another man bearing what were clearly complimentary bottles. Sensible, she thought, good customer relations, and returned hastily to her plate to avoid the man's questioning look. Not a waiter, but a floor manager, and she feared he had recognised her, though hopefully not as wife to Detective Chief Superintendent McLeish.

Tristram, four places away from her, on the other side of the table, suddenly coughed, touching his throat, and she looked over at him, alarmed. He reached for a glass of water, downed it, coughed again, drew in a breath and started to cough seriously. Someone slapped

119

him on the back which made it worse, and Francesca was on her feet and round his side of the table, in a flash. She looked round for more water and blinked; the lighting appeared to have gone dim and there was a mist in the restaurant. Other diners had started to cough and fan themselves.

'Tris. Out, now,' she said, urgently; one glance at Jeremy and he was with her, picking up Tris's jacket and urging him out. She drew breath and started to cough herself; the smog in the restaurant was thickening and patrons were gesticulating and waiters rushing ineffectually around. She looked up at the ceiling and saw that black smoke was rolling from every crack in the pine planking. Jeremy seized her arm and she grabbed a napkin, poured water over it and gave it to Tristram who took it wordlessly and clapped it over his mouth. Jeremy would not even expect the same treatment, but Tristram's throat must at all costs be protected. She glanced up at the ceiling, coughing herself, to see that the thick black smoke was no longer billowing out, but oozing, reluctantly. A small door, marked 'Private', opened beside them and Matthew Sutherland's client, the chef, emerged, his arm round a white-faced shocked man, who was stripped down to a greying vest above battered jeans with both forearms wrapped in tea towels.

'Got the air-conditioning off,' he shouted to the floor manager, across the backs of retreating patrons.

Francesca almost opened her mouth to point out that air was what was needed before she realised that it was the ventilation system which had been blowing smoke to every corner of the restaurant through the ceiling. Behind the slatted pine panels must be tubes and pipes carrying air and music, and if things went wrong, black smoke.

'Ze sprinklers?' The floor manager had arrived at Chef's side.

'No, for God's sake, Jean-Pierre. It's the grease filter over the grill. Fire's inside the pipes – I've called the fire brigade out, but it's dying down.'

She found herself on the pavement with a firm brotherly arm around her. Jeremy, six years her junior, scolding in an entirely middle-aged way about pregnant women who exposed themselves to risk. She managed not to snap at him, recognising that she was a surrogate for her sister-in-law in far-away Hong Kong, but occupied herself wrapping Tristram, pale and anxious, into a jacket and finding the cough sweets she always carried. The floor manager, Jean-Pierre, was outside attempting to reassure and placate customers, milling around on the pavement. It was a fire in the kitchen, he was explaining, not serious, no bills would of course be charged, and any patron here who had paid should submit the bill for reimbursement in the morning. Indeed, any patron whose evening had been disrupted would be received for a complimentary meal on any evening of his choice during the next week. It was nicely done, a neat piece of disaster recovery. But disaster it most certainly was for a restaurant. And another potential crisis was threatening here too, she realised grimly, setting herself to the task of getting Tristram, still coughing, to the expensive stand-by medical adviser to the English National Opera. And achieving some kind of explanation to her husband as to how she had been an eyewitness of an unexplained turn in the case he was professionally charged with investigating.

9

'Good morning, Miss Delves – I shouldn't say that, should I? It can't really be a very good morning for you. Sorry we couldn't get here for eight, but eight thirty's not bad, not with this traffic, thought it was going to be a lot worse.'

Judith managed to raise a smile; Mac Troughton, relentlessly chirpy, rubbing his hands and gazing appraisingly at the blackened ceiling of the Café, was general foreman of the heating and ventilation firm which had installed the system, and his availability the key determinant of whether the Café could reopen in the foreseeable future. It was a devastating scene: long strips of the pine ceiling in the restaurant were blackened and cracked and all the paintwork was covered in greasy black. The kitchen was a wreck. They had not been able to use the washing-up machines last night and a couple of wash-ups were wearily stacking blackened, greasy plates into them. Saucepans of food stood where they had been abandoned, and Tony Gallagher, in the middle of it, was engaged in disposing of everything that was left. Anything not already securely in a deep freeze would need to be thrown out. The char grill, with eight wizened blackened steaks sticking to the iron bars, was the centre of the destruction. Above it the huge fan hood hung, crooked and twisted by the heat of the fire.

'Grease filter caught, then,' Mac Troughton said, smiling brightly at Tony Gallagher, who gave him a look that ought to have caused him to shrivel like the steaks, but which bounced off that armour-plated personality.

'That's where it started, Mac,' Judith acknowledged. 'One of the steaks caught for a minute, the grill chef turned it over to put the flame out and thought nothing of it until drops of flaming grease started to fall on him. Then he ran. No, he's not here, some of it went through his jacket and he had to go to casualty. We don't expect him in.'

'Took you a bit of time to get the emergency switch off, then.'

'Bloody right.' Tony Gallagher passed a tray of pastries speckled with soot to an underling for disposal. 'It's way down the end of the corridor.'

'As required in the regulations. And stated in all the notices. And illuminated as, I hope, you found.'

A snort from Tony Gallagher, but Mac Troughton was not giving an inch.

'Doesn't take long to spread, of course, that's what you get with an efficient ventilation system, sorry about that, I'm sure.' He was studying the damage, moving to consider different angles.

One put up with Mac, she reminded herself, because he was the best, and they had had cause to be grateful to him many times for his system.

'Yerss. I can have a crew here tomorrow, and I'll pick up the parts myself. Give you time to clean up.' He drew two fingers along a blackened, greasy counter and wiped them on one of the wash-ups's towels, leaving two parallel black smudges. Judith followed him meekly into the restaurant, while he opined it wasn't worth pulling the pipe through, all that bit of panel would need replacing anyway, so if a builder could be secured just to pull it off, his skilled men could go straight there after the kitchen. And no, he wouldn't like to offer any view, not just now, not until a chippie cleared things for him, like, as to how long it would take, or how much it would cost, but he'd put a holding order on for two hundred metres of trunking if she could let him have a cheque now for £1000. She sat down to write it, on the spot, as he watched her.

'I expect you was due to have the filter cleaned.'

'Overdue. Well overdue,' she said, bitterly, concentrating on making the figures and the writing on the cheque match.

'You might not want to say that to everyone. If you take my meaning.'

She looked up at him, but he was gazing at the ceiling, and she understood the full extent of the problem. They were heavily insured for everything including loss of profit if the restaurant was closed for more than a few days. But the insurance company could reasonably object to paying out if a necessary precaution against fire had been omitted. She looked gratefully at his overalled chest and pressed the cheque into his hand, and he talked his way out of the front of the restaurant just ahead of a Jaguar which deposited Michael Owens at the door.

'How's it going?'

A phone call had summoned both of them from a sound sleep at 1 a.m. and he had driven her back to London, and helped her calm the staff, sort out their injuries and secure the building. He had finally insisted on taking her to her own flat at five o'clock. He had gone on to his flat and was immaculately dressed in expensive casuals in contrast to her boiler suit and trainers.

'It actually looks even worse this morning, doesn't it? Christ, what a mess. I think I might give Brian Rubin a ring.'

'Why? So he can come and gloat?'

'Darling.' He pulled her a little away from the procession of curious passers-by. 'There really is now a case for cutting our losses. Give Rubin the problem, let him claim the insurance and have all the hassle, rather than us – you – do it all and then hand it over. No?'

She looked at him, appalled, and he looked back at her, his face drooping. 'You really hadn't accepted we were going to sell.'

'No, I haven't.' They both heard the change of tense, and she winced as the hand holding her arm clenched. 'Please don't ring Brian Rubin.' It was not a request and he looked back at her. 'We'll talk at lunch, OK?'

John McLeish was in his office reading, again, the forensic report on the Café de la Paix lift. The stain on the carpet was indeed blood and had belonged to the dead girl. So, at some point she had been in the lift, dead presumably, and blood from her nosebleed, since there was no open wound on the corpse, had dripped on to the carpet. The lift was rich in fingerprints belonging to Judith Delves, Michael Owens, Tony Gallagher, Richard Marsh-Hayden, Brian Rubin, and indeed the dead girl herself. There were other unidentified prints and it would now be necessary to match them up with staff and see what, if anything, was left over. Depressingly, there were also the characteristic bubble marks left by rubber gloves, so it was most likely the murderer had not taken them off until he – or she – had got rid of the body. He looked up to find Bruce Davidson, also in a suit, watching him from the door.

'I came in,' he said redundantly, 'I thought you'd need some help what with the fire at Café de la Paix?'

'I had an eyewitness present. As I did not know, Fran was there, eating with her brothers and the cast of *Tosca*.'

'Ah.'

'Yes. She hadn't, of course, any idea whether it was accidental or not, so no useful purpose was served.'

A chastened Francesca was cooking lunch for her mother and John.

He had been extremely angry when she had rung him, guiltily, from Tristram's flat at midnight, to confess where she had been and to report the fire, but she had been so penitent that he had managed to forgive her.

'The fire brigade lads say probably accident not arson. They've seen one of these before. There was a lot of grease inside the hood and the pipes above the charcoal grill, so when a flame went up from a steak it caught. Like a chimney going on fire. And then, of course, the fans took the fire right through the ventilation which runs above the ceiling. They got them switched off pretty quick. Bloody complicated way of setting a fire. I mean, you'd have to have six months of grease to start with, stuffed inside the cooker hood.'

'Doesn't sound likely, does it?'

At Café de la Paix, Judith had reached the same conclusion. She put her head through the kitchen hatch.

'Chef. A word, please. Out here.'

He came slowly and reluctantly, but underneath the masculine foot-dragging she could see he was deeply uneasy. She had placed herself at a hastily cleaned table at the back of the Café, well out of range of the clean-up squad who had reported for duty that morning, imagining they were going to spend the day in clean uniforms, waiting on tidy, clean people. They were nonetheless working with a will; they got time and a half on Sundays anyway, and Judith had promised everyone double time and a £10 bonus over. Nothing could be more important than to get the thick black greasy stain off tables, chairs, cruets, vases and floors as quickly as possible. She considered her chef, who was slumped, looking at his hands.

'I know something has gone wrong for you, Tony. What is it?'

He looked up at her briefly, then hunched his shoulders and looked down, the big hands moving restlessly.

'Is it money?'

His hands twitched and his head turned away; it was like dealing with someone of about seven years old. She tried again. 'The police – Mr McLeish, the Chief Superintendent – he saw you being followed. So they know something's wrong. You might as well tell me.'

He flung himself round in his chair, in an agony of physical frustration, she realised. He would have liked to hit someone, or be lifted from the scene by helicopter, but he was cornered. She reminded herself there were at least fifteen people within easy call and waited until, gripping the table, he managed to tell her about his gambling debts.

'Five thousand,' she said, involuntarily, and understood immediately from the quick look she got that this was not the whole story. She sat, dismayed, working out how to say what had to be said. 'I finished the last three months' accounts before I went away for the weekend,' she said, finally, and saw his shoulders slump.

'I had to get cash.'

'From the till?'

'Nah.' He was obviously surprised and managed to look her, briefly, in the eye. 'Sold some food at the back.'

'*That*'s what happened to the plate costs? They're up to thirty-eight per cent, thirty-nine last month. The difference between profit and loss.' A long miserable silence fell.

'We was selling the place, see, and it wouldn't matter. I mean, Rubin wasn't going to reduce the price, he was that mad to buy us.'

She glanced at him, and he went quiet again and looked longingly at the kitchen door. 'This is what Selina was talking about.'

'Yeh.'

Judith sat up. 'She accused you of it?'

'Yeh. But she didn't really know how to find ... a ... well, anything wrong, so I wasn't much bothered.'

'You waited to do all this until I was out of the way, over the river?' she said, bitterly.

'It wasn't like that.' He was scarlet and sullen, but he was still sitting in his chair. 'They was after me – are after me. I didn't want a beating, OK?'

'You could have said, you silly cuckoo.' They stared at each other, Judith as startled as he by the emergence of the childhood epithet. 'We might not have wanted our chef incapacitated either.'

He looked back at her, very carefully, the blue eyes narrowed. 'Doesn't matter now, though, does it?'

'More than before,' Judith, who had been working and thinking with only a short break since 2 a.m., assured him. 'We have to get open again, quickly. How do I replace you in a hurry, you ... you ...'

'Stupid bog-trotter?' His jaw was gritted.

'Silly idiot was what I was struggling for.'

126

'What are you going to do?' He managed to look her briefly in the eye.

'It's what are *we* going to do.' She stared back. 'First thing we have to get the wolves beaten back from your sledge. We throw them something, like say £3000.'

'It'll take a bit more than that, and I'll tell you true, I've not got it.'

'Not even from three months' selling our supplies?' She watched him go scarlet. 'Pity. I'll lend whatever you need to you personally, but I'll take your shares as security. And you pay back my estimate of what you've taken from here out of future wages, or out of your shares if we do have to sell.'

He was watching her lips, pale now, like an anxious child. 'And I get it in cash?'

'Yes. But I want a proper agreement. Your lawyer can do it, but I want it done. And you do your damnedest to make sure we make the profit we should.' She put out her hand, and after a second's hesitation he shook it hard, unsmiling.

'I'll do that now, ring the lawyer.'

'Tony. Do we have to change our butcher?'

'We do, yeh, but no need to pay his bill on time, and I know another.' He caught her eye. 'Maybe you'd like to choose the next one.'

'I would. And someone else to supply olive oil?'

'Mm. Yeh.' He hesitated, and struggled with himself. 'I'm sorry,' he said, managing to look her in the collar-bone, and fled to the kitchen and the telephone.

Matthew Sutherland, summoned for the second time in two days to Café de la Paix, got out at Trafalgar Square and walked crossly up past the Coliseum. He stopped to look and found himself face to face with Tristram Wilson, looking maliciously amused. 'Sorry if you were meeting Frannie. She's at home in disgrace. I lured her out to the Café de la Paix last night and all would have been well, but there was a fire.'

'You were all there, were you?'

'Absolutely. Lots and lots of black smoke pouring from the ceiling. Very bad for the throat.' Tristram Wilson touched his neck, cautiously.

'Not very good for trade either.'

'Indeed not. I suppose we all think of our own trade first.'

Fair enough, Matthew thought, amused by encountering Francesca's speed of response coming out of a man's face. 'You're rehearsing, are you?'

'Yes. This production is having a bad time – Alan O'Meara is fighting a cold, and poor old Scarpia just about managed yesterday. If there were any justice in the world both of us understudies would be singing tomorrow but, life being what it is, Alan is croaking through and they had a spare Scarpia. We're just walking through it with the new Scarpia who happens to be in the country, make sure we don't all bang into each other.' Tristram's eyes flickered past him and Matthew realised that several other people had stopped, including two very good-looking young women. He would have to leave them to Francesca's brother; it was already past noon. And not much chance of lunch, Matthew understood, as he was admitted to Café de la Paix – an unlit cavern, blackened with smoke, with grime-encrusted figures labouring assiduously in every corner.

'Where was the fire?' he said, by way of greeting to his client who had appeared, hands black to the elbow.

'In the kitchen. An accident. Grease filter caught fire. Never mind that, I need you to write an agreement.'

Raised voices could be heard behind them and they turned to look. A waiter, less than immaculate in a filthy kitchen tunic over battered jeans, was explaining, voice raised in frustration, that the restaurant was closed, there had been a fire. A familiar, slurred voice responded that it owned half the fucking place and it was coming in, sunshine.

'Richard.' Tony Gallagher, tight-lipped, indicated to the waiter that he should be admitted.

'Just heard about it. Fuckin' hell.'

Not a bad description, Matt thought, fading as far backwards into the scenery as he could. Richard Marsh-Hayden was in a vile temper, and he himself just wanted to talk to his client and get out of there. Not only was it a profoundly depressing scene, but he had an uneasy feeling that any unemployed spectator would find themselves in a dirty tunic up to the eyes in black grease before they had time to protest.

'Bugger, isn't it?' Tony Gallagher agreed, looking round for someone to take Richard away from him.

Judith Delves came out of the gloom, very pale and as filthy as everyone else.

'Judith, for Christ's sake.' Matthew realised abruptly that Richard was just this side of drunk. 'We have to get out of this. I'll call Brian Rubin.'

'Will you shut up,' Judith hissed, furious, as heads turned among the labour force.

Richard Marsh-Hayden opened his mouth to protest, looking to Tony for support.

'Listen, Richard, you want to talk to Judith, better be in the office. We're all working our arses off here. You can go through the kitchen if you want to see the worst, but keep your mouth shut.' He summoned Matthew, inadequately camouflaged behind a stepladder, and took him to a table close to the front which had been more or less cleaned.

'What's going on, Tony?' Matt asked, and saw over Tony's head Judith Delves coming back towards them.

'I've put Richard in the office with coffee,' she said, wearily. 'We'll have to talk to him later. Now, Mr Sutherland. Has Tony explained?'

After the first two minutes Matthew managed to get his mouth shut, and to start taking notes. 'OK,' he said, after ten minutes. 'I'll set up a meeting as soon as I can with Mr Abbott, or his associates, and offer them a settlement, for which my firm will be put in funds by you, Tony.' He considered his notes. 'I'll draft the loan agreement and the charge on the shares. You need to be separately advised, Miss Delves, I can only act for Tony here, not both of you.'

'I'll act for myself. I can read.'

She was very pale and tense but had herself well under control. He would clear all this with Peter Graebner; a situation where one person – and a female person at that – was lending money, uncounselled by a solicitor, to someone who did have proper legal advice, was uncomfortable however they might formally disassociate the firm from her. And Peter would have to set up the meeting with the bookie's reps and hold his hand on this occasion, though next time he would know how to do all this by himself.

'Right,' he said, thinking of the quiet office and the word processor and the precedent file which were what he needed right now. He realised he had lost his audience; both were staring over his head.

'He must have found some more booze.' Tony had half risen from his seat. 'You stay out the way, Judith.'

'There wasn't any in the office.'

'Brought it with him, didn't he?'

Richard Marsh-Hayden, moving unsteadily and clumsily, barely missing knocking over a stepladder complete with young woman and bucket, sank into a chair, the hem of his jacket hitting the edge of the table with a solid clunk.

'Judith, you're fucking insane. It'll take weeks to get this place open again, and the customers will have buggered off somewhere else. Rubin doesn't give a shit, he just wants it. His offer still stands, just as it was. Same dosh.'

'When did you speak to him?'

'I didn't. Michael did. He told me. Must have been this morning.'

Two blotches of colour appeared on Judith Delves' cheekbones. 'He shouldn't have done that.'

'Oh, Judith. Get off. He owns more than thirty per cent, so do I. Anyway, Rubin rang him. Rang me too, I just wasn't there – it was on the answerphone. He'd heard.'

Yes, of course he had, Matthew thought, and saw the same understanding in Judith's face. He was very sorry for her, she was fighting hard, but it didn't really matter who rang whom in this situation.

'Bugger all that anyway.' Richard Marsh-Hayden, echoing his thought, leant unevenly across the table. 'If you won't see any business sense, Judith, think of your mates. It was bad enough when this place was running OK, but now . . .' One wavering sweep of the hand indicated the desolation around them, as an ant line of people filed past them, carrying chairs and tables, barely adequately cleaned up, out the front to a removal van so they could sit in temporary storage 'Well now, it's all gone. Like Selina.' He gazed round them. 'You've all forgotten her, but I haven't and I just want out of here. And I can't afford to bugger off. Every fucking thing reminds me, and I want out.' He looked round their faces, sighed, leant forward and crashed on his forehead on to the table, causing three coffee cups to add the rest of their contents to the general disorder and disarray.

Curtain, Matt thought, irresistibly, and let out the breath he seemed to have been holding. The only thing a conscientious lawyer could do about any of it was to get out and get on with the work he was being paid to do, so he picked up his briefcase and left with a muttered explanation to Judith and Tony who were grimly cleaning up spilt coffee. But as he passed the Coliseum, he stopped to look at a man putting up the new cast list for the next day and decided he would have lunch well round the corner from the Café de la Paix and all its works. He stood for a moment to watch the man putting up posters, wondering if it was double time on Sundays in his trade, unlike the practice of the law, and working out where to eat. A door at the side opened and Tristram came out, calling over his shoulder. He saw Matthew and blinked.

'I take it you've not been there since I last saw you.'

'No. In the Caff, but I need lunch. Where else do I eat round here?'

'Pub. I'll come with you, I've been let out while Scarpia and Tosca do the supper scene where she makes a deal for life. Good voice, Scarpia, but his English is terrible.'

'I forgot it was sung in English here.'

'I'm not sure anyone told this Scarpia either. I did suggest, quietly you know, that the poor bugger might as well be allowed to do it in Italian, like he's used to. That's when the director sent me out to lunch.'

The bar was crowded, but they both ended up with a substantial pie and chips, washed down with beer in Matthew's case and tonic water for Tristram. Matt eyed the drink askance and Tristram grinned, looking exactly like his sister. 'They'd know what to think in New Zealand, I expect, but you can't drink and sing. Alcohol opens the throat temporarily, then you're buggered, or I am. When my voice started to break, Frannie kept me going with slugs of gin for recordings, but we only got away with it for three months.'

'You've done well on it, anyway.' Matt was eating with hangover-inspired hunger. 'Will I get a ticket tomorrow?'

'No, apparently. But I'll get you in if you want to come. Fran's got two and I'm not sure my brother-in-law's going to make it. He's not really into opera. But either way I'll see you in. Maybe in a box.'

'Are you sure? I haven't seen – heard – much opera, but I'm interested. Implausible plots, though. I've never understood quite how Tosca could be so dippy.'

'Oh, I don't know,' Tristram said, tolerantly, showing all his sister's capacity for arguing a case from either side. 'I daresay a lot worse happens in police states. There's a very good aria where she says she's always lived an artistic life and been kind to people and lovers, and brought flowers for the Virgin, so what has she done to deserve all this? Lot of ordinary people, trapped in police states, must have felt like that.' He grinned. 'I have to say Fran thinks that whole aria is just whingeing self-pity, but then she doesn't like Puccini.' He looked carefully at Matthew. 'Chap who wrote the music.'

'I did know. But the bit I find really peculiar is that Tosca believed this Scarpia, when he said the bullets wouldn't be real. He was a policeman, for heaven's sake.'

131

'Like my brother-in-law? Not that I find it easy to imagine John in a similar situation.' Tristram was sounding dismissive, and Matt understood that he was a little jealous.

'Can't be easy for him with you lot,' he said, mildly, and Tristram looked up, sharply.

'Lucky to have us,' he said, indignantly, and met Matt's amused stare. 'He's got our Fran, barefoot and pregnant and not keeping up her piano, and we need to rescue her every now and then.'

'Get her out to the opera?' Matt asked, deadpan.

'That sort of thing.' The blue eyes under the dark hair were considering him, alive with mischief. This of course was the wayward sibling whom an unmarried Francesca had rushed to rescue from the clutches of the New York State police, abandoning John McLeish and all other obligations. No wonder she found Tosca prey to unnecessary self-pity, he thought, with affection; she would undoubtedly have been prepared to sleep with anyone she had to in order to get a brother, never mind a lover, out of the nick.

'Well, I suppose she's out of it for a bit, with this latest sprog,' her brother said, stretching and collecting his wallet. 'Give her a ring, check if she's using both tickets tomorrow,' he suggested, smooth as glass. 'If she is, let me know here and I'll leave one for you.'

John McLeish and Bruce Davidson looked up as their driver pulled to a halt behind a high-sided van outside the Café de la Paix. Three men were fitting a glass pane into one side of the van and three others were following, carefully, across the wide pavement with another.

'Taking the glass out,' Davidson observed, redundantly.

'Why? Vandals?'

'More like they want to carry things in without breakages.'

Davidson was right, he understood, as they edged their way past a gang of three carpenters starting work on the gaping hole that had been the Caff's largest floor-to-ceiling glass window. They stood and stared at the echoing, dirty room and the blackened ceiling.

'Lot of material to bring in,' Davidson pointed out, helpfully.

'Indeed.' McLeish, hearing footsteps, turned to see Michael Owens and Brian Rubin, both of whom checked on seeing him.

'Afternoon. I'm sorry, this looks terrible.'

Michael Owens glanced past him. 'Not quite as terrible as it did at three o'clock this morning. Judith and I were in the country in bed

132

and drove up as soon as we'd managed to wake up. I've had some sleep, but she hasn't.'

McLeish gazed at him expressionlessly, and he sighed. 'I suppose you were woken up too? But I'm trying to take Judith home as soon as I can.'

'We'll try not to be too long,' McLeish said, non-commitally, and stepped into the wreck of the Café.

'Darling.' Judith Delves emerged from the confusion to greet Michael warmly and faltered, seeing the police presence. Brian Rubin, McLeish observed, had shrunk his considerable presence into a corner behind a stack of timber and two carpenters.

'We've just had to send Richard home in a taxi,' she said, hurriedly to her fiancé. 'In a very bad way.'

Michael Owens opened his mouth to ask a question, then visibly remembered the police standing politely waiting and said that he would go and talk to Gallagher or something and fix a coffee, if that was all right, until she was finished, and went off, Brian Rubin scuttling unobtrusively after him.

'If you have time, Miss Delves, we would like to establish who had keys to the back door.'

She was looking a bit wild-eyed, and small wonder with the mess around her, but they had a murder to solve and no one's business problems could be allowed to interfere. John McLeish had already talked to the London Fire Brigade and the loss adjuster representing the insurers, and the fire had been undoubtedly accidental. There was, the loss adjuster had made it clear, an area of dispute over contributory negligence. The grease filter over the grill should not have caught like that had it been cleaned out regularly, but the evidence was no longer there to see; any excess grease that might or might not have been present had disappeared in the fire. And when all was said and done, no lives had been lost, or even endangered, the sous chef's injuries were not at all serious and apart from some expensive replacement of ventilation pipes the rest was smoke damage, tiresome to clean but not structural.

John McLeish understood that he would have to allow Judith Delves a little time to settle. By his calculation she had managed on two hours' sleep in the last thirty-six and was showing it.

'Keys. Well, I've already explained that we keep one in the till. It shouldn't have been copied. It's a Banham key and you have to send them one as a sample. But it's not impossible. I have one. Selina had one. Tony has one. So does Gérard, the night manager.' She counted on her fingers. 'That makes four and there were six. Oh yes. One in the till and one with Mary, our bookkeeper.'

'Did you – have you – got Mrs Marsh-Hayden's key back?'

'No. For some reason it didn't seem very important.' Furious sarcasm is part of the day's work for police officers and McLeish ignored it.

'Do you have yours here?'

She blushed scarlet, the colour incongruous on the pale face. 'No, as a matter of fact.'

'When did you last use it?'

'Oh. It must be ten days ago.' he sighed. 'The thing is, Mary gets here at eight thirty, before I do, and I leave before the night manager except if I'm the night manager, which I only am in an emergency, and the last time was ten days ago. Otherwise I leave the key at home. In my flat.'

'Would Mrs Marsh-Hayden have carried her key with her?'

'She didn't need to either. Unless it was an emergency.'

So Richard Marsh-Hayden had access to a key and so did Michael Owens as well as the official keyholders. He glanced at Davidson who had written 'Rubin?' in his notebook.

'It would be unlikely then that Mr Rubin would have a key?'

'He doesn't need one. He comes in here, or the kitchen, whenever he wants as far as I can see. Like a vulture, waiting to pick our bones.'

'I suppose that the damage is such that he might want to withdraw his offer.'

She stared at him. 'You cannot possibly be thinking that anyone would do *this*' – her hand swept round the devastation around her – 'just to put a purchaser off?'

He did not comment, and she looked at him, every ounce of her saying that she would have expected better from Francesca Wilson's husband.

'In any case it would have been a mistaken tactic. Both Richard, who was in earlier, and Michael are even more keen to sell now, because they think I can't get the place straight again. Well, they'll see. And bloody Brian Rubin knows better – look at him there looking round, he knows it can be done if I keep my nerve, and the insurance pay quickly.' She stopped, suddenly, looking blank, and McLeish looked at her enquiringly. 'Sorry, a passing worry. Look, I have to finish ringing up the customers booked for tonight to explain what has happened – I know you've got things you need to do, but could we do it all tomorrow? I need to keep the business going for when we can open again.' They stared involuntarily up at the smoke-blackened ceiling and the filthy walls, and she saw them look. 'It will reopen, let no one doubt it.'

'That's fine, Miss Delves.' McLeish decided that pressing her at this point was counter-productive. 'May we just have a look round and then we'll get out of your hair.'

In the first-floor office, which was untidy but looked like an oasis of peace and tranquillity after the chaos on the ground floor, Michael was watching Brian Rubin.

'What do we do now?'

Brian Rubin sat down, having looked cautiously at the bentwood chair and rejected it in favour of a solid metal piece. 'It'll cost £100,000 plus to put that lot downstairs right,' he said. 'Take £100,000 off the price – or don't, and let me deal with the insurance company – and I'm still on. You keep the loss of profits if you get any.'

'I'll have to talk to the others. But that's a fair offer. You did look in the kitchen?'

'As I went past. £20,000 of the money's in there – the grill's gone and the hood and a couple of the hobs.'

Michael nodded, thinking that this man would make an excellent corporate finance client; knew his own mind and how to do a deal, no messing around salami-slicing on a bargain. 'Well, Richard's very keen to proceed.'

'What about Judith?'

Michael sighed. 'It's her baby, that's the trouble. All she can think about is making it better. She may insist on getting the place open again before I can get her to see sense.'

'But you will? Get her to agree, you think? In some timescale I can live with.'

'I'll have to.'

John McLeish was also a man to make up his mind. 'Not a lot we can do here, but I'm glad to have seen this.'

They were in the kitchen, standing in the middle of a wet, greyish floor, and he could hear Judith Delves on one phone and Tony Gallagher on another, talking to customers. It was the same speech each time, friendly, matter-of-fact apologies, followed by assurances that the restaurant would reopen 'as quickly as possible' and the

135

offer of transferring the booking to Caff 2 with a complimentary bottle of wine per two people. A neat exercise in hanging on to a business; Caff 2 was not Café de la Paix geographically, but the offer of free wine was precisely calculated to sway those who had no particular reason for needing to be in Covent Garden. He waited till she was between calls and told her they would be back tomorrow and, on an impulse, wished her luck. She reminded him of Francesca, he realised, cross with himself for unprofessional behaviour. Well, he would get himself home and chase his wife's family away and spend a peaceful evening with her and his son.

'Judith? It's time to go home. Tomorrow is another day.'

She lifted her head from the table where she had been briefly asleep and the whole depressing mess swam into her vision.

'You'll be ill if you go on like this. I need to get you out of this bloody place. No, don't look like that, I mean tonight, for a rest. I know you've got Mac Troughton and his merry men tomorrow.'

'And a few more booked customers for tomorrow night to warn off.'

He was urging her into a coat, but she stopped irresolute, looking for the list. 'Judith, come on.' His voice went up, raggedly, and she remembered that his weekend had been ruined and with it his hopes of getting her to concentrate on the house in the country. She let him help her into her jacket and smiled, wearily, on Tony Gallagher who was emerging from the kitchen, looking exhausted, hands grey shading to black under the fingernails.

'I'll get here for seven and let Mac's people in, Judith. You have a bit of a lay-in.'

'Thanks, Tony,' she said, grateful for the thought rather than the reality. She was most definitely going to be in for seven herself, or there was no way of getting through the labours facing them all the next day. He nodded and went up to check the street door before vanishing into the kitchen on his way out.

'Funny about disaster,' Michael observed, surlily. 'Put him in better temper than he's been in for weeks, hasn't it?'

She opened her mouth to tell him that the reason for Tony's restored equanimity was nothing less than the removal of the threat to his life, but decided against it. There would have to be an explanation of what she had done, but not tonight, not when they were all so weary and on edge.

136

10

Francesca, juggling William on one arm, made tea one-handedly and irritably called to her husband to hurry if he was going to work at all today. The weekend had been the usual crowded rush, with family and, as often, conducted against the background of her husband missing for large parts of it. She was aware, however, that the legitimacy of her grievance was seriously undermined by the fact that she had involved herself in the latest development of his case, even if she had not meant to do so. And she wanted to go again to hear Tristram the next day and persuade John to come with her. She tried to put Will into his high-chair, but he resisted, clinging to her with all the strength of a solid, long-legged twenty-one-month-old. He must know there is a usurper on the way, she thought, wearily, bracing herself against the chair to ease the pull on her back muscles.

'Will. Stop that.' Blessedly, John was by her side, shaved and mostly dressed, his hair still damp from the shower. He prised Will off her and threaded him into his high-chair.

'He had breakfast? Sit down, I'll get it.'

She subsided into a chair; a second pregnancy at thirty-four was making her very tired, though she had, she reminded herself, nothing to complain about, no sickness, no blood pressure troubles, her own remaining some twenty-five per cent below the normal for her age, and none of her teeth giving trouble.

'I'm not going in till lunch,' her husband said. 'Thought we'd have a morning together to make up for the weekend since it's your day off.'

'That's very nice,' she said, taken by surprise, then rallied. 'They'll all ring you up.'

'No, they won't. Unless someone else gets murdered there, or the place bursts into flames again. Anyway we'll go out for a bit, take this one to the park.'

'Park,' William cried, hopefully, and splashed his spoon in the plate, depositing cereal in his mother's hair. She opened her mouth to complain, but John had reached for a clean tea towel and was carefully removing cornflakes from her parting before she could formulate a grievance. He passed her a cup of tea, took the spoon from Will and got breakfast down him in double time, the child charmed by having his father's attention. He then scooped him out of the chair and put him on the floor with a couple of saucepans and settled down with his own cup of tea to look at her carefully.

'You're looking tired.'

'I'm pregnant,' she reminded him. 'And my husband doesn't get home weekends.'

'Except to babysit while you go out with your brothers,' he pointed out, and they eyed each other, acknowledging a stand-off. 'Anyway, I wasn't missing long yesterday, but I had to go and look.'

'I agree it would have been a bit casual not to. How bad was it? I mean, did the fire destroy anything you needed?'

'Not unless there was some unexpected evidence lurking in the ventilation system. We did check and my chaps are there this morning to see there is nothing in the ventilation system but ventilation, as it were.'

'Like another body?'

'Anything's possible in that place,' McLeish agreed, sourly, then looked at her. 'Damn, you've gone all pale. Here, quick, have some more tea.' He came anxiously round to her side of the table to put an arm round her.

'It's the baby. Just like with Will. I can't manage anything violent. I'll be found giving up newspapers again. Sorry, go on. You didn't find anything stuffed into the pipes?'

'No, and I came away yesterday because the place was such chaos and everybody so busy trying to get straight they weren't going to pay any attention to me. It'll be the same this morning, so I've left Bruce in charge. I have to go in to the shop after lunch because I've got interviews set up. And I'll drop by the Café on the way home, see how they're getting on.'

'Was it an awful mess?' She watched, indulgently, as Will clawed his way up his father's trousers and struggled to get on to his lap.

'Yes. Looks terrible, and the insurance assessor apparently reckons they'll be in for £100,000-odd.'

'And of course the place will be closed. That'll cost them.'

John looked at her carefully over their son's dark head. 'I needed someone to ask. How much profit do they make there?'

She closed her eyes, the better to recall what she had gleaned from Judith Delves. 'About £100,000 a month, but they weren't making that recently. Anyway, profit isn't the point in an emergency. It's

138

cash that matters.' She considered her statement. 'Actually, with small companies it's always cash what matters.'

'Profit is a statement of opinion . . .'

'Cash is for real,' she confirmed. 'So what they're looking at, oop at that particular mill, is outgo of £100,000 on the conversion at least, and no income at all.'

'What about the other site – Caff 2?'

'Not doing better than break-even in profit terms and still swallowing cash. I bet they haven't paid all the bills on that conversion, it's pretty recent.'

John McLeish thought about what he was being told. It was always worth consulting Francesca on any matters of business or accountancy, and identifying the financial pressure points would be particularly useful in this case. 'So how are they going to find £100,000 plus to put Café de la Paix right? Does the insurance company pay as you go?'

'More likely weeks after you needed ready cash. I mean, think of domestic insurance. When we had that plumbing leak we got the insurance months after the whole thing had been fixed and the kitchen ceiling put back up. Didn't matter that much, because we both have steady incomes, arriving in our bank accounts every month. But one of the ways these people make money is to hang on to the cash for as long as possible.'

'So not much joy there.'

'Not a lot. And, actually, a restaurant must be in a much worse position than a factory-type business to withstand a disaster like this.'

'Why?'

'No debtors. A factory that went on fire would have supplied goods to people who haven't yet paid for them, and could be called on to pay. A restaurant – or a shop – doesn't have anyone owing money to it – oh, well, a bit on credit cards that they haven't yet got from the credit card companies, but not a lot. But, and here's the problem, they have lots of people they owe money to, butchers and bakers and candlestick makers who supplied on, what, thirty days' credit, and who want paying as that thirtieth day arrives.'

'Add what on to the conversion costs?'

'Turnover is about £4m on that side, food costs say thirty-three per cent, so that's £1.3m a year. £100,000 a month. So plus £100,000. Plus staff costs – you can't fire all of them and expect to get them back a month later – plus rent, rates, lights, gas, heating. Plus another £100,000 a month, I guess. Will is eating one of your buttons, darling.'

'It's anchored to me, but I agree, better not. Pass a biscuit. So, if the place was closed for a month they'd have to find £200,000 for bills and running costs plus £100,000 for the conversion.'

She considered the point, reaching for a pencil. 'Not quite as bad as that; you could postpone paying for some of the conversion until you get something from the insurance. But you'd need £250,000.'

'Where would you go for that?'

'Your bank. And if they won't play, the shareholders.'

'And if *they* won't play?'

'You go bust. Or you sell up.'

They stared at each other, the silence broken only by Will's humming.

'Well, most of the shareholders wanted to sell anyway,' John McLeish said, slowly.

'They did, didn't they?' She was gazing at him, shaken. 'Surely people don't go round burning down the main cash-generating asset of a business in order to force a sale?'

'Depends how much they needed the money.'

'You and any other policemen who come my way always remind me that most murders are domestics. Driven by living in families, not by money at all.'

'Mrs Marsh-Hayden's husband is in serious financial trouble, remember?'

'I do, I do. But if you remember, Mr Rubin of Gemini is in serious need of a deal, or he may not be able to go on. He has at least got a business, it may not be that bad for him, but he's under a financial cosh as well.'

So is Tony Gallagher, he thought, but it would be indiscreet and unprofessional to share this detail with his wife. Will, whose humming had been getting louder, took his father's cheeks in both hands. 'Dadda. Park.'

'I agree. You come along with me, my boy, while I finish getting dressed, and let your Mum get ready.'

'Michael . Have you time to have a word?'

It was the bastard Simon, and it would have made sense to say, immediately, that nothing would give greater pleasure, but it would, alas, have to be the day after tomorrow. But he had been taken by

140

surprise, as Simon had intended, and there was nothing to do but indicate that he was available.

'Terrific. I've got a meeting in an hour. Do you mind my office?'

Of course he did, rule one in merchant banking, as in war, was to choose your own ground, but Simon had not left him time to reply, and was already half-way back to his palatial corner office, the one Michael had been covertly looking forward to occupying.

'Thought it was time we talked.' The courtesies were being observed, Simon had motioned him to a seat at the large round table which took up much of the space not occupied by the oversized, overpriced desk which had been brought in especially for a new head of corporate finance. Jugs of coffee sat in a tray, with elegant bone china cups, so there would be no pauses while bank servants were summoned to fuss with trays and jugs and cups. Michael lowered himself into a seat, feeling his heart thump, and carefully relaxed his clenched hands.

'Bad luck about Grindels.'

It had been all over the *Financial Times* that morning; his deal being done by bloody Lazards. The justifiably shamefaced finance director of Grindels had rung him at eight o'clock, claiming to have tried to get him on Friday. If the man had tried at all, it had been well after five o'clock when, indeed, he himself had given up hope of getting his call returned.

'Bad faith, more like. We'd done all the thinking and half the work.'

'You decided not to go for a fee arrangement, didn't you? Pity.'

Two weeks ago, Simon Rutherford had urged him, in front of all his fellow directors, not even to consider doing more work without being sure the prospective client was signed up, at least to a drop-dead fee.

'They wouldn't have agreed.'

'Perhaps. But that would have told us something.'

The bastard was right of course, and in his younger, more confident, more successful days he wouldn't have moved to do that much work without having lured the prospective customer into a fee large enough to discourage him from doing the deal with anyone else's help. He didn't have anything else to say and if he had, Simon Rutherford would not have given him time; this meeting was being conducted to his agenda and at his pace.

'I'm not going to be able to put you forward for a bonus this year, Mike. As you know, the department hasn't made a lot this year and

141

what there is to be split up has to go to the lads and their teams, who've brought in the fees.'

If this was all he had to say that was all right. 'I understand that, Simon. I've not had a good year. Unlike last year, or the year before that.' As well that this arrogant sod should be reminded that he had been the one of the highest fee earners any year in the five before this.

'I know that, Mike. You've had a very good run. But the Plockton flotation was a disaster, wasn't it? No matter how good a face you all put on it, not a lot seems to have gone right for you since.' Michael opened his mouth to speak, but the other man waved him down. 'I've got another six months to get this department really buzzing, as it should, and I need every one of my directors to bring in £3m of fees this year. And we're six months into the year and you've managed just under £50K.'

'I've had personal difficulties,' he heard himself say, panicked. The bank was his home, he made £300,000 a year there and typically doubled it in bonus, it could not just be vanishing. He saw the other man hesitate, and got his mouth open. 'I have taken my eye off the ball a bit, but I am cooking another deal. Be a £5m fee all on its own if I can bring it off,' he adlibbed wildly, seeing the other man looking disbelieving.

'I understand you're having to spend time on a restaurant you apparently own. You did tell Compliance about it, did you?'

'No. It was a passive shareholding – a tax deal. I wasn't a director till a year ago. I just ate there. And I don't own a majority.'

'But you're a director now? Yes? And you own thirty-two and a half per cent.' He had a note, you could just see it, tucked under the newspaper.

'Yes.'

'You know the bank rules of course.'

'I do. But the company is being sold – should have been completed by now, but it's just taking rather a long time.'

'One of the shareholders was found in a deep freeze, I understand. Are you going to be able to complete a sale? In those circumstances?'

'Oh yes. And I'm not involved in the actual sale, I just sign bits of paper when I'm asked. You know.'

'What I know is that private companies are buggers, things are always going wrong. Usually not, however, involving key workers stuffed into the deep freeze. You need to get rid of it, believe me, Mike.'

The bastard looked at him steadily, and he resisted an urge to salute; as if he was his commanding officer. 'I hear you,' he said, getting to his feet. 'I'll do that. And I'll come and talk later in the week about my deal, if I may, always glad of another view.' He had managed to reach the door, but Simon Rutherford was watching him, unmoving.

'Thursday, please. Ask Gloria to put you in after the Executive Committee.'

Judith had escaped to the office; Mac Troughton's men had arrived at seven and unloaded at high speed for the best part of an hour, even with the whole of the front of the Caff removed to facilitate the entry of objects like twelve-foot lengths of ducting for the ventilation system, and a cooker hood. The morning traffic in St Martin's Lane had had to snake past the two big vans, but as one of the drivers observed, there weren't any policemen around that early. From eight o'clock onwards the big restaurant had become a hell, its size and emptiness converting it into an echo chamber for the operations being separately conducted, all of which involved steel, or large pieces of wood and hammers. No one had been able to hear themselves speak, but Mac Troughton's men had not required much instruction. Tony Gallagher had rendered himself hoarse inside an hour, supervising the installation of a new grill and agreeing the siting of the new cooker hood, then they had gone off site for breakfast and to see young Matthew Sutherland in order to be taken through a draft of their agreement. It had, she reflected, been the only enjoyable bit of a catastrophic day, telling that cocky young lawyer exactly what she would and would not accept.

What needed doing, fully as urgently as a cooker hood or ventilation system, was the documentation of an insurance claim. Mac Troughton was still, grittily, refusing to discuss a timescale or a cost estimate for his part of the repair work, observing that it depended on what else they found, but it looked like weeks rather than days, and would cost what it cost. The only bit of it she could do, here and now, apart from opening a ledger on the computer for rebuilding, was to sort out how much profit the Caff could be postulated to have made in the four weeks before the fire, in the hope that the insurance company would be prepared to make an interim payment. This was, she knew, unlikely, but she could not leave the site, a steady stream of decisions, large and small, would be required of her throughout the day, and she might as well do something to bring order out of this painful chaos.

It was slow, iterative work, and she was in the depths of it when the office door opened, cautiously.

'Richard.' She looked at him, carefully, sheltering behind her PC. He looked ill, thin and red-eyed, but he had shaved, she saw, and combed his hair. There was much to be said for a military training; the prescribed shave, shit and shower, as Michael said, did put you on course for the day, even if, like Richard, you had spent the day before sodden with drink. 'Come in,' she invited, trying not to sound unwelcoming. 'I'll put the kettle on.'

She had bought three electric kettles first thing that morning, one for the office and two for the toilers on the floor below. And several boxes of tea bags and three jars of coffee, and milk and bread, butter and jam, which were reposing in the bar fridge. The army below, like any other, marched on its stomach and they would get a shock if they started to forage for provender in high-rent Covent Garden, where workmen's cafés were in notably short supply. She cleared a chair for her erstwhile partner's husband, and made him a black coffee as he had asked, and retired behind her desk prepared to repel boarders. He was having difficulty formulating whatever he had come to ask, and she was not going to help. Her neck was painful with tension and she shifted her shoulders to ease it.

'You and Selina.' He took a gulp of coffee while she waited, unmoving. 'You sometimes bought clothes – to wear for when you were working here, I mean.' He was digging in the light leather briefcase he carried when he was trying to impress bank managers.

'Yes,' she said, impatient, as he went through the contents a second time.

'I've got a bill here. Harvey Nicks.'

He handed it across the table and she looked down without touching it; she was quick at figures and picked out at once that this was a long-running account, off which amounts had been paid, irregularly, succeeded almost at once by a further purchase which had only increased the amount due. Some of that, to be fair, was interest at twenty-three per cent. The whole now stood at £7306, the credit limit being £8000. At one shop, she thought, incredulously; her Visa card limit, on which she bought everything, was £2000, the whole bill paid off automatically every month. She looked at Richard enquiringly; he was watching her over his coffee cup, simultaneously hangdog and anxious. She felt slightly sick.

'I'm afraid that we can't pay that from here. We used occasionally to buy a suit each through the restaurant accounts. You know, something we actually did wear to work here. But we had to stop doing that – the Inland Revenue got very strict about the definition of workwear and we couldn't persuade them that Nicole Farhi or Yves St Laurent fell within it.' She tried a smile but it died in the face of Richard Marsh-Hayden's hostility. 'So we haven't done any of that for, oh, the last year. I'm sorry.'

He was still looking at her with that peculiar mix of hangdog pleading and simmering rage, and she wished that the office were not so effectively insulated from the ground floor. 'Selina said quite a lot of clothes found their way on to the accounts.'

'Did she?' she asked, feebly. She stared at the PC, rage threatening to choke her. Where had Selina managed to hide payments for expensive suits? What was a trained bookkeeper like Mary thinking of to allow it? She took a deep breath and her mind cleared. There was no way. She had been analysing accounts for the last three weeks, the suppliers were all names known to her as well as her own family and none of them were dress shops, they really were supplying meat, olive oil, paper napkins, glasses, spaghetti, greengrocery, and all the myriad requirements of a large restaurant. And Mary was a good bookkeeper, limited though her capacity for analysis might be. It hadn't happened, just as she had told Richard.

She paused to think, and her mind cleared. 'That's not your problem, surely, Richard. You don't have to worry about it, you just send it to the lawyers. It's a debt of the estate.' She had missed the point, she saw, in a flash of revelation, just as he put his coffee cup back in the saucer, with the overprecise movement of rage.

'So she was paying for all those clothes herself then?' he asked, the voice tight.

'Well, the restaurant wasn't.' She was suddenly furiously angry herself at being hassled by a man who was uselessly, self-indulgently unable to control his financial affairs and yet in a position to control her life, with his substantial shareholding in her restaurant. She watched, grimly, as he absorbed that message, and wondered how to get him out of the office. 'I see it's ten thirty,' she said, crisply, 'and I am expecting an electrician.' There were three of them, or had been when she last looked, gloomily applying their testers to various parts of the walls downstairs.

'I'll sit here a minute, have some more coffee.' He had gone white, she saw through her own rage.

'Right,' she said, bad-temperedly, and switched off the computer and moved the piles of bills into the big safe that stood open beside her. 'Damn,' she said, involuntarily.

'What?' Richard Marsh-Hayden looked up dully, but he could not have missed the bundles of notes, cheques and chits cascading on to the floor.

'Saturday night's take,' she said, furiously, picking up notes. 'We don't bank on Saturday nights, we wait to put it into the night safe on Sunday morning when there are people about. Not the first thing I thought of yesterday, but I should have.' She looked at the big safe and hesitated, very conscious of Richard's eyes on the cash; he looked like a starving man outside a bakery. And the combination of the safe had not been changed in eighteen months. Mary was totally unmechanical and had refused to try, and she herself had kept forgetting, and she was not prepared to leave cash, even in a safe, anywhere near Richard Marsh-Hayden. She looked at the note on the top bundle; in fact there was only £1400-odd, the rest were cheques and credit card receipts. And cash would be needed on site, there was no point banking that, she would only have to get it out again. If she was allowed, indeed, given the state of the overdraft. She hesitated.

'You'll need cash for that lot,' Richard Marsh-Hayden said, jabbing a thumb at the floor, in echo of her own calculations.

'I will,' she said, putting the cheques and credit slips back and banging the big safe shut and twisting the combination.

'Don't carry that much cash about, for heaven's sake.'

'I wasn't going to. I'll put it in the little safe in the inner office, save it falling out every time I want to get at the accounts.' No need to alienate Richard even further by making it clear she would not leave cash in a safe to which he might know the combination. She waited for him to go, but he was filling the kettle at the little sink, staring drearily out of the window, so she retired, crossly, to the inner office and, glancing over her shoulder, pushed the cash inside the old, out-of-date safe, which they had never thrown away when the big new one had replaced it.

Brian Rubin glanced anxiously across a lunch table at his wife. It was still warm enough to eat outside, on the terrace, and even to haul up a sun umbrella. She had arrived, unexpectedly, at ten that morning, having left her mother's place at 7 a.m., the car loaded to well beyond

146

the Plimsoll line, with two children and their accoutrements. He had indicated, feebly, that he ought to be at his office, but she was having none of that, and had lumbered him with both children while she got the house straight. His five-year-old son was fidgeting to leave the table while his three-year-old daughter was, infinitely slowly, finishing her melting ice-cream.

'All right, Annabelle, that's enough. Eat it, or leave it. Joshua, you can get down too.'

Janice had firm standards about behaviour at meal times and most other things too, which he mostly found a deeply reassuring nuisance. He waited, apprehensively; she was working to a timetable and he wasn't going to be allowed to interfere with it. She watched as the children flashed away to rescue an interrupted game involving mud and water at the bottom of the big suburban garden.

'Right,' she said, pouring him coffee. 'Now you can tell me what's going on.'

'What do you mean?' he temporised, anxiously.

'I had to pay cash at the garage for petrol. Lucky I had some, or you'd have had to come down to Ashford.'

'Ah, well. See, what with the delay on the sale going through I had to pay some of the business bills on the Visa, didn't I? I didn't realise I'd got so close to the credit. The business is paying some of it off this morning. Or would,' he added, inspired, 'if I was there to sign the cheque.'

She looked at him, unimpressed. 'I'll need cash then. Now.' She held out her hand and he stood up, crouched awkwardly, to get cash out of his back pocket where he always carried a reserve.

'A hundred do?'

'For today. I'll need to get some food in. And tomorrow I need to put down a term's fees, or we don't get Joshua in to Stonefield. That's £1700. And I don't want any yes, no or maybe, Brian. We agreed.'

'We did. It's just this hitch that's left me a bit short. But you'll be able to use the Visa tomorrow ... well, perhaps not tomorrow,' he said, reluctantly. 'Day after, anyway.' He expected an explosion but she simply poured herself some coffee.

'Explain it to me, Brian. You were buying these restaurants and we were going on the market, so there'd be a lot of extra cash, and you could take more salary. Then this Selina changes her mind, and next thing I hear she's dead. Then there's a fire. So what's going to happen now? You aren't going to buy a burnt-out place, are you?'

'Oh, it's not that bad,' he assured her, grateful that he could offer honest reassurance. 'And it means the whole place'll be redecorated and look fresh. No, that's all right, in fact it may work out better.'

His daughter came rushing up to show her mother a mud-covered treasure, which she gravely admired, and Brian sat admiring them both, particularly the curve of Janice's neck above her cotton dress, the blonde hair neatly tied back. She dispatched the child back to the orchard and he watched her with love.

'You and she had something going, didn't you?'

He dropped his coffee cup, smashing the saucer, and looked at her, seeing his own shock reflected in her face, understanding that she had not really seriously suspected him. 'I don't know what you mean,' he said, far too late, and she burst into tears of combined rage and shock.

'Pet, I'm sorry.' He cast around wildly. 'It was everything got to me, stress, I suppose.' He looked at her, hopefully, but her face twisted again and he lunged to take her in his arms.

'Bugger off, Brian. You don't get out of it like that.' She pushed him away, the rejection absolutely unmistakable, and scrubbed at her eyes. 'Now, let's have it, full strength. Do the police know?'

She was staring at him, as if he were a mess the dog had made.

'You don't need to look like that, I'm not the first bloke to make an idiot of himself.'

'The other idiots aren't married to me. I knew there was something wrong, only I never really thought of . . .'

'It doesn't mean anything, honestly. She was making difficulties about the sale and I was just trying to jolly her along.'

'And one thing led to another, I suppose,' she flashed, furiously, and he fell silent; the noise of his children playing seemed to be coming from hundreds of yards away.

'I'm sorry,' he said, humbly, when he thought she might hear him. 'Even if . . . well, even if she was still around, I'd have stopped it, soon as you came back.'

'Oh, so now it's my fault for taking the kids to see my mother?' She started to cry again, angrily, and he looked desperately towards the children who were still contentedly playing.

'I didn't mean that. I meant she didn't matter. I'm sorry.'

'You ought to be ashamed.'

'I am.'

She looked at him, sharply, and he just managed not to say anything more, biting back anything he might have been going to

148

explain about the tensions of living from day to day, trying to keep all the fucking balls in the air, to keep his business life from crashing around them. She had stopped crying, he saw with relief.

'Who else knows? About her and you?'

'No one. I promise.' He felt an uneasy pang. 'Diana may have wondered.'

'But *she* isn't going to tell the police. She thinks the sun shines out of your backside.' The vulgarity was unlike her, but this was not the moment to object.

'They won't be talking to her, anyway – I mean, she's nothing to do with Café de la Paix, and they haven't asked to see her. But Jan, I never lifted a finger to her, though I felt like it sometimes, I can tell you.' He laughed uneasily, but she was stone-faced.

'The police don't need to hear anything about it, then.' She looked across at the garden, alerted by a cry of rage; Annabelle had hit Joshua with a spade and he was retaliating. 'You go and sort that out, while I wash my face, then you can have them for a change while I go off and do the shopping and get my hair done.'

'So he wasn't *anywhere* between, what, 1 a.m. and 3 a.m. on that night?'

'That's right. He didn't get to the Turkish baths until three. They put the time on, see, when people come in. And the doorman at the club says he left at one, or one fifteen at the latest. No, he didn't sneak back in again. He left.'

'He must have known we would check on him,' John McLeish said, incredulously. 'Good work, Willis, but it wasn't that difficult to find the gap.'

'No,' Detective Sergeant Willis agreed, amicably. 'Not at all.'

They all gazed at their copies of Richard Marsh-Hayden's original statement in which he had claimed to have been at a gambling club until 'about two', then gone to the Turkish baths.

'Perhaps he didn't notice that they write the time down there?'

'Or perhaps he was in a panic and thought he'd just get through,' McLeish said, grimly. 'Where is he?'

'Try the Caff. Miss Delves will be there, or thereabouts.'

Davidson reached for a phone and made his enquiry, holding the phone at a little distance from his ear. 'Mr Marsh-Hayden is with you? In the office?' He covered the phone. 'Bring him in?' McLeish shook his head. 'Could you, or someone, tell him Detective Chief

Superintendent McLeish will be passing the Café shortly and would like a word? Pardon, sorry, Miss Delves, I missed that.' He winced as he listened, and they could all hear a crash, echoing from the phone. 'Oh, well, I daresay Mr McLeish will manage. Thank you.' He put the phone down, pulling at his ear. 'Out of it. Pissed. Holed up in the office with a bottle. She can't get him out. Very grateful if we can, she says.'

John McLeish was outside the Café de la Paix ten minutes later, having told the driver to use the siren to get them through the rush-hour traffic. They pulled up behind a chauffeur-driven Jaguar, which was disgorging Michael Owens, bad temper and anxiety in every line of him. McLeish caught up with him and explained his presence.

'Oh. Well, I'm here because Judith asked for my help in getting Richard out of the office before he smashes it up, or sets it on fire. Fuck. If I'd known you were here and wanted to see him I'd have finished a couple of things up before I came. I'm meeting Rubin here, but not till seven thirty.'

He stood irresolute, hands clenched, and McLeish was reminded that this was a big, powerful man, only a couple of inches short of his own six foot four inches and in much better physical nick, with the controlled restlessness of the fit and well exercised.

'In any case, there's enough people on site, including Tony Gallagher. I can't think why Judith couldn't just ... oh, well, yes, I suppose I can, bit tasteless, given that Selina ... Sorry, Chief Superintendent, go ahead – if you need a hand sobering him up, I'm here.'

They walked through the long room, stepping gingerly to avoid the workers and the piles of material, to be greeted by Judith Delves and Tony Gallagher.

'He's in the office. I took coffee in but I'm not sure he's drinking it. He's got a bottle of whisky with him – I tried to take it, but he snatched it back.' Judith was sounding harassed.

'You should have asked me, Judy,' Tony Gallagher said, crossly.

'Well, I didn't want a fight.'

This argument had obviously been going on for some time, Mc-Leish noted. 'May I use the office to talk to Mr Marsh-Hayden?' he asked.

'I'm not sure how much you'll get out of him, but you're welcome. The rest of us are here, using the kitchen phone, if you need us.'

Richard Marsh-Hayden was sitting, one hand on the bottle, gazing blearily out of the window and was indeed on the edge of sleep, or collapse. McLeish considered him uneasily, and changed his plans;

this was the murdered woman's husband, and an unexplained hour and a half on the night she had disappeared was the stuff of which murder convictions were made, that, and the fact of his access to the key. But any mistakes in handling would leave a loophole big enough for a good barrister to leap into.

So he cautioned him, and offered him the chance to acquire a solicitor before answering, and Marsh-Hayden waved him away.

'No. I'll tell you. Been thinking I ought to. I came back here that night. Yeh, one thirty or so, if you say so. Thereabouts. I've got a key. Selina's key.' He dug in the pockets of his jacket while they sat, unbreathing. He produced two grubby handkerchiefs, a silver hip flask with the top dangling from its chain, a wallet and a Banham key. 'The door was locked, so I got myself in. No one there. No one in the office.'

'Did you use the lift?' McLeish kept his voice dead level.

'No. Walked up. Didn't want to make a noise.'

McLeish drew breath, carefully, and heard Davidson do the same. 'Why did you come back?'

'I wanted to see Selina.' Richard Marsh-Hayden sounded simply surprised. 'We had a row. I told you. Wanted to make up.' He looked across at them and his mouth went tight and pulled down, and his eyes blurred and he reached unseeingly for one of the grubby handkerchiefs.

'How long did you stay on the premises?' Davidson had got too anxious to sit still.

'Mm. Well, I was a bit pissed, so I had a slash in the men's downstairs. Did that first. Then went up to the office, sat there for, oh, ten minutes or so, just thinking. Then I looked around and found some water in the office fridge, I needed something. Then I decided I'd better go.'

McLeish sat, in silence, considering this history. Davidson was fidgeting again, unobtrusively, but he didn't need reminding of the difficulty.

'So you didn't go home? Although you were trying to find your wife?'

'Had a chance to think about it. Didn't want to get home pissed and have another row. So I was sick – made myself – in the gents downstairs and went to the baths. Thought I'd only be an hour or so, but I went to sleep. Got home around ten, but she'd gone. Like I told you.'

This bit accorded with the records at the baths. It was a deeply

151

unconvincing recital, but the man appeared to be unconscious of its deficiencies. Well, he was, utterly, soddenly, drunk and McLeish hesitated. It was a temptation to take him into custody, now, but no matter how much Richard Marsh-Hayden was estranged from his family, they were a powerful lot, and there would be an expensive solicitor round his neck inside a couple of hours, hampering investigations. As he deliberated, Richard laid his head on the desk and slept, fitfully snoring. McLeish leant over, abstracted the bottle and jerked his head at Davidson who followed him out. 'I'll do this in the morning, but put a watch on him. This lot can get him home.'

They clattered downstairs and found Michael Owens, huddled in the kitchen with Judith and Tony. 'It'll be quiet in a minute,' she called over the noise. 'Mac's people are going off to eat, and the joiners who are coming to clear the next lot don't come in till nine thirty.'

He waited, with acquired patience, as a blessed silence fell and the crew in the kitchen unhuddled and went to make coffee and sweep the dust off a couple of tables while McLeish addressed himself to Michael Owens. 'Can you get him home? Yes? If you give him an hour to sleep it off you can get him into a cab.'

Michael Owens sighed, exasperated. 'Cabs won't take him and I don't blame them. I'll have to take him.' He chewed his lip in frustration. 'Anyway. Our problem. Nothing more we can do for you, Chief Superintendent?'

McLeish confirmed that he, too, was on his way home, and went, leaving Davidson to make sure the watchers were in place.

11

'Judith. The safe's open.'

Mary, plump and blonde, neat in short-sleeved top and pleated Terylene skirt, was standing, irresolute, looking at the big safe, the heavy door an inch or so open. 'Were you in earlier?' she asked, as Judith, in clean boiler suit, deposited a briefcase on her desk.

'No. I must have left it last night. I had it open two or three times yesterday, but I did think I'd left it shut.' She sat down behind her own desk and thought about the safe. Mary had had yesterday off, so it was no good asking her. 'There isn't any cash in it,' she explained to Mary's reproachful face. 'I put the cash in the little old safe . . . oh . . . yesterday.'

Mary blinked at her.

'The cash from Saturday's take. I thought we'd need it with all this lot on site. Indeed, we will on Friday, but I haven't actually used it yet.'

'But you put it in the old safe.' Mary was honestly puzzled, and Judith felt herself redden.

'There were a lot of people about.'

'And you didn't want them to know we kept cash in the safe.' Mary obviously felt she was getting closer to understanding, but to Judith the whole explanation sounded less and less likely. Where did sane business people keep cash if not in a safe? Why have a safe if it was not used as a depository for cash? But it would be wholly unfair to Richard to share her suspicions with Mary.

'Well, anyway, I put it in the old safe, but I could swear I shut the big safe. I did put the management accounts and the back-up disks in there. We'd better look.'

They looked and Judith sat back. 'It's all there. I must just be going round the bend.'

'You've had too much, and now this awful fire. I'm ever so sorry I had to take a day's holiday, but Liz couldn't change.' Mary, in addition to her other burdens, shared the care of an increasingly old and forgetful parent with her only sister. 'Shall we check the old safe?' She was making for the small inner office as she spoke, and Judith followed her meekly. 'It's moved,' they both said, simultaneously, and stared at it. It had been pulled away from its corner and turned slightly towards the light, but it was closed. Judith, hands trembling, turned the wheel, counting to get the combination right, and swung the door open. The cash was there in a pile on top of a heap of papers, as she had left it yesterday. 'It's all right.'

'We'd better count it,' Mary suggested.

They did that, and it was all there, and Judith sat back, pale with relief.

'What's that file?' Mary had squatted beside her, and reached over to pull out a red envelope file, labelled 'Insurance policies; old'.

'I suppose what it says? Better look, though. I've been finding papers in all sorts of places they shouldn't be.'

Mary struggled to her feet, apologising for the creaks, and opened up the file while Judith sat on the floor, irresolute, trying to decide what to do with the cash.

'Oh. Oh dear, Judith.'

'What?'

'There are letters. To Selina.'

'What sort of letters?'

'Well, very personal ones.'

They looked at each other.

'Mr Marsh-Hayden ought to have them . . .' Her voice trailed away as she looked down, distressed, at the file.

Judith clambered ungracefully to her feet. 'Let me look. Oh.' She read the first one, feeling a blush come right up from her neck. 'We can't,' she said slowly. 'The police were here over the weekend, checking Selina's desk for anything personal. They'll want them.' She considered the file, anxiously. 'I suppose Selina thought they'd be better in the safe and the police didn't look.'

'But they did,' Mary said. 'I opened it for them on Friday and they had a look through. It was only rubbish. This – these letters weren't there, I mean, they'd have found them.'

Judith gaped at her. 'We've had all sorts through the office, when we were moving things around on Sunday, but I couldn't get in here most of yesterday.'

'You were too busy, I'm sure,' Mary said, helpfully.

'No. Richard was here, getting drunk. We couldn't get him out.'

They stared at each other, and Judith, moving like a sleepwalker, went to find a telephone.

*

'It's ten thirty. The Hon. Richard was due here at ten. Will I get the lads to fetch him out?'

'Ah. So it is.' John McLeish, dictating to his secretary, was two-thirds down the in-tray. 'I wondered why I was doing so well, I've had an extra half-hour. Have you rung him up?'

Davidson retreated to do that, and McLeish took a run at the Annual Leave table, neatly summarised for him by his secretary on a Post-It.

'No one below the rank of DI plans to be here at all from 20 December to 5 January, I see.' He dictated a note to four detective inspectors, reminding them of the minimum practicable level of staffing needed, and asking for a plan agreed between all four of them by the end of next week. The trouble with all administration was that you had to keep on top of it; ignore the stuff that didn't immediately need doing for a couple of weeks and it all needed doing at once. And it would have taken the opportunity to multiply, somehow, inside the pile of papers like neglected weeds, as Francesca had observed one exasperated day when they had dug jointly down to the bottom of the domestic in-tray to find multiple compounded problems.

'No answer.' Davidson appeared in the doorway. 'But he's there unless he's managed to get past a sergeant and a DC.'

McLeish looked up at him. 'I'm getting old. I forgot we had a team on him. Get them to ring the bell, looking as if they have been just sent out from the local nick.' Davidson gave him an old-fashioned look and he grinned. 'You were going to tell them that?'

'I was, aye.'

McLeish was reading, slitty-eyed, a tricky proposal about second-ment, which appeared to be a method of avoiding giving him the two extra detective sergeants he needed. 'Where's he live? Fulham? I've got at least an hour.'

Ten minutes later Davidson reappeared. 'He's not answering the door. Nor the phone.'

McLeish sat back, his attention engaged, and they looked at each other.

'And he's nowhere, you're sure?'

'I'm sure. Will we break in? Get a warrant?'

'Hang on. Jenny, get me Mr Owens – Michael Owens, will you? At his office.'

'He's in a meeting.'

'Get him out, would you?'

They drank coffee, catching up on the morning's information, while Jenny struggled with a range of secretaries and assistants, and finally rang through with Michael Owens on the line. McLeish explained the problem.

'You don't have a key to the house? No. Well, we can get a warrant, or go through a window, but I'd like someone who knows Mr Marsh-Hayden there. Well, that would be helpful. Certainly. Inspector Davidson will meet you there.'

He put the phone down. 'He's worried. Says Mr Marsh-Hayden was in a bad way last night, very low, very depressed, still not sober. He got him into bed or rather he and Gallagher and Rubin made a joint effort, but he – Mr Owens – didn't stay, although he felt he ought to have done. He wanted to get Miss Delves to leave the restaurant and go home. And the other two had places to go to of course.'

'Now he feels badly?'

'Now he feels badly. So you and he are going to have a race to get there. Take a car and get someone from the local shop to meet you.'

'I'll take my wee pickaxe.'

'Mr Marsh-Hayden's probably just sleeping off yesterday. But hurry.' This last was addressed to Davidson's back as he left the office, shouting to a passing detective constable.

McLeish called his secretary and bent his mind to the problem of secondments, but realised he wasn't going to crack it this time, not with half his mind on it. So he went down the corridor and did some useful staff work, congratulating the team that had found the gap in Richard Marsh-Hayden's account of his movements, and stopping to read a painstaking report on the Marsh-Hayden financial position.

'A good bit of this is guesswork,' the man who had done it warned him. 'He could have some assets hidden away. But I don't think so. If you're in business you don't want CCJs – that's County Court Judgements, sir – on your record. I think he'd have paid those bills if he could. Oh, phone for you, sir, Inspector Davidson. On that line.'

'The good news is he's alive.' The gritty Glasgow accent, emphasised by the telephone, informed him. 'But no' at all well. Another few hours and he'd have been gone, they say.' A scuffling noise and voices in the background intervened. 'St Stephen's, is it? Wait for the lad, he'll go with you. You're going too, Mr Owens? Ring us up later, will you?'

'What had he taken?'

'Empty packet of paracetamol by the bed. And a bottle of whisky. I didna let the paramedics take it. I'll get them printed.'

'Good man.' The attending paramedics would have been trained to take with them any bottles or pills found by the side of an attempted suicide; Bruce Davidson was trained not to let any clue out of his sight, except for forensic examination, and the clash of training must have been interesting. And Davidson had sent a DC to the hospital so nothing Richard Marsh-Hayden managed to say would go unrecorded.

He sat back, feeling flat. After several days of intensive work on this murder the statistically likely solution, that the husband had done it, seemed to be right. Ninety per cent of murders of women are committed by their husbands, or their lovers. And many of these men understand, in horror, that they cannot live with the result, either because they had not meant to kill at all, or because, having willed the death, they cannot live without their victim. Richard Marsh-Hayden's suicide attempt was a classic piece of behaviour. And, he thought grimly, it would have saved a lot of police time had Davidson and Michael Owens got there a few hours later when it was all over. If Richard Marsh-Hayden did recover, all precedent suggested that he would then decide in favour of life and would fight like a tiger to avoid responsibility for his wife's death. So there would be no point just now in telling the labouring teams down the corridor to stop work. He would wait and see what a modern casualty hospital could do, and in the meantime he would settle, finally, these blasted secondments.

Matthew Sutherland, uncharacteristically, was feeling about twelve years old as he tagged after his senior partner. 'Why didn't you invite them to the office?' he asked, trying for a grip on the situation.

'I would not want anyone to think these people might be clients of the practice.' Peter Graebner, five foot six inches in his shoes, forged across a road, regardless of traffic, looking like something out of the Old Testament.

'Well, I'm sorry a client of mine has brought us to deal with them. But it was you they knew.'

'Such men are always with us.'

This silenced Matthew who, following in Peter's wake, observed that the crowds on the pavement around the market stalls parted like the Red Sea for his senior partner. And the stall-holders all acknowledged him, unperturbed by the fact that this morning Peter did not see or hear them. He stopped so abruptly that Matthew nearly fell over him and looked up at a pub sign.

'It's on the first floor. Ring the bell, please, Matthew. Twice, quickly.'

Matthew complied with a strong feeling that he ought to have been wearing asbestos gloves, and was unsurprised to have the door elaborately unbolted by a heavy man with a big head worn well forward and a look of having received one punch in the face too many.

'Graebner and Sutherland,' Peter said, gloomily, and they were led up to a first-floor room, sparsely furnished with a large battered table, two four-drawer filing cabinets and a substantial safe. It also contained two enormous unattractive dogs, of a breed that Matthew had believed to be outlawed, and two smallish men, dark-haired, low-browed and plainly brothers, sitting at the other side of the table. He waited for Peter to sit, which he did uninvited, and sat beside him, silent.

'Coffee, Mr Graebner? You won't? Right. You got something to offer us, I understand.'

'Our client in this matter is Anthony Gallagher. Who owes you £9000.'

'Bit more than that, I'm afraid, Mr Graebner. There's interest accrued.'

'The offer I am authorised to make includes reasonable interest. That is, interest which a court of law would consider reasonable.'

Neither brother moved, but the air in the room seemed to vanish, and Matthew found his hands clenched. Peter Graebner's hands, he saw, rested on the table, quite relaxed.

'We don't go to court much,' Brother One said.

Peter Graebner looked at him thoughtfully, and transferred his attention to the other brother.

'We've had enquiries about this particular debt,' Brother Two observed.

'Presumably as a by-product of the murder investigation at my client's workplace,' Peter said, politely.

'They got anyone for that yet?'

'Not to my knowledge.'

'Your client's in for that, is he?'

'Not particularly, as I understand the matter. Matthew?'

158

'No more than anyone else there.' It came out husky, as if he had not used his voice for a very long time, and he fought to sit still and deadpan as the two pairs of black eyes opposite examined him in detail. Their gaze shifted to his senior partner.

'So what's your offer, Mr Graebner?'

Peter Graebner, unhurried, extracted a piece of paper. 'The capital sum had risen over six months, I understand, to £7800 at 3 September. We have added interest at twenty-two per cent – the standard credit card rate – making some assumptions about the dates at which various monies were outstanding, and arrive at a total of £9100 rounded up.'

Brother Two moved his right hand to look at a scrap of paper underneath it. 'We have £10,600.'

'Our offer involves payment of £9100 in cash, if you prefer, later this week.'

'It's not enough.'

'It is our final offer.'

'Your client thought about all this, has he?'

'Extensively.'

His senior partner and the senior brother looked at each other steadily, and Matthew understood that this was an old relationship.

'I wouldn't do it for everyone, but for you, Mr Graebner, I'll take it. He's a lucky man, Gallagher.'

'Surely not. Or I would not be here.'

A sudden smile which got nowhere near the black unwinking eyes moved the tight mouth. 'That's very good. You tell him he doesn't invest with us again, that's part of it. Far as we're concerned he didn't pay what he agreed and we won't deal with him, understand?'

'I will tell him you are not prepared to do business with him in the future. But our offer is conditional on your agreement not to interfere in any way with my client.'

'That's understood, Mr Graebner. So your associate delivers the cash – when?'

Matthew found he had got down the stairs and out of the building before he breathed in. His chest felt stiff and his shoulders ached. Peter Graebner looked just the same, small, greying and rabbinical, trotting along the pavement, absently throwing out suggestions about a landlord/tenant case in which they were both involved.

'I'll come back alive, will I, after handing over the money?' Matthew asked, breathlessly.

'Good gracious, yes, my boy. And they'll be willing to deal with you alone next time, if need be.'

'I can't wait.'

'No, he's still unconscious. I'm going to come back – will you get a couple of sandwiches? Anything I need to know?' Michael Owens had waited while Richard Marsh-Hayden had been taken away to have his stomach pumped and put into an intensive care bed, wired to about twenty different pieces of equipment. No one had been prepared to give an opinion. The houseman had called out two senior consultants whose views were not available. There were nurses doing little bits of rewiring round the unconscious Richard every five minutes, and it was clear he might as well not be there, and would indeed be in the way when the family arrived.

'Brian Rubin called?' he said, surprised. 'You didn't tell him where I was? Oh, you did. To get rid of him. No, don't worry, Susie, he'd have known soon enough. I'll ring him. Or better yet, I'll go by his office – it's on the way. Sort of.'

He only got in by ringing the bell for two minutes solidly and identifying himself. He had not expected that resilient tough to be looking so distressed. He was unshaven, the shadow very dark on the olive skin, and the thick curly hair had not been brushed. The office was full of dirty coffee cups, and both telephones were ringing at once, continuously and unanswered.

'Diana's having a long weekend,' he reported gloomily. 'Not that anything would help today, but at least I could have sent her out to buy more coffee. Shut the door – the phones will drive you mad otherwise. Your girl told me the bad news – it means the deal's buggered, doesn't it? Someone warned me – chap who did it can't benefit.'

'He isn't under arrest,' Michael said, stiffly. 'Or wasn't when I left. There's a policeman with him. I feel terrible – poured him into bed last night, with no goodwill at all, I just wanted to get back to collect Judith. And then he tries to kill himself.'

'If he'd brought it off then presumably he'd never have been charged? And the estate would get Selina's shares and could sell them.'

'I really don't know.'

'Sorry, sorry. Forgot you'd known him since you were kids. Fuck it, though. I had a couple of weeks' grace from the bank to see if I could bring this deal off, but they're losing interest. In every sense. And anyway, what with the fire, I'd need a bit more cash.' He ran both hands through his disordered hair which parted unbecomingly. 'Just at this moment I don't see a way through. I need coffee.' He got up, peered hopefully into two of the mugs which littered his desk and took them with him, opening the office door on the ringing telephones. 'Gotcha.' He pounced on a half-open drawer in the desk and extracted a small jar of coffee, unplugged the electric kettle and carried it and the mugs back with him. He poured hot water into both mugs, rinsed them round in a desultory way and poured the results on to a wilting pot plant, then put in fresh coffee and water. 'Sorry about this. What are you going to do? I mean, I'm still in the market for this deal for about a week, I suppose.'

'You've got a charge on Richard's shares – no, he told me, he had to. Couldn't you go ahead and take the risk on Selina's fifteen per cent?'

'I would, if it were my decision. But it isn't – I have to have the bank's and the broker's support, or I don't have the cash. And they find it too difficult, because it's not a bog standard deal.'

'It *is* too difficult,' Michael said, soberly. 'You'd need to be ICI or near offer to get them to do that kind of funding. It's a bugger for me too, I'd love to be able to sell.'

'Particularly after the fire.'

'As you say. Judith and Tony Gallagher hope to be able to open again next week. I've seen the schedule.'

'She's nuts, sorry, excuse me. I keep forgetting you two are engaged. And Tony Gallagher is one of the reasons the place wasn't making any money.'

'What?'

'He's been ripping you off. Has to have been him. Don't look like that, mate, I told Selina.'

'You told Selina?'

'Yeh, and that was a mistake. She came to me, said she wasn't happy with the deal and her position, yatter, yatter, yatter, so I told her she was lucky to be getting it at a good price, because she couldn't control her staff, and her chef was into a scam. I thought she'd take the point, sell out and take a greeter's job with me. She was good at that. But no, what does she do? Talks to Judith, and those two decide they can turn the whole thing round and get on to the market. Only I've got nine other restaurants and years' more experience than they have and I only managed to get on to the market last year.' He peered at his guest. 'I was offering a fair price too, and not chiselling on it.'

'Yes,' Michael said, slowly. 'Yes. Sorry, I can't get this straight. You were the mystery businessman who told Selina about the scam. And Selina told Judith?'

'Must have, mustn't she?'

'And Judith now thinks she can turn Tony Gallagher and get the restaurant open again in a week. After the fire, which was his fault.'

'Sorry, come again?'

'It may have been an accident, but he was responsible for making sure the grease filter was cleaned. And he was too busy robbing the till.'

'Probably not the till,' Brian Rubin demurred. 'Food sales at the back, or a supplier fiddle.'

'Why on earth did Selina think she could cope with the likes of Tony Gallagher, if he turned against them?' He stared at Brian Rubin, who looked back at him, got up and poured some more coffee.

'Well, I'd assumed – I mean, I could be wrong – that she had something going with him.'

'What? She was in it too!'

'I thought it was simpler than that. Good-looking bloke. Don't look like that, Michael, I could be wrong, I mean I never saw them at it, but well, Selina was the sort of girl who likes a bit of rough.'

'Tony Gallagher!'

'Wouldn't be true of Judith of course,' Brian Rubin pointed out, hastily. 'He's got a lot of respect for her. I bet you he only started on the fiddle when she was building the new place.' He looked anxiously at his guest. 'I mean, she'll be making Tony sweat for it. She knows what she's doing, believe me, and I'd rather she didn't. I want her to sell out.' He paused to consider this statement, and Michael, still dazed, found the flaw in the argument.

'But Tony wanted to sell.'

'Now that is true. And he didn't just want to sell, he needed to. Made that clear to me. He was in money trouble – no, he didn't say what but he was scared. Well, maybe he solved it some other way.'

'Like stealing from us.'

'Well, well, it's maybe not that hopeless.' Brian Rubin was sitting up, the mind working, displaying the qualities that had enabled him to claw together his first restaurants from scratch. 'I've *got* Richard's shares, if he doesn't repay the loan in another six months, and he's not going to do that, is he? Selina's shares we can't do anything

162

about, but if you could buy Tony's off him and we could somehow persuade Judith she isn't going to manage to get the Caff open again before she runs out of cash, then we're home.' He looked hopefully at his guest, then considered him more closely. 'You OK?'

'I've got a headache. Now I know why everyone tells you not to get involved with private companies, or do business with friends. I'll tell Judith. I can't wait to be out of this.'

'You remembered it's *Tosca* again tonight? I asked Tris to get two tickets for us.'

John McLeish looked at his desk diary in dismay. 'I can't. I'm sorry. It's the Bramshill reunion dinner.'

'Oh.' Francesca knew that this was not only a prior engagement but completely inescapable. 'Oh, pity. In which case I'll tell Tris he can have the tickets back – they're booked out. I was not, of course, going on afterwards.' She was sounding virtuous and injured and McLeish reflected, as he had often done before, on the marks left by the relentless competition between siblings.

'I should hope not,' he said, briskly. 'It's a weekday and you're pregnant, remember?'

'Very difficult to forget. How are you getting on?'

'Not too bad.'

'You arrested someone?'

'Not exactly.'

'I see. Do you have to stay and get absolutely pissed with the lads? No? See you around eleven then.'

He put the phone down and looked up; Bruce Davidson was in the doorway, all but dancing with excitement.

'What?'

'There's more letters. Being fingerprinted as we speak, but it looks like more of the same. Only up to date.'

'To Selina? How many?'

'Four from gentlemen friends. Quite a lot of others from women friends, or her mother, as well. Found at the Café de la Paix, in a folder in a safe.'

McLeish looked at him, scandalised. 'Was it not searched?'

'Yes, and I've talked to the bloke who did it. It wasn't there, when he looked, it was put in later and Miss Delves says so too. That for me? Thanks, lass.' He snatched up the phone, blue eyes bright with excitement. 'Mr Marsh-Hayden's, were they? Good, good, good, just

163

keep going.' He put the phone down, beaming with pleasure. 'Richard Marsh-Hayden's prints all over them. My bet is – and Miss Delves thinks so as well – he found them yesterday somewhere in the Café de la Paix office and sat reading them all day, getting more and more pissed. Mrs Cameron had a day off and Miss Delves was busy downstairs after the first hour or so. And in any case she said no one wanted to be in there with him – with Richard – they just left him there hoping he'd go home.'

'So he hunted around,' McLeish said slowly, 'because he thought there were some more letters – some more men. And then he found them. Why didn't he take them home with him?'

'Why not make himself really bloody miserable?' Davidson agreed. 'Wait a minute, though. He didn't go home by himself, did he? Owens, Gallagher and Rubin took him, and he mebbe didn't want to risk carrying the folder, dropping it in the car whatever, so he popped it in the safe.'

'Yes,' McLeish said, seeing it. 'Yes. That's what happened. And he went home, took a lot of paracetamol and passed out.' He looked across at Davidson. 'When are we going to be able to ask him about all this?'

'Well, now, there's the problem.' Davidson had calmed down a bit, but the excitement of the chase was still on him. 'They were running more tests but his liver function is very poor.'

'Very poor?'

'That's what they said. You've to talk to the consultant at lunchtime when he finishes his rounds, or a meeting, or whatever.'

'Where did he get all this paracetamol?'

'Packet by the bed, remember. The story is that Rubin and Gallagher and Michael Owens took him back – took all three of them to get him into the car and put him to bed. Owens says he got him to drink some water, not enough but some, and had left a glass and a jug beside him. He didn't see the paracetamol, and didn't give Marsh-Hayden any drugs at all. They had a discussion and agreed he'd only sick them up, and he was better left propped up in bed. They took all the alcohol they could see and put it in Michael Owens' car. Didn't find it all, though; there was a half-bottle of whisky with the paracetamol by the bed. I've only talked to Owens, but I'm seeing the other two later.'

'How was he? Owens, I mean?'

'Terrible. Feels awful, he says, about leaving, but he was fed up and desperate to get back to his fiancée, Miss Delves, and make her go home. Well, you can see that, she's having a bad time.'

'So Richard Marsh-Hayden read the letters, got pissed, went home, drank a bit more and took everything he could see,' McLeish said, thoughtfully. 'Well, no point speculating. We need to look at the letters, and I'd like to talk to Mr Marsh-Hayden.'

Davidson eyed him. 'You think we've got a conclusion here?'

'That he killed his wife, then attempted suicide? Not unlikely, is it? I'd just rather ask him.'

'Any tickets? Anywhere?'

The man in the Coliseum box office indicated that his only hope lay in someone being so lost to all sense of propriety as to return a ticket an hour before the performance. Matt only just managed not to swear aloud; he had been too busy during the day even to remember to ring up Francesca, in too much of a hurry to get to the Café de la Paix with his hastily drafted loan agreement and charge over the shares to stop on his way. Altogether it had been a difficult day, starting with meeting two people who still made his blood run cold when he thought about them, and continuing through a painful redraft of his original thoughts. And it had got no easier; when he got to the Café de la Paix he had had to beat on the door for five minutes, making gestures eloquent of his wish to be admitted. Men on ladders, manhandling lengths of aluminium ducts, either ignored him or made gestures back indicating that the restaurant was closed, as if anyone could think otherwise. Performance restaurant, perhaps, he wondered, trying to recover his temper, eat your lunch while workmen erect the roof above your head. At the point where he was considering a frontal assault on the door, Tony Gallagher, dodging tubes and ladders, had let him in and he and Judith had signed the agreement against a background of crashing noise which penetrated to the first-floor office from the massed labour force on the site. He had attempted to console and met the usual fate of the well-meaning underinformed; cash, Judith had told him, was pouring out to the expensive groups of fitters and joiners working at time and a half and to the thirty regular kitchen staff and waiters who must not be allowed to drift away to work for other restaurants. The regular suppliers were all expecting their bills to be paid on their normal schedule, but there was no cash at all coming in.

'Won't the suppliers wait?' he had asked when these facts had been explained.

'Well, they have to,' Judith Delves had said, irritably. 'But they won't go on supplying except for cash. So when we need to get supplies in to open we have to find more cash. Which we haven't got.'

All in all, it was a bad time for the chef to have got himself in a position where he, too, needed cash, Matt reflected, but Judith Delves had shown no hesitation at all in arranging a banker's draft from her private funds for him to hand over to Tony's appalling associates. He considered her as he stood, disappointed, in the foyer. She was indeed determined; the odds against her were considerable. Even though she now owned, or controlled, twenty per cent of the shareholding, recent events could only make the others keener to sell and get shot of the whole mess. Well, she had his client tied hand and foot, and he must be one of the key – if not the key – elements in getting the restaurant open and trading again. And if Brian Rubin was forced out of business, then none of the other shareholders had anywhere to go if they really wanted out. That had been the point of recruiting the late Mrs Marsh-Hayden to her side of course; there was a good chance that Brian Rubin would not be able to hang on and the other shareholders would just have had to row along with them. The two women might have been in some practical difficulty without his client, but now Tony Gallagher was committed; Judith Delves controlled his shares.

He sat down, heavily, on a seat just inside the door, barely seeing the early arrivals leaving coats and greeting each other in that braying English way which still fell oddly on his ear even five years out of New Zealand. Judith Delves was taking a huge financial risk, but her ability to carry on the business was much strengthened. Would Selina Marsh-Hayden have been showing a similar resolution? No, emphatically, on what he had known of her, she was at best an uncertain ally, sexually volatile and without any of Judith's capacity for sheer grinding hard work. But Selina was dead, and the man investigating that death, Francesca's husband, even if he knew Tony had been in trouble, certainly could not know how it had been resolved. He cast one reluctant backward glance at the man behind the counter, who shook his head sympathetically, and rose to go; Peter Graebner would clear his head for him. He marched down the steps, unseeingly, and cannoned into a woman.

'Matthew. Do you mind?'

'Francesca. Sorry. What are *you* doing here?'

She was looking up at him, frowning. 'Are you all right?'

'No. I wanted to hear your brother but I couldn't get a ticket.'

'Ah-ha.'

'Wonderwoman! You haven't!'

'I have. I've been trying to find you. Tristram told me you wanted one. It's John's ticket. He's at some Old Policemen's outing. It's a box seat with whoever else has comp tickets. Agents. People's Central European aunties.'

'Is that really OK?'

'Yes, you cuckoo.'

He hugged her to him, suddenly enormously pleased with life. She felt warm and smelled of lily of the valley as she always had.

'I had lunch with your brother on Sunday, see,' he said, following her through the gathering fashionable crowd, full of faces he half recognised.

'He said. We'll go round afterwards, but I'm not going on to supper. Too pregnant.'

He understood the reminder perfectly and smiled at her reassuringly, he hoped, as they arrived at the door to the box, occupied by two heavy duty Central European ladies and an immaculate American in his thirties. The man looked at him thoughtfully before dismissing him from consideration, leaving Matthew to wonder, again, how gays could know, so unerringly, who was straight. Francesca took a front seat, bowing politely to the rest of the box, and he wedged himself awkwardly into one of the rear seats, noting that a box seat was not quite the privilege it might appear from his normal position in the gallery. He peered down over Francesca's shoulder to the auditorium which was boiling with people.

'The merchant banking community,' Francesca said, nodding towards the front stalls. 'They all have a deal whereby you can book twice a week in exchange for a vast subscription.'

'How do you know?'

'I am Bursar of Gladstone still. I invest our funds, such as they are. Or rather I don't, but I am part of the mechanism for choosing those who do. Our current lot of advisers brought us here.'

'Does John like opera?'

'He's only been to two. But he would have come to hear Tristram, 'course he would, given notice.'

'I'm sure he would.' He was aware he was sounding distracted.

'Matt?' She had always been quick, of course, to read your mind. 'Your client OK, is he?'

'I hope so. Yes. Well, it's a difficult time.'

'Not like you to resort to generalities.'

'All I can do at the moment. Your policeman friend making any progress on the murder, is he?'

'I have no idea, he wouldn't tell me. But he sounds different when things are moving.' He felt her head turn as he stared down at the stalls. 'Do you want to tell me anything? Or tell John?'

'Don't know yet.'

'If in doubt, speak, I know that's what he would say,' she said, warningly. 'I talk to Judith Delves, you know.'

'Do you now? When?'

'She came and talked to me after the murder about how to hang on to her restaurant when her boyfriend really didn't want her to. I didn't think her chances were that good, but counselled procrastination on the basis that on the whole delay caused a deal to go away. Rotten advice, given what has happened. She'd have been better out of it.'

Matthew thought about it, slowly. 'Rich bloke, Mr Owens, or isn't he?'

'Oh, must be. Directors in banks like that make hundreds of thousands. Every year. We're in the wrong trades, Matt, you, me, *and* John. Good-looking too – I saw him at the restaurant. Quite a hunk. I quite see why Judith fancies him. She says his taste used to run to dazzling blondes, like the late Selina. I hope I was right to reassure her that chaps grew out of that.'

'Oh absolutely,' Matt said, promptly. 'You might want to fuck a Selina, but they give you trouble. The less flashy ones don't. There's an English type – no, get off, Fran, we have them where I come from – good sports, do anything for you, don't fuss, keep the firm running. Judith's one of those.'

'No, she isn't.' He grinned affectionately at the familiar profile. 'She's one of the other sort of troublesome ones. The ones who want their own careers, eccentric things like that. Like me.'

'Not like you,' he said, quietly. 'Doesn't look like you do.'

'That's not the point.' She was blushing and resolutely not looking at him. 'First time round I was married into a merchant bank. You're right, they want women who, like crusaders' wives, keep the roof on the castle and the swine in the pens and the passing strangers out of their beds. They absolutely do not want raving beauties with wandering tendencies and they equally do not want bloody-minded women who want their own castle. So Michael cannot have understood quite what Judith is like. She fancies him rotten and can't quite see how she's been so lucky, with one part of her mind. With the other she's tackling the real issue.'

'Which is?'

'Like Trollope said of one of his heroes: "It is the internal qualities of a man that make a marriage." Not whether he earns enough for any six people.'

He sat watching her, but she would not turn to look at him, and leaned out further to look at something.

'Here we go.'

The house lights faded and a single light brightened at the front of the curtains which opened a crack to reveal a man in evening dress. The circle and balcony groaned and the stalls buzzed. Francesca scowled in disapproval and the man explained, deprecatingly, that a bug had finally felled one Rumanian bass baritone Scarpia, but that they had been fortunate enough to be able to replace him with another, similar. A scatter of polite applause followed, and Francesca nodded, smiling, to the larger of the two women in their box.

The conductor came on, the curtain went up, finally. Matthew had been to operas before, but not with a cast like this, or a stage or a tradition like this. But through it all he still found himself back in the mess that was Café de la Paix, watching his client signing the charge on his shares, seeing again the two dogs and the two brothers from this morning. He did manage to get away from his thoughts for the brief moments while Tristram was on stage; star potential that one, he thought, momentarily painfully jealous of a man who at not much older than he had his feet so securely on the ladder. And who had the devoted Francesca, lost in concentration, unmoving, as a supporter.

The lights went up for the interval, leaving him blinking, guiltily. Francesca leant across to say something in German to the women who both beamed at her, but he managed to extract her after a minute or so.

'Didn't know you spoke German.'

'I don't really, but then nor do they. They're Rumanian.' She was relaxed and happy. 'Good, isn't it?'

'Terrific.'

It must have lacked something, because she looked at him, carefully.

'Did you know Selina's husband, Richard, is in hospital? Tried to top himself.' He had not known he was going to say that, he thought.

'Mr Marsh-Hayden. Ah.'

'What does that mean?'

'John says it's usually the husband in these cases. Or the resident man. And they very often feel terrible when they've done it. That must be why he feels progress is being made.'

'He's wrong.' He looked down at her, but she did not seem to feel he had gone barking mad.

'Why is he wrong? Who do you fancy?'

'I don't know.'

She looked back at him, patiently. 'Are you a bit too close to this? You could try listening to the music, you know.'

'Fran. Sorry. I was, sort of.'

'Concentrate. It clears the brain.' She patted his hand in a sisterly way, nothing sexual there at all, and he laughed.

12

Francesca woke from a stunned sleep as the bed shifted under her. She rolled over to see her husband padding towards the bathroom. It was light, it must be morning. She lay, collecting herself; William had woken at 2 a. m., wet, and she had changed his bed and put a nappy on him, deciding that whatever Susannah thought he wasn't really ready to be dry at night. But, she remembered, John had not been there, had still been out. She sat up, crossly; true, her husband was under forty and not yet in the heart attack danger zone, but he really could not drink until past two and get up again at 7 a.m. without risking turning her into a widowed mother of two. The Metropolitan Police would have to be forced to understand his limits.

He came back from the bathroom, staggering with sleep and rolled heavily on to his side of the bed. 'How late were you?' She sounded like all nagging wives everywhere, she realised, and scuttled over to his side to give him a cuddle.

'*That*'s nice.' He rolled over and gathered her into his arms. 'Four o'clock. I'm not going to the office yet.'

'What a party.'

'No. Or rather it was turning into one, but I was called out of it at eleven thirty.'

'What happened?'

'The Café de la Paix case. Richard Marsh-Hayden took an overdose on Monday night and died in hospital early this morning. Liver failure.'

'How?'

'Well, he'd taken too much paracetamol, but his liver was shot anyway. They're doing a PM, but he was a boozer with a history of hepatitis. So it wouldn't have taken all that much to finish him.'

'How awful. Or I suppose not, if he killed his wife.' She moved against him as his hands went under her nightdress. 'You don't want me to go on talking about it, right?'

'Right. Will's asleep. I looked.'

'Let me lock the door.' She slid out of bed, and padded across the room, turning the key silently, holding her breath as she listened for their treasured child who seemed miraculously still to be deeply asleep. She stopped momentarily to watch, with love, the sight of her husband fighting his way out of his pyjamas, enmeshing himself with the duvet, and pulled off her nightie preparatory to burrowing in from the other side. They both fell deeply asleep afterwards and Francesca surfaced to a room full of the autumn sun and the comforting muffled sound-track of William's nanny, getting him dressed. It must be past eight thirty which was when Susannah came on duty, having got up at about eight twenty-five. She rolled over to find her watch and stared at it unbelievingly. Nine thirty, and she was due at Gladstone College at the very latest for a meeting at eleven o'clock. She looked, irresolute, at her husband, sprawled over two-thirds of the bed, and was just deciding to leave him to sleep, and the hell with the Metropolitan Police Force and all its works, when his eyes opened.

'It's nine thirty,' she said, anticipating the question, 'and I have to get up. Stay there.'

'No. Can't do it. Lots to fix. That was nice.'

'Wasn't it? I feel human again, not just cross and pregnant.'

'I never asked. How was the show?'

'They had a substitute Scarpia who did well. Much rapturous applause, dressing-room full of excitable people in four languages. The tenor lead, Alan, wasn't singing nearly as well as he did on Saturday; he's got a throat and he was terribly constricted at the top of the range. Forcing it. And the orchestra was all over the shop, particularly the woodwind. Clarinettist kept going sharp. But Tris was OK, bang in tune unlike most of them.'

John McLeish, after six years with the Wilson family, was still disconcerted by the detachment with which they assessed all music. Indeed, he was regularly brought up short by the amount they knew instinctively, the appalling ease with which any of them could perform, even the ones like his wife, who had not made their career in music. He looked across at her; she was standing in a patch of sunshine bent over, shaking her breasts down into the cups of her brassiere. She straightened up and caught his appreciative eye.

'Yes, well, I know you like it, but I don't feel I need all this extra presence. It's only a couple of months but already I can't get it all in comfortably.'

'That's what I like.'

She laughed and came over to kiss him, and he padded off contentedly to the shower, while she unlocked the bedroom door to let in William who had finished breakfast and realised he was being excluded from his parents' room.

'So is that it, with the case?' she asked as her husband came out of the bathroom, wrapped in a towel. William rushed at him and he scooped him up, effortlessly.

'It's certainly the prime suspect gone.'

'Is that policemanly caution, or nagging doubt?'

'Oh, he was certainly favourite. By some way. No, it's just loose ends. Bits that don't fit. You get those in any case. That should be it, we'll tidy up and do the next one. And the next. Are you planning to go to Gladstone? Because you'll need a bit more on than that.'

Michael Owens sat at his desk in the large, air-conditioned office, with the echo of the conversation he had just had in his ears. He had rung St Stephen's Hospital at nine thirty, after the morning meeting, and the response he had got had alerted him. He had rung the Café de la Paix where no one had any better information and persevered until he had run Detective Chief Superintendent McLeish to earth, in a car, on the way to Scotland Yard.

'That's the strength of it, I'm sorry to say. He died about three this morning.'

'Why didn't you get to me before?' he had asked, outraged on discovering that Richard had died almost seven hours earlier.

'I didn't leave the hospital till 3.30 a.m. and neither did his parents and sister. I expect they got up late too.' McLeish was sounding just this side of tart, and Michael mentally acknowledged the point.

'Did he . . . was he able to . . . to say goodbye?'

'He never recovered consciousness at all. Acute liver failure, nothing to be done, in the end. That tends to be what happens with a paracetamol overdose. And a not very good liver anyway, I understand.'

'He'd had hepatitis. In Cyprus.'

And he drank, in excess, which no hepatitis survivor should do, as neither of them said.

'Chief Superintendent, is that . . . I mean . . . are you still investigating Selina Marsh-Hayden's murder?'

'We have not yet reviewed all the evidence.'

Michael had opened his mouth to try another question, but understood that he was not going to get an answer.

*

173

Francesca surfaced from her morning meeting – a review of the domestic bursar's management accounts – to find two messages, both from Judith Delves.

'She really wants to talk to you,' the secretary who looked after the whole of her department observed.

'Yes, I see.' She sat at her desk, but it did not take long to decide that everything from common charity to duty to a Gladstone Old Girl required her to return Judith's call. The Café de la Paix statistically probable murderer was dead, by his own hand, and her husband's interest in the case presumably therefore over, except for his usual conscientious job of tidying up. And Judith, who was her own age and had appealed to her for help, had an impossible job to do, her principal place of business ravaged by fire and her all-male shareholders in fundamental disagreement with her. It was the duty of all good women to come to the aid of this particular party.

'This is too difficult to do on the phone,' Judith Delves said, against a background of shouted conversation, along the lines of 'Up your end a bit, Mick' punctuated by crashes and hammer noises. 'May I come and see you?'

'Actually, I have a meeting at the Department at three,' Francesca volunteered. 'I could pop in afterwards, assuming there is anywhere we can talk. Right?'

She went through a college lunch for their increasing number of women lawyers, most of whom seemed to be hollow-eyed and devoid of friends or lovers as a result of working fifteen hours a day, every day, in prestigious City law firms. This kind of slavery was hardly what the feminist movement had sought to achieve, she reflected, treacherously; in some sense these young women, the most intellectually distinguished and envied of their generation, were not a lot better off than the women locked on to weaving machines in nineteenth-century factories. True, of course, that this was an apprenticeship, that in ten to fifteen years' time those who survived could be partners, paid astronomically well, but how and when were they going to find husbands and have children? Or were they simply going to decide against all that, as she herself so nearly had, in favour of being captains of their own destinies? It was perfectly possible that these pale girls, whingeing about their conditions of employment, were also mildly sorry for her, on a civil servant's pay, married and totally earthbound by a toddler and a bump. For everything there is a season, she told herself, maturely, only to be jolted out of her comfort by the cleverest of all the recent graduates' drawled, mischievous, sharp account of a drafting meeting on a recent high-profile company flotation.

The after-taste stayed with her through a particularly uninspiring meeting with Department for Education officials, and she arrived at the Café de la Paix in a mood to help Judith Delves to keep her own business against all comers if required. Large metallic objects were being carried through the glass door by men whose every movement said that they were on highly bonused piecework and she doubted whether they even saw her as she slipped in between parties. She stopped, daunted; the elegant, cool restaurant, all brightly polished glass and brass, and bright clear colours, had become one big, dusty, dirty, echoing shed. She stood blinking, trying to decide what was happening, and saw that the position was not as hopeless as a first glance had suggested. The last bits of aluminium ducting to replace the ventilation system were being fitted, as she watched, and yards behind the four-men team came another team; carpenters were sawing narrow planks to replace the false ceiling that covered the bunking. Of course, even once the carpenters were done, varnishing and repainting remained, but Francesca, used to supervising build-ers, reckoned it could be done in a couple of weeks. She considered the sheer numbers on site and the speed and concentration with which they were working, and reduced her estimate. In ten days, given a following wind, and suitcasefuls of cash, Café de la Paix would be ready to go. Allow another day to get chairs, tables, tablecloths and staff back in, by the week after next the site would be trading again.

She shared her conclusion on timing, tentatively, with Judith Delves, who emerged from a huddle of site management to greet her, and Judith agreed, crossing her fingers. They smiled at each other.

'So. What can I do?'

'It's very good of you to come, Francesca. I'm afraid I was in a panic when I rang. Michael had just rung to say that Richard had died, and *that* was a shock for both of us. And then he was assuming that this was the final straw, as it were. That we had no choice but to sell, and I just . . . I just . . .'

'Needed another head,' Francesca supplied, unwilling to cast her-self instantly as an ally.

'Yes. Come up to the office. You can come through the kitchen.'

The kitchen, although in serious need of repainting, was in good shape. The heavy duty stainless steel equipment had all survived,

175

with nothing more expensive or difficult than a good clean-up. The grill and, of course, the extractor duct over it had been replaced in their entirety, and a young man was laboriously washing the spectacularly dirty floor.

'Ah.'

'Ah, indeed. I come and look at it to cheer myself up. Tony – Chef – is coming in later. He was here at five thirty to receive the new grill and make quite sure it went in right, so he's gone home for a sleep.'

'What can he do, now the kitchen is in?'

Judith Delves looked at her, and she realised she had opened the mouth without engaging the brain. 'Menu planning. Recosting. Talking to suppliers.'

'Of course,' she said, meekly. 'All new menu?'

'Not necessarily. But one on which we can make a decent profit and which can be kept simple. We've lost two sous chefs and a couple of commis as well, and it'll take a while to get up to full staff. Tony needs to make some phone calls too.'

She opened the door of the office and Francesca blinked. It became clear that every object which could not be sent to store had been put up here for safety. There was a narrow pathway to Judith's big desk and she followed her hostess gingerly towards it, and they sat down on two chairs by the window behind the desk, ready, as Francesca pointed out, to defend the office against any number of circling Indians. Judith laughed, politely, but seemed to be having difficulty formulating her request, so Francesca decided to help.

'So your chef is working hard?'

'Yes. Very.'

'Does that mean he has changed his mind about wanting to sell?'

The right question, she saw, and Judith gratefully told her exactly what had changed his mind, including her knowledge of the scam he had been conducting.

'So that's what Matt Sutherland was doing up here on Tuesday. I took him to the Coliseum, I had the only spare ticket. He found a dazzling blonde backstage so I left him to it.' She drew breath. 'I've always wanted to be a blonde. They do seem to have more of the fun than is wholly reasonable.'

'Like Selina,' Judith said.

'I only saw her the once, but she did look like someone who had all of everything that was going.'

'Yes, but we never had problems over men. She could get anyone she wanted, but she never fancied the same men as I did.'

Francesca, who had understood that Tony Gallagher would never have got away with a scam had Judith Delves not been off site for a critical six months, then wondered aloud how good a business-woman the late Selina Marsh-Hayden had been. Or had she been better at brightening the lives of those around her than at the minutiae of administration?

Judith nodded, sadly. 'I should never have left her running the place on her own. I should have put in a heavy-duty general manager – I knew it wasn't Selina's skill. But we were spending all the spare money on the conversion across the river and we couldn't afford to add to the overheads.'

'What was Selina paid, if I may ask?'

'Same as me. £20,000.'

Francesca felt her eyebrows go up; that was the going rate for a secretary in a merchant bank.

Judith had noticed her reaction. 'In the private sector you have to slave now in order to be a fat cat later. We were going to make real money when we had grown the group a bit. We would each have made six times our original capital over four years as it was. But we can do much better.'

'If the others are prepared to hang on,' Francesca observed. She stopped and gazed at her hostess. 'But with the Marsh-Haydens both gone, there aren't many others around, are there? Tony, who you say is co-operating, and your Michael. Is he still objecting?'

Judith Delves looked out of the window, biting her lip. 'Yes. But, of course, we haven't talked about the restaurant since he heard Richard had died. That was a terrible shock, I thought he was all right. You see, I thought people *were* if they got to hospital alive and got pumped out.'

'Not if they took paracetamol twelve hours before, as I understand it. It gets the liver and that is irreplaceable.'

'Paracetamol?'

'So I understand.' Francesca was uneasily aware that she had got her information from the inside but, after all, Richard's family must have been told what he had taken; it wasn't a secret.

'But he never took paracetamol,' Judith objected. 'He wouldn't let Selina buy it either. He'd read about an awful case – a teenage girl who had had a fight with her boyfriend, took half a bottle of paracetamol and then was revived. She apologised and the boy apologised and everyone promised not to do it again. Then the doctor had to tell them all it was too late, the girl was already

177

effectively dead. It gave Richard the shivers. Well, it gave me the shivers. It was only about ten tablets.'

'What a terrible story.' Francesca moved in her chair, suddenly very conscious of the bump which was making her neat skirt uncomfortable at the waist. 'I think for the future I might find some other way of fixing a headache.' She looked across at the other woman, still haunted by the vision of a repentant teenager, surrounded by friends and family, looking hopefully to a future that she was not going to have. Judith was looking equally haunted, and Francesca remembered abruptly how the conversation had started. 'But, Judith, it *was* paracetamol, or something like it, that he took. I'm sure about that.'

'Then, I suppose, he did really mean to kill himself,' the other woman said, slowly. 'It wasn't an accident, or a cry for help, or any of the things I was thinking.'

'Mm.' Francesca acknowledged mentally that this piece of information was potentially useful in tying off a loose end and ought to be shared with her husband. Given his objections to interference by her, it would be nice if it got to him from someone other than herself. 'His family would have known about his objections to paracetamol?'

'I'm not sure they're that close. Richard was a black sheep, and he had quarrelled really seriously with his father.'

They let a moment elapse in memory of the Hon. Richard Marsh-Hayden, and it was Francesca, conscious as always of the pressure of time, who found her way back to the purpose of her visit.

'So, where are you on the sale?'

'Well, I don't know, which is why I wanted to talk to you. Richard's shares, I know, were left to Selina, but . . .'

'Mm. Do you know where they go now that – as the lawyers say – the bequest has failed? No? Probably back to his family in some way. Oh dear. What a mess. Sorry, Judith, I only meant that the whole thing will disappear into limbo while they sort that one out. And, of course, there's a problem about Selina's shares. If they passed to Richard they go with his estate.'

'*If* they passed?'

'You usually have a clause saying the beneficiary must survive thirty days – that's to avoid two sets of estate duty.'

Judith looked at her, appalled. 'So Selina's shares may go back to her family, and get lost there?'

'Indeed. But, sorry, there is no way of avoiding bad taste in this conversation, this confusion may help you. At the moment, so far as I can see, no one can pass good title to Richard or Selina's shares. Not to Mr Rubin, not to anybody until in some indeterminate future both Richard and Selina's estates get probate. *Then*, of course, executors will want to sell – what are they going to do with unquoted shares in a small business? But Mr Rubin may have gone away.' Francesca was momentarily carried away by a vision of the future. 'Then you'd have the chance to make an offer for both lots. With the restaurant here open again you could raise the money.'

'You've forgotten Michael.'

'Ah. I *had* forgotten him. But Judith, surely, if Mr Rubin goes away then it's all quite different. Unless there is a purchaser banging on your door it must be right to buy in any loose shares and trade on. Your Michael's a banker, after all.'

They looked at each other and Judith nodded. '*If* we could just get the place open and trading, at a proper margin, I could put in an expensive general manager here which would give me more free time.' She had gone pink with excitement, her mind obviously racing over the detail. 'Michael may still not like it much, but . . .'

'In the situation we envisage, he won't have a lot of choice – I mean none of you do. So a few graceful concessions on your part, like a general manager . . .'

'Yes. Oh yes. Now all I need is someone who wants a long-term investment in a restaurant.' She stopped and looked guiltily at Francesca. 'This is awful – I can't be doing this.'

Francesca considered her. 'Did you like Richard?'

'No. But I wouldn't have wished that on him.' Her voice went shrill and her eyes were bright, but she steadied herself and smiled across at the silent Francesca. 'Thanks. You're right. Now all I have to do is talk to Michael. And pray that Tony doesn't break an arm in the next four weeks.'

'Or a leg?' Francesca wondered.

'He doesn't need legs to cook with.'

Matthew arrived in the crowded reception room of Graebner Associates, full of the usual mix of every race under the sun, mostly with the kids as well, and made for his senior partner.

'Was that all right? You rang them and told them day after tomorrow?' Peter Graebner was ushering out one client, a sullen

Caribbean, fifteen years old, hair in elaborate plaits, and collecting another, a small anxious Chinese man and wife, but paused, seeing Matthew's face.

'Yes. I'd have liked to get it over with, but we can't get a banker's draft till tomorrow, at the earliest. So Friday's safe.'

Peter smiled gently at the Chinese couple and indicated that he would be with them shortly and they sank back on their chairs, watching him intently.

'That will be all right though. They are men of their word. In their field.'

'Yeh. Sorry. I'm still having trouble with the idea of handing over near on £10,000 to people like that.'

'Better than drug dealers.'

There was a message here, as Matt well appreciated. Not for those who had indulged in soft drugs and dealt with the people who purveyed them, to be unduly censorious about bookmakers, whose trade was not illegal.

'Gimme a break, Peter.'

His senior partner's spectacles glinted at him. 'Ring your client, won't you? He'll be glad to know he can go to work safely.'

Judith, completing a slow tour of inspection, picked her way through wood shavings and cardboard boxes to the door and was surprised to find the late evening sun shining. She stood, watching the home-going traffic thirty feet away across the broad pavement and the early evening theatre crowds, some stopping hopefully to look at the front of the restaurant, faces falling in disappointment as they realised it was closed. She sighed; she, too, wished it was open to welcome in all these passers-by. She reminded herself that, disaster as the fire had been, when they reopened the Caff would be sparkling new; after four years it had been getting shabby despite persistent maintenance and some of the kitchen equipment had been wearing badly. No one could welcome a fire and a restaurant closed for two weeks, but it was not all loss; at some time in the next year they would have had to close to refurbish for at least a week.

A Jaguar, chauffeur driven, pulled up by the kerb and she watched incuriously as the driver got out. His passengers were not waiting to be released and she stepped back involuntarily as Brian Rubin, expensively attired in a baggy linen suit and fashionably tieless, unfolded himself on to the pavement. Another man, conventionally dressed, was walking round the car from the off-side, and she saw it was Michael. He said something to the driver who nodded and slid back into the car, and she braced herself for whatever was to come. Brian Rubin came over to her, hand extended, so she had to take it.

'Judith. How are you? I am so sorry about Richard . . .'

He was, she saw, incredulous; he was looking haggard, and his eyes were watering. He produced a handkerchief and, unembarrassed, mopped them. 'Terrible thing to happen. The poor bugger, excuse me.'

Michael had come up behind him and kissed her, pressing her to him. He was upset too, she could feel it right through his body.

'What a bloody day.' He was holding her as if he had reached home after a shipwreck, and Brian Rubin looked away, tactfully. 'I need a drink. But I don't suppose we've got one in there, just at the moment.'

'We do in the office, if you don't mind fighting your way through the whole of the bar fittings which are parked there.' She was pointedly not looking at Brian Rubin, but saw from Michael's expression that he was going to form part of the conversation. She took them through the Café; Brian Rubin, professional that he was, would understand that they were not all that far from being able to reopen.

'You've done brilliant, Judith,' he said, as they went through the kitchen. 'Wouldn't have believed it from when I saw it Sunday.'

'Thank you,' she said, demurely. 'Tony has worked like a Trojan. He's just catching up with his sleep, but he'll be in again later.' She wanted the besieging general to know that the inmates of the citadel were all of one mind and preparing to repel him. Brian's eyebrows lifted but he took the point, and so, she saw, did her lover. He was looking wretched, shoulders slumped in the good suit, walking heavily. She distributed drinks and they stood awkwardly in the crowded office, Michael gazing silently out of the window. He came back from wherever he had been and looked across at her in appeal, and she stiffened her back, feeling her rigid defences being undermined.

'Brian came to me this afternoon because he has something important to tell us. Important to all of us.'

'I can't imagine what.' She needed to discharge the hostility she felt to both of them. Brian, leaning against the dismantled bar, looked at her steadily.

'Thing is, Richard's death means his shares pass to me. Or rather to my company. We made a deal, six months ago.'

181

'What?' She felt dazed and stupid.

'He needed money. So he borrowed from me, and I took a call option on his shares, which I could exercise if he didn't repay the loan within a year. Or, of course, if he died. That's a standard clause in these agreements, only no one thought – I certainly didn't – that it was actually going to happen. You know.'

She did indeed, she thought, appalled. The agreement she and Tony Gallagher had signed only on Monday had exactly that clause in it; Tony had observed, not wholly in joke, that he'd better watch his step with her, to which she had countered that she was doing the deal to keep her head chef alive and on the job not in order to murder him. She looked at Michael who was examining the contents of his glass.

'*You* knew he had mortgaged his shares.'

'He only told me last week. And to be frank I thought Brian was very ill advised to lend on the shares. He can't make the other shareholders accept the transfer. The Articles say we don't have to. As he knows.'

He was still not quite looking at her and she watched his fingers clenched on his glass.

'Did Richard ask you for a loan?'

'No. Well, only on Selina's shares and only in the most general terms and he knew we wouldn't do it. I've never been prepared to lend money myself, and there was no point asking the bank to do it. Not with Richard's track record. He wasn't asking seriously.' He managed to look at her and her heart twisted. He was miserable and on the wrong foot, and so was she.

'I'll bugger off.' Brian Rubin finished his drink in one swallow. 'You two need to talk. But look, Judith, we are where we are. I think you're terrific, and we'd be better off cooperating than fighting. You can have any deal you need – shares in the combined group, joint managing director, whatever. And I need Tony too, tell him. You're both as good as or better than anyone I've got, just say what you want.' He put his glass down, tidily, and considered her, and swept her into a warm hairy embrace to which she could not but yield. 'Either way,' he said, seriously, disentangling himself, but still holding her hands, 'you've got a great future in the business – I'd just like it to be with me.' He kissed her cheek and took himself off, having achieved an unimprovable exit.

'Bloody cheek,' she said, gazing at the swinging door.

182

'Oh, I agree. But he did what I wanted to. Come here.' Michael had crossed from the window and turned her to him and wrapped his arms round her. 'God, what a day. Poor Richard. I can't get it out of my head.' He was crying, she realised, as she held him, and found herself weeping too. 'We need to talk, but I don't want to now. In fact, there's only one thing I do want and there isn't anywhere here, so I want to take you home.'

Agonised, she thought of the specialist lighting man, due in forty minutes, and absolutely needing to be seen if the restaurant was to be lit for next week. Her head cleared. 'There's a bed here. In the back room. I don't think it's got things all over it.'

'Still?'

'We never got rid of it after the rush to get set up here. We – Selina and me – used to kip here if we couldn't get home.' She tugged at his hand. 'Come and see.'

'No.' His grip on her tightened. 'I want to be with you out of here, for God's sake.'

Tony, she thought, gratefully, hearing a familiar voice, shouting the odds. Tony could cope with the lights man; they had agreed that morning what was wanted and marked the catalogue subject only to questions of price and delivery. And she could go back with Michael and get into bed with him which she needed and wanted. 'Darling, it's all right. We'll go. I just have to have ten minutes with Tony, then I'm free. Sit here and have a coffee, I promise I'll be back by the time you've finished it.'

She was back just outside the ten minutes, but he had got himself a coffee, and was standing, leaning on a filing cabinet. She kissed him and collected her handbag, checking for keys, and sorting quickly through the odd bits of paper that had accumulated during the day, pausing to scribble another message for Tony while he watched.

'You're relying pretty heavily on Gallagher, aren't you? On a chap who's been stealing from us? And who can't wait to sell?'

'It's a bit different now. And he's going to repay what he took.' She decided that now was not the moment to reveal the rest of her arrangements with Chef. 'We need him, yes. We could open the doors without him but no one would get anything to eat. There are no spare head chefs who can manage a kitchen turning out four hundred covers a day. Conran was the final straw, they're all working for him.'

He was looking hostile as well as miserable, and she sought to distract him. 'I'm throwing away the paracetamol – I'll find something else to fix a headache.'

'Because of Richard?'

'Because of Richard. He never would use it, or let Selina. And even though I don't have his liver I think I'll find something else.' She looked at him. 'What is it?'

He was staring at her incredulously. 'I didn't know he didn't – normally – use paracetamol.' He looked past her unseeingly, then spread his hands. 'Well, that clinches it, doesn't it? He *meant* to do it. Thank God.'

'Darling?'

'I've been feeling terrible. I thought he just blundered out of bed, still pissed, after I'd gone and took a handful, and it was all a ghastly accident which I could have stopped. But if he knew about paracetamol, then he did it deliberately. He killed Selina, and he meant to kill himself. Christ, what a relief.' He pulled himself out of the chair and enveloped her in a bear hug. 'Home. Quick. I could even fancy something to eat. Afterwards, I mean.'

Francesca crept silently out of Will's room, holding her breath. He had been tired and fretful when she got back from a long day at Gladstone, worn out by attendance at the birthday party of a fellow toddler. He had practically slept in his bath and managed half a cup of milk before being rolled into his cot. He turned on his back and complained briefly, but then his eyes had closed and he had disappeared into the utterly silent sleep of childhood. She remembered, wryly, as she slipped away that the first night they had brought him home from hospital, aged six days, she had sat outside his bedroom listening to his quiet breathing, tense with anxiety. John had finally had to take her firmly downstairs, pointing out that there was no reason for Will to stop breathing, once he had started, and in any case she could not spend the rest of her nights on the stairs, it was impracticable.

She would not be so tense and so anxious with a second whatever it was, she assured herself, it would all be much easier. She found she had sat down on the stairs at the very thought of a second sleeping baby, and got hastily to her feet again. She had something on her conscience and if the information had not already reached John by another route, she would have to tell him, even if he was angry. Alcohol would help, she hoped; one of Perry's Christmas presents had been a case of really good Beaujolais, and a bottle was sitting near the warmth of the stove.

He was home on time, but looking tired and harassed, and she gave him a glass with the soup while the griddle heated, ready for steak *au poivre*. She asked after his day generally and more particularly, about progress in the Café de la Paix case. She busied herself with the steaks – the sauce needed careful timing – and put them on the table with green beans and courgettes. He ate, ravenously; he must have missed lunch again, but she was not going to nag. She waited for her moment, which she had calculated would come just before the raspberries and cream.

'There's something I'm not sure you will have picked up. At Café de la Paix. Judith told me that Richard Marsh-Hayden knew all about the risks of paracetamol on a duff liver. He never bought it, or let Selina do so either. So he must have meant to do himself in.' She looked at him. 'I thought that was helpful in case you were in doubt.'

'He never used it? Or bought it?'

'Apparently not.'

'Had he been told not to use it? Did Judith Delves say? Was this medical advice?'

'No, no.' She told him about the awful story of the repentant teenager; it made her feel queasy even in the retelling, but she knew that her policeman husband had seen most horrors in the course of his career and he would not be put off his dinner. He was sitting very still, eyes narrowed, and she looked at him enquiringly.

'So he chose the most frightening way to die he could think of,' he said, slowly, and she sat down, slowly.

'Put like that . . .' she said, hesitantly.

She passed him his raspberries, understanding he was still preoccupied, which he started to eat. She watched, with love, as he suddenly tasted what he was eating and looked at them to check. 'Raspberries.'

'And cream and sugar; I put them on for you.'

'Very good.' He grinned at her. 'I'm not that cross with you for pointing out something we'd missed. And I'd have got there tomorrow, I hope.'

'Of course you would.' This was not simply support for male ego, which she as sister to four brothers knew was much more frail than was generally understood. It was not luck that had propelled her husband to his present eminence, nor intuition, although his was highly developed, but sheer hard work and patience and never neglecting the obvious, even though his well-trained team hadn't seen it. He stretched out a hand.

'Now come on, you're a good useful girl and a credit to the Force, but I got home early so we could have an evening together.'

13

'Mary, what are you doing?'

Mary Cameron, on her knees on the floor of the inner office, looked up at her, pink and flushed. 'I can't stand it any more.'

Judith felt the blood go from her face. 'But Mary . . .'

'Oh, Judith. No, I didn't mean *here*, I only meant the mess in the office. Oh dear. Sit down, I'll make us some coffee.'

She rose clumsily to her feet, and Judith let herself be pressed into a chair. 'It's just depressing, being in this office,' Mary said, firmly, finding the kettle. 'I thought I would tidy up and pile all the menus and the paper napkins and so on in the inner office so that we aren't falling over them all the time. We'll both feel better.'

'Miss Delves? Inspector Davidson here.'

He was looking through the door, the bright eyes interested.

'Just having coffee,' Mary said.

'Someone been in?' He glanced round the office, small objects on every surface.

'I'm afraid it just looks like that, Inspector,' Judith said, grimly. 'What can we do for you?'

'My guvnor's here. Chief Superintendent McLeish. Be up in a moment.'

Judith, tired to the bone, managed not to say that this was a rare pleasure, keenly awaited. Mary, who had a soft spot for good-looking Scots, was organising coffee for Bruce Davidson, sniffing at half-empty cartons of milk and fussing about getting some fresh from the men working downstairs, or going out to the corner café. Judith was listening for the lift and was taken aback when the latch on the office door clicked and John McLeish was in the room, carrying something small in a plastic bag.

'Good morning, Miss Delves, Mrs Cameron. Bruce.' He held up the bag. 'There's a sergeant downstairs somewhere. Find him, would you? I wanted to ask Miss Delves and Mrs Cameron about it first. Ah.' His attention had been caught by something and Davidson checked on his way to the door. 'Is that bottle kept up here all the time?'

Judith looked blankly at the crowded desk. 'Bottle? Oh. The paracetamol, you mean? No. I turned it out of my handbag.'

'When?'

'When I heard about Richard.'

He considered her, and she felt small and stupid, like a child. 'Right. After he died. Yesterday.'

'Yes.'

'But you had it in your handbag?'

'Yes. It is my drug of choice for a headache. And I've had a few of those.' She had one now, suddenly, but she could not, of course, take a pill for it. Or not until there was a moment when Mary could be asked to get some aspirin.

'That's what I take as well,' Mary volunteered, and for a moment John McLeish's attention shifted, then returned like a searchlight. He held up the plastic bag.

'There were two packets in the kitchen.'

'What, still?' She had surprised him, she saw, and was momentarily cheered. 'With all the workmen, I mean. There is – was – always some there on a shelf to the right of the second hob. Next to the omelette pans. Usually the soluble sort. I know because I used to get them there if I couldn't be bothered to go up to the office.' She hesitated. 'There are normally a couple of packets at the reception desk too, but I don't know if they're still there.'

Nothing seemed to pass between John McLeish and his sidekick, but Davidson was gone, his footsteps audible on the stairs. In the background the kettle had boiled, and Mary was hovering, trying to decide whether she should make coffee.

'I need coffee. Will you have some, Chief Superintendent?' She looked up to where he was standing like something carved from a tree trunk.

'Yes, please. Two sugars,' he said to her relief, and moved to perch on the edge of a desk.

'You think Richard took paracetamol from here?' she ventured.

'Not necessarily.'

The phone rang and she picked up, then handed it to him.

'Three packets and two bottles.' His eyebrows moved. 'Right. Yes, take them all, give them to the DC down there, tell him to get them off.'

'What are you going to do with them?'

'Tests.'

She thought about it. 'Fingerprints. But everybody's will be on them. I mean, they're communal. The ones at reception are in case a customer comes in with a headache.'

'We have most of yours on file, I believe.'

They did, she remembered; on the day after Selina's body had been discovered they had all had their fingerprints taken. It had been just another not quite real event of that awful day. She was suddenly overcome with exhaustion; this had all been going on for ever. 'Why does it matter where he got the paracetamol? Is it worse if he picked it up here than if he bought it?' She was sounding shrill, she could hear, but it provoked no reaction at all. He was listening to something, she realised, and heard voices on the stairs.

'I didn't fucking *know* he shouldn't take the stuff, did I?' The door opened to reveal Tony Gallagher in a grubby tunic with 'Chef' on the pocket, with Davidson and another big man in the inevitable grey suit and white shirt; they really might as well wear a uniform jacket and helmet, she thought.

'Mr Gallagher says he gave Mr Marsh-Hayden four paracetamols dissolved in water on the Monday around 8 p.m.'

'He'd passed himself out, then he came round with a thick head. We wanted to get him out of here, so I gave him something I take when I've got a head. Soluble, see, they work quicker.' He looked across at Judith in appeal. 'Oh Christ! I only meant . . .'

'He'd had more than four,' John McLeish said, matter-of-factly.

'Tony, did he know they were paracetamol?' Judith asked.

John McLeish's head lifted, sharply, but he did not intervene.

'He wouldn't have known if they was fucking arsenic, Judy. He had a bad head, he needed to shift the pain, he just drank it down without asking questions.'

'Did anyone else give him anything? Or did he take anything else while he was here?' John McLeish was somehow managing to sound only casually interested.

'I dunno, mate. Look, he was here, pissed, and in the way. I wanted him gone, Michael wanted him gone, so did Brian Rubin, so they could have a little get-together. If he'd wanted some more, they'd have given him some. Why don't you ask them?'

'We shall. Did you leave the packet with them?'

'Didn't *take* the packet. I mixed the stuff in the kitchen, put the packet back next to the Bandaid. Can't operate a shift without that stuff; or the Alka Seltzer.'

Yes, Judith thought, and if you looked at anyone's workplace you would find, along with the materials for doing their job, the particular medicaments they favoured. Along with Chef's favourite knife and his best omelette pan went the headache pills and the barley sugar sweets he sucked. And no one in Tony's kitchen would take even one without his consent, and it was quite inconceivable that anyone would remove a whole package. She cleared her throat.

'You'll find another bottle in my top drawer, Chief Superintendent. Along with other necessities.' She watched as Bruce Davidson and the other policeman, wearing thin plastic gloves, went through all the desks, hers and Mary's, ignoring sanitary towels, packets of raisins, wine gums, old combs, and producing, finally, five bottles of paracetamol, varying from full to half empty, two packets of the same, soluble, and three packets of Anadin. 'Selina didn't take paracetamol,' she said, wearily. 'Richard wouldn't let her. I kept aspirin and the Anadin for her.'

'We all went in the car to get him home, Michael and Brian Rubin and me. That night.' Tony Gallagher was pale and sweating around the hair-line.

John McLeish nodded; he'd known that, she understood.

'I'd like to get a statement from you, Mr Gallagher, now. Just about the events of Monday evening.'

'I'd like my solicitor here.'

'Matthew Sutherland? Certainly, if you wish. Ring him now.' He looked round the crowded office. 'Get him to meet you at New Scotland Yard, will you? As soon as he can. Can you use another phone? I want another word with Miss Delves. No, not you, Mrs Cameron, thank you, you weren't here on Monday as I understand it. You could come to New Scotland Yard, Miss Delves, if that suits you better?'

'No,' she said, through a tight throat. If Mary would not mind going and perhaps getting in some more supplies, tea, coffee and milk, if she would? The big sergeant helpfully offered to escort her, and Davidson held the door open so Mary had no choice but to leave, making only two forays back, first for her bag then for her coat. Bruce Davidson, in answer to an invisible signal from McLeish, followed the party out.

'This doesn't need to be formal, yet,' McLeish said, surprising her. 'And I've understood about the paracetamol. Tell me about the safe. Mrs Cameron found it open; she told one of my people.'

She told him promptly about the scene with Richard, and how she had not liked to leave the cash in the big safe.

'But you shut the big safe then?'

'Oh yes. And put the cash in the old safe.'

'And you think you closed it?'

'Yes, I do.'

'Do you know the combination by heart?'

'Of the big safe, yes. The old safe – the little one – happened to be open when I wanted to put the cash in. I had to look it up to open it yesterday.'

'And where would you look it up?'

Her heart sank; she had hoped that somehow he would miss this point. 'In the card index, on the desk there.' She made to pick up the old red leather box.

'Don't touch it, please.'

Her hand checked, and he waited while she got herself back in place.

'Under what would the number be filed?'

'Well. Under S, I'm afraid.'

'S for safe.' He sounded only mildly surprised, and she looked at him with despair.

'I know, I know. And if – when – we get back into order all that will be changed. Selina could never remember the number of the big safe and there was a panic one morning, so we put it on the card. We put the number of the old safe there as well.'

'Who else would have known that?'

'Well, Richard obviously did. He put the file of letters in it.'

'Yes.' McLeish was used to people under stress explaining the obvious, but he was also in a hurry and she blushed.

'I imagine everyone did. Or could have, which must come to the same thing.'

'Mr Gallagher?'

'Yes,' she said, reluctantly. 'He's in and out of the office all the time, and he and Mary work together a lot . . .' Her mind was not entirely on him, she was worrying away at something, he saw, and waited. 'Those letters. Were they . . .'

McLeish decided she could be helpful. 'Those letters are still being scheduled. But some are from men, and make it clear that she was still having affairs after her marriage.'

'Yes. I think I knew she was. She got letters here marked "Personal" which no one would have opened.'

'If we asked you to identify handwriting, would you be able to?'

She winced and he considered his statement. 'On an envelope, that is. She kept them too.'

'I would be glad to try.' She paused for thought. 'But, you know, unless you work with someone, or live with them, you don't see their handwriting. So I may not be much use.'

This had not been, he saw, what she was really thinking about, and he sat on the edge of a desk to give her time to elucidate her next worry.

'There is something I need to tell you.'

'What?'

She went to her bag and got out a letter which had the look of having been read a dozen times already. 'Selina and I are – were – of course insured as key men. As people of key importance to the business.' She looked at him to see if he understood and saw that he did. 'Originally for £30,000 each. That was four years ago, when we started.'

'Yes?'

'Then two months ago, I was looking at the insurance on the building and I found the policy and thought it really seemed too little. £30,000, I mean. So I put it up to £100,000 each.' She looked at him, but he was registering nothing. 'I'd forgotten about it. I can't believe it, but I had. Mary sent a copy of the death certificate to our insurance broker, because we needed to get him to change the signatures. Only she didn't know I'd increased it. So this morning my broker's asking me to fill up a claim form and saying what a good thing we had increased it.'

'So you will get £100,000?'

'Not me personally. It's the company's money. But it means we can pay the outstanding bills and get open again.'

'And without it?'

'I have a meeting with the bank manager this morning. And we weren't paying any bills and I wasn't sure ... well, what he would do. I'll go to the meeting, but now I only have to give him this letter.'

She looked at him, in appeal, but he was remembering his conversation with Francesca. With the restaurant closed, cash poured out, bills poured in and your only hope was the bank who might well have been unreceptive to a request for a substantial loan. But surely no competent person running their own business could actually have forgotten how much insurance they had? Failed to remember to take insurance perhaps, but forgotten how much it was? He considered her; she was sitting on her big chair, defiantly drinking coffee, a big capable young woman in her workmanlike navy boiler suit. Her late partner, attention only half on the business, forever being distracted by her admirers, must have sometimes annoyed her beyond bearing. And it must have been about the time she was renewing the insurance that Judith Delves would have realised that this partner had managed so badly as to leave the business perilously short of cash and that they might be in a position where they had to sell.

'When did the sale negotiations start? I mean, was that what triggered a reconsideration of your insurance position?'

She had got the point, he saw, as her hands went still and her neck tensed. 'No. No, it was an annual routine. Delayed as it happens, because I was off site, but we did it every year. The auditors insist.'

Now that was true, in general, but a word with the auditors generally was well overdue.

'Right,' he said, having waited to see that she had said all that she was going to. 'I'll ask you to say all that again, as a formal statement. No, don't move, I'll ask Inspector Davidson to come up.'

Michael Owens had arrived much later than he meant to, but he was sleeping badly and having corresponding difficulty in getting up. If he couldn't get in some days at nine thirty rather than the 8 a.m. start which was *de rigueur* for the younger directors it was ridiculous, he told himself as he went past the bank reception. It was a new man on the desk who insisted on seeing his pass, so he had to stop. He was feeling quite alienated and surly enough to have refused, but the bank's head of personnel was there behind him, waiting for the lift. So he had to dig papers out of his briefcase and find the pass, with its annoying little tag with which the young and keen attached it to the pockets of their jackets, and then put it away again. The head of personnel, Peter Redfern, a sardonic forty-year-old, had just whisked into a lift, the doors closing in Michael's face, so he had to wait for another one.

And when he reached his own office his secretary was there to remind him that he had a date with Simon in half an hour. He hadn't forgotten but he had pushed it to the back of his mind, and no wonder, he thought self-pityingly. He looked again at the outline notes he had, of three ideas which just might work, but they looked even thinner and less substantial than they had on Tuesday when he had cobbled them together. A junior had done some research on one of them, but he had all too clearly not found the idea carried conviction and the three neatly typed pages and six tables got no one any further. He had read the *Financial Times* which seemed to be full of enviable deals being done by other people, but he flipped through the four papers that arrived for him every morning, hoping for inspiration. GIRL IN FREEZER CASE: HUSBAND DIES he saw on page two of the *Mirror* and read it carefully. It had a definitive elegiac quality, much more restrained than the paper's original reporting of Selina's death. A spokesman for the Metropolitan Police Force must have indicated pretty strongly that no one need expect any more excitement or new developments in this particular case.

'Five to, Michael.' His secretary came in to take his out-tray away, but he had not even looked at his morning mail. He fell on it, hopefully, but there was nothing there, except invitations, appeals for charity and booklets from solicitors on the latest developments in company law. Well, so what if he didn't have a lot to say to Simon Rutherford, he could confess as much and creep, crawl, add that Simon had been quite right about the distraction potential of the Café de la Paix and ask for a week's leave now to sort it out.

Peter Redfern was coming out of Simon's outer office as he went in and gave him a constrained smile. Simon's secretary was seated in front of her PC, watching the blinking light on the telephone, and he opened his mouth to say he would go away if now were not convenient. The light blinked off and she waved him in without looking at him. He checked, instincts alert, but there was no other place to go, so he went forward, heart hammering.

'Come and sit down, Mike.' The bastard wasn't looking at him either. He took a chair and launched into his prepared speech, but Simon Rutherford held up his hand after the opening sentence. 'Mike. That isn't . . . well, it's not what's been agreed.' He ploughed on, not looking at him. 'I've consulted the rest of the Executive Committee and they are supporting my view that the department needs thinning out at the top. You've had a good run, your contribution's been appreciated, but you're obviously developing other interests, and I need to bring in some new people. And I need to make some space.' He managed to look him in the face if not the eye. 'We'll honour your contract of course, help you as much as we can to find somewhere else, but it's not working for us here, or for you.'

He sat, feeling ill with rage, staring at the man, wanting to hit him, but understood that he would have to salvage what he could. 'I'm entitled to a year's notice,' he managed to say, fairly calmly. 'I'd like to work six months of it; easier to get a job from here than if I'm sitting at home.'

'You won't be. We'll pay for outplacement, to give you the best possible chance.'

'I don't want that. I'd rather be here.' Under notice or not, if he made a deal work they'd keep him, they'd have to. The bastard was sweating, he saw, and he felt marginally, fractionally less desperate.

'I'm sorry, Mike, that option's not on offer. The Executive Committee are quite clear on this, we don't want people who have every reason to be unhappy still sitting around. Bad for morale.'

He felt such rage overwhelming him that he had to grip the table. 'So what is your plan?'

'Peter Redfern is waiting to go through all that with you.'

He should have known that nothing short of firing a director got the head of personnel out of his cosy fifth-floor office. He sat, trying to assimilate what was happening to him. 'You've got someone coming in?'

Simon Rutherford hardly blinked. 'I was going on to tell you. Martin Withers. From Schroders. Young but promising, and a retail specialist. We're announcing it tomorrow.'

'And when are you announcing me?'

'That's negotiable, and Peter Redfern is the chap to talk to, OK? I'm sorry, but I hope you'll come to feel it's a new start.' He stood and extended his hand, but Michael ignored it, he was so choked with anger that he knew he would pull the bastard's arm off if he touched him. He walked blindly out of the door, into Peter Redfern; Simon's secretary had vanished.

'I can't talk now,' he managed to say.

'Come and have coffee.' The man was shielding him from the passers-by in the corridor and he understood that he would have to hit him to get rid of him, so he walked with him, dumb with rage and grief, to the lift.

'I bet they've got this place wired.'

Tony Gallagher and Matthew Sutherland were having a conference in the tiny cramped coffee-bar just over the road from New Scotland Yard.

'We don't have time to worry about that,' Matthew said, firmly. He had fixed up this meeting in a hurry, not thinking carefully enough. The place would not be wired, but given its location some of the customers probably worked at New Scotland Yard. But he had to talk to Tony; several elements of the confused recital he had already received over the phone worried him considerably. The vital thing was to calm his client down. 'Tony. For a start, if Richard died of paracetamol poisoning, of course they're going to check what he had. They do that even if they think he took them deliberately. They don't think any different now, it's just that the bloke's dead, right?'

'Came straight to me though. There was three of us took him home, got him to bed. Michael, Brian Rubin and me. It was Michael's car, see, and Brian and me just wanted to get home, we both live that way, and he offered us a ride. 'Course, once I got in the car they had a go at me about getting on with the sale, could I talk to Judy?'

'Did you tell them? About the agreement?'

'None of their fucking business.'

That was hardly fair as well as being literally untrue, but Matthew let it pass. It was true that the banker's draft from Judith had only reached the client account that morning, and so the transaction had not formally been completed on Monday when this conversation had been held. The real reason for Tony not wanting to talk to Michael Owens, or Brian Rubin, was that he was feeling a fool, as he should more usefully have felt months ago. He was wishing to postpone, hopefully for ever, confessing the extent to which he had handed over control of his destiny.

'Did any of the others give Richard anything to take?'

Tony hesitated. 'Didn't see them. We all went upstairs, but it was Michael who got him into bed – he's strong, that bloke, carted Richard up the last bit where the stairs are narrow by himself. He said he'd left water beside him – Brian asked.'

'Was Richard right out of it then?'

Tony thought. 'I've seen blokes like that, they get up good as new after a few hours' sleep.' He took a mouthful of his coffee. 'This is good, what machine are they using?' He got up to peer over the counter while Matthew caught up with his notes. He waited while his client exchanged words with the proprietor and came back, tucking a slip of paper into his top pocket. The truly interesting thing about Tony Gallagher was that, by luck, he had found something that worked for him, that did not involve violence; a man who could check out a coffee machine while waiting to be interviewed by the police was truly interested in his subject. A thought struck him, sparked by the coffee.

'When Richard was at the Caff, and you were sobering him up, did he have anything else to drink, or eat?'

'Wouldn't eat, but he had about eight cups of coffee. Michael kept feeding them to him, and walking him to keep him awake. Brian Rubin helped too. 'Course, Richard had been in the office a lot of the day, we was too busy to care provided he was out the way. And he must have had a skinful there, but I don't know what. We put the bar supplies up there, Sunday, so could have been anything.'

Matt looked at his watch. 'I can't think you've got a lot to worry about, Tony. Just tell them all that.'

His client looked at him sideways. 'You're saying I got you out of your cot for nothing? I don't trust them buggers.'

'No, I wasn't saying that.' He was watching his client's hands, fiddling with a teaspoon. 'Tony. Anything else you're worrying about?'

'Nah. Not really.'

'You'll break that.' As he spoke there was a snapping noise and they both gazed at two bits of metal which had been a perfectly good teaspoon.

'Jesus.' Tony palmed the bits, one large hand swallowing them. 'This whole thing, it's got to me.' He looked sidelong at Matthew, who froze. There was, as Peter Graebner had always reminded him, a real danger in being close to the clients. You could not do your real work of defending them to the best of your ability if they had honoured you with their confidence in a way that made it clear they were guilty as charged. 'There is one thing.'

Matthew breathed again; no one prefaced a confession to murder in those terms.

'Last time we saw the big chap, McLeish, he was going on about what happened the last night Selina was around. When we had a row in the kitchen. He didn't believe what I'd said.'

'About the row? No, he didn't, but he didn't think it mattered, did he? After all, she wasn't killed then.'

Tony fidgeted, reaching for another spoon, which Matthew captured. 'Fuck. Well, it didn't have anything to do with Selina, but thing is I was in the office. Just for about twenty minutes.'

Matt waited but nothing seemed to be coming. 'What were you doing?'

His client gazed at the sandwich counter. 'Maria. This waitress. She was there too.'

Matt started to laugh. 'Like when I came round that Saturday.'

Gallagher grinned. 'Yeh. That's right. Only on the bed. In the inner office.'

'Why didn't you say?'

' 'Cos she's married.'

Matt gazed at him, trying not to let his jaw drop. 'To one of my sous chefs. Yeh, I know. Anyway, I didn't want it, you know, on paper anywhere. And I didn't want her having to be interviewed, like. I mean he'd of wondered. Jean-Pierre.'

'There's a bed up there?' Matt asked, to give himself time to think.

'Yeh. It's always been there. I wouldn't like Judy to know either, know what I mean?'

From everything he read about successful chefs, this behaviour was probably not out of line. But involving, as it did, the wife of a sous chef, and coming on top of excessive and stupid gambling, it might indeed worry an employer and Matt could see why his client might prefer to keep it to himself. The police were not that careful about keeping information confidential either.

'They want to talk about Richard Marsh-Hayden,' he pointed out. 'If they ask you again about Selina's death you have to tell them. Better be embarrassed than nicked.'

'All right.' Gallagher, like all clients, was happy to put the responsibility for a decision on to his lawyer; that, as Peter Graebner used to observe, was the trap. 'And talking of embarrassment, I signed the thing – the draft – and left it at your office, this morning. Can you hand it over today?'

'I've got a date for tomorrow. They know it's coming, don't worry.'

'They're fucking dangerous, these people.'

'Not if you don't owe them money.' Matt decided he was entitled to the last word. 'Come on then, let's get this over with, it's half-past.'

Tony Gallagher turned his key in the back door of Café de la Paix, hoping that the massed building trades had not left something heavy against it. There were no lights showing in the floors above, and he grinned to himself as the door yielded, smoothly.

'Come on Maria, it's OK.'

The very tall, pale blonde behind him blinked at him and smiled, tremulously.

'Or we could go back to my place? There's no one there till the morning, but it's a bit of a way out.'

'No, Tony, I mus' go home not too late. Jean-Pierre knows I finish at twelve at Caff 2.'

'So we've got an hour and a half. Lucky if I can keep going that long.' They were through the door, inside the silent, dusty building and he wrapped his arms round her, gently biting her ear while he listened for voices, or noises. 'Come on then. No, hold on a minute, I'll go up by myself just in case Judy's up there working late – don't think so, but you never know.'

He looked momentarily at the lift but he had not yet been able to bring himself to go in it after the police had indicated that it could be used normally. And now wasn't the time to start, so he took off up the stairs, two at a time, arriving, chest heaving, outside the office. Another snag occurred to him, but the door handle turned easily and the door opened on to a darkened room, the shapes of the desks and filing cabinets illumined by the display boards of the theatre opposite, and by a street light somewhere to the right. He hesitated, then took two steps towards the left-hand side of the room and the door which was the only access to the smaller inner office, and froze, because the door was open and there was a faint light reflecting on the piece of wall he could see. He walked towards it, hesitantly. 'Hello?' I must be daft, he thought, but his pressing need for the little bed which was housed in the office overcame caution and he pushed on to see who had left a light on.

It was coming from a desk lamp, sat insecurely on the floor, and there was no one by it, or visible. Someone left it on, he thought, not stopping to examine why anyone would want a light placed so that they and whatever they were looking at would have to be on the floor with it. He reached for the switch at the right-hand side of the door when an appalling pain started above his left ear and he saw a string of stars as he fell to the floor and into unconsciousness.

'Tony?' The pale blonde girl, waiting in the darkness below, heard the heavy thud of his fall. She called again but there was no answer; she heard running steps, then the lift gates clash. She stood, stupidly wondering why Tony was coming down again, then realised, her danger understood, where the lift would stop and fled up the stairs, terrified, hearing over the gasps of her own breath the whine of the lift as it went down and the ping as it stopped. The back door banged as she pressed herself against the staircase wall, sick with fright, and it took several minutes of silence for her to be able to gather herself together and decide that she dared not run into the tiny back passage where horror might be lying in wait, but must force herself upwards. She was gasping with fright as she found the light switch, but there was no one there. She saw the light in the inner office and gasped for air, ready to run, but then she saw a familiar pair of legs on the floor.

'Tony,' she screamed, and ran to him, but he was limp and his head was covered with blood. 'Oh Tony.' She started to cry, helplessly, shaking with fright so that the task of dialling 999 eluded her trembling hands the first twice she tried. Then every word of English seemed to have deserted her and she poured out the story in a mixture of French and sobs, so that it was a good twenty minutes before ambulance men and an accompanying paramedic were thumping up the stairs, carrying their heavy equipment.

14

'No, it looked much like this yesterday, except the safe was closed.'
John McLeish had been woken at one thirty that morning to be told
that there was another development in the Café de la Paix saga, but
on finding that Tony Gallagher was in St Thomas's, unconscious but
stable, that the young woman who had found him was also there, in
shock, with policemen at both their bedsides, and that the office
premises at the Café were properly secured, he had decided to get
up at an ordinary time. As a carefree bachelor, he reflected, he might
have made a different decision, but rushing to his post at one thirty
in the morning now meant abandoning a pregnant wife to cope with
a child who was probably not going to sleep through the night until
he reached secondary school. His audience, Bruce Davidson, one
sergeant and a DC, gazed at the mess in front of them; papers
covered the bed and the whole of the floor in the inner office.

'The tape on the safe is unbroken, sir. Forensic took all the contents
except the cash, which should be in the big safe in the outer office.'

'It is.' Judith Delves, hollow-eyed from lack of sleep, had got the
main safe open.

'We'll need to seal this office and take everything out,' McLeish
said, raising his voice. 'I'm sorry,' he added, seeing Judith Delves'
face. 'Someone must have been looking for something, you see.'

'Cash, presumably. Someone knew we were a building site here
and closed up after dark.' She was very near the end of her rope, and
McLeish remembered that it was her chef who lay unconscious in St
Thomas's, without whom reopening the restaurant must be difficult
if not impossible.

'Miss Delves, could we have a word?'

He led her back into the main office, indicating to Bruce Davidson
that he should attend while the DC deployed himself elsewhere. He
could hear someone coming up the stairs and turned to dispose of
the interruption, but it was Matthew Sutherland, in a suit, a sight
sufficiently unusual as to give him pause. The lad looked older and
more sharply focused, the dark red hair short and tidy.

'Chief Superintendent.'

'Good morning, Mr Sutherland. How is your client?'

'Still unconscious. I need to tell you without his formal consent about an agreement he has recently made. If Miss Delves has not already told you.'

'I haven't. Is it relevant, Matt?'

The relationship had obviously become easier between these two, he noted.

'It feels as if it is,' Matt Sutherland said, uncompromisingly, and she sighed, made coffee and they sat, she and Matthew perched on desks, and McLeish and Davidson disposed uneasily on the bentwood chairs.

He listened to their joint recital, Matthew's customary spare, economical clarity of explanation, somewhat blurred by Judith Delves, who was exhausted and repeating herself, and adding superfluous detail.

'So you haven't actually handed over the money, Mr Sutherland?' he asked, when he was sure they had finished.

'No. But they knew it was coming today. And Peter – Peter Graebner – made a call this morning and says he is reasonably sure they – the bookies – had nothing to do with the attack. Distressed to have their good faith called into question.'

'The lass with him makes it clear that they were here for other reasons, and surprised an intruder,' Bruce Davidson observed and got a direct look from Matthew.

'My first thought, however, was that he'd been followed. Or that someone who knew his habits was lying in wait for him. It seemed better for the police not to waste time going down that track.'

'I would have been glad to know about Mr Gallagher's financial problems – and this agreement – a bit earlier.'

Judith Delves, blushing, started into an incoherent defence, but McLeish had addressed himself to Matthew and was waiting for an answer.

'My client would have told you as soon as the money had been handed over.'

'Why would you have advised him to wait until then?' McLeish intended to remind young Sutherland that he was professionally an officer of the court, and saw from the way Matthew was gritting his back teeth that he had succeeded.

'It was the best I could do,' he said, baldly, and McLeish only just managed not to laugh. 'And besides,' he added, recovering ground fast, 'we had no reason to believe that my client was your prime suspect in the murder of Mrs Marsh-Hayden. Quite the contrary, in fact.'

From Tuesday morning, when Richard Marsh-Hayden had ended up in hospital full of paracetamol, it had indeed been the case that the police were not seriously looking for anyone else for the murder, as McLeish mentally conceded.

'I was instructed on Sunday in relation to this agreement.' Matthew, who was fully as quick and observant as a good policeman, pressed his advantage.

'You knew, however, before then that he was in financial difficulty.'

'So did you. He came to me because the police had been stirring up his creditors.'

'It's not the same as being told, in good order. You don't get the same answers.' McLeish, stung, spoke evenly, and Matthew sat up straight on his uncomfortable perch.

'I accept that. And you would have been told had we been asked, or had the information seemed relevant. As it now does.'

McLeish, accepting the formal stand-off, thought of delivering the weary speech about the life of investigating officers being made intolerable by people concealing information they did not think relevant, the innocent having nothing to fear, but desisted. It was the wrong audience; the majority of the Graebner Associates clients were guilty, and probably of more than what they were charged with. Matthew's first duty, now and always, was to present his client's best side and suppress the worst without actually misleading the police, and he knew it. But Bruce Davidson's controlled fidget reminded him that all this was a bit more relevant than Matthew was admitting; Judith Delves now controlled twenty per cent rather than fifteen of the Café de la Paix shareholding. Well, it wasn't the magic twenty-five per cent that you needed to get effectively in the way of the majority, but with the Marsh-Hayden shares in limbo, she had twenty per cent to Michael Owens' thirty-two and a half, and could not at the moment be swept aside. He looked cautiously at Judith Delves; she was drinking coffee without tasting it, hands trembling on the cup, eyes fixed sightlessly on some internal obsession, still in shock.

'Miss Delves, have you been up all night?'

'Yes.' She came back to herself and looked at him over her coffee cup. 'And I must start ringing round to see if I can borrow a head chef. Just for a week from next Friday, just to get us open.' She looked longingly at the telephone, then at her watch and reached over for more coffee, spilling a bit as she poured it.

Matthew Sutherland's eyebrows had gone right up and McLeish mentally agreed with him. It was by no means a foregone conclusion that Tony Gallagher would recover consciousness, never mind be fit to turn out 250 covers in two weeks' time. A tap at the door distracted him and he got off the chair carefully to open it.

'Sir, excuse me. A Mr Owens is here, says can he see Miss Delves?'

'Send him up.' It would be a good moment to see where the relationship stood between the only two shareholders in Café de la Paix who were neither awaiting burial nor unconscious in hospital.

'I've come to collect Judith,' Michael Owens announced, uncompromisingly. He looked bigger out of a suit, dressed much as McLeish's brothers-in-law, in jeans and a beautifully cut leather jacket. Only, McLeish observed, big lads like him ought not to wear leather jackets. His brothers-in-law had once dragged him to the excessively expensive shop which provided their jackets, and all, including the cutter, had agreed that no one of six foot four inches and built like the ex-rugby player he was could wear a leather jacket without looking as if they had just got off a motor-bike, no matter how careful the cut.

'You'll be at your office later?' McLeish was prepared to let him sweep Judith Delves away; she was hardly likely to have been implicated in an attack on the chef, she needed him to reopen her treasured business. There was a difficult pause, and he sat up mentally.

'No. I won't be going in today.' Owens was sounding constrained, and Judith Delves was looking agonised. She opened her mouth, visibly remembered Matthew Sutherland's presence and closed it again.

'Mr Sutherland. Thank you for coming. Where can we find you later today?'

'I'm going to my office.' Matthew was sounding unbearably smug, and McLeish gave him a look which got him out of the room, escorted by Davidson.

'Mr Owens?' he prompted, when Bruce Davidson had returned.

'I won't be going back to my office at all. I resigned yesterday.'

No one is fired in the City, Francesca had told him, unless found with both hands actually in the till. They resign, typically 'to follow their own interests'. Like reading the newspapers and sullenly taking the children out for walks, she had added The events at Café de la Paix seemed to have claimed another victim.

'Have you been up all night as well?' he asked, cautiously.

'No.' He realised Owens was in a rage. 'No one told me what had happened but I got worried when I rang Judith this morning to wake her, as I had promised last night, and she wasn't there. So I rang up here and heard what had happened.'

'I'm sorry, Michael, but there wasn't anything to be done. That couldn't wait, I mean. And ... and I knew you hadn't had a good day, so I thought ...' Her voice trailed away and McLeish waited, poised to intervene; Judith's reference to the events of yesterday had served only to inflame.

'You thought wrong,' Owens said, rudely. 'But you're not making sense generally, and you need some sleep. Come home, leave this lot here to get on, and they'll call me at your flat if there's any change in ... at St Thomas's.' He reached for her hand, awkwardly. 'Come on, darling. Home.' She was sitting, unmoving, and looked at McLeish in complicated appeal, which Owens noticed. 'Wait a minute. What was Matt Sutherland doing here? Looking for compensation for occupational injury for his client, I suppose?' He looked enquiringly at the policemen who gazed back, stolidly.

'No,' Judith said, putting down her cup and visibly nerving herself to her task. 'Although we may owe Tony, he did chase someone away. No. He had come to tell Mr McLeish ... Chief Superintendent McLeish ...' She stopped and put a hand to her throat.

'What?' Michael Owens obviously wanted to shake her, but confined himself to glaring at the policemen.

'That he had drawn up an agreement under which Mr Gallagher charged his shares to Miss Delves in return for a loan sufficient to pay off his gambling debts,' McLeish said without expression.

'You what?' Michael Owens rounded on his fiancée. 'You're mad. You won't get that back.' He stared at her. 'You were buying his shares. Or buying control of them at least.'

McLeish, out of sheer humanity, might have intervened, but Judith, exhausted, at war with her boyfriend, and having lent a substantial sum to her chef now lying unconscious in hospital, was weeping silently and pathetically, tears pouring down her face.

'Oh God. Judith.' Michael Owens scrabbled for a handkerchief and wiped her face for her with great tenderness, desperate to give comfort. 'It'll be all right, we'll get through this, I'm here,' he said, with love, totally unconscious of McLeish. 'Come on, let's get you

205

home and into a bath, and it won't all seem so bad.' He looked round wildly, and McLeish handed him a box of Kleenex. 'Right. Thanks. Look, Superintendent, you can see she's not in shape to deal with anything. I'll take her back and you can talk to her later.'

'That's fine,' McLeish said, placidly. 'I need also to take a statement from you.'

'What about?'

'We need to know where everyone was earlier this morning. At the time of the attack.'

'Oh that, yes.' He turned distractedly to Judith who was weeping silently but continuously down his shirt. 'Well, I can tell you now if it will save bothering us later. We had dinner together, went back to Judith's flat and I left, oh, about one o'clock I suppose – I wanted to get back to my own place. I drove myself.'

Only a rich man would have felt it necessary to state that qualification, McLeish thought, then pulled himself up. He, too, was driven more often than he drove, as senior policemen are.

'And you didna drop by the Café for anything?' Bruce Davidson asked.

'No. It's on my way home and I probably glanced at it, but I didn't see anything out of the way. Or I would have stopped.' He cradled Judith against his shoulder, stroking her back gently, making Mc-Leish for all his experience feel like an intruder.

'Was it all dark there, or did you see any light?' Bruce Davidson, made evidently of sterner stuff, was pressing on.

'I really didn't look but I'm sure I would have noticed a light. So I guess there wasn't one. Better now?' This was addressed to Judith who was showing signs of recovery and feeling for a handkerchief. She looked up at him and nodded.

'I ought to stay,' she said, weakly.

'Rubbish. Lots of competent people here.'

'Tony isn't.'

'I've never quite trusted him, as you know.' Judith's face crumpled. 'Sorry, don't start again. But Marco is here, I saw him as I came in, so's Mary, and those carpenters don't need telling, they're going like the clappers. It's all all right. Come on.'

McLeish and Davidson, left in possession, waited a decent minute upon their exit and looked at each other.

'Loves her, it seems.'

'Oh aye. Thought he was going to carry her downstairs.' Davidson brooded. 'Wonder why he lost his job?'

'We'll need to check. But this lot can't have helped. I don't suppose merchant banks like their directors involved with murder.'

'Or suicide.'

'If that's what it was.'

'You're no' happy, John?'

'Not quite, but you know how it is.'

'This one was mebbe just an intruder, coming in to see what he could nick, hit out because Gallagher was between him and the door.'

'Well, he knew what he was doing, didn't he?' McLeish said, slowly. 'One blow, then another to make sure, Doc says – sorry, I had a message too – that's what the X-ray says. He was looking for something, I don't know what.'

'He'd have had a job with the mess in there.' Bruce Davidson objected. 'Besides what was he looking for? Something in the accounts? They're in the big safe. Miss Delves checked this morning.'

'I don't know, Bruce, but that's what I think. Get Forensic on the blower and tell them we want that file of letters back soon as they can so we can look at them.'

Bruce Davidson was going through his case, methodically 'Got it. A wee message from the Marsh-Hayden solicitors, asking if we can release both bodies. Both families want a funeral. 'Course they do.'

McLeish sighed. 'No. We can't. I'll talk to them.'

'You're really worried then, John?'

'I'm not sure, but I'm not going to be hurried. We'll go back now, and you make bloody sure no other bugger is taking any of the team away.'

Judith Delves woke from the deep sleep of physical and mental exhaustion and blinked at the familiar curtains. The light had shifted and she sat bolt upright, beset by anxiety. She scrabbled for her bedside alarm clock, couldn't find it, and shot out of bed, panicked. She was wearing a nightdress, she observed, in her rush to the door and she remembered having a bath.

'Michael,' she said, 'what's the time?'

'Just past six o'clock.' She stared at him, distraught, and he raised a hand. 'No need to panic. The carpenters should finish tomorrow, and I've told the decorators they're on for Sunday. We need the time to clear up. Mary has rescued the management accounts from something called Forensic. I tried to go in and tidy up the back office, but it was full of policemen and I was told to go away.'

He was sounding justifiably smug, and she sank into a chair. 'Tony?'

'Still unconscious but no worse at three o'clock. Stable seems to be the word. I wasn't allowed to see him either.'

'But you tried. Thank you.' He was boiling the kettle, his back to her and she remembered belatedly that he had only been free to do all of this because of his own professional disaster. She had been less than sympathetic too, she thought wearily, but yesterday nothing mattered to her much except getting the restaurant open and trading. 'Darling?' she said to his back. 'Thank you for bringing me away this morning. I just ... well, when I heard about Tony I seem to have gone a bit mad. It just all seemed impossible.'

He turned, with the neatness of the athletic, and put the tray down on the table and she saw that he was keeping his temper with an effort. 'You are a bit mad, darling. I brought you home because you were going to collapse and you will have a breakdown if you go on like this. Can you not accept that it is just too difficult to go on? It's an enormous management responsibility even in normal times and when you're trying to restore one restaurant at the same time, it's just ridiculous.'

'I do know,' she said, gabbling in her anxiety. 'I have to get a general manager, I do accept that, there just hasn't been time.'

'And a head chef. And a new sous chef, and two commis.'

'A sous chef?'

'Jean-Pierre resigned, not surprisingly. He wasn't under any illusion about what his wife was doing there with his boss at one in the morning. She's gone too, if you care about that. It's just too much for you, and the more so if we are ever going to get married.'

She stared at the table, unable to marshal much of an argument, but suddenly heard Francesca McLeish telling her, with relish, the story of the convicted felon and Louis XIV's horse, as an argument for procrastination when no advantage could be gained by action. 'You've been very patient,' she said, meekly, 'and I will think about it all again. But we will all be in a weak position if we don't get this place open. I feel I owe it to Richard and Selina. And Tony, who may be going to need money very badly. And us,' she added, and wished she hadn't when she saw his face.

'There is no way,' he said, teeth gritted, 'that I could need the extra cash we just might get badly enough to put up with this kind of hassle. I should have got out a couple of years ago. I stayed in because I liked the people and felt, God help me, some loyalty to the place. But if you are thinking that I might want to work in this place, or to get the last sixpence out of selling it, forget it. I'll be back in a job easily, you wait and see. I can earn several times what you'll ever get out of here.'

I have still not quite understood, she thought bleakly, how much he hates the restaurants, or how unwilling he is for me to go on working. And I am not ready to deal with all that this entails, not now. She felt the easy tears of exhaustion start, and it did the trick, he fussed over her and poured tea, and she agreed not to go anywhere near the restaurant, but to go instead and have a quiet dinner cooked by someone else at somewhere solid, exquisite and expensive like the Connaught.

'Terrible thing. Poor Judith's having a very bad time.' Brian Rubin was sincere in his concern, McLeish saw, interested. It must be to his advantage that Judith Delves should be driven into a position where she had no option but to sell, but he was nonetheless distressed for her. Or perhaps he had given up his pursuit of the Café de la Paix and was now pursuing some other goal. He asked the question cautiously.

'No, no, no, no. Which is why I'm very glad to see you. The police, I mean. I don't know whether anyone's told you, but Richard's death means I own his shares. They were charged to me in return for a loan. And perhaps Selina's too, the lawyers are looking at it.'

McLeish just managed not to gape at him. 'Does Miss Delves know?'

'I told her, and Michael. I wasn't sure she'd quite taken it in, I know what it's like when you're doing an opening.'

'Tell me why *Mrs* Marsh-Hayden's shares are involved.'

'Left to Richard in her will, you see, and the deed covers all shares owned by him. Mind, I wouldn't push it and I wouldn't try and get Selina's shares for free, that wouldn't be right, but well, how shall I put it, it'd be difficult for them to be sold to anyone else. If you see what I mean.'

McLeish did, and considered his man carefully. He was indeed looking less harassed, and he had had a haircut, in McLeish's personal experience an important sign of personal organisation. But the signs of financial pressure were still there; he and Davidson had been admitted to the office only after scrutiny and the weary secretary on the switchboard was still telling all callers either that Mr Rubin had just stepped out, or that he was in a meeting.

'In a way it doesn't help,' Rubin said, reading his mind disconcertingly. 'Unless I can get everyone to agree I can't go to the market and complete the deal.'

'Everyone, including Miss Delves?'

'Yeh. My financial advisers, so-called, say that because of all the publicity we can only do it if everyone is signed up and saying it's the best thing to do. Before all this, see, we could perhaps have afforded to have Judith not too keen, but having to give up. Now she's got to be keen. Which she isn't.'

The man was still, however you looked at it, more cheerful despite this gloomily realistic recital. Presumably, despite his genuine concern for Judith Delves, he expected the loss of Tony Gallagher to be the final crushing blow, which would lead her to the endorsement of any sale.

'We are, of course, asking everyone for a statement of where they were from eleven o'clock onwards last night.'

'I thought you would be. Violence isn't my style, Chief Superintendent, I thought you knew me better than that by now. Mind, although in theory I would willingly have killed Judith, or Selina, the problem always was I wouldn't have been able to do it when push came to shove. And I certainly wouldn't have taken on Tony Gallagher, he's bigger than I am.' He gazed, wide-eyed, at McLeish. 'And, as I should have said first off, I was at a charity do last night, on a table with the mayor and the headmaster of the school my son's going to. Left there just before one and got home about one thirty. In St Albans, this is.'

Given that Tony Gallagher had been coshed at 1.25 a.m. that was conclusive. But at the team meeting an hour earlier they had all agreed that the attack on Tony Gallagher was not necessarily linked to the murder of Selina Marsh-Hayden; it could well have been an intruder bent on theft who had felled Tony Gallagher. But another piece of evidence that most definitely linked the cheerful man in front of him to the late Selina Marsh-Hayden had also come to light that morning.

'We'd also like to ask you about your relationship with Selina Marsh-Hayden, and I want you to consider your answers carefully.' He had, as he had intended, changed the atmosphere in the room and Brian Rubin was suddenly very still.

'What do you mean?' It came out husky, and he cleared his throat. 'Were you having an affair with her?'

Brian Rubin opened his mouth, looked at them, and understood it was too late. 'Fuck.' He scrubbed his face with his hands, trying for composure, the policemen sitting absolutely still. 'I suppose it was the letter. I thought at the time, never write, but ... but, well, she liked that, see.'

He looked over at McLeish, who kept his face straight, but only just. None of the four letters from three different men found in the red file was in Brian Rubin's handwriting. This had surprised the team not a little, since admirably thorough investigation work had turned up Rubin's credit card records for the last four months and established that most of them related to purchases at Harvey Nichols, or Gucci, or Harrods. The next bit had been easy, the detective sergeant who had done the work assured the team, everyone at Harvey Nichols knew Mrs Marsh-Hayden, didn't they? And doubtless derived both profit and amusement over the years from the men she had brought in to buy her clothes, the team had agreed.

'Does your wife know about her?'

Davidson had decided his boss was winded, evidently.

'Now she does. She guessed. But she doesn't know I wrote a letter.' He looked at McLeish pleadingly. 'Will they ... I mean, will they ... well I expect you've seen it all before.'

McLeish agreed mentally that those letters he had read were indeed not outside his experience, but graphic written descriptions of intended sexual activity are not that unusual in a policeman's life. Unless Brian Rubin's as yet undiscovered letter contained something very different, of course.

'Yeh, but look.' Brian Rubin, though chagrined, was recovering strongly. 'I didn't *kill* her. Never lifted a hand to a woman, ever. It was just a bit of fun.' He looked at them. 'I mean, she wasn't threatening me.' His voice changed on the sentence, and McLeish looked in enquiry. 'Yeh, well, no, I mean ...' He stopped. 'I want to talk to my solicitor.'

'By all means. Ring him up now.'

Brian Rubin made to get up, then sat down again. 'Oh shit,' he said, from the heart, and they watched him struggle with himself. 'She wanted a better deal for herself,' he said, finally, looking at the table, hands clenched. 'She'd agreed to the sale, but she wanted to get some little extras out of it. She was pissed off with Richard, because he was broke and always telling her she couldn't have things. And that rang a bell, and all, I've had a bit of that from Janice. My wife. So I gave Selina what I could, clothes, meals out and, well, one thing led to another, as they say. Then it turns out that she wants a directorship in the Group – my company – with a three-year rolling contract. That means she'd always get three years' notice, and I promised her that. In what circumstances I would think you could imagine.'

McLeish just stopped himself from nodding sympathetically.

'But I couldn't deliver, could I? The brokers who are doing the float said no contracts, there's all these committees, Greenbury, Cadbury, Banbury – no, that can't be right, can it? – but three-year rolling contracts are out of order apparently. I mean, even I couldn't have one and it's my group. Neither the institutions nor the non-executive directors would have it.'

McLeish nodded; he was on familiar ground here. It had been Francesca's employers, the Department of Trade and Industry who had initially been responsible for organising the Cadbury Committee on Corporate Covenance. In order, she had explained, to keep corporate snouts out of the trough, or at least to achieve a situation where shareholders could shoulder their way in alongside. Ironic that the very feminine Selina Marsh-Hayden should have run into a heavy-duty structure designed to corral the worst excesses of senior Corporate Man.

'So I had to tell her no. She thought I was bullshitting her and she told me she wouldn't sell. So I lost my temper. I told her she was a bloody fool and couldn't run a business, and I told her Gallagher was ripping them off. Which he was, by the way, and I can make a pretty good guess how and where. There could be a few people wanted to hit him over the head, I tell you. Anyway.'

He fell silent, lost in some disagreeable memory, so that finally McLeish had to prompt him.

'Yeh, right. Sorry. So then she flounces out, leaving me in a right state and with £8000 of bills on the plastic, but I don't see her again until we have that meeting the day of the night she went missing. And you know about that.'

One of the things they knew, of course, McLeish reflected, was that Brian Rubin had no alibi for the hours between eleven thirty and about seven o'clock the next day, when he had bought a paper on his way to work, Mrs Rubin being absent with her mother at the time.

'Where was my letter, can I ask?' Rubin was watching him carefully and he looked back expressionless. Rubin sighed. 'I was hoping, see, that Richard hadn't . . . well, hadn't found it. I liked him. He was a complete bloody fool with money – yeh, well, I know what you're thinking' – McLeish was not aware his face had moved – 'but I'll get through this patch, you'll see, and he *wasn't* going to get through. Even if the sale had gone through he'd have been broke again in six months.' He broke off and visibly recalled where he had started the speech and what he had meant to say. 'But he was a nice bloke and I felt fucking terrible when he topped himself. I'd just . . . well I'd be happier if it couldn't have been because of . . . well, a letter I wrote.'

He looked at them pleadingly, but they both gazed back stone-faced. The truth was that his worst fears were probably justified even if it was not his letter that had been involved. The most likely scenario was that Richard, encamped with a bottle in the office on Monday, with everyone too busy, or too exasperated, to go near him, had found the red file of letters that his wife had been keeping and made himself thoroughly wretched. Bruce Davidson and a Special Branch sergeant had stood over Forensic, chivvying them. The man from the Special Branch had been carrying a file with specimens of his royal client's eccentric and sprawling handwriting and it had not taken long to establish that he had not written any of the four. 'At least he's got that much sense,' the man had observed dourly. Analysis of the file's contents revealed that they were all letters to Selina Marsh-Hayden, but only four spoke of love or assignation. The rest were ordinary correspondence going back to the date of her marriage: letters from girlfriends, from her mother, and notes from her brothers. But the four would have made unhappy reading for her husband; as Brian Rubin had observed, the letters were recent and all described very varied sexual activities, though mercifully very little to suggest a particular interest in sado-masochism. While two of them they had been able to identify quickly, two correspondents remained mysteries, but they matched none of the specimens of shareholders' handwriting collected from documents at the Café de la Paix – neither Tony Gallagher, nor Michael Owens, were the authors. Brian Rubin had also at that earlier stage been eliminated; a specimen of his handwriting was available in a note to Judith. Specimens of handwriting were now being sought from every man employed in the group, their style and content rendering it clear that the authorship had to be male. McLeish had wondered how he would have felt stumbling on a similar file after the death of his wife, but imagination had failed to sustain Francesca urging on a series of lovers to such essays of fancy. Or indeed, he had reminded himself, of him actually getting to the point of strangling her no matter how furious he was.

The best theory, the one which covered most of the known facts and made emotional sense, was that Richard Marsh-Hayden had murdered his wife, whether out of rage at her sexual peccadilloes – and he could well have found the red file at an earlier stage, read its contents and left it there to come back to – or fury at her refusal to sell, or a combination of both. And then, suffering from grief, regret and guilt, had either found these letters, or rubbed salt into his wounds by disinterring and rereading them, it didn't much matter which, and decided to end his own life.

'How many letters did you write in all, Mr Rubin?'

'Just the one.'

Well, one might have got lost but equally it was possible that there were more letters they had not yet found, more recent than the four they had.

'And when did you write it?'

'What – two months ago. Then I remembered, didn't I, that writing is dangerous. So I never wrote another. She didn't mind that much, she liked getting the letter, but a trip to Harvey Nicks did just as well, really.'

McLeish looked sideways at Davidson and was reassured to see that he was finding this explanation convincing. He sat and thought, ignoring Rubin's fidgeting; at least one letter was missing and must for the case's sake be found. The team would need to go back to Café de la Paix and take the place apart if necessary. His conscience was clear about not telling Brian Rubin immediately that his letter had not been found; the secondary evidence from the credit cards would have been good enough, and in any case the man had not sought to deny an affair.

They got the formal statement organised and he left Bruce to deal with the typing and the signatures. He had a driver waiting and was intending to get home for family supper when he got a call from St Thomas's, which caused him to collect Bruce and abandon all intention of going home.

'I gather we're lucky to be able to talk to you at all, but thank you for seeing us.'

214

A half-closed suspicious eye was slanted at them from underneath a sizeable bandage which covered Tony Gallagher's head and his left eye. 'Well, I knew you wasn't going to go away, didn't I? But I don't remember a fucking thing, not after I come into the Caff. What day is it now?'

'Friday evening,' McLeish said, watching his man carefully. He sat on a chair on one side of the bed, his view severely obstructed by a set of tubes and wires plugged into Gallagher's head, chest and arm. Davidson was arranged uncomfortably just behind him, and Matthew Sutherland, who appeared to have been woken from a deep sleep, was seated on the other side of the bed, trying not to scratch.

McLeish and Davidson had been forbidden to stay more than twenty minutes, or to press their witness. Tony Gallagher's swift recovery from unconsciousness had surprised his doctors. It had been, as a member of the surgical team had explained, one hell of a clout – a technical term, no doubt, as Davidson had observed – but a thick skull and a strong constitution combined with the latest medical technology looked like ensuring that Gallagher would be fine if carefully nursed and watched for complications. He was severely bruised, his right eye was closed but the swelling under the skull was dissipating nicely.

'No matter,' McLeish said, calmly. 'Anything you remember now or later could be useful, but don't struggle. You had a young woman with you, who raised the alarm.'

'I don't remember her.' The other eye had closed, definitively, and McLeish sighed inwardly. If Gallagher had really forgotten the girl he had been with then he was worse off than all had feared. He looked thoughtfully at Matthew Sutherland who was watching his client.

'Tony,' Matt said, suppressing a huge yawn, 'can I just tell you Jean-Pierre resigned this morning and went back to France. Took Maria with him.'

The eye opened again and fixed itself on his lawyer. 'Oh. Right. Well, yeh, it was Maria with me, we'd been having a drink.' He hesitated, looked sideways at McLeish. 'We came in,' he continued, finding a formula, 'didn't we, just to see everything was all right. Then I heard a noise and told her to stay where she was and I started up the stairs and *that* really is the last thing I remember.'

'Nothing after that?' McLeish asked, carefully.

'No. Honest. I lie here trying to think and it's all gone.' A tear escaped from the eye they could see, and he coughed while they watched him anxiously. 'Christ, that hurt.' He was moving fretfully, and Matthew Sutherland put a large hand gently on his arm.

'S'all right, Tony, don't sweat it. It'll come back.'

'Yeh. Can you get the nurse back? She said if it hurt to call her.'

Matthew reached for the buzzer on the bedhead and McLeish noticed how neatly he avoided the tubes and wires while still gently holding Gallagher's arm.

'We'll go,' McLeish said, quietly. He had seen enough head injuries to know that the man wasn't faking it and that any strain risked destabilising him. He backed out, avoiding tubes, and he and Davidson made for the door, standing aside for the incoming nurse. He glanced back; Tony Gallagher was even paler than when they had arrived, tossing uneasily, but Matthew Sutherland was steady as a rock, matter-of-factly helping the nurse with the drip while talking soothingly to his client. They repaired to the hospital canteen, an enormous, fundamentally inhospitable room done out in shades of green and yellow, with three heavily overweight women behind the counter. But the tea was strong and hot and the Danish pastries fresh, and they found themselves a quiet corner.

'Not much joy there,' Bruce Davidson observed.

'No. Sorry to have kept you.'

He stirred his tea. 'Nae bother. Now, Wednesday evening, we reckoned that the perpetrator was dead. You were a wee bit doubtful but that was the general view. Mine too,' he added, stolidly.

'But then we found those letters. Which could widen the field, if she – Selina – was using them. As she was with Mr Rubin.'

'It wasna the *letters* she was using there,' Davidson objected. 'It was herself, by his account. I mean they were in full swing. He couldn't get enough of it.' He took a huge bite of his pastry.

'That's true. But those four letters – I had them typed up to make life a bit easier.' He reached inside the old climbing jacket, which Francesca didn't like him to wear in London, and handed over several folded bits of paper. 'Look at the dates.'

Bruce Davidson looked, then looked again, checking back. 'The latest is dated six months before she died.'

'Brian Rubin wrote one two months ago, so there may be others from someone else.'

Bruce Davidson considered him severely. 'Running two of them at the same time, ye mean?'

'Perhaps not?' McLeish said, meekly.

'Not impossible,' Davidson allowed. 'I had a lass once had me and another lad on the go at the same time. Neither of us knew. Found out over a drink, years later.' He shook his head, sombrely. 'Married now with four kids, the lass, I mean.'

'We need to find that letter from Rubin,' McLeish said, soberly. 'And to be sure there aren't any more. She'd surely have been keeping them at the office too.'

'But why keep them separate?' Davidson asked.

'Maybe she kept them all together but someone else extracted a few of them.'

'Like Mr Marsh-Hayden?' Davidson uncrossed his legs, knocking the unstable little table, and cursed at the remains of his tea distributing itself over his pastry.

'He was off his face with drink,' McLeish said, slowly. 'Everyone agrees about that. But he was not too shocked or too drunk not to hide the file. So he may well have taken some out and put them somewhere else. But, of course, the next day he was dying in St Stephen's.' McLeish stopped, deciding he wasn't being any more convincing than when he had first thought about it.

'And it wasn't him breaking in to look for them either, because he was cold by then, God rest him. And it wasn't Rubin, because he was playing footsie with the local mayor.' Bruce Davidson was a patient and methodical thinker who followed a thought to its conclusion.

'No.' McLeish sat up. 'But it could have been the man who wrote the missing letters. Took them out, was disturbed by Tony Gallagher, clouted him and ran like hell. If there were any letters. If there was a man,' he added, wearily.

'No one to ask, is there?' Davidson pointed out.

'No. Do you want another tea?'

'I'm all right.' He caught his superior's eye. 'You mebbe want one, John?'

'No. I want . . . well, I want just to talk something else through. It's quite simple, but it's worrying me. It's the usual question of who benefits? Who is better off because Selina and Richard Marsh-Hayden are dead?'

'Mr Rubin, surely? He has Richard's shares and mebbe Selina's.'

'Mm. Do we think Richard was going to be able to pay Mr Rubin back? No? Well, then Mr Rubin would have got them anyway in another six months. And we know that Selina's death actually delayed the sale.'

Bruce Davidson plodded his way through the sequence. 'You're saying anyone who wanted to buy or sell was in practice screwed by Selina's death.'

'I suppose they might not have realised that in advance,' McLeish said, stirring in sugar. 'But what about the one who *didn't* want to sell? She's got her way, as it turns out.'

'Judith Delves. Aye, but now Brian Rubin has Richard's shares, the enemy is through the gates.'

'True,' McLeish conceded. 'But she didn't *know* Rubin would get Richard's shares on his death. Go back to Selina's death. That delayed the sale to no one's advantage except Judith's. *And* she got £100,000 out of it as well to keep the business going. She couldn't have foreseen the fire, but she did know the business was in trouble because Selina hadn't been doing her job and Gallagher had been robbing them. With Selina dead, the sale is delayed and she's got the cash to go on.'

'Now you say it . . .' Davidson said, slowly, '. . . it's no' a bad case to argue.'

'Indeed not. And Judith only increased the insurance on Selina two months ago.'

'I'd not quite seen that. But where does that put Mr Owens? You saw him, he's not best pleased.'

'No, but he can't actually force a sale. Or not *now*, maybe in a few months' time. And I am reminded that Frannie advised Miss Delves to delay by all means possible on the basis that something might change.'

Bruce looked at him, appalled. 'Before Selina died, she advised this?'

'No, no, thank heavens – this conversation happened after Selina's body had been found. It's an analysis Judith Delves could have managed for herself in any case, I just wish my lovely wife hadn't helped her to it, if only because I can't get it out of my head. Look at it, Bruce, everyone else is worse off after the killings. Rubin can't buy, Owens and Gallagher can't sell.'

'Yes, but Gallagher's been bought out, as much as he needs to be.'

'True. But Owens wanted to sell, and now he can't. Mind you, we know he doesn't need the money, for all he's lost his job.'

'No indeed. We're in the wrong business, John, when a man younger than us turns out to be worth the thick end of £3m.'

They finished their tea in contemplative silence.

'I'm not getting anywhere, Bruce. You go off to the pub, or whatever single blokes do these days, and I'll go and eat humble pie and dried-up supper, and read the same book over and over again to the kid.'

15

'Frannie? Are you sitting down?'

'Yes. I'm in the kitchen where I always sit down. What's *happened*?'

'Don't panic. It's a good news day. *Guess who* is going to be rich and famous?'

'Tristram. You've not . . . you aren't . . .'

'Yes, I am. Poor old Alan – God bless him and keep him safely tucked up in bed – has a temperature of 103 and can't do more than croak. So I'm singing Cavaradossi tonight and Monday.'

'But couldn't they have got someone else?'

'There is absolutely no support in the world like one gets from devoted family. Who could be better than lovely *moi*?'

He was sounding wildly overexcited, as well he might, but she was still dazed. 'But, darling, you always said they wouldn't use you, that you were only rehearsed in case Alan dropped dead in Act One. You always assumed they'd borrow a tenor from somewhere.'

Her brother laughed; she could hear conversation and people passing. 'Oh, they tried,' he said, lowering his voice. 'Absolutely everywhere – I can't tell you what yesterday was like, but I wasn't even going to hint to any of you until I knew they'd drawn a blank everywhere. The big names are either working or far too grand, you see, to come and do a couple of nights for the ENO at the end of a run. The money isn't that good. Then all those who are a couple of steps ahead of me are either ill – there's a sort of Eastern European flu about, bless it – or working, or totally unable to manage the job in English. So in the end Management had to confess they'd called all over Europe yesterday, as well as up and down the East Coast, and ask me to do it. I graciously said I would.'

'Wonderfully decent of you,' his sister agreed. 'Are you nervous?'

'Not particularly. Or not yet.' Tristram, unlike the nerveless Perry, had occasionally suffered from crippling stage fright. 'I've sung it a lot before.'

Indeed, she agreed, reserving to herself the thought that singing the lead at the ENO was not quite the same as doing it when touring Eastern Europe.

'We're rehearsing all morning, or at least Elena and I are. You want tickets?'

'How many can we have?'

'Six. A box. So that's you and Mum. Will John come?'

'Of *course* he will. Who else are you asking? What are you doing for women?'

'She's in the chorus.'

'Then she doesn't need a ticket. What about Perry? He must be on his way home – yes, he's landing this morning.'

'Perry then. He'll enjoy it.'

Not necessarily, she thought, but let that pass.

'And your nice friend Matthew, perhaps? Or is it awkward with John?'

'Good heavens, not in the slightest,' she lied, promptly. 'But he's seen it very recently.'

'Not with me as Cavaradossi. I'll ask him. I must go, Fran, they're calling me.'

'Oh, darling, good luck. I'm sure you're going to be a smash hit, I really am. Just stay calm.'

The two people in the Café de la Paix office were not talking but were very much aware of each other. Judith Delves was quietly determined to stay at the Café to work on the insurance claim and to deal with questions from the small group of electricians and tilers who were working – at double rates – to stay ahead of the decorators also at double rates, who were racing through the front half of the restaurant. She had been at her desk since leaving Michael's flat at 9 a.m. and he had been in twice, once to insist on taking her out to lunch and now to try to get her to agree to leave at 5.30 p.m. to go back to her flat and get into something more formal than a navy boiler suit to accompany him to *Tosca* at the Coliseum. And he was apparently prepared to sit without as much as a newspaper until she yielded the point. She was finding herself unable to keep up her end of the hostile silence and cast around mentally for something to occupy him and break the tension.

'I had a call from John McLeish. He wants a team to come in tomorrow.'

'Oh, for God's sake.' Michael was sounding irritated but not ungrateful for a break in the silence. 'Why? What's their problem?'

'That file of letters they found. They're obviously wanting to check there aren't any more.'

'Any *more*? Weren't those enough? I understand there were a few letters suggesting Selina had been, well, a bit free with her favours.'

'They weren't all love letters, I gather,' she said, stiffly. 'Anyway, he sounded as if it was a routine thing, and I reminded him that the police had taken everything out of the inner office. I offered to look through all the cabinets, but I really didn't think there was anything but accounts and old conveyancing files and so on. They either don't believe me or they don't think I'll bother to look.'

'Nor you should. You've more than enough to do, let them do their own dirty work.' He got up. 'I fancy a coffee.'

He made them both a cup and she looked up at him gratefully. It was a perfect October day outside; a lime tree, its leaves tinged brown, blew in the wind against a background of faded blue sky, like a poster for the Fall in New England. He looked down at her. 'Actually, I could look, couldn't I? Can we make a deal? I'll do this chore for the police, save you being harassed tomorrow, or as much as I can, and you go home and change in an hour. I'll wait for you here and get on.'

She was already a little ashamed of herself and accepted the compromise eagerly.

'Where is the best, or the most likely place to start?' he asked, gazing around him. 'Did Selina ever go near any of these?'

'Of course she did. All of them.' There were ten heavy four-drawer cabinets arranged in a bank. 'Or try the bookcases, or the cupboard where the bank statements are. I mean, if she was keeping anything else here it could be anywhere, except her desk because the police cleared that. Keys are in the safe.' She nodded towards the big safe, which sat half open.

'Did you change the combination?'

Her pen stilled in her hands and she looked up aghast. 'I forgot. I'd better do it now.'

'No need, don't stop now. I'll remind you.' He unlocked a filing cabinet and looked into the top drawer. 'This isn't filing as I know it,' he observed, and she got up wearily and peered over his shoulder.

'Oh dear. I think it's just old Visa receipts, but they ought to have been thrown away. I'll do it.'

'No, for heaven's sake.'

She sat down guiltily and forced herself back to the insurance claim, very conscious of him as he sighed and banged his way through drawers. He was disturbing her, but equally he wanted to help and it was really not reasonable to refuse to go to the opera when he had got tickets as a treat for them.

She sat up and stretched her back and found he was watching her.

'It is five thirty,' he said, firmly.

'And a good time to stop,' she assured him. 'I'll go and come back here.' She peered, dismayed, into the chaos of a filing drawer. 'I'm sorry, it's awful, I never realised. Mary and I will have a go.'

'I could attempt a tidy-up. Throw some of it away – I don't have anything much better to do.'

'Absolutely not,' she said, firmly. 'It's our mess, we'll clear it. I'm ashamed of us.'

'Never mind that. Do we have a shredder hidden away?'

'A what? Oh, I see. No, we've never thought of it, perhaps we should.' She stood, irresolute, and he turned her round gently and pointed her towards the door.

'Darling. Go.'

She went, taking the stairs for exercise, and stopped off just to see how the work was progressing. Half an hour later she looked at her watch and fled, hoping against hope for a passing taxi. She was standing, anxiously peering up the street, when a big dark red station wagon, which seemed familiar, came past her and parked outside the Café's boarded-up frontage. She looked but no one seemed to be getting out and then, blessedly, there was a taxi, his light illuminated, and in the press of telling him where she was going she forgot to look again, and it was not until she reached her own front door that she remembered that Brian Rubin drove a dark red Volvo Estate.

'If it's dinner jacket, I'm not going,' John McLeish warned, over the head of his small son. 'I can't, my shirt's not back after the Bramshill party this week.'

'No, it's all right,' Francesca assured him. 'It's not a first night for anyone but Tristram. I just hope people aren't going to be terribly disappointed to miss Alan, but I understand Tris may be rather a draw. Being fashionable and happening and *now*, as he is. No, Will, the fashionable, happening *now* outing for you is a bath full of warm water, come on.'

She bore their son, protesting, from the room while McLeish unloaded the dishwasher and loaded it up again, marvelling that any two of his in-laws could use so many plates. Perry was on the sofa, sleeping off jet-lag, and his mother-in-law, bless her, was assisting in bathing William, preparatory to leaving him with Susannah, who was in a sulk because she had hoped to be invited to the opera. He had tried to volunteer to babysit instead, but this suggestion had been poorly received, and Susannah consoled to some extent by a load of autographed CDs and a cuddle from Perry had been called to the colours.

Francesca was still distractedly doing her eyes as they all piled into the studio's Rolls, with Perry drowsing in a corner. His bodyguard prodded him and enquired whether he needed an upper or what, and McLeish bent his most forbidding scowl on the man. They had had to wait a couple of minutes outside the Coliseum to let an even bigger Rolls disgorge its cargo, but the waiting photographers wasted very little film on the two emerging minor royals, devoting their attention to Perry, who emerged from his latest nap smiling and pleasant, exuding gracious confidence in his younger brother. McLeish, blinking in the flashlights behind Francesca, could only be relieved that Tristram was safely immured inside and couldn't hear any of it.

'Matt,' he heard her call joyfully and saw that, indeed, young Sutherland, wearing a suit and tie, was grinning at them from their box.

'Tristram invited him. He's taken rather a fancy,' Mary Wilson explained, watching his face anxiously.

'He's a good lad for a solicitor,' McLeish assured her, remembering Matt's efficient tenderness with Tony Gallagher, and greeted him civilly. In a lull in the cries of greeting, he managed to ask if Matt had any later news and was unsurprised to hear that Gallagher was still away rather than present much of the time.

'Doctors are pleased, though,' Matt assured him. 'But they've no idea when he'll be fit to work. There's the rest of the team.' He pointed out Judith Delves and Michael Owens in the middle of the stalls, Michael's head bent in conversation with a large man in the next seat, and Judith looking tired and reading her programme. McLeish scanned further back and saw Brian Rubin with a pretty blonde whom he was treating with anxious deference.

'If Tony were here, we'd have all the extant shareholders and the Principal Suitor,' Matt pointed out, and on that thought the lights went down.

A small man in a dinner jacket appeared in front of the curtain, and Matthew was this time not surprised when the audience groaned. Francesca, he saw, was furious, looking like a ruffled eagle, and he watched as John McLeish patted her hand. The man on the stage was embarked on a more elaborate apology, starting with the news that the substitute Scarpia was still in place – this news received in silence – and going on to explain the disaster that had befallen Cavaradossi. Matthew waited, with real interest, for him to describe the frenzied telephonings which, as, he knew from Tristram, had occupied two entire days, but he did none of that. Management had evidently decided to take a bold line and to make a virtue of necessity, so that their spokesman was explaining that they had been greatly and peculiarly fortunate in having among the existing cast the brilliant young tenor Tristram Wilson who had sung Cavaradossi in major opera houses in Europe. A sporting round of applause, led from the gallery, broke out at this point and he saw Francesca breathe again. 'Spoletta,' Management added, conscientiously, 'will be sung tonight by Giles Raven,' and the audience, reminded of its manners, applauded that too.

Management retired, and the overture started and, after what seemed to John McLeish quite a lot of that, the curtain went up on an old man – or rather, he realised, quite a young man doing his best to simulate the slow, careful movements of old age. Then Tristram bounced in, and set up, elaborately, an easel and a painting, dropping a brush as he did and bending awkwardly, stiff-legged, to pick it up. Stricken by nerves, McLeish realised, and glanced at Tristram's siblings, both of whom were staring at the stage, their backs rigid with tension. He took his wife's hand, seeing her lips move in prayer, but plainly she did not even notice, her whole heart and mind fixed on the brother struggling on stage. Tristram had got his mouth open and he was singing, but McLeish could hear that it was stiff and constrained, quite unlike the clear, high, effortless tenor he was used to hearing. He found he was tense too; if Tristram could not take this God-given chance, no member of the Wilson family would be tolerable to live with, except possibly his mother-in-law, who was sitting calmly and quietly, watching her youngest with love but without anxiety. It was to be hoped that his own Francesca, who was looking like a model for a tragic mask, would manage, with age, to feel with less intensity.

A large and sumptuously attired lady had joined Tristram on the stage and McLeish slowly recalled that this was the plump, frumpily

225

dressed, middle-aged lady he had seen at the understudy rehearsal. Well, she was still a big girl – and giving away twenty years to Tristram – but, got up to kill and superbly lit, you could believe in her as a successful beauty and an inspiration for artists. And she was, he realised, being the greatest possible support to her young cavalier; Tristram had relaxed a bit and the superb voice could be heard again, at least in several passages. The general easing among the audience, particularly the bit of it with which he was walled up, reassured him that he was right. And then the duet was over; Tristram was gone, and the Rumanian Scarpia with his henchmen – including the Tristram-substitute who was singing Spoletta – were on, and then they were gone and the lights went up to polite applause.

He turned cautiously to look at the Wilson siblings, but they were deaf and blind to everything but each other.

'One of us had better go round.' Francesca was very pale.

'We never do before the end. It could rattle him worse.'

They gazed at each other, and McLeish cleared his throat, hoping to attract his wife's attention.

His mother-in-law leant forward. 'Darlings, we should leave him alone. He's got all his friends there, they're all experienced. He'll settle down in the next act.'

Her children gazed at her, obedient but stricken, and totally unconvinced by this eminently practical view, and Matt Sutherland decided to take a hand.

'Look, I'm invited round to Anna – this girl I know in the chorus. I could tell him we all think he's doing great.'

'He knows you don't know.' The normally tactful Perry was too distressed for his sibling to be careful, and McLeish grinned inwardly. Welcome to the club, Mr Sutherland, of those whose opinion on anything musical is simply not worth having.

'I think we should all go and have a nice drink,' Mrs Wilson said, firmly, catching his eye, and between them they levered Francesca and Perry out of their seats and into the bar, where Perry was instantly restored by approaches from a couple of awe-inspired and smitten young women. Francesca, however, a picture of misery, was backed into a corner refusing to be diverted.

'Francesca?'

He looked round, startled, prepared if need be to get rid of the intruder before his wife could bite them, but Judith Delves had outflanked him, and was kissing her. 'A wonderful voice. He was terrific in the duet.'

'Well, he was better,' Francesca allowed. She lowered her voice, looking round for enemies. 'He'll have to relax.'

'He will surely? Now he's got the first act behind him. The second act is much easier because it's so dramatic.'

'That's perfectly true,' Francesca agreed, and John McLeish silently blessed Judith Delves as he handed his wife the drink she had been furiously refusing. 'And he does get over stage fright, it's just always been a problem for him.' She downed half her drink and looked round her, colour returning to her face. 'Is that your young man?'

'Yes, it is.' She looked over the bar and Michael Owens came reluctantly towards them. He was looking irritable and was very tense, the big hands clenched and the shoulders set. Not surprising, McLeish thought, you don't expect to meet the Detective Chief Superintendent in charge of investigating the deaths of two of your associates when you're trying to have a night out at the opera.

'Came to hear my brother-in-law,' he said, easily, extending a hand, and introducing Francesca.

'Of course.' Michael Owens' face cleared. 'I'd forgotten the connection.' He hesitated, obviously searching for words. 'He's doing well.'

Michael Owens possibly did know what he was talking about musically, he decided, and saw from Francesca's look that she had reached the same view.

'Not yet,' she said. 'But he will.'

'It's a great voice,' Michael Owens said, and they smiled at each other.

'Three-minute bell.' Perry reappeared from behind a wall of admirers, trailing his bodyguard. 'Let's get there.'

And the second act, he could see, was indeed better. Everyone seemed to have relaxed. Tristram didn't seem to him to have all that much to do, but he was doing it very well; something had released him from care and the superb voice was back in full working order. He was removed, bloodstained, hurling defiance. Tosca settled down to bargain for his life and to murder Scarpia, and the curtain came down again, to real applause this time. Disconcertingly, it went up again, and the bloodstained Tristram, Tosca and the murdered Scarpia appeared hand in hand to take a series of bows. Only Scarpia got to bow on his own, but Tristram was standing relaxed and smiling.

'I know that's not the end, don't I?' McLeish asked, puzzled, under cover of the applause.

'That's right,' Perry said, across Francesca. 'Continental habit of having soloists take a bow after Act Two. I always find it confusing, but in this case it has a bit of sense in it. Scarpia can bugger off home rather than kicking his heels through Act Three to take a bow.'

'Ah.' He caught Matthew Sutherland's sympathetic look and loyally refused to return it.

'OK. I can face the bar,' Francesca said, blithely, and he stood to let her and Matthew go past him. He waited for his mother-in-law and made sure she had a drink and a chair, and that Perry was at hand before looking round him. A familiar face, looking amazed, swam into his view and he nodded to Brian Rubin.

Instead of disappearing down the stairs, as he had rather expected, Rubin came over towing a pretty blonde woman.

'Chief Superintendent?'

'My brother-in-law is Tristram Wilson.'

'I just remembered, after I saw you. My wife Janice.'

Ah yes, McLeish thought, considering the strong jaw and bright eyes, and the firm grip on Brian Rubin's hand. Yes, I do see.

'He's wonderful. Your brother-in-law,' she said, earnestly.

'He's relaxed a bit.' McLeish thought it safer to adopt his in-laws' careful and grudging approach.

'I can't *wait* for Act Three.' Janice Rubin was saying, undiscouraged, and just as the five-minute bell went, he saw, over her head, Michael Owens and Judith Delves; some kind of argument was going on, and Judith was near tears. She looked up and caught his eye, and he looked away, embarrassed, but she came over to the group, greeting the Rubins briefly.

'Tristram very nicely asked us to come round afterwards. Michael's got rather a headache, so we may not make it. Will you tell him it wasn't rudeness, if that happens?' She glanced over to Owens, who was watching her moodily. 'Or I might just come by myself, just for a few minutes.'

Several bells rang and the bar cleared, and McLeish only just made it back to his seat. The curtain went up and a pure high treble voice sang from the battlements, then Tosca came on. Tristram was brought out from his cell and the two of them sang of love and freedom. It was, this time, unquestionably superb, you really did not have to be musical, or sitting in a box with two singers, to understand that. He looked sideways, cautiously; there were tears rolling unregarded down Francesca's cheeks, and Perry, hand locked over hers, was weeping gently as well. It was, of course, a *silly* plot, he thought, crossly, tears in his own eyes as the firing squad filed out and Tosca tried, disbelieving, to get a dead man up and on his way to freedom.

228

'Music critic of *The Times*,' Perry said, *sotto voce*, blowing his nose as Tosca disappeared over the battlements. 'Down there, running for the exit.'

'How do you know?' McLeish asked, over the torrential applause as the curtain went down.

'It's been the same man for yonks. He was doing it when I was the treble here opening Act Three, what – fifteen years ago.'

One forgot, McLeish thought, that this peacock star had once been a serious classical singer, and had abandoned it for a life of public adulation and knicker flinging teenagers.

'Means Tris will get a review – doesn't always happen with an understudy.'

He was looking just perceptibly smug, and McLeish raised an eyebrow at him.

'My agent had a word,' Perry confirmed. 'Mind you, he deserves it.' He sighed, looking suddenly ten years older and a stone heavier, then peered downwards and rose to his feet, shouting as the curtain went up and the chorus took a bow, then all the minor parts, then Tristram and Tosca together, at which point the applause became deafening. Other boxes, emboldened by Perry, were on their feet, and the stalls limbered up patchily. Tosca received, graciously, a vast bouquet of flowers, and Tristram another. There was a pause, then Tosca gave Tristram a firm, motherly shove between the shoulder blades and he shot forwards, startled, to take an individual bow, to dense, generous applause. He stepped back, kissed Tosca and went forward graciously so that, as was her right, she took the last call in a storm of applause and shouts and flying flowers.

They sat in the box while the theatre cleared, giving Francesca time to get her face back in order. Matt Sutherland was fidgeting, so they let him out to see his girl in the chorus, then finally they made a dignified exit and fought their way – Perry, Biff the bodyguard and McLeish in the lead – into the madhouse that was the stage door.

Amid the weeping, champagne-drinking, rejoicing throng in Tristram's crowded dressing-room, Perry formed a second centre of attention, ignoring Francesca's reproachful scowl. They all had a drink and embraced Tristram, collecting a generous supply of stage make-up as they did so, and Francesca was just scolding him into dry clothes – he was pouring sweat and high on relief and exhaustion – when McLeish noticed Judith Delves peep in, looking stricken.

He got over to her on Matt Sutherland's heels, sharing exactly the same thought.

'Is it Tony?'

'Oh, Matt. What are you doing here? No, no, no, nothing like that. I rang the hospital just before I came and they said he was going on nicely. I'm a bit tired.' She turned to greet Francesca who had followed her men.

'Where's your Michael?' she asked, looking round.

'He's gone home. He had a splitting headache. He wanted me to come here.'

A quarrel, McLeish thought, and saw his conviction echoed in Francesca's over-expressive face.

'Oh dear. I'm sorry. Come and have a drink. Tris is just changing in someone else's dressing-room.'

It might have been better, McLeish thought, if his wife could avoid sweeping into her sympathetic wake one of the principals in a current, live case, but it was evidently not to be. He saw Brian Rubin, his wife's hand firmly clasped, hovering hopefully and decided that at the moment there was no way of getting this party back on the rails of orthodox investigative procedure. He would just have to wait his chance, and scoop Francesca up and take her home as soon as she felt able to leave her brother.

He allowed her another twenty minutes and half a glass of champagne in Tristram's crowded dressing-room before declaring that he needed to take her home, and was gratified when she disentangled herself immediately from a knot of brothers and Matthew Sutherland. He was a good deal less pleased to find that she had offered Judith Delves a ride home. Uncharacteristically his face must have reflected his views, and he found that Judith was firmly rejecting the idea and saying she would get a taxi, good heavens, there were plenty of them and Francesca needed to get home to bed. So he took Francesca away, feeling mildly curmudgeonly, but after all Judith Delves was still a suspect in a murder case and moreover it was not his fault that Michael Owens had found it necessary to go home early. He peered anxiously at his wife; she was very quiet and rather pale and he resolved to get her home quickly and prevent her going to work too early the next day.

Judith Delves watched them go, giving them a few minutes to get away in order that they might not be embarrassed by her inability to find a taxi straightaway; it was never that easy late at night. Her fears were justified; there were no taxis and in the rush she had left her mobile phone in the flat. She looked round for a public phone and saw that there was a queue for it, in which Matthew Sutherland

and his girl were prominent. Brian Rubin and his wife had gone, not that she would have been happy about asking them for a lift, but there was a simple answer: she could go up to the Caff and use a phone there to call out Radio Taxis to come and take her home on the restaurant account.

McLeish, three miles away, gently patted his wife's knee. 'We're nearly there.'

'I wasn't really asleep, I just had my eyes closed.'

'Like your Mum, listening to opera.'

She grinned in the dark. 'I know. She's not exactly unmusical and she knows a lot. She just, well, she can do without it. Any of it. I can't imagine how she produced us all, or lived with Dad in perfect amity. Anyway, I was actually thinking about Judith.'

'I'm sorry I was less than forthcoming about taking her home.'

'Well, I was a bit embarrassed and I'll tell you why. That relationship is coming unstuck under the strain; I was next to them at the bar at the second interval. He was absolutely pissed off, and picked a quarrel with her – I don't think he even stayed for Act Three. So she was left like a lemon. That's why I wanted to rescue her.'

'I'm sorry, I didn't know.'

'How could you? And you'd had enough for one day, anyhow.'

Judith Delves shivered. It had been such a perfect day she had not bothered with a coat, assuming Michael would drive her home, but it was now cold, and her light wool short-sleeved dress was not warm enough. She would not have been surprised to find some of the workmen still in the Caff, since they were all on piecework, but the whole building was dark. Even the outside light by the basement entrance, which was always left on to discourage derelicts camping there, was off. She approached cautiously, checking that no one was huddled in the doorway, but it was clear and she felt for her keys, using the light of a street lamp to penetrate to the bottom of an awkwardly shaped evening bag. She went down the steps, making a mental note that the empty paint pots, blackened pieces of pine and twisted pipes piled in the rubbish cage must be removed on Monday before they caused complaint, and stopped, three steps from the bottom. She was on a level with the neat metal covering of the ventilation outlet and she could smell smoke and hear the fan.

'Oh no, no, no,' she heard herself moan aloud, as she forced the key into the lock. 'Not *again*, please God.' It was dark and she felt for the light switch to the right of the door, hand trembling. But there was nothing to see, and only a very faint, acrid smell of smoke. A wire burning through somewhere, she thought wildly; the kitchen perhaps. She went up the shallow stairs two at a time, the smell in her nostrils stronger now, and she could see a faint flicker of light. She banged on all the light switches she could see and rushed through the door. Flames flickered on the big grill beneath the hood and she gaped at it, trying to understand what she was seeing. Blackened paper was scattered around and more was burning merrily, fluttering on the metal bars above the hot gas jets. Some *fool* must have left papers on the grill and they had caught fire, she thought, furiously, and then she heard the lift move, passing behind the panelling and ducked instinctively behind the big central counter listening to the descending whine and the jolt as it reached the floor below her.

'Please go away, please, please . . .' she found herself whispering on an indrawn breath. 'Just go away . . .'

The door below banged and she held her breath, praying, but there was no sound at all and she leant back, shaking, against the solid central counter. Her legs were suddenly cramping painfully, and she stretched them out in front of her, bracing the muscles. She could hear the hiss of the grill and told herself she must get up and switch it off and call the police, but her heart was still hammering and the central counter gratefully cool, so she waited to get her breath and picked up a piece of the debris as it came past her.

The writing was familiar, she realised, she knew who formed an 'm' like that. Another piece fluttered by her and she reached for it; it fell apart into black flakes except for one corner, and she felt her face turn scarlet as she read what was written. She got to her feet, clinging to the counter, and held on to it as she moved slowly down and turned off the gas. She was going to be sick, she realised, and lurched towards the basin and threw up comprehensively. She retched again, miserably, resting her head on the cool tiles and suddenly understood her danger. She turned, still swallowing, towards the kitchen phone which was by the door, barely able to breathe from fright. The door was half open and she stood, frozen, watching it, but a change in the light made her half turn. Behind her stood a figure in a white chef's jacket, features unrecognisable under a black Balaclava, holding something white in its hands, then a band was tightening round her throat and she was fighting for her life.

*

'Darling? Lights gone green.'

'Fuck. Oh, fuck.' He very rarely swore, and Francesca gaped at him, but he was wrenching the wheel round, tyres crunching. The big car bumped off the pavement opposite and he pushed it through the gears and through an amber light.

'Phone. Red button, and say it's me.'

He did not see her, Francesca knew, she was just a more or less competent body to be instructed, so she did precisely as she was asked. He snatched the phone from her, using the other hand to get round a corner, and she closed her eyes in prayer, knowing that the duty of a policeman's wife was not to distract her man in times of trouble. It was medieval, or at best mid-Victorian, she thought, clinging to the bar above the passenger window and checking her safety belt, but there it was. She listened uncomprehendingly to her husband ordering units into place as they screamed up the Edgware Road, headlights flashing. The phone, which he had dropped into her lap, rang and she seized it up, trying to work out what to press.

'Green button,' her husband instructed, squeezing through a traffic light, the flat of his right hand on the horn.

'Matthew? A fire? At the Caff?' She looked helplessly over at her husband.

'Can he get in? No? Has he done 999? Yes? Tell him to wait there.'

They were going up Piccadilly at seventy miles an hour, snaking among a few bewildered cars, and she choked back a scream as they hurtled round into Haymarket, barely missing a wavering pedestrian. She apologised, palely, for her lapse, but they were through Trafalgar Square, going the wrong way up St Martin's Lane, the horn a continuous scream, and blessedly they had stopped and John was out of the car running, like the big prop forward he had once been. I am not, she thought, going to sit here with cars swerving around me, feeling sick. I shall get out and try and breathe. She watched her moment and got out between cars and ran round on to the pavement as two police cars, sirens blaring, halted either end of their Volvo. She pointed wordlessly to the side of the building where John had been running and policemen poured after him. She stood, knowing she must keep out of the way, and saw the blue wave check, then come running back again, John in the middle with Matthew's red head beside him, and congregate around the boarded-up frontage, then shockingly came the noise of gunfire, and they were in, disappearing through a narrow door in the boards, each man briefly silhouetted against the light.

She waited a minute then reached in and switched off the Volvo, collected her handbag and walked across to peer cautiously through the door. The huge room, brightly lit and littered with ladders and paint pots and trestle tables, was deserted. The whole hunt seemed to have been swallowed up, and she edged down one side, keeping to the wall where she could until she reached the kitchen, which was full of men, several talking on telephones. In the middle her husband in his shirt-sleeves was kneeling by a girl who was lying very still on the floor with another man working on her. She recognised Judith Delves and watched in shocked silence as John took over, calmly, while the man who had been working to revive her got up and dusted himself, gratefully. There was another cluster of people around another recumbent body, male this time, the other side of the big central counter, but they were not working on him; he was dressed in a white jacket, lying on his face in the classic recovery position. She stood on her toes to see who it was, wondering why he appeared to be wearing a black woolly cap; edging forward to get a better look, she slipped and had to save herself by seizing at a rack which rocked and rattled. She drew in breath, horrified, but John had not even heard her, locked in the struggle to save Judith Delves. The whole place smelt of smoke and there were black fragments every-where, fluttering round the body with the black hat who was beginning to stir. She opened her mouth to shout but two of the attendant policemen squatted instantly to turn the man over and help him to sit up. She saw Michael Owens' bright blond hair as someone pulled off the black hat and he seemed to have a tea towel clenched in his left hand.

A noise on the far side of the kitchen distracted her; three men, armed with assorted oxygen canisters and stretchers, arrived at Judith Delves' side. They hooked her on to an oxygen line and felt for her heart and took her away as swiftly as they had arrived, and John stood up and stretched and looked across the kitchen. Men surrounded him, waiting for instructions which he gave, briskly, and Michael Owens was removed, hung limply between two policemen. It was Matthew, finally, who saw that she was there, and made to come over to her, but she shook her head at him and waited for her husband to finish doing what he did so well.

EPILOGUE

'That's John now, Tris. I'll talk to you tomorrow.' She banged the phone down and ran to the door, getting it open as her husband's key turned in the lock. He must, she knew, be exhausted. She had driven the Volvo home at 2 a.m. that morning, pausing only to remind her husband she existed and to tell him where the family car was going. She had felt a guilt-stricken sympathy with her little son who had developed a habit of climbing on to her knee and taking her face in both hands to make quite sure she was listening to him; only deference to John's position in the Metropolitan Police hierarchy had prevented her from doing the same in the crowded kitchen of Café de la Paix. He came through the door, white with exhaustion, and she waited impatiently while his driver deposited two briefcases and a coat in the hall and said goodnight.

'I haven't eaten,' he said, kissing her, and she led him to the kitchen and installed him at the table with a huge whisky while she clattered about. He had been on his feet since the morning of the day before and was done, physically, but he was engaged in the little activities of a man settling himself in his home, peering suspiciously at the post, fishing a piece of junk mail out of the waste-paper basket to reassure himself he was not being deprived of some life-changing treat.

'Will in bed?'

'Only just. Could you wait to look at him in case he wakes?'

''Course.' He finished his whisky, rose to get another, and stopped beside her at the stove. 'You got home all right?'

'The earthquake was a bit of bother but it was fine otherwise.'

'Good.' She waited, flipping over the steak, while he poured a drink. '*What* did you say?'

She laughed. 'I wondered if you were with me. Your supper's ready, get outside it so you can talk.' She sat opposite him, with a soda water with a dash of white wine, which was all the baby would let her drink.

'What made you do that spectacular U-turn?' she asked, when she could stand it no longer, and most of his plateful had disappeared.

'You said Owens had picked a quarrel.'

'That was true.'

'I realised why.' He finished the potatoes and sat back in his chair, stretching, less pale now but eyes heavy with tiredness. 'He needed time in the Caff office by himself to find what he was looking for.'

'Ah. Which was?'

Her husband considered her and she realised she was being slow. 'A letter, or letters to Selina?'

'That's right. He found the two he wanted – the two he had written and took them downstairs to burn them on the grill. Another few minutes and he'd have been away.'

'So he was one of Mrs Marsh-Hayden's lovers.' She looked at her husband cautiously. He was blinking in the lights; she probably had about five minutes before he fell asleep, and she needed to get him upstairs before that happened. 'Did he kill her?'

'Yes.'

'Did you get a confession?'

'Not to murder. He claims accident. He says he meant only to frighten her.'

'Darling, sorry, but *why*? I've heard of *crime passionnel* but it was – is – surely Judith he wants.'

'I agree. Selina was blackmailing him.'

'What for? And could he not just have paid?' She had understood that Michael Owens, at thirty-eight, had already made a substantial fortune.

'It wasn't money, or not only. According to him she'd got pissed off with her own husband being always broke and she wanted a more reliable and shrewd one. So she seduced him, he says, and was putting on pressure for him to give up Judith and marry her instead.'

'But she was married.'

'Indeed so, but she wanted out. And Marsh-Hayden would apparently have divorced her, given . . . well, given the letters.'

'Were his like the others?'

'Well, yes, up to a point.'

'Only he liked something even more peculiar and embarrassing?' She knew better than to ask for further and better particulars. 'At any event, Judith would have been put off if she'd been shown them.'

'That was the threat of course,' her husband said. He hesitated. 'Was he right to worry? Would she have been so put off as to ditch him?'

He waited while his wife, very slightly pink around the cheekbones, consulted some earlier experience.

'It's different with a husband,' she said, finally. 'A lover who liked something a bit out of the way might be fun – I mean, so long as it wasn't torture or doing it with dogs – but speaking personally I'd feel uncomfortable if I discovered you really, really only liked it if I tied you to the stove and beat you first. Or the other way round,' she added, conscientiously. 'It might indeed have put Judith off, particularly if she was – as she was – having doubts about whether she really wanted to be married if she wasn't going to be able to run her own shop.' She reflected for a moment, saddened. 'So he panicked and killed Selina without even trying it the other way – I mean, without even trying to confess to Judith.' She stopped. 'I never asked. Is she still recovering?'

'Yes. In fact she's in reasonable shape for someone who was half strangled by her fiancé.'

'*That* wasn't an accident, of course.'

'No. But by then he was in the business of saving his skin. He killed Selina – by accident or not – and he killed her husband. We may not be able to make that one stick, but I'm clear about it. He knew that paracetamol could finish off someone with a rotten liver; he watched Tony Gallagher put four into a glass, and it gave him the idea. He could have given Richard another slug at the restaurant – they kept it everywhere – or even later; it was him who saw Richard actually into bed the night he died, when he was out of his head.'

'Why kill Richard? Was he becoming suspicious?'

'Don't know whether he was actually becoming suspicious of Owens. But he had found more letters, and Owens might reasonably have feared he would go on looking.'

'Where *were* the other letters? I mean, did you ever find them?'

'In scraps in the kitchen. They came out of a drawer containing four-year-old bank statements.'

'Ah. If you want to hide a tree, a forest is a good place. What would Richard have done if he had found them?'

'Confronted him? Told Judith? In the end he'd have shown them to us, I assume, and then we'd have had a more careful look at Mr Owens, who didn't seem to have a motive. He wanted to sell, of course, to get Judith out of the business, but it wasn't as if he needed the cash. But if he didn't get the letters back, he knew he was at risk of losing her, and you're right, she's what he minds about. Asking after her even now, when he's put her in hospital.' He had finished his steak and was gazing at his empty plate, thoughtfully.

She got up and put her arms round him. 'Come upstairs. I'm not going to be able to carry you, now I'm pregnant.'

'Did you tell Will?' he asked, following her, heavily.

'Yes. He doesn't believe it.'

'Poor kid's got a sad disillusionment ahead,' her husband said, stumbling to the bathroom, pulling off clothes as he went.

'Madame? Jacques on reception. Mrs McLeish is here and Mr Sutherland.'

'I'll come, Jacques.' Judith considered the two men at the big table at the other end of the office. In the massive clear-out they had finally achieved last week, four years' worth of papers had been boxed and put into storage against the unlikely contingency that anyone would want them again, and empty filing cabinets sold or given away so that there was now space. And light, made brighter by glistening white paint and a couple of large abstracts. That had been Brian Rubin's doing; he had been uncompromising about the need for a decent uncluttered office and he had been absolutely right. Everything seemed easier, including the management accounts; and there again his advent had been a liberation; the Gemini Group's accounting system was modern and easy to operate, and the price of updated computers and a software licence had been trivial in comparison to the time it saved.

'Francesca's just arrived. Do you want to come down for tea, or are you and Tony still busy?'

'Nah, we've cracked it, haven't we, Bri? Francesca's husband decided to let her come here then.' Tony Gallagher in street clothes got up and stretched.

'Well, after all, we've been open two weeks now,' Brian Rubin observed, carefully, not looking at her. 'And the case is closed as far as he is concerned.'

Judith didn't look at him either; it was still difficult to talk easily about the fact that Michael Owens was in a prison hospital, officially unfit to plead but unofficially understood to be guilty of two murders and two failed attempts.

The three of them trooped downstairs; by common unspoken consent no one was using the back lift and plans for reorganising the kitchen would see it eliminated in the quiet period after Christmas. The restaurant sparkled, immaculately redecorated, as fresh and clean as when it had been opened first, four years before. It was the dead period of the afternoon but staff were deployed setting up for the evening; Café de la Paix had been booked to capacity at lunch since it reopened, was well filled from 6 to 10.20 p.m. and markedly overbooked after that when the post-theatre crowds arrived, exposing mercilessly the limits of a too small kitchen. Tony Gallagher who, four weeks ago, had come straight back to work from hospital to get the Café reopened, was in serious need of a week off but even that seemed not impossible given the quality of the sous chefs he had managed to recruit.

'You're looking tired.' Francesca McLeish rose to greet her and Judith smiled at her gratefully. It had been Matthew Sutherland, most visibly, and Francesca, working undercover, who had kept the show on the road while she and Tony had recovered from their injuries and all parties had absorbed the first stunning shock. It had taken a little time to understand that a friend and partner had been responsible for the death of two partners and for putting another two – one the woman he had expected to marry – into hospital. Matthew Sutherland had conceived it as part of his duty to a client to take over supervising the conversion, taking leave from Graebner Associates to run from hospital bed to site office, bearing cheques, instructions and materials for days until Judith had discharged herself from hospital, still shocked and muffled in polo-neck sweater and scarf to disguise livid bruising. Tony Gallagher, pale, thin and having to sit down heavily every twenty minutes, had got back on site three days after her.

Francesca, who had been on the verge of collecting William from the base of a potted plant, realised with relief that Matt was going to pick him up. 'Going to have a baby,' he was announcing, pulling Matt's hair to make him pay attention.

'Congratulations, old boy. That'll be a real treat.'

Not what he'll get, his mother thought, sadly. She could still remember her own disappointment when her brother Charlie arrived and she had found that not only did he absorb much of her mother's attention but he was also not at all interested in playing and appeared to spend most of the day asleep. She watched sardonically as Matt, easily bored by small children, unloaded her son on Brian Rubin who received him with the ease of the experienced father. She grinned at him; she had come to like him very much over the last five weeks. She had gone on visiting Judith Delves in hospital despite John's involvement in the case, feeling strongly that her support must not be withdrawn. She had been startled to find Judith refusing to contemplate giving up a place which must be full of bad memories, and where the shareholding was in an inextricable mess, mostly held in the nerveless hands of trustees or executors. But in practice, as she had advised long ago, confusion and legal uncertainty had played into Judith's hands. She had had to accommodate Brian Rubin who was the legal owner of Richard Marsh-Hayden's thirty-two and a half per cent shareholding, but she had strong cards to play as well, given her own fifteen per cent, her control over Tony Gallagher's five per cent and the fact that Michael Owens, when coherent, was insisting that his thirty-two and a half per cent should be hers. Selina's fifteen per cent was still in the hands of her executors, but they had no idea what to do with it and it had been possible to reach agreement that her trustees should hold it as a passive shareholding. It was not perhaps a classic company structure, but it was stable, after a fashion, and would certainly hold while the restaurants were trading profitably.

'Brian,' she said, under cover of an animated discussion between Matt, Judith and Tony, 'how is Gemini doing?'

'A lot better, for all I've been busy here. Well, it's the run up to Christmas, isn't it? January's going to be the difficult one.' He was looking cheerful, despite it all, and she considered him.

'You all seem to be getting on well here.'

He glanced at the others, but seeing them engrossed, lowered his voice. 'In a few months' time I think we'll get it right and put the groups together.' He saw her face. 'I'm not banking on it, Fran, but it'd be better for her.'

'If she had a decent shareholding.' Francesca, who had stuck by Judith through the negotiations, went automatically into that mode, and he laughed.

'She would. It'd pay me.' He reached past her, obedient to Will's demand for crisps.

That probably *was* how it would come out, she thought, slowly, and it would indeed be better for Judith to be a treasured managing director for this lively tough. She smiled at him, and held out her arms for her son, and they bent together to put him into his pushchair. A good man, for all his excursion with Selina, and a kindly father.

'I must go – I'm meeting John.'

Brian Rubin was looking over her head. 'He's come to fetch you.' He tightened the last strap conscientiously round Will and turned the pushchair so they could both see the big man in the grey suit coming past the glittering mirrors towards them. And then she had to get Will out of his violently rocking pushchair again so that he could greet his father, and then they were on their way, passing the first of the pre-theatre clients.